Praise for *The Request*

"Fast-paced and thrilling, with twists at every turn, *The Request* kept me guessing until its satisfying conclusion."

—Catherine McKenzie, author of *I'll Never Tell*

"David Bell more than delivers on the shocking premise of *The Request*, which is a gripping exploration of guilt, loyalty, and desperation. [It] combines complex characters, social commentary, and expertly meted-out plot twists that will keep readers guessing—and gasping—until the final page. Bell is a master."

—Robyn Harding, international bestselling author of *The Party*

More praise for the work of David Bell

"[Bell is] a bang-up storyteller, armed with enough detours and surprises to keep the pages turning." —*The Cleveland Plain Dealer*

"David Bell is a definite natural storyteller and a first-class writer."

—*Suspense Magazine*

"Filled with twists and turns. . . . Bell is a master of suspense with well-fleshed-out characters." —*Midwest Book Review*

"[A] twisty, realistic thriller. . . . [Bell] is a skilled storyteller."

—*Houston Chronicle*

"A tale straight out of the psychological thriller territory blazed by the likes of Harlan Coben and Lisa Gardner." —*The Providence Journal*

ALSO BY DAVID BELL

Cemetery Girl

The Hiding Place

Never Come Back

The Forgotten Girl

Somebody I Used to Know

Since She Went Away

Bring Her Home

Somebody's Daughter

Layover

THE
REQUEST

DAVID BELL

BERKLEY | NEW YORK

BERKLEY
An imprint of Penguin Random House LLC
penguinrandomhouse.com

ISBN: 9780440000907

The Library of Congress has catalogued the hardcover edition as follows:

Names: Bell, David, 1969 November 17– author.
Title: The request / David Bell.
Description: First Edition. | New York : Berkley, 2020.
Identifiers: LCCN 2019055517 (print) | LCCN 2019055518 (ebook) |
ISBN 9780440000891 (hardcover) | ISBN 9780440000914 (ebook)
Subjects: GSAFD: Mystery fiction. | Suspense fiction.
Classification: LCC PS3602.E64544 R47 2020 (print) | LCC PS3602.E64544
(ebook) | DDC 813/.6--dc23
LC record available at https://lccn.loc.gov/2019055517
LC ebook record available at https://lccn.loc.gov/2019055518

Printed in the United States of America
1   3   5   7   9   10   8   6   4   2

Cover images: woman by Robin de Blanche / Shutterstock;
man by Terry Bidgood / Trevillion Images
Cover design by Eileen Carey
Book design by Elke Sigal

For Molly

PROLOGUE

Of all the things I never thought I'd say about my life, there is this—I have a blackmailer.

The blackmail started for a simple reason—I was guilty.

And over the years the guilt has taken a strong hold of me. Like a giant iron fist.

I used to do things differently. Before the blackmailing started.

I used to hand over the money voluntarily. And on my own schedule. I would head to my bank branch and withdraw a couple hundred dollars from the savings account Amanda and I share. Once, after I received a one-thousand-dollar bonus at the PR firm where I worked, I handed the entire amount over. I always placed the crisp stack of cash in a manila envelope. I wrapped the envelope with tape, making sure it was secure and tight, and I drove thirty minutes away from my home and arrived in another town, where I traced the familiar path to a modest two-story house in an old subdivision.

Sometimes I arrived before daylight, telling Amanda I had an early meeting in my office. Other times I rolled up to the house late at night, headlights off, radio silent, claiming a social obligation from work or having made some other plausible excuse.

In those days, before everything else happened, Amanda never questioned me. She believed what I told her.

I always found the house dark, the porch light extinguished. I quickly pulled open the mailbox that sat at the end of the driveway, felt the coolness of the morning or night air against my face, slipped the envelope inside, closed the mailbox tight, and drove off. I'd mastered the smooth transaction, accomplishing my task in mere seconds.

I didn't write on the envelope. Or leave a note.

But otherwise I did nothing to conceal my identity. It was there if someone wanted to find it.

My fingerprints were on the envelope, the tape, the money. My DNA was on the flap I licked.

I knew for a fact the family was getting the money.

I knew because just six weeks ago, the local paper ran a story. It detailed the anonymous gifts of cash that appeared randomly in the mailbox. The article's author theorized that the person leaving the money was a Good Samaritan, someone moved by the plight of the family and the medical expenses related to the accident six years earlier that left their middle daughter with permanent disabilities and their youngest daughter dead. In the story, the family explained that the cash helped keep them afloat when times were tough by allowing them to purchase much-needed medical supplies or household items.

"We have insurance," the father said in the article. "And the government helps some. But it's never enough. These envelopes are a godsend."

He went on to say they were initially reluctant to tell anyone about the money. More than anything else, they worried the publicity might scare off the anonymous donor. Clearly this person didn't want attention or recognition of any kind.

But eventually the family couldn't stand not saying anything.

They wanted the donor to know how much they appreciated what he or she was doing for them. They wanted the donor to know how much the money helped.

And they insisted they would never test the envelope for finger-prints or DNA. They would never set up a hidden camera to try to catch the person in the act.

And if the donor ever stopped leaving the money for any reason, they would understand. He or she had already been more generous than anyone could have imagined.

"I truly believe the person who gives us this money is an angel," the mother said. "I know it sounds corny to say that in this day and age, but I really believe it's an angel."

Just under a month ago, I got caught.

Not by the police. Not by the media.

And not by Amanda.

No, I got caught by the family's eldest daughter, the one who wasn't quoted in the article about the anonymous angelic donations.

I'd been reluctant to go back and make another delivery. I feared that the article might have stirred up too much attention and might drive someone—another reporter, a neighbor, a random fame seeker who wanted something to brag about on social media—to stake the place out and catch me. Over time, my guilt grew greater than my fear. And I went back with another envelope.

After I dropped it off and was two miles from their house, a car pulled alongside me on the empty road. The sky was gray, just light-ening toward sunrise. No one else was out.

At first I ignored the driver, but they paced me, and then made an aggressive move—increasing their speed, pulling ahead, and cutting over into my lane so I had no choice but to slow and then stop unless I wanted to go into the culvert that ran on my right.

The other driver stopped as well, blocking me in and allowing me no path forward.

I sat frozen in the car, my hands gripping the wheel. I was ready to slam the car into reverse and back up, turn around if I had to.

But then the driver stepped out. Instead of a cop or a menacing figure, I saw a woman about my age. She wore a long-sleeve T-shirt and jeans. Running shoes. Her dirty blond hair was pulled back in a ponytail, and she walked briskly toward my car, her stride long and confident. She twirled her finger, telling me to roll down the window. Which I did.

"Is everything okay?" I asked. "Are you hurt?"

"Just listen," she said. She spoke in clipped sentences, her voice husky, with a trace of a Kentucky accent. "You know who I am, right?"

I hadn't seen her photo in six years. But the face wasn't that different. A few smile lines around the eyes. A few gray strands in the hair. But it was her.

Dawn Steiner. The elder sister of Maggie and Emily Steiner. Maggie was killed in the accident, and Emily was left with a permanent injury to her leg, one that hindered her ability to walk and work.

My heart thumped. Triple time. The morning was cool, but beads of sweat popped out on my forehead like I was a sick man.

"What do you want?" I asked.

"Shhh. You know me, then. And I know you. So, like I said, just listen."

Her tone was flat as the road. Calm. Clear. Precise.

"I need money. I need my cut of what you have. In fact, I need more than that. I lost a sister here. And what you give to my parents . . . Let's just say it doesn't trickle down to me. And I have things I need the money for. I have obligations to keep up with. And you seem to be doing just fine. Help me out, and I'll keep my mouth shut."

"About the money?"

"About why you do this at all. My parents believe what they want to believe about their anonymous Good Samaritan. It helps them deal with the shit sandwich they've been given to eat. They can open up the envelope of money when it shows up, and they can turn to each other and say, 'See, the world's not such a bad place.' But I'm not like that."

"I'm going to go."

"You'll stay. You'll listen. See, I had to ask myself, my cynical self, why would someone give money to my family this way? If you wanted to help them out, you could just donate to the fund that was set up after the accident. No, whoever is coming in the middle of the night and leaving money is up to something else. And what could that be?" She snapped her fingers. "Guilt. That's the only explanation. Someone with a lot of guilt. A lot. Now, your friend Aaron, the one who went to prison, he's done his time. And his life on the outside can't be that great. He couldn't just go around like Santa, leaving goodies for a struggling family." She shook her head, a look of amusement on her face. "And your friend, the other one? The rich guy? What's his name?"

"Leave my friends out of it."

"One look at him and you can see he wouldn't give his money to somebody. He's a jerk through and through. He looks like the type to have an accident. Not the type to care if anyone got hurt. And not the type to feel guilt."

"You're wrong," I said. "I'm just trying to help. You can't conclude anything from my gesture."

"I can't? Okay. I'll go to the police and the press and tell them it's you leaving the money. I'll tell them there's something fishy about the accident. You riding in the backseat of your own car. They'll want to look into that now that the story is back on everybody's minds. If you want to take the chance that they open it back up, I'll go do it."

She turned to go, her movements possessing a military crispness.

"Wait." Heavy resignation pressed down on me, like bricks piled on my back. "I don't know what you want."

She told me the amount. Ten thousand dollars.

And she told me she needed it in one month. Thirty days.

"That's the deadline. Thirty days. Round up the money or I go to the police and the media and tell them you've been leaving the envelopes. From there . . . like I said, they'll start digging into everything in your life. You're a pretty well-known guy in this town. It could be embarrassing for that kind of thing to hit the news."

"You're asking for too much. Far too much. I can't come up with that much money on such short notice. I have a family. And we just . . ." It sounded silly to mention it in contrast to her lost and injured sisters. But I said it anyway. "We're having work done on our house this spring. I put down a deposit. That was a lot of what we had saved."

Dawn gave me a stare as cold as ice. She used her left fist and rapped on the hood of the car twice. "Cry me a river. I think you'll find a way. I don't believe you have a choice. Ten thousand. Thirty days."

She drove off, leaving me sitting in the road as the sun came up. Just like that—I had a blackmailer.

I thought back to that article, the one in which Dawn's mother had called me an angel.

Everything I'm about to tell you proves how wrong she was. . . .

CHAPTER ONE

"Ryan."

Someone called my name. I was leaving the Juniper Pig and stepping into the parking lot, heading for my car. The voice that came through the dark was sharp and husky, a knife swipe through the night, and I jumped.

I couldn't tell if a man or a woman had spoken.

After work I'd stopped by the Pig, the microbrewery I'd owned a small stake in for the last sixteen months. I was one of three partners, and my contribution had been the smallest, but we took turns going by in the evenings to see how things were running. And that night was my turn.

I hadn't wanted to stop by the bar. Amanda was waiting at home with our baby, Henry, and thinking of seeing them made my stomach flutter with anticipation and joy. My time away from them felt longer than the hours that passed on the clock, and returning to them every evening was sweet relief. Since Henry had been born, I'd been trying hard to curb my tendency to overwork. But it wasn't easy. Since my dad died while I was in college, leaving my mother and me high and dry, I'd been compelled to keep going forward, to keep pushing at work. . . .

I hoped Henry would change that. I hoped I could slow down.

But a shadowy figure came toward me in the darkness, freezing my progress. The person was short, the face in shadow.

It was early April, the air still cool, the days still lengthening. I waited, watching. I'd just posted to my Instagram account, sharing a photo of the beer I'd just sampled, one of our brewers' latest concoctions, the HopPig IPA.

"Who is that?" I asked.

"Ryan?"

Dawn Steiner? Her deadline loomed that week, just two days away, but I hadn't seen or heard from her since that morning almost a month ago. And I'd made almost no progress on finding the money for her. Had she decided to come looking for me?

But then I saw who it was and slipped my phone back into my pocket.

"Is that really you?" I asked the figure still standing in the shadows of the building. Relieved.

He stepped closer, moving into the crisp light that spilled from the windows of the Pig. "It's me," he said. "Indeed."

Blake Norton. My best friend from college. And also my most challenging. He was loyal, fun, and charming. He was immature, reckless, and juvenile. He was Butch Cassidy crossed with Bluto from *Animal House.*

I hadn't seen him in six months, even though we lived in the same small city, Rossingville, Kentucky. He held out his hand, and we shook.

Blake looked thinner, healthier, like maybe he'd dropped fifteen or twenty pounds. His face was less puffy. I wondered if he'd stopped drinking and started exercising more, if he was on one of his periodic health kicks. He was shorter than me by two inches, and he wore a neatly trimmed beard. His shoulder-length hair was off his face and combed into place for a change, and his flannel shirt appeared to be free of stains, the sleeves rolled to his elbows with a measure of precision.

"Why are you skulking around in the parking lot?" I asked.

I realized I was happy to see him. Years of friendship, countless memories big and small, and an endless supply of fierce loyalty brought a smile to my face.

"Skulking." He smiled as well. "I could always count on you to come up with a ten-dollar word like 'skulking.'"

"I got one of those calendars for Christmas," I said, "the kind that gives you a new word every day. Today's was 'skulking.'"

Blake shook his head. "No, you know all the fancy words. You always have. I remember you were an English major when we started college. You switched to marketing later, but I know what your real passion was."

"You know why I switched to something more reliable as well as I do," I said. "I minored in English. And before Henry was born, I read a lot. And you're still not answering my question."

Blake turned to the side, his brown lace-up boots scraping against the gravel of the lot as he did. He looked at the Pig, then faced me again. "I shouldn't go in there. Too much temptation."

"You quit drinking?" I asked.

"I *stopped* drinking. I'll never quit." He shrugged. "It's been about six weeks now."

"That's good. I'm glad to hear it."

"Yeah. It is. I even joined a gym." He held up his right arm and flexed, even though there was no way to see anything beneath the shirt. "Bright-eyed. Bushy-tailed. That's me."

"A gym? You couldn't run twenty feet in college."

"Ten if I was lucky. And that was only if someone was giving away beer or pizza."

I laughed. "True enough. Well, I'm happy for you."

Cars passed on the street, their headlights making us squint. The air smelled like rain, and some thick clouds obscured the early-emerging stars. I wore a denim jacket but felt a shiver as the wind kicked up.

Blake pointed across the street to the coffee shop. "I was hoping we could talk. Just a few minutes. I know they don't sell anything stronger than caffeine over there."

I checked the time on my Apple watch. Amanda expected me. And I really wanted to get home before Henry went to sleep. Being home for his bedtime mattered to me. A great deal. Taking part in the bedtime ritual helped ease my sense of missing out during the long hours I was away at work.

"I can't," I said. "Really, I just can't. Amanda's been with Henry all day, and I already got delayed here. One of our servers is going through a breakup, and he wanted my advice. That took longer than I expected. You know how seriously college kids take breakups. How about lunch tomorrow? That would work a lot better."

"I know, I know. You've got a family now. And you're dedicated. And juggling a lot. I get it. And I know these kids who work here look at you like you're their sensitive big brother. I'm sure they bring you their problems all the time."

"It happens. They're away from home. They have crises. . . ."

But he started shaking his head. "But I kind of need this. It's an emergency."

"An emergency? What are you talking about?"

But he simply pointed across the street. And smiled, a look I recognized and remembered well. The look said, *Come on. You're going to want to hear this.*

It was certainly tough to say no to an old friend. And it was tough to say no to Blake. Sometimes it felt like he could convince anyone of anything. And while I'd learned over the years to recognize when he was stretching the truth or attempting to lead me down some path I shouldn't take, a part of me always felt a little thrill at the thought of taking the ride.

Blake knew me so well. And he knew so much about me.

What emergency was he contending with tonight? Six months since we'd last talked and he looked like a man transformed?

"Ten minutes," I said, pointing at the watch. "Talk fast when we get there."

He nodded, and we went to the curb, waiting for a break in the passing traffic, and then crossed the street side by side like when we were in college, doing every damn thing together.

CHAPTER TWO

The place was called the Ground Floor, and the weeknight crowd was light. Most of the students from the state university in town went to a coffee shop near campus, one run by some recent graduates. The bell dinged over our heads as we pushed through the glass door, and Blake stepped aside, allowing an elderly couple to pass. They thanked him, and Blake gave them his brightest smile.

"You two go straight home now," he said. "And don't do anything I wouldn't do."

"We're too old for that," the woman said, placing her hand on Blake's arm.

"I doubt that," he said, leaning in a little.

And they all laughed.

The Ground Floor catered to a professional crowd, one that came in early in the morning and during the afternoon and then drifted away when the sun went down. But I stopped in there from time to time since it was across the street from the Pig, and it seemed neighborly to support each other's businesses. And I also knew the Ground Floor because my small PR firm had helped the shop with a branding campaign two years earlier. One of our designers had redone their logo, giving it a more modern look, and while I hadn't worked on that job, I figured anyone who gave business to our slowly growing outfit deserved to receive my coffee patronage.

At the counter I ordered an Americano while Blake opted for a blend, and we settled in at an isolated table in a corner of the room. Al Stewart's "Time Passages" played overhead, and the steamer hissed as it blew froth behind the counter. I loved the rich smell of the roasting beans, the lingering scent of the pastries baked that morning. I pulled out my phone and texted Amanda, telling her I was delayed but wouldn't be long. It took a lot of willpower, but I ignored the flurry of notifications that came up, real-time responses to my beer photo from the Pig and a post from earlier in the day, a shot I'd taken of Henry being bathed.

Be there soon.

And as soon as I hit SEND and heard the swooshing sound of the text heading her way, I wished I'd just told Blake no, that I'd stuck to just going to lunch with him.

But he'd used the word "emergency." Why?

I had my suspicions. When we'd met in college, we quickly settled into roles. Blake was wild, and I was serious. I studied too much, and Blake would get me to loosen up.

Then Blake would go too far, and I'd rein him in. Blake would have a crisis—a girl, a professor, his parents—and I'd advise him on the best way to handle it.

I expected a crisis. An irritated boss. A new relationship gone wrong.

I waited a moment, hoping Amanda would respond. But she didn't.

I'd tried calling her an hour earlier but hadn't gotten an answer. Sometimes she tried to catch a nap at the same time as Henry. Sometimes she just got too busy with Henry to bother with the phone. But I wanted to make sure she knew I wouldn't be home when I'd said I would. I felt a little like a fool admitting that I'd had no idea how much strain having a newborn would add to our lives. I don't think either one of us had. Amanda felt it more because she was on the front line with Henry every day, and I wanted to get home to help as fast as I could.

"I bet you didn't mention my name," Blake said.

"What's that?"

"To Amanda," he said. "You texted her, but I'd bet you every beer I've ever drunk you didn't tell her you were with me. I know she's not the forgiving type."

"There wasn't any need to mention you." But he was right. I had intentionally left Blake out of the message. Amanda and Blake had fallen out, which had caused me not to see him for six months, and there was no need to stir that pot. I sipped my coffee. "But, seriously, ten minutes."

"Sure. I understand." He lifted his steaming mug and drank. I expected him to wince from what must have been the scalding temperature of the coffee, but he didn't flinch. One brown droplet clung to his beard.

I studied his eyes. It had been a long time since I'd seen them as clear as they were in the bright light of the coffee shop. No red. No fog or glaze from alcohol. Or weed. He looked more like the fresh-faced guy I had met during our first year of college than he had at any time since. And when I'd seen him laugh with that older couple, I understood what had been appealing about him in the first place all those years ago. His natural ease with everyone he met. His jokes that always seemed organic. His ability to get along with just about anyone. Almost everyone at our small college knew his name. Partyers and studiers. Football players and honors students.

And I wasn't different from anyone else who had met him back then. He was the flame, and I was the moth.

"You seemed a little jumpy when I said your name." Blake eyed me over his mug. "Everything okay?"

"Just busy. You know."

"How is the PR firm?" he asked. "On steady ground?"

"Steadier every day," I said. "Three years since we opened, and we're making it. We're hoping to land a contract with the Warren Manufacturing Group. You know, the outfit that makes screen doors."

"Sexy."

"They have a lot of money. And I think it's going to happen. A whole social media and branding campaign for them. That would be a nice shot in the arm."

"Look at you," he said. "A businessman."

"Kind of."

"And you're looking good, Ryan," he said. "As always."

"Bullshit. I've gained five or ten pounds since Henry was born. They don't tell you that when you have a kid everybody on earth brings you food. And you eat it. And then you just sit around, taking care of a baby. Maybe when he starts crawling I'll lose a little."

"Five or ten pounds?" He looked me up and down, even dropping his head and peeking under the table as though the extra weight might have been hidden there. "Where? You've always been so trim. So disciplined. In college, two slices of pizza when the rest of us ate four. Usually just two beers when the rest of us . . . Well, you know. Some of us had far too many."

"I didn't always stop at two," I said, looking down at my own steaming mug. My face flushed, and not from the heat of the coffee. "You know that better than anyone."

"It was rare."

"I'm flattered you think of me as such a model of virtue and restraint, but usually I didn't eat or drink as much because I didn't have enough money to buy it. Unless you bought it for me."

"No charge," he said. "How's your mom? She good?"

"Yeah, she's good. She's busy teaching. She's going to come and see Henry in July."

"Will you tell her I said hello?"

"I will. She always asks about you. And speaking of Henry . . . I really need to know what this emergency is. I have a growing baby who likes to poop and cry. And a wife who's been stuck with him all day. And I don't want to miss bedtime."

"Sam has shown me the pictures. Instagram, Facebook."

"Sam has? You mean . . . ?"

"That's what I'm here to talk about. But, yes, Sam has shown me the pictures."

"And she hasn't convinced you to join the social media world? You're still a Luddite?"

He dismissed me by waving a hand. "That's your thing, not mine. I just don't need to put all my business out there. Some things are meant to be private. But he is a beautiful kid. You all look pretty damn happy. And you sure post often enough."

"Well, you know, first child and all that. If we have another, we'll be too tired to take pictures. Although I don't know if either one of us can be more tired. But you've got me curious. . . . Sam? Did you bury the lede when you asked to talk? What's going on with Sam?"

He smiled and scratched at his beard, swiping that drop of coffee away. "Yeah, okay, I have good news of my own. Samantha and I are getting married."

It took me a moment to respond. His clear brown eyes were beaming like a child's, and I knew he wanted me to be happy for him. As happy as he appeared to be for himself.

But . . .

"Are you surprised?" he asked.

"Kind of. But that's not an emergency, is it?"

"Didn't you see it on Facebook?" he asked. "You're on there all the time. Sam posted about it today."

I stalled by taking a big drink of my Americano, which suddenly tasted less appealing than it had a few moments before. I felt Blake's eyes on me the whole time I swallowed, as he anticipated my reaction to his big news. If Sam had posted that day, I'd missed it.

"Well, come on," he said, impatient. "Aren't you happy for me?"

"I am. I am. Congratulations." I put the mug down and offered my hand across the table. We shook, which felt as strange as it must have looked to anyone who saw us. Two men shaking hands across a table in a coffee shop as though they'd just closed a business deal. "That's great, man. Really. You know I think very highly of Samantha. She's wonderful."

"You think she's too good for me," he said.

"I didn't say that—"

"It's okay. Everybody thinks that. Hell, I do. She's organized and proper. She knows which fork to eat with first and how to fold a fitted sheet."

"It's not that," I said. The caffeine made my heart run faster, like a galloping wild horse. My fingertips tingled. And if I couldn't be honest and forthright with an old friend, then what was the point? "This is the . . . Is it the third time you've been engaged to Sam now? And the other two times it—you know—didn't work out. So, I just . . . I'm wondering if it will stick."

Blake nodded. "Right, right. I get it. And you called it. We've been here before, and then something stupid always happens. Usually it's been me screwing it up somehow. I know. I hear you." He leaned forward, his eyes zeroing in on me. "But this time it's different. I mean it. I'm better. More mature. And I get it. I understand how great Sam is. How supportive and loving. I'm really on it. You know, there comes a time when we all have to grow up. It happens at different times for all of us." He pointed at me. "You had it figured out sooner. I'm a slow learner. But I got there."

He seemed sincere. He really did. His clear eyes looked completely serious.

And I knew Blake well enough to know this was something he did.

He'd always latch on to some new enthusiasm—a new job, a different major, a girl he met—and claim that everything was suddenly different, that *this time* everything would work out perfectly.

But it never did. He always blew it up or broke it down and went back to being the same old Blake doing too much of everything. Drinking. Smoking. Eating.

But I could see how desperately he wanted me to believe it would work this time. How desperately he wanted me to approve and share his happiness.

And for all I knew, this would be it. He might have grown up. He might be a fully formed adult.

I wasn't lying when I said Samantha was wonderful. She was. Pretty and optimistic. Considerate of others. Warm. Enthusiastic. But with none of Blake's tendency toward recklessness. She was a schoolteacher, and she walked the straight and narrow. I couldn't count the number of good causes she'd managed to get Amanda or me to volunteer for or donate money to. She wanted to run for the school board someday. She'd already said she wanted my firm to help with social media when she did.

But I understood what she saw in him. I knew how charming Blake could be. How bighearted. How much he could make anyone feel like the center of his world, how much his attention and energy could focus like a spotlight. Samantha was as smart as I was. She could see everything I could see—the good and the challenging.

I knew she played some of the role in Blake's life I used to play. She told him when to back off, when not to play so hard. And he kept her from working on lesson plans until midnight.

I got it.

And I *wanted* to be happy for him.

And I *wanted* him to be happy. I really did.

Still, I suspected I knew why he'd sought me out that night. If he and Sam were going to get married, then he needed groomsmen. A best man, even. He'd asked me during his second engagement to Sam, the one that lasted the longest of the first two, and I'd said yes, had even gone so far as to begin to plan a bachelor party weekend in New Orleans before things were called off. Their first engagement had ended after three weeks, well before any groomsmen had been asked to join the wedding party.

"Well, that's great," I said. "You look great, and I'm glad you two have worked things out."

"Thanks," he said. "Really."

But he didn't say anything else. He stared at me, and the silence settled between us like a leaden cloud.

The clock ticked. Ten minutes were up. I knew Amanda was waiting at home. I knew Henry was falling asleep without me.

"Is that all you wanted to tell me?" I asked.

"Right, right," he said. He tapped his index finger against his lips. "There is just one more thing I need to ask you. Just a small request."

CHAPTER THREE

Amanda and I had both been in several weddings over the years. They caused a lot of stress, and it always seemed as though the wedding party ended up growing irritated with the demands of the bride and the groom. Being in someone's wedding could end even the most enduring friendship.

Still, if Blake wanted me by his side, there was no question I would do it. We'd been friends for too long. We'd been through too much.

My dad had died suddenly during our sophomore year of college. He just dropped dead of a heart attack with no warning signs at the age of forty-eight. He'd been in the garage moving some boxes around, come back in and told my mom he was hot, and then gone facedown onto the kitchen floor like a falling piano, his head against the dishwasher, his feet under the table. I found out pretty quickly that my parents didn't have life insurance and that they hadn't set aside enough money for me to continue in school.

The private college I attended was expensive, close to forty thousand dollars a year, and before I even went home for the funeral, my mom told me I might not be able to stay. I was still processing the reality of my dad's death, so the news that I might have to leave college and all my friends nearly paralyzed me.

It was Blake who stepped up. He drove me home and went to the funeral with me. He bought me a new sport coat and helped me knot my tie. When we got back to school, and I was ready to pack my room and return home to work and enroll in community college, it was Blake who guided me through the morass of financial aid forms, helping me find a scholarship that allowed me to stay in school. I wouldn't have made it through all that without him. And I wouldn't have the life I had now if I hadn't stayed in school.

And he'd stood up at our wedding as my best man. It felt like he'd been by my side through many of the most important events of the past ten years.

"What do you need?" I asked.

Blake carefully picked up his coffee mug and moved it to the side of the wooden table. Then he leaned forward so his head was more than halfway across the table. There was something about someone doing that in a public place that seemed odd but also inviting. So I leaned forward to hear him.

Why so much solemnity for a request he'd already made once before?

Blake spoke in a low voice. "When I say that Samantha and I have figured things out, that we're really going to make it work this time and work for real, I mean it. I really mean it. I need her. And I think she needs me. It just . . . feels right between us."

"I believe you."

Up close his lips were cracked and dry, his teeth not quite as shining bright as I remembered.

"Well, the thing is, there's a problem . . . ," he said. "A loose thread. One that could turn into a noose around my neck if it isn't taken care of."

I tried to make sense of what he was saying, but I couldn't. The confusion must have shown on my face, because Blake went on.

"You know I haven't always been perfect, Ryan. I've really struggled with the idea of committing and settling down. It works for me up to a point, but then when we get engaged, and we start to talk about wedding dates, I start to get itchy. My skin literally crawls." He shrugged. He seemed to be admitting defeat in the face of the kinds of problems most of us outgrew or pushed aside as we got older. "That's why this is our third go-around. I haven't quite been able to take that last step, to just accept my good fortune and happiness with Sam and go for it."

"I know, Blake." I held his gaze, seeing in his face the college kid I'd met ten years ago. "But I'm not sure what that has to do with me."

Blake lowered his voice even more. "I was involved with a woman, Ryan. This . . . thing lasted a short time. And I want to be clear: It happened when Sam and I were broken up. And it ended once Sam and I were putting things back together. You know Sam. She wouldn't stand for infidelity, even when we're dating, and I wouldn't do that to her. I'm a commitment-phobe but not a cheater."

"I know that," I said. "You wouldn't hurt Sam that way."

"But I did spend time with this other woman. We had some really good times, to be honest."

"I still don't see the problem," I said. "If you were broken up when you dated this woman and then ended it to get back together with Sam, what's the issue?"

Blake leaned back in his chair. His cheeks flushed deep red above his beard. "You're trying to oversimplify it, Ryan. You're trying to fit things into a neat little box."

"Isn't that exactly what you're telling me?"

"You've got the perfect marriage and the perfect kid. You've got your PR firm, for God's sake, and you have a stake in a hipster brewery. You've made every correct step since we finished college. You could have gone in a lot of different directions when your dad died, but you went into a higher gear and haven't looked back." He shook his head. "Sam and everyone I see tells me about your posts. The fund-raisers and the charitable donations and the pro bono work. You've got the world by the short ones. Your life is always shown through just the right filter, isn't it, Ryan?"

"Okay, I'm not sure where all of this is going. You said you wanted to ask me something, but instead you're going on about this woman who you didn't cheat on Sam with. Are you looking for advice?"

"I don't need advice. Maybe I've outgrown that part of our friendship. I can go to Sam. I can talk to her. Isn't that what you have in your marriage? A partner?"

"Of course."

"Well, I'm not looking for that here."

"I'm in a hurry." I pushed back from the table, the chair scraping against the concrete floor so loudly that the other people in the coffee shop turned to look. "Amanda's waiting for me. I have to help her put Henry down. You think everything's perfect. I'm going to go home and have to change a shitty diaper. I can't put that on Instagram. Nothing's perfect. I'm happy for you, Blake. I really am. I'm glad you told me about this. Sam's amazing. I hope you're happy. But you're not really telling me anything—"

"You can't go."

His voice was flat, slicing like a steel blade through the Cat Stevens song now playing overhead and the murmured conversations around us.

I looked around, and the other patrons continued with their own conversations. The barista, a college student with fuchsia-streaked hair, and what looked like thirteen piercings in her left ear, chatted with a customer while she sloppily poured milk from a gallon jug.

We stared at each other for a moment, Blake and I.

I scooted forward.

"Why not?" I asked.

But I already knew.

And so did he.

"You haven't even heard what I want you to do yet, Ryan," he said. "The request. And you know—and I know—you have no choice but to do whatever I ask you to do."

CHAPTER FOUR

I braced myself for what was next.

No choice indeed. I stayed rooted in my chair, my spine rigid as a board.

"Things didn't end well between this woman and me," he said. "I broke it off abruptly. To get back with Sam. This woman didn't like that. You know, things with Sam, the clarity I acquired about our relationship, that came to me kind of suddenly after all of our fits and starts. Sometimes you just have an insight about your life—an epiphany, I guess you could call it. And then I knew what I wanted, the direction I needed to go. This woman I was with is so carefree. So fun. I love Sam, but her background, her family—they're all so . . . serious. So proper. I love them all, but I also never quite feel like I can be myself with them. Sam, yes. But the family . . . It was a relief to be with this other woman. It was liberating, and I really let my guard down."

"How did you do that?" I asked.

"I got carried away in the things I said."

"Did you promise her something? A commitment? Marriage?"

"No, not that."

"Who the hell is she?"

Blake shook his head, affecting a casual, devil-may-care approach to such mundane facts as the woman's identity. "I don't want to get into all the details, Ryan. Her name is Jen, okay, and she lives here in town. She has a good job. She's smart too. She's getting her MBA online. It's not important to know more, and I don't want this to be embarrassing for her. No more than it already is. It's over. I've told her that in no uncertain terms. She knows about Sam. She knows I'm getting married." A slightly amused look crossed his face, as though something had surprised him. "In fact, Sam and I are getting married on Saturday. This Saturday."

"Saturday? That's two days from now."

My own reaction to the news confused me. On the one hand, I felt relieved I hadn't been asked to participate. On the other . . . one of my oldest friends was getting married, and he hadn't bothered to tell me about it until the very last moment.

And he hadn't bothered to invite me either.

As I said, we'd been by each other's side for everything important up to that point. We'd depended on each other, just not lately.

Blake must have read the look on my face, because he jumped in to explain.

"It's a small wedding," he said. "We've planned it quickly. Sam's mom knew someone who could get us in at that place on Deer Valley Road. You know, the Deer Valley Barn. That's where the ceremony and the reception are going to be. They had a cancellation, so we got in."

"Yeah, okay."

"Hey, look, we didn't invite you because of all that stuff Amanda said about me the last time we saw each other. You can understand that, right? I mean, if Sam went off on you that way, you wouldn't invite her to your wedding. Not that Sam ever would say those kinds of things, of course."

I understood what he was saying. And why.

Six months earlier, not long after Henry was born, Blake had come over to the house to see the baby. When he came in, Henry was still asleep, and Blake made a grand entrance, carrying a gigantic stuffed elephant. It had taken us what felt like a long, long time to get Henry down, and Blake spoke in a booming voice that immediately woke the baby up. We were new parents, and Amanda was dealing with changes to her body—sleep deprivation, a painful breast infection, the soreness from the delivery itself—so anything might have put us both on edge. Not to mention the whirl of emotions that came with having a baby. I whispered to her that I'd get Blake out of the house in under an hour. And I almost did.

But he insisted on holding Henry.

We tried to put him off. We said Henry needed to be fed and then go to sleep. But Blake insisted, saying we were like family, that he was "Uncle Blake" since neither one of us had siblings, and it wouldn't be right for him not to hold our baby. I said we wanted to get him back to sleep. Blake wouldn't let it go.

Due to loyalty and years of friendship with him, I finally relented and said Blake could hold Henry if we set him up on the couch.

Amanda's eyes turned into more than daggers. They were giant icy broadswords directed right at me.

Blake was a good friend. I thought by showing trust, by sharing with him, we'd be showing him how we really felt.

Amanda took over then. She propped a department store's worth of pillows around Blake, and then gently set the baby in his arms. She sat six inches away, watching with the vigilance of a new mother. She made a mama grizzly look laid-back and calm.

And it all went fine for ten minutes. Henry lay still, gurgling happily. Blake talked to him in a soothing voice. I even managed to take a photo, which I immediately posted on Instagram.

But then Blake decided to stand up. Without asking. And when he stood, he bumped Henry's head against the glass lampshade next to the couch.

Immediately Henry began to wail. And Amanda moved to take Henry back so fast that a brief little tug-of-war ensued, as they both tried to hold the baby. For a second, I really thought Henry might end up on the floor.

But Amanda wrestled him from Blake's arms. And a quick examination of his head showed that the bump against the lampshade had left only a small red mark. Henry quieted down, and Blake offered a halfhearted apology.

If he'd offered one that had sounded remotely sincere, he might have avoided Amanda's wrath. And mine.

But he sounded so casual, so unconcerned about Henry's well-being and the stress his actions had placed on us, that something had to give.

And Amanda hasn't always been one for suppressing her feelings.

Amanda called him selfish and self-centered. Immature. Irresponsible.

Inconsiderate.

All the bad things we'd both thought about Blake for years but had never dared to say.

It all came pouring out that evening in our living room.

And I knew Amanda was mad at me too. And I couldn't blame her.

I pushed Blake toward the door, trying to send him on his way and defuse the situation as much as possible. I told Blake he'd made a mistake, that all he'd had to do was stay on the couch and everything would have been fine.

Then Amanda told Blake he had no regard for anyone or anything. That he was careless and destructive. And she didn't care if he never came back to our house.

Before he left, Blake turned back and said, "You think *I* don't care about anyone? I have something to tell you, Amanda—you should talk to your husband about that."

"What do you mean?" Amanda asked.

"Forget it," Blake said. "I'll just go."

After I guided him out and went back in, Amanda told me she didn't know if she could stand the thought of him coming back in the house when Henry was still a baby.

"Blake can see him again when Henry goes to college."

Things cooled between Blake and me. We texted but didn't see each other until that night when he'd appeared out of nowhere, saying my name in the dark.

CHAPTER FIVE

"Okay," I said, "you're getting married on Saturday, and we're not invited. That's okay. If you need me to do something to help you with the wedding, I will. You said you planned this all at the last minute. Do you need a photographer or something? A guy I know at work might be able to do it on short notice."

Blake shook his head. "We've got all that covered. Band, photographer, flowers. It's really going to be nice. I mean, if it happens."

"If? What do you mean, if? I thought you'd patched it all up with Sam, mended the fences, and rebuilt the bridges."

Blake started to say something, then stopped. His cheeks flushed again. He almost looked embarrassed.

I'd never seen anything embarrass Blake. And plenty of things over the years should have. But maybe not drinking allowed him to feel shame more acutely.

"Like I said, I was really open with this woman," he said. "I could tell her anything about myself."

"What did you tell her that's a problem?"

"I put my thoughts and feelings about her down in writing. In some letters. If you follow me. It's actually kind of romantic and old-fashioned. I mean, who writes those kinds of letters anymore? A hell of a lot better than changing your Facebook status to say you're dating someone. Or to post something on Instagram with some gauzy filter. It was a grand gesture, right?"

I shook my head, trying not to say too much. But I couldn't help myself. "It would have been grand if they'd been written for your future wife. Yes."

Blake had always fancied himself something of a romantic. I was never sure he understood what the word really meant. From his point of view, being romantic meant falling in love easily, telling a woman whatever she wanted to hear in the moment, and dealing with the consequences later. In college, he had preferred to communicate with everyone, including his romantic interests, through the phone or face-to-face. He'd hated to text or e-mail. He'd never joined social media. He once showed me a note he wrote to a woman he dated casually in college. The flowery, sentimental language made me feel queasy, but it worked to convince the woman to date him for a month. Blake spun all of these choices as something romantic as well. He occasionally referred to himself as a man born in the wrong time, and he liked to mock my social media habits.

"Well, this woman has those letters. And I don't."

All of a sudden, I got it. "Are you saying she's threatening to show them to Sam?"

Blake's face unclenched for the first time in a few minutes. "More or less, that's what she's told me."

"So what? You and Sam were broken up. You dated someone and gushed at her. Sam can't hold that against you forever. Just get married and move on."

Blake nodded. "I really laid it on with her. Look, I don't know what all I said in the heat of the moment. I was just spilling my thoughts."

"Then just come clean with Sam about what you may or may not have said, that you may have gotten a little carried away, and she'll forget it. This is really odd behavior for you. Worrying so much about this. You're all tied up in knots over what you said in a letter to this Jen. It's no big deal."

"Sam does like to see the best in people. Everybody, not just me."

Blake's assessment of Samantha rang true. She struck me as one of the most guileless people I'd ever met. But I didn't believe she saw Blake simply as a reclamation project, a chance to show that her empathy and patience could outlast anything he could throw her way. When Sam and Blake were together and things were good between them, she did smooth his rough edges. She brought things out in Blake—patience, calmness, sensitivity—that no one else did. And Blake helped tether Samantha to the ground, helped her appear less naive. Despite everything they'd been through as a couple, they struck me as a good match, the best I'd ever seen Blake part of.

And what would happen if Sam saw a note written by Blake pledging his devotion to another woman?

It would be awkward and strange for them. For Sam.

But not worth ending a relationship over.

My phone buzzed in my pocket. I took it out and saw a text from Amanda.

Are you coming soon? Sleepy baby.

Sorry. Hurrying.

"Just ask for the letters back?" I asked as I put the phone away.

"I've tried that. Many times. But she won't really take my calls anymore. It's been a few weeks since I've called her or talked to her. We're at loggerheads. She won't budge. As the wedding approaches . . . I just don't want anything to blow this for Sam and me. We're almost to the finish line."

Maybe I was slow off the mark. Maybe the wheels in my mind didn't turn as quickly as they should have.

Maybe I just couldn't comprehend that Blake would ask me for the kind of thing he had dreamed up.

But I didn't see where any of it was going.

I had no idea.

"Do you want me to recommend a lawyer or something?" I asked. "I'm not sure a respectable attorney would get wrapped up in something this insignificant. Or petty. Or whatever you want to call it."

Like I said, Blake was several steps ahead of me. He shook his head, his eyes slowly closing and then opening again. They remained clear as a mountain stream.

"No, *you're* going to get the letters back, Ryan," he said. "You're going to go into her house and bring them back to me."

CHAPTER SIX

I felt my eyes widen. If anyone in the coffee shop had been looking at me, they would have thought I was joking around, making some kind of ridiculous face, the kind of thing I did to entertain Henry at home.

But the emotion was real and genuine. What Blake was saying sounded completely and utterly nuts.

"You want me to go talk to this woman on your behalf? Why? She doesn't know me—"

But he shook his head. "You're not going to *talk* to her, Ryan. It's past the time for talking. You're going to go into her house and take the letters. And you're going to bring them to me so Sam never has to see them. I didn't say anything about talking to her."

It seemed as though the music, which had been playing softly over our heads, dropped to an even lower volume. And across the room someone broke out laughing, a sharp, mocking sound that caused me to look their way and then back to Blake.

"You're crazy," I said, shaking my head. "Seriously. I have to get home. I can't believe you dragged me over here for this bullshit."

Blake acted as though he hadn't heard me.

"It's simple," he said. "Tonight at ten o'clock. She'll be out. She always is on Thursdays. I know the door code. I know where the letters are. She has a keepsake drawer in her bedroom. The letters were there the last time I was in the house. That was a few weeks ago. They've always been in there. I should have taken them, but it would be too obvious. You just go over, go in, and get them. Easy as pie."

"You want me to break into a complete stranger's house?"

"Not break in, Ryan." Now he shook his head at me. "I said I know the code. At least, I think I do. Unless she's changed it." He scratched his chin distractedly for a moment. "But you just *go* in. No breaking in. No busting down doors. Nothing like that. And you're not stealing her TV or her computer. Just taking the letters I wrote. They're my property, really. They're my words."

"If you go into someone's home without permission, it's breaking in. Even if you know the door code. The cops won't make that distinction. Besides, maybe she's scanned or copied the letters already. It could all be for nothing."

"I can't take any chances."

"Why don't *you* do it?" I asked. "Why drag me down into your mess?"

"I can't. What if someone saw me? What if something went wrong, and I got caught? Then it would all come out. And Sam's parents . . . her dad . . . even the smallest hint of impropriety, and he'd lose his mind. I can't have that happen. Not when Sam and I are so close to the finish line."

"But I can? *I* can risk getting caught? You think it's okay if I get arrested. I have a child. A wife."

"You won't get caught, Ryan. And I know I can trust you. I'd ask someone else, but who else can I count on as much as you? You're one of the few honest people I know. Shit, maybe the only one. You and Sam. But I can't ask her."

"If I get caught breaking into someone's house—my job, my reputation. What would people think of me? What would Amanda think of me?"

"That's why you'll be careful. And you'll do it right."

I picked up my mug and drank without thinking. The coffee had turned lukewarm and too bitter. I almost spit it out, but I choked it down and pushed the mug away with the back of my hand.

"It's been nice seeing you again, Blake," I said, although I no longer felt that way. "I guess. I know you don't want advice, but since we're friends, I feel compelled to offer some. Just talk to Sam. Start your marriage in a good place, with none of this craziness. That's the best shot you've got. Not this cloak-and-dagger shit that can only lead to more problems."

I scooted my chair back again, but before I could stand, Blake's hand came across the table, landing on top of mine like a handcuff. I felt the coolness of his skin, the roughness of his palm. He locked eyes with me.

"Are you going to do that with Amanda, Ryan?" he asked. "Are you going to go home tonight and sit down with her while your son sleeps in his nice room upstairs and wipe the slate clean? Are you going to tell her everything she doesn't know about you? She's pretty no-nonsense. She's a tough nut."

"I've never done anything like this."

"You know that's not what I'm talking about. You know what I mean. Hell, you're so worried about your reputation and your position, you'd have to come clean to everybody in this town to feel safe, wouldn't you? And if everyone knew . . . well, there's legal jeopardy."

"What are you saying? Are you threatening me?"

"You'll do this for me, Ryan. You'll do it or every single person in this town will know the one thing you don't want them to know about you."

CHAPTER SEVEN

Blake Norton and I met during our freshman year at Ferncroft College, a small liberal arts school in the rolling hills of central Kentucky with about two thousand students, thirty minutes away from Rossingville. We first got to know each other when we joined the same social club during the fall of our freshman year.

These social clubs weren't really fraternities. Ferncroft didn't allow the Greek system on its beautiful, stately Gothic Revival campus. The college took itself too seriously for that. They wanted to be like Harvard and Princeton. They wanted to be considered the "Ivy of the South."

So, going all the way back to the school's founding in the nineteenth century, students, both men and women, joined social clubs. Ostensibly, they were philanthropic organizations in which students raised money for worthy causes, volunteering their time on weekends and evenings at soup kitchens and blood drives and tutoring programs.

But the social club members engaged in all the things someone might associate with a fraternity or sorority. We drank. We held parties. We carried out elaborate pranks.

Our club was called the Sigil and Shield and, like all of the clubs at

Ferncroft, it was coed. Had been since the nineteen sixties. And, during our time at Ferncroft and largely due to Blake's influence, we became known as one of the hardest-partying clubs on campus.

We threw large blowouts for every occasion—Arbor Day, Groundhog Day, Easter, fall break, you name it. If someone farted or went to the bathroom, we threw a party. Everyone drank at these events. Everyone danced and yelled and let loose.

Sigil and Shield also made a big deal out of being exclusive. We admitted only the right kind of student, someone we all believed would fit in with the rest of us. Someone with the right degree of coolness, intellect, and ironic detachment. To that end, we made anyone wishing to join go through a rigorous series of tests.

In other words, we hazed.

We didn't call it that, of course. Especially not after one of our rival clubs, the Kings and Queens, was disbanded by the university during our sophomore year when one of their pledges was rushed to the hospital with alcohol poisoning.

So we told our pledges we had to "interview" them.

We all knew what that meant. The pledges knew. The members knew. Even the administration knew. And they were willing to turn a blind eye as long as the tuition dollars rolled in and the enrollment stayed up. As long as the alums who went on to successful careers opened their checkbooks and gave back to the school.

Blake and I were never ringleaders in the club. We never bothered to run for or hold important positions. We went along for the parties and the fun, but otherwise we flew below the radar.

Aaron Knicely was an awkward kid who wanted to get into Sigil and Shield. Desperately. His desire to be one of us oozed out of every pore on his body.

He was a small kid, a freshman when we were seniors. His clothes never looked quite right. He never knew the right thing to say. At parties he stood around, shifting his weight from one foot to the other like a nervous child.

He was never going to get into Sigil and Shield. Never. As soon as members laid eyes on him, they wrote him off.

But for some reason, he stuck around through the pledge process. He took whatever the members dished out and came back for more. He showed a lot of spine, to be honest, and while I never said it out loud to anyone else, I found myself with a growing sense of admiration for him.

The night before the official invitations to join went out, we spent one final evening with all the potential members. One more party, one more chance for those supplicants who the current members of Sigil and Shield were on the fence about to make the right impression.

The rest of what I have to tell you about that night I've had to reconstruct by talking to others, including Blake, and reading things in the news. To say I had too much to drink would be an understatement. I'm not sure I ever drank more in my life.

Or remembered less.

Snatches still come back to me.

I remember the party starting. I remember doing shots of tequila until I couldn't see straight.

I remember dancing with . . . someone.

And I remember going outside. Blake and me and Aaron Knicely.

I know we had more tequila as we walked.

I know Aaron drank more than the rest of us. I know we egged him on.

I know we should have stopped. But we didn't.

CHAPTER EIGHT

Blake's hand remained clamped on mine. The contact between our skin started to feel unpleasant, like I'd touched something cold and unknown in the dark.

But I didn't pull away.

We remained connected in more ways than one.

"Let me ask you something," he said, sounding casual. "Do you still make those nocturnal visits to the Steiners' house you told me about? You must, right?"

"You know the answer to that."

"I wonder if they really don't know it's you," he said, amused. "When they did that cheesy newspaper story, they claimed not to know who the Good Samaritan was. But if they thought about it, if they really looked into it, couldn't they figure it out? When a crime is committed, the cops ask, 'Who benefits?' Well, who benefits from trying to buy off the Steiners?"

Blake didn't know about Dawn. No one did. I'd gone from assuaging my guilt by giving money to the family to being blackmailed by Dawn. I was being squeezed like a piece of fruit. The small profits generated by the Pig had been mostly going to the Steiner family. What had started as a fun project with friends and a bit of a tax shelter—own a business, brew some beer—had turned into a wellspring for guilt and blackmail money. And now Dawn wanted a big, fat chunk I didn't have.

And none of the money I'd given them had lifted the burden of guilt I carried. I still saw the accident in my dreams, still saw Maggie Steiner's face. . . .

"People do good things for strangers every day," I said. "It's not an aberration."

But Blake rambled on.

"The lucky thing for you is that Aaron couldn't remember much of anything from that night," Blake said. "He was wasted, and then he bashed his head so hard against the steering wheel, he was concussed, so the whole night was a blur. He knew he'd been at Sigil and Shield, which meant a one-year suspension for the club. We all had the fear of God put into us by the dean. I remember that." He shook his head at the memory. "They chose to come down on the whole club rather than in-dividuals. After all, Aaron wasn't actually a member. . . ."

"We were lucky they didn't," I said.

"Damn right. I remember you holding your breath all the way up to graduation. You were so worried they were going to jump on us, expel us, and not let us get our degrees. Man, you were obsessed with cov-ering your ass. 'What if my mom finds out the truth? What about all the sacrifices she made for my education after my dad died? She went back to school. She became a teacher.'"

"Yeah, I know. I was scared."

"Everybody knows who was in the car that night. It was in the papers. So if a reporter really wanted to dig deeper into those gifts to the Steiners, they could."

"The reporter called you and me. You know that. And we both told them the same thing—we didn't know about the money."

"They'd have to subpoena bank records to really prove anything. And who wants to do that?"

"It's in the past," I said. "Aaron did his time."

Blake pulled his hand away and laughed in a low, snuffling way. When he finally stopped and wiped his eyes, he said, "Did you really just say, 'It's in the past'? Really? You're still bringing the Steiners envelopes of cash, and you don't want anyone to know about it, but you think it's in the past? Let me ask you something else, Ryan. . . . Does Amanda know *everything* about that night yet? Have you ever told her? Does she know about the money you give to complete strangers?"

I didn't answer. I didn't need to because he knew I'd never told her my role in the accident. Amanda hadn't attended Ferncroft. We'd met after graduation, and she pretty quickly knew about the accident. After all, what does someone do when they meet a new person? They Google them. And the information about the accident was right there for all to see. Aaron driving drunk when he hit the other car. One person killed, one injured in the second vehicle. Two of Aaron's passengers—Blake and me—injured. One—me—injured seriously enough to require hospitalization. Amanda didn't know that the bad dreams I had several times a year were images of Maggie and Emily passing across my mind during the darkness of the night.

It had been Blake and I who suggested Aaron go perform one of the oldest rituals known to students at Ferncroft College—drive fifteen miles out into the countryside, down winding state roads, and take the sign announcing the entrance to the small town of Gnaw Bone, Kentucky, population 343. Almost every dorm and social club on campus had a stolen Gnaw Bone sign in it.

I knew it all led Aaron to think he had an iota of a chance to be admitted to Sigil and Shield when he really didn't.

"So Amanda knows all about the accident," Blake said, "but she only knows what was in the papers. The official story. You were in the car and got hurt. . . ."

"Blake—"

"Oh, yeah. I remember now. There's the thing with Amanda's sister. How old was she when she died?"

He waited until I answered.

"Fifteen."

"On her bike, right? Hit by a drunk driver. Didn't you say that was one of the things you and Amanda talked about when you first met? How you both had drunk-driving accidents that affected your lives? It would be tough to tell her the truth now, wouldn't it? You'd have to admit to her that you were behind the wheel in an accident that killed a seventeen-year-old girl. You wouldn't be any different in her eyes from the monster who killed her sister. If you thought Amanda was pissed over me bumping Henry's head against a lamp—"

"It's over, Blake."

"How does Amanda accept you owning a stake in a bar when her sister died in a drunk-driving accident?"

"We talked about that before I ever got involved with the Pig. I wasn't going to do it if it caused problems for her or her family. But she said it was okay with her, that people have to move on. It's over, Blake."

His face suddenly grew serious. "Is it over for Emily Steiner and her family, Ryan? Limping around with a shattered leg and a speech impediment? Having to live with her parents all these years instead of finishing high school with her classmates and going off to college? Their other child dead."

"You've made your point. I haven't forgotten them. I never can."

"Things are tough today, Ryan. The political climate. Everything is so politically correct. If the people you worked with, the clients at your company who you help with their social media and branding campaigns . . . Would they want a PR guy who had his name smeared all over the news for killing someone? Would Warren Manufacturing want their screen doors being branded by someone who committed vehicular homicide? Or the people who buy your beer at the Pig—would they buy your beer if they found out the role you really played in that girl getting killed? If they found out you were the one driving and not Aaron. Think of the clients you'd lose, Ryan, the money. The business. The charities you've supported. Which ones are they? The local chapter of MADD, right? The women's shelter?"

"I said you made your point."

"What if everyone found out, Ryan? Hell, the police. There's no statute of limitations on felonies in Kentucky. Did you know that?"

But he'd lost me. I was shaking my head.

"I'm not going to do it," I said. "And the only person who could expose me is you. Are you saying you're going to tell everyone I was driving that night if I don't do this . . . this asinine request?"

Blake remained silent for a moment. A new scent reached my nostrils . . . a burning pastry, something left in a toaster too long. It acted as an irritant, almost causing me to sneeze. The barista waved a towel around behind the counter, fanning smoke, her face creased with disgust.

"I'm not going to tell anyone, Ryan," he said, the words coming out slow. "These letters I wrote to Jen, the things we shared and talked about . . . You see, that accident and the truth about it, the truth about you—well . . . I haven't been able to tell anyone about it either. Ever. I can't even tell Sam because her parents would flip. It's a secret I'm keeping too. So that article came out in the paper, and it brought it all up for me again. You know, I was in that car too. So . . . when Jen and I were still dating back then . . . and because I felt freer with her, looser, I felt liberated to tell her things I couldn't tell anyone else. Telling her . . . It was like when you meet a stranger in a bar or in an airport. I unburdened myself to her because she was separate from the rest of my life. I knew we weren't going to get married, so I spilled my guts."

The door to the Ground Floor remained closed, but I'd have sworn it had opened, letting in a cold wind. Some chill gripped me, creeped over every inch of my body. The feeling made me nauseated, and I struggled to say anything. But I finally managed to.

"Blake, no."

"She knows. And I mentioned it in one of the letters. . . . I told her how much it meant to me that we could speak freely about everything, all the things that matter to me. So it's in there. In writing. The truth about that night. The truth about who was driving. The truth about you."

The cold feeling gradually turned warmer. It felt like a small fire was burning in my chest. Dead center.

"Blake." My voice was low, bitter. I looked around but no one paid any attention to us. "She knows? And you put it in writing? Are you the biggest damn fool who has ever lived?"

"So you see," he said, "it's in your best interest to get those letters out of there. We both have a lot at stake. You'd be exposed and put in legal jeopardy for driving the car. My relationship with Sam and her family would be in jeopardy."

Blake started fishing around in his pants pocket. He brought out a piece of paper folded into a tiny square. He handed it to me, and after a short pause, I took it from him but didn't open it.

"The address is on there," he said. "So's the door code. It's a small house, and you just need to get into the bedroom and look in the top drawer of the dresser. She doesn't have a dog or a roommate or anything, so you don't have to worry about that. Just get in and get out. She goes to a late-night yoga class on Thursdays. She'll be out of the house until eleven. Maybe later if she gets a drink with a friend or something, like she sometimes does. But you don't want to dally. Just get in, get the letters, and get back out."

"Maybe this woman wouldn't do anything with the letters," I said. "Maybe she's just bluffing."

"She might be. You're right. Maybe she just wants to make me sweat. But can either of us take that chance?"

"Why does this have to happen tonight? Why such little notice?" I still held the folded paper in my outstretched hand.

"I just told you, Ryan. The wedding is Saturday. And Jen knows that.

So if she wants to stick it to me, she'd do it before the wedding. She'd blow everything up now. And tonight is the only night this week I know when she's out of the house. You tell Amanda whatever you want to tell her to get out of your house at ten. But do take care of it tonight if you don't want everyone in town to know about who was really driving that night."

My hand, the one holding the paper, shook, causing the paper to quiver.

I don't know if Blake noticed or not.

For the distraction more than anything else, I put the folded paper into my pocket. I couldn't look Blake in the eye.

I thought of everything I'd done in the six years since college, in the six years since the night of the accident. The one that ruined Emily Steiner's life. The one that killed Maggie.

The one I caused but didn't get caught for.

Could that bring everything all down?

Did I intend to find out?

"I don't ever want to see you again," I said.

"What's that?"

Maybe I'd spoken quietly, too quietly for him to hear. So I said it again, making sure he understood.

"I'll do it," I said. "But then after I bring you these letters, I don't ever want to see or hear from you again. Ever. This is the end between the two of us. Do you understand?"

He looked a little surprised but not completely.

He nodded, and I turned on my heel like a soldier and left the coffee shop without looking back.

CHAPTER NINE

Amanda was in the kitchen when I came home. It was eight fifteen, and she sat at the table with a mug of tea and a book, her phone resting right next to her. The kitchen smelled like the meal I'd missed. Grilled chicken, sautéed onions and peppers.

Amanda's face, her presence, always brought me relief. I wanted, needed to see someone normal. Someone with their feet on the ground.

But she didn't look up right away when I came through the door. She kept her eyes fixed on her book for a beat longer than normal, so I knew she was irritated by my late arrival. And I couldn't blame her. After five years together, two of them as a married couple, we recognized the slightest ripples that passed across each other's face. I could tell by the way her brow creased and the set of her jaw when something was bothering her. And she always spotted the way I pursed my lips or squinted my eyes as a sign of trouble.

She picked up a bookmark and stuck it in the book. "Is everything okay?"

"It is. And I'm sorry I'm late. I know I missed bedtime."

"I was mad when you didn't come home on time." She tended to be philosophical and analytical about her moods, often taking a step back and examining herself from a careful distance. "I've been trying to get myself into a reasonable frame of mind since then."

"I'm sorry." I leaned down and kissed her, tasting the tea. "Mmmm. Peppermint."

"You want some?" She wore her brown hair pulled back off her face. Her skin was clear, her lips red. The light showed the flashing brightness of her teeth when she spoke.

"No, thanks. And I really am sorry. It was my night to check on the Pig, as you know."

"I do. I know you have obligations there."

"And then when I was leaving, Tony—you know that kid who's been waiting tables there for the last six months? The one with all the tattoos?"

"Don't they all have a lot of tattoos?"

"Yes, they do. But Tony is the one with the mermaid tattoo on his arm."

"I remember him. He's a cute kid."

"Well, he broke up with his boyfriend and wanted relationship advice. So I listened and gave him some. I guess he sees me as a wise old man."

"You are to a college kid." She winked and picked up the tea mug. "Look, I'm really not mad, okay? I think this is the first time you've missed putting Henry down since he was born. Life happens sometimes. You can change two diapers full of poop tomorrow to make up for it."

I withheld the conversation with Blake. What he'd asked me to do made me sick and nervous. I felt a heavy, dense pressure in my gut, and I tried to distract myself by turning it into something else.

"I need to eat," I said.

And I did suddenly feel achingly hungry. I opened the refrigerator and found a cold piece of grilled chicken. I took a couple of bites, not even bothering with a plate, and washed it down with a glass of water from the tap. It was cold and hurt my teeth.

I stared out the window above the sink at the backyard even though it was dark. I'd been fantasizing ever since we'd found out we were pregnant about installing a swing set and someday being able to push Henry on a swing out there. We'd contracted with a local company to add a patio and landscaping first to make the yard, which had been badly overgrown when we moved in, the kind of place we could really spend time. We could think about the swing set in a few years. . . .

That was why I had almost no extra money to just hand over to Dawn.

I turned back around, wiping the corner of my mouth with my fingers.

"Hey," I said, "it looked like the car was moved. Was there a doctor's appointment today? I tried to call you earlier."

"Oh, that." She put the mug back down. "I ran to the store for a little bit."

"The bane of your existence, going to the grocery store. Did you take Henry?"

"No, Mom came over. She stayed with him while I went. It was no big deal."

"I just wish you could go out and do something more exciting than a trip to the store."

"I am. Next weekend. Or have you forgotten already?"

"Is that next weekend already?" Since Henry's birth, time moved with the speed of a rocket. But I knew what she was referring to. "Your trip to Nashville with Holly and Kate? My weekend as a single dad?"

"I think you can handle it. You change diapers better than I do. That's why I was so quickly able to get over you not being here for bedtime. Yes, you missed the ceremonial changing of the dirty diaper, and I had to do it myself. But next weekend"—she rubbed her hands together—"it's all yours. Every dirty diaper."

"That sounds like revenge."

"No. It sounds like a mom who needs to get away. I'm sure I'll bawl when I leave him though. Didn't we both cry when we went away to Lexington in January and left him with my parents?"

"You cried."

"Okay, tough guy. I didn't see you wiping your eyes. Right. Anyway, I think he definitely has some teeth coming in on the bottom. He could be getting real cranky real soon."

"Can't we just rub whiskey on his gums? Isn't that what we're supposed to do?"

She laughed a little at my suggestion. "If you're from the old school." She turned her chair to better face me. She wore yoga pants and flip-flops with my old Ferncroft College sweatshirt. "You know, if you want to make it up to me for being late and missing diaper duty, we can watch that movie tonight. The one about the former FBI agent who tracks down missing kids? I feel tired but not quite as exhausted as I normally do, so I've got a chance to stay awake until the end."

I wished more than anything the night could have been a normal one. The two of us could have curled up together on the couch and watched a movie, even if one or both of us ended up falling asleep halfway through. I even wouldn't have minded if Henry woke us up, or if I changed a dirty diaper or took the trash out.

All of those very normal things sounded too good to be true. Because they were.

I picked up a napkin and wiped my hands.

"Oh, crap. I'm sorry. I forgot I promised Eric and Ron I'd play basketball with them tonight. At the Y. They're down a man, and I'm on their sub list. The game's at nine forty-five."

"Really? That late?"

"Yes, really. The league goes late on Thursday, and I've been telling them no for a long time. Kind of like you were telling Holly and Kate no for so long about the girls' weekend until they practically forced you to say yes."

"You got me to say yes."

She let out a long, disappointed sigh. And she placed her hand on the book, absently riffling the pages, the only sound in the quiet kitchen. Lately our ability to find time to spend together was always compromised by work, Henry, and the accompanying exhaustion. We'd been trying to find a good night to watch a movie together for over a week, and my encounter with Blake had ruined it, like an infection spreading through every aspect of my life.

"Can we try for tomorrow?" I asked. "I'll be sure to get home early. Maybe Henry will go down earlier."

"It's okay," she said with a wave of her hand. "Don't worry about it." She didn't sound convincing as she nodded at the book. "I need to finish this for book club next week anyway. And it's actually good. Someone picked a book I like for a change."

I went over to her again and placed my arm on her shoulder, pulling her close. "I'm sorry, Amanda. Really. I'd bail, but I promised, and they need another guy. And I've been putting them off for so long."

"And you're such a good basketball player."

"You know that's not true."

"You're right. You're terrible. I've seen you play. You're the living, breathing embodiment of the phrase 'White men can't jump.'" She forced a smile. "It's all good, I guess. You and I can have a night together tomorrow."

"Thanks for understanding."

I released her from the hug but stood there, staring down at her. Her natural beauty. Her shining hair, her hazel eyes. The life we'd built together—home, careers, a baby. I felt a tearing in my chest, a wrenching ache. I wanted to stay home. I wanted to be there with her and Henry.

But if I stayed and everyone found out about my role in the accident, I could lose it all. I'd face legal jeopardy, civil jeopardy. I'd lose my job, my ability to provide for my new family.

"What is it?" she asked, her brow creasing with curiosity.

"Nothing."

"Something's on your mind, Ryan."

"Anticipation," I said. "I'm looking forward to tomorrow night more than tonight."

She reached up and cupped her hand against my cheek. "Tomorrow night?"

"Absolutely."

"But," she said, stopping me in my tracks, "you need to tell me something."

"Sure."

She sounded serious. Did she know something? Had Blake come by the house?

"Am I turning into one of those boring mothers who only talks about her kid's sleeping and teething? Is that what I've become? I used to have a career, before the little bundle of joy came along. I made almost as much as you do."

"You're not boring. I promise. Remember just this morning we had that talk about the election, and you gave me that long, complicated theory on why people vote against their own interests. That wasn't boring. Not at all."

"So you're saying I still have some intellectual heft?"

"Absolutely. More than I do." I kissed her again. Our lips lingered for a long, sweet moment. "And you can go back to work whenever you want. You actually made a little more money than I did a couple of years when you hit those bonuses. And you know they'd love to have you back, even as a consultant."

"I know. I'm thinking about it. I see all my friends on social media, posting about their fabulous work trips and high-pressure meetings. I feel cut off."

"You should do whatever you want, Amanda."

I had started up the stairs to the bedroom to change when her voice stopped me.

"Hey," she said, "do you know what I saw on Facebook today?"

I came back down. "I don't know. What?"

"As you know, I don't get on there every day anymore. It's tough to keep up with all of it these days, and I'd rather be focused on the little guy."

"Of course."

"But I checked it out today. Did you see it? Sam posted that she and Blake are getting married this weekend. Did you know about that?"

I tried very hard to keep my face neutral and stoic.

"No, I didn't see that on Facebook," I said.

"Blake didn't tell you about it?"

"No."

"I know he's stayed away ever since I chewed him out over the lampshade incident. But I can't believe he didn't invite you. They're getting married, and we just don't know about it or get invited?"

"Isn't that what you wanted?" I asked.

She thought about it, tapping her fingers against the cover of her book. "I guess so. It's just strange the way people can pass in and out of our lives. Maybe that's all Facebook is good for—reminding us of the people we're no longer close to."

"That's one way to look at it."

"Are you sad?" she asked. "If we don't go or even get invited? I've been thinking. . . . You and he were such good friends, and while he's not my favorite person, he means a lot to you. I know you leaned on him a lot when your dad died, and I can't underestimate that." She shrugged and looked reluctant to admit what she said next. "I mean, he has his charms. I have to admit that. He's always been very kind to me outside of the lampshade incident. He's funny, for one thing. And thoughtful . . . at times. And I do like Sam a lot. We were really starting to become friends. I guess what I'm saying is if you want him back in our lives, if you want to try to have a better relationship with him, we can do it. We all have difficult people in our lives, and we have to remember all the good things about them too. . . . Am I making any sense?"

"You are."

"So I could ask Sam about the wedding if you want. . . ."

"I will be very happy not to attend their wedding," I said.

And I meant every word of it.

Before I went up the stairs again, Amanda said my name. "Ryan?"

I waited. "What?"

But she didn't say anything. She studied me, her brow creased.

I tried to make my face blank. I tried not to purse my lips or squint my eyes.

"It's nothing," she said.

"Are you sure?"

"I'm sure. Tomorrow night."

She went back to her book, and I went upstairs.

CHAPTER TEN

It took ten minutes to reach the address Blake had given me. The house sat in the middle of a block in a relatively new subdivision, the houses midsized and almost identical. SUVs and sedans filled the driveways, and soccer balls and swing sets occupied the backyards. Someone Amanda used to work with lived a few streets away, and we had gone to a Fourth of July party at her house shortly after it was built.

I arrived at nine fifty. It wasn't clear to me if the woman in question was leaving before ten or right at ten on the nose, so I rolled past the house, taking a look. The front porch light glowed like a tiny moon, illuminating the house number, but the rest of the place looked dark. She'd probably already left for her yoga class, but if Blake said ten was the time, I intended to stick to that. I circled the block one more time, hoping against hope I drove in a nonsuspicious way.

The second time around, the stress started to get the better of me. My palms grew wet where they pressed against the steering wheel. Sweat trickled down my side underneath the gym clothes I'd put on to perpetuate the lie I'd told to Amanda. My mouth was dry, my heart fluttering in my chest like that of a scared kitten. I needed gas too, but I ignored the gauge. I could deal with that on the way home when all the nonsense was over.

Between Blake's request and the looming threat of exposure from Dawn Steiner, I was a jangled tangle of nerves.

I studied the houses lining the street, houses where families slept or watched TV or read together in comfortable family rooms, and I wished more than anything I could be home with Amanda, watching some silly movie, each of us with an ear trained toward the baby monitor and the sound of Henry's gentle breathing.

Just leave. Just turn around and get out. Tell Blake to go to hell.

I passed the woman's house, still dark, still empty looking.

Just hit the gas and go.

Did I know for sure Blake would really tell anyone and everyone about the accident from college, the one that had killed Maggie Steiner and injured her sister Emily?

I couldn't say anything with certainty.

And that was always the problem with Blake—his unpredictability. If he wanted to, he could tell my coworkers. He could tell my partners in the Pig. He could go to the media.

He could tell Amanda. Far too easily. All he had to do was drive over, knock on the door, and tell her. He could be sitting in front of our house right now, waiting to tell her.

But it was more than just Blake now. For whatever reason, he'd said in those letters to this woman something that incriminated me. And those words put everything in my life in jeopardy.

And the risk to everything I held dear made me willing to do something as crazy as going into a stranger's home and removing something—*stealing it*, for all intents and purposes—just to preserve my family, my freedom, and my reputation. I'd spent the six years since college, every single day since the night of the accident, trying to leave it behind and create a life I could be proud of.

One Amanda and Henry could also be proud of.

I couldn't risk any of that. And the option of going into a stranger's house for a few minutes when she wasn't home and grabbing a stack of letters that included the most incriminating one sounded pretty easy.

I checked the clock on my phone. Two minutes before ten. If I was going to do this thing, it was time.

I'd formulated a plan for how to pull the job off. I parked a block and a half away, at the end of a street so I wasn't directly in front of anyone's house. When I'd dressed at home, right after peeking in on a sleeping Henry and wishing I could trade places with him in blissful slumber, I'd selected a dark shirt and shorts, the better to blend into the night. I'd even pulled a baseball hat down low on my forehead, the band exerting a squeezing pressure against my scalp.

I checked myself in the rearview before I climbed out of the car.

The person I saw staring back at me looked exactly like someone going to break into a house, like a guy who didn't want to be recognized. So I pushed the hat back a little on my forehead, hoping it made me look more casual and less like a creeping cat burglar.

I'd simply have to walk like a normal guy strolling through the neighborhood without a care in the world.

I turned the car off and got out.

CHAPTER ELEVEN

The night was strangely quiet. The moon overhead slipped in and out of clouds like a moving spotlight. I instinctively reached for my phone, itching to capture and share the image, but I pushed the urge away. Instead, I simply stopped and made sure my phone was set to silent.

I tried to walk softly, but even with my sneakers, my footfalls sounded like gunshots in the quiet night. A few early-spring bugs chirped in the grass, and a car drove by a couple of blocks away, its engine emitting a low hum in the darkness, but otherwise there was almost no sound. No voices, no music. Nothing.

The silence unnerved me. The spring night seemed sinister, a cauldron of lurking dangers.

I turned onto a street that ran north and south, one that connected at the next intersection with the street where this woman Jen lived. On that street I'd turn right and go down a few houses before reaching the correct address. I looked at the houses as I passed, envious of the quiet lives going on behind their closed doors and drawn curtains. I felt like an interloper on their average lives, dragged there as the result of a horrible mistake I'd made six years earlier.

And one Blake had made in the past few months.

A man came around the corner of a house on my left. I saw him first, then heard something like keys jangling. His small fluffy dog bounded ahead of him, straining against the leash, and when the dog saw me, he strained even harder, pulling against the man until he stumbled slightly forward.

I looked to my right and briefly considered cutting sharply across the street to the sidewalk opposite me. But there wasn't time to do that, and if I had, wouldn't I have created suspicion?

So I walked on, head down slightly, and as the man came abreast of me, the fluffy dog's tail going like a metronome, I tried not to make eye contact. But the man said hello to me, a friendly greeting, and without thinking too much about it, I said hello back to him.

Then my eyes trailed up, ever so quickly, and our gazes locked for a split second. The man smiled at me as we passed and looked like he wanted to say something, but I turned my head away and looked down at my shoes.

When I was well by him and almost to the next street, the one I needed to turn right on in order to complete my mission, I wondered if the man knew me from somewhere. Had I seen recognition in his eyes, however fleeting? Or had I just allowed my paranoia to get the best of me?

He might have seen me on one of the many social media spots we'd done for the Pig. Or he might have met me at a chamber of commerce meeting. I told myself to keep walking past the woman's street and then to loop around and return to my car. To abort the mission, as they would have said in a spy movie when the spy's cover was blown.

But when I reached the corner, I told myself to calm down, that a momentary glance in the dark with my hat and basketball clothes likely wouldn't stick in an older man's mind. Even if he had seen me somewhere before, I was now appearing before him completely out of context.

So I kept going and made the right turn.

I quickly came in sight of the house, which sat at the top of a front yard that sloped up slightly. The houses on either side of it were mostly dark as well, and on the drive over, I'd decided not to hesitate or slow down at all. I'd walk up the driveway as though I belonged there. I got to the back of the house and turned around the corner and into the backyard, where I saw the small patio and French doors.

The house directly behind me was screened from view by a privacy fence, so I breathed a little easier. But I still felt exposed, like an athlete on a field with everyone in the stands watching to see what he would do. At that point, I felt more eager to get inside the house and out of sight of any potential witnesses.

Blake had told me that the woman frequently lost her keys, so she'd installed keypads on all the exterior doors. Since he'd spent so much time coming and going—at odd hours of the day and night—he knew the code, which I'd memorized so I wouldn't have to fumble with paper while standing outside the house. Four digits. Easy enough.

But then I noticed something Blake hadn't told me about.

A pretty big detail.

Not only did the door use a keypad, but a sticker on the door indicated the keypad was connected to an alarm system. I'd heard of those setups before, and it meant that if someone tried to enter an alarm code that didn't work or if they messed up several times in a row, the alarm automatically sent an alert. The warning might go to the alarm company, who might then call the police. Or it might go to the home-owner, buzzing them on their phone.

Either way, it reduced my margin for error to almost nothing.

If I rushed and messed up the code . . .

Or if the code had been changed, and Blake didn't know. After all, wouldn't it make sense for a woman to change her keypad code after a breakup?

"Damn it, Blake," I said, muttering in the dark.

It was the kind of detail he would have overlooked. Or failed to mention.

I could have left.

No one held a gun to my head. No one was forcing me to do anything.

But I already had the code memorized.

And the longer I stood outside, the greater the chance a neighbor would glance out the window and see me.

1-7-9-2.

1792. I knew from growing up that was the year Kentucky had been admitted to the union. Maybe this woman Blake was involved with was a history buff.

I typed it in one number at a time and went for the handle, hoping nothing went wrong.

CHAPTER TWELVE

The door refused to open.

I turned the handle once, twice, and then a third time, pushing against the door at the same time, but it didn't budge.

"Shit."

My hands started to shake ever so slightly. It felt as though someone had turned up the temperature of the night by ten degrees, even though it was actually cool and pleasant. Almost growing chilly.

I entered the code again and turned the handle.

Still nothing.

A dog started barking a couple of houses away, sharp, insistent yelps that pierced the night. Could it have seen or heard me?

Then a voice cut through the darkness. "Knock it off, Sparkle!"

For some reason, I wondered why anyone would name their dog Sparkle.

But I shook that thought from my head and refocused. I knew I'd already tried twice, and my margin for error might be gone.

I guessed three made for a good magic number. Three failed attempts might trigger a response from the system. So I had to make the next one count.

Had I been wrong about the code? Was I missing something?

I reached into my pocket and brought out the paper. It was creased and limp, and my sweaty hands made it stick to my fingers and difficult to open. I unfolded it quickly, using the ambient light from the stars and the reappearing moon and the houses nearby to read Blake's note.

1-7-9-2.

Hadn't I entered that?

Had the code changed, and Blake didn't know?

I decided to try one more time. And if it didn't work, I'd get the hell out of there before the police were summoned.

Or before Sparkle came over and bit my leg off.

I took a deep breath, wiped my sweaty hands on my shorts, and carefully entered the code.

When I tried to turn the handle again, it stuck, refusing to open. And my mind raced, imagining at that very moment an alarm ringing like a fire bell in the police station just two miles away.

I tried one more time and felt the handle give a little. I pushed against the door, leaning my shoulder into it, and it gave more.

With a little more pressure, the door opened, and I almost fell across the threshold and stumbled inside the house. But I stayed on my feet, took one quick look back to make sure nobody saw me, and then I slipped inside, pulling the door shut behind me.

CHAPTER THIRTEEN

Everything was dark.

Since I'd spent so much time walking through the night, my eyes had mostly adjusted, so I could pretty quickly see where I was.

I stood in a family room. I saw the dark outlines of sleek modern furniture—a couch, two recliners, and a large TV. Everything looked neat and orderly, everything in its place. A shelf full of highbrow fiction and nonfiction books I claimed I wanted to read but never did. A framed diploma from the University of Louisville. News and decorating magazines fanned out on the coffee table.

I listened. In the kitchen off the family room, a ceiling fan whirred, the pull chain rhythmically clacking with each revolution, which seemed somewhat odd for an empty house. But Amanda and I frequently left home with fans going, and otherwise, I heard nothing. I wanted to move fast, and get out. I doubted my slow work and multiple tries on the back door had alerted anyone, but in case they had, I needed to move quickly.

And something else could go wrong. What if the woman who lived here decided to leave yoga early? She might decide not to go at all. She might say, *The hell with being healthy and flexible. I want to go home and watch TV and drink a glass of wine.*

I knew the bedroom sat at the front of the house, the windows facing the street, so I headed that way. I still walked quietly and sleekly, even though I felt pretty certain no one was inside the house.

Why risk it?

It felt bizarre to be in a stranger's home. Like the gravest violation of someone's privacy. And I again cursed Blake for forcing me to do it, for putting me in the position of being an intruder.

Remember, he didn't hold a gun to your head. . . .

You made this mess by driving that car that night. . . .

You made the mess by never coming clean about the accident. . . .

This night . . . and Dawn Steiner . . . all because of you . . .

The voice in my mind was right. Again.

If I felt like an intruder, a violator of a stranger's privacy, it was my own doing. My own choosing.

I moved toward the front of the house, through the family room and past the kitchen, the floor gently creaking beneath my feet, and before I turned left down the hallway that led to the bedrooms, I saw something on the floor that made me stop.

At first I thought it was an animal. A large mouse or even a small rabbit.

Then I saw it was cloth. I bent down. A sock? A bandanna? Something that might have fallen out of a gym bag as the woman rushed to get to yoga?

No. It was a glove. A black glove.

I picked it up and examined it in the light that spilled through the small window at the top of the front door. Who would have a winter glove out at the beginning of April? Spring hadn't fully erupted, but there was no need to wear gloves.

I decided to put it back down and leave it where it lay. If the woman who lived here had dropped it for some reason, then she would want it again.

But it was strange the way an innocuous accessory unnerved me. Something seemed off about the glove being out in the middle of the foyer in the empty and quiet house.

I needed to get out.

I went down the short hallway to the master bedroom. When I got there, the door was closed. It seemed strange to me that someone would leave their bedroom door closed when they weren't home.

Maybe everyone did it. Maybe I'd be the only one to find it odd. But it unnerved me just as the random dropped glove had.

Then I wondered if there'd be an unexpected problem. Would the bedroom door be locked somehow? Something Blake hadn't thought of and didn't have an answer to?

I swallowed hard and reached for the knob. It turned freely, and the door swung open.

CHAPTER FOURTEEN

Bright light spilled through the large bedroom window that faced the street, creating a rectangle pattern across the bed.

I took a step inside and my foot brushed against something. I looked down and saw clothes scattered across the floor. A lot of clothes.

The sheets and the comforter were bundled up and halfway falling off the mattress. The air felt close and stuffy.

The room stood in stark contrast to the neatness and order of the rest of the house. But, then again, if someone was going to have one messy space, it might as well be the bedroom. It would explain the closed door, to prevent any visitors from seeing it.

The dresser sat on my left, so I started that way, gingerly stepping over the strewn clothes. As I approached the dresser, I saw that several of the drawers were open, and more clothes spilled over their edges.

My foot bumped against something solid.

I looked down and took a step back. Something was buried under the clothes.

I would have gone on, not needing to know what object—a shoe, a book—sat beneath the mess. But some of the light reflected off something buried in the clothes, so I took a closer look.

It took a moment, but I saw the light was reflecting off a watch. I saw the second hand had stopped, the other hands frozen at an incorrect time: twelve fifteen. The crystal was cracked. Some part of me couldn't stand the thought of the watch being on the floor, exposed to the possibility of someone coming along and stepping on it, further crunching the face or destroying the watch altogether.

So I bent down to pick it up and place it on the dresser.

But when I pulled on the watch, I felt resistance. That's when I realized the watch was attached to someone's wrist.

CHAPTER FIFTEEN

I don't know if I cried out or jumped back.

I must have.

But I was too shocked to notice.

I stood in place, staring at the watch face and the exposed portion of skin. The hand and the fingers were illuminated in the glow from the streetlight. The nails were painted a dark color. And a silver ring with an intricate scrollwork design circled the middle finger.

She's asleep, I thought. *Asleep on the floor.*

But my mind quickly shifted from the irrational to the horrific. She wasn't asleep.

She is . . .

While my heart thumped and the sweat on my body turned cold as lake water, I stepped forward again, bent down, and felt the wrist. I pressed my fingers all over, searching for a pulse, but as soon as I touched the skin I knew.

She is dead.

The hand and wrist were slightly cool. I moved the clothes that covered the rest of the body, and as I did, a face emerged, the eyes staring vacantly toward the ceiling. I touched her cheek with the back of my hand and felt the same unnatural coolness.

She was dead. *Definitely dead.*

And some reptilian part of my brain took over, sending a message to the rest of my body that said, *Run. Run. Run.*

But I resisted. I studied her face because . . .

I pulled out my phone and activated the flashlight. I no longer cared if anyone saw the light from outside the house. There was something about the woman's face. . . .

The flashlight lit her face and neck. A trickle of blood marked her forehead, and her hair was clotted and tangled with sticky gore as though she'd taken a hard blow. The stream of light reflected off her dead, glassy eyes, the irises a bright blue even though the lids were partially closed.

I knew her.

It took me a minute, but I recognized her.

Jennifer Bates.

Blake had said "Jen," but I knew her as Jennifer.

We'd met through work, and while I hadn't spoken to or even seen her for months, I knew it was her. I couldn't forget because—

My phone vibrated in my pocket.

Blake.

It had to be Blake. It had to be him telling me what was going on, explaining how it was a terrible misunderstanding. Letting me know the whole thing was a joke, that he couldn't have sent me into a house with a dead woman.

But when I looked at the screen, things only grew stranger and more confusing.

It was a Facebook friend request.

From Jennifer Bates.

The woman dead on the floor in front of me.

CHAPTER SIXTEEN

Was somebody watching me?

I clicked off the flashlight, my head turning to the bedroom window. All I saw were the starkly shifting limbs of trees silhouetted against the streetlights.

I felt like a hamster in a cage, and outside someone might have been observing me, seeing how I reacted to the bizarre events unfolding before me.

Was it Blake? Had he killed the woman, then sent me in? And was he now seeing how much he could screw with my life?

Immediately I thought about calling the police, but then how would I explain my presence? If I was worried about my involvement in the accident from college coming to light, how would it look if the police found me standing over the dead body of a female acquaintance?

I needed to get the hell out of this house.

But before I did, I walked over to the dresser, where the letters were supposed to be. Had someone else come into the house for the same reason I had? If the dresser was open, the drawers emptied and searched, could it be we were after the same thing?

I peered into the top drawer, where Blake had told me the letters would be. It was nearly empty. Only a hairbrush and a wadded-up pink tank top remained inside. Everything else was spilled on the floor. I checked the other drawers as well, but it was the same thing every time. Empty or almost empty. No letters. No personal effects. No notes or diaries. Almost nothing.

I looked around the room, the debris scattered at my feet and over Jennifer's body. It was too much of a mess to sort through. And I felt no desire to paw around Jennifer's clothes, knowing her dead body lay beneath them.

I asked myself if the killer had used the clothes to intentionally cover her body so he wouldn't have to see her. Or had the scattering of the clothes been an accident?

My thoughts were cut off by a distant sound. At first, I thought I'd imagined it. Maybe Sparkle had started to howl. Or maybe someone had triggered a car alarm.

I froze in place, listening more intently, my head cocked. Another moment passed, and then I heard it again.

A siren.

A distant siren growing closer.

It could have been something besides a response to Jennifer's death. *Her murder.*

Maybe someone had left their oven on. Maybe an elderly person had suffered a heart attack or a fall.

But could I risk it? Someone had sent me that friend request, almost as though they were watching me. If I was being set up, then wouldn't it make sense for someone to call the police as well so they could catch me inside the house?

I took a step to go, my foot brushing against the side of Jennifer's body. I pulled my leg back and stopped. A human being lay there at my feet, someone about my age. Hours before I'd come into the house, she'd been as alive as I was. Breathing, thinking, dreaming. And now . . .

She lay on the floor like a piece of discarded furniture, something I stepped over and tried to ignore.

The siren grew ever closer. I started to go again, but then I saw something under the bedside table, something that caught the ambient light. I went over and picked it up. An iPhone, one that presumably belonged to Jennifer. Impulsively I took it with me as I retraced my steps out of the bedroom, hoping it might provide some information that would explain everything that was going on. I dashed down the hallway, across the foyer, and over the random black glove, which I carefully avoided.

I went through to the back of the house, and before I went out, I took a look through a window that offered a view of the yard. I pressed my head against the cool glass, turning to the right and left as far as I could. I saw nothing. Heard nothing.

Except the increasingly close siren that sounded as though it was less than a mile away.

Since I had no idea if anyone waited outside, but I did know that the siren grew ever closer, it didn't seem like much of a choice. I needed to go and risk being seen by someone. Sparkle's owner or someone else looking out their window late at night.

I used the end of my shirt to cover my hand and turned the handle. As I did it, I tried to remember if I'd touched anything else in the house. Maybe one of the dresser drawers. But they'd already been open, so had I avoided any real contact with them?

I couldn't know. And I couldn't go back.

I slipped outside into the cool night, a blissful relief from the tight air inside the house.

I pulled the door shut, and then used my shirt to wipe off the outside handle and the keypad. For all I knew, the police were responding to a summons due to my fumbling with the code when I'd first arrived.

It didn't really matter. I wiped the handle off as best I could, took one more look around, and saw no one. Then I went down through the neighbor's yard rather than coming out at the front of Jennifer's house. If the cops were pulling up, I couldn't be seen. In fact, I went down a few yards until I reached the street I'd walked up before, the one that ran perpendicular to Jennifer's. The one where I'd seen the dog walker.

As I came to the street, a blue glow bounced off the fronts of all the houses, and the siren grew louder, almost deafening. The police car sped by in a white streak, and I stopped in place until it was past. It turned right onto Jennifer's street, its tires squealing, and I knew I had to get out of there and back to my own vehicle.

So I did.

I retraced my steps as quickly as possible without looking like I'd just stolen something. Or committed a murder.

I kept my head down and walked back to the car. By the time I opened the door and flopped into the driver's seat, my forehead was covered with sweat, and I could barely catch my breath. But I didn't have time to wait or recover.

I started the car and drove out of there, leaving the neighborhood—and Jennifer's dead body—behind me.

CHAPTER SEVENTEEN

On my way out of Jennifer's neighborhood, I passed another cop car zooming past in the direction of her house, a blur of blue light and screeching sound.

"Crap. Crap."

The word seemed inadequate to the situation I found myself in. Any words would have been inadequate.

I realized I was driving in the direction of my house, where Amanda and Henry waited for me. But I couldn't go there. I would have to explain why I'd left the basketball game early. And I'd be returning there without having any idea of what was going on with Blake and Jennifer.

On my right I saw a strip mall, so I pulled in and parked the car far from the stores, which were mostly closed, the windows darkened, the lot empty. My hands shook as I took my phone out. Jennifer's Facebook request was still on my screen.

The image of Jennifer on the floor—her dead-eyed stare, her chilled flesh—flashed in my mind. I tried to push it away, to concentrate on the task at hand, but I knew I'd be seeing those images and feeling those sensations for a long time. For the rest of my life. How could anyone forget something like that?

I called Blake, hoping he'd tell me something that made sense. That it was all a joke or a misunderstanding or a social science experiment gone too far. As the phone rang and rang, it occurred to me that Blake was the only person I could confide in about Jennifer's death. At least for the moment.

It scared the shit out of me to have to put so much faith in him.

The call went to voice mail. I hung up and dialed again. Again and again.

The phone kept ringing and ringing until Blake's tinny recorded voice came on, asking the caller to leave a message.

In frustration I said, "Where the hell are you? Call me."

I hit REDIAL a few times, jabbing the phone with my finger as hard as I could, as though that would make the call go through. What do they say about insanity? Doing the same thing over and over and expecting a different result? I knew deep down Blake wouldn't be answering. I knew it as surely as anything, but I kept dialing until I grew so sick of the ringing sound I wanted to throw the phone out the car window and crunch it beneath my tires.

I ran my hand through my hair and opened my Facebook app, intending to see if there was anything on Jennifer's page that might tell me what was happening. I went there and looked, but since I hadn't accepted her request, I couldn't see much. Just a profile picture of her at the beach holding a beer. No posts or other photos I could see. No relationship information.

And there was no way I was accepting that creepy friend request.

I again wondered if someone—Blake?—had been watching me while I was inside the house. Had the friend request been a test to see how I'd respond? Or was it a threat, an indication that someone held some power over me I couldn't see?

I shifted my weight a little and felt the bulky object in my left shorts pocket. Jennifer's phone. I'd forgotten I'd grabbed it as I left the house and drove away, and it made no sense to look at her social media pages when I could look directly at the source.

I slid the phone out, silently hoping it wasn't password protected. But it was.

"Damn it."

I slapped the steering wheel in frustration. I wanted to throw the phone out the window and forget it.

But then I thought of the code for the back door. Was it possible? 1792.

So I entered it into the phone. And it worked.

"Thank God."

I was happy to see Jennifer was as lazy as I was and couldn't be bothered coming up with a new password for every device.

I went right to her text messages and saw Blake's name at the top of the list. I opened the conversation between him and Jennifer and started reading, moving backward from the most recent messages. And right away I saw that Blake had lied to me.

At the coffee shop, he had told me he hadn't seen or spoken to the woman—who I didn't know was Jennifer Bates at the time—in several weeks. But the text exchange showed they'd traded messages just that morning. And Blake wanted to come over and see her before she left for work because he wanted the letters back. And he didn't want her to show them to anyone. The messages were terse and blunt, but when Blake said he was coming over to see her, Jennifer responded: It's a free country.

She didn't exactly tell him not to come, but it didn't sound like she wanted him there either.

It was safe to assume Blake had gone to her house after the message. And what had happened then . . . ?

Then my phone began vibrating, and I nearly jumped out of my skin.

I fumbled my phone when I tried to pick it up, and it fell into my lap.

As I finally corralled it, I wondered if the message was coming from Jennifer. Or whoever was controlling her account. And whoever was controlling her account and sending requests must be the killer.

Right?

But when I checked the screen, I saw it wasn't from Jennifer.

It was a text from Amanda.

I know you're at the game. But if you get this can you give me a call?

She knew I sometimes brought my stuff to the gym floor with me. There'd been a few break-ins in the locker room, especially late at night, and some of the guys I'd played with brought their valuables—wallets, keys, phones—to the court, where they were safer.

My throat was dry as dirt, and I swallowed as I called her.

I told myself to keep my voice steady. Calm.

"Hey," I said when she picked up. "What's up?"

"I'm sorry to interrupt the game. Can you talk?"

"I can talk."

Would she notice the lack of noise in the background? No cheers or shouts? No bouncing balls?

"Look, I'll make this fast, okay? Hell, maybe I shouldn't have even called."

"Go ahead. I'm glad you did. It's nice to hear your voice."

"Oh, okay. Thanks. Well, I just wanted to tell you something."

Once again, I was amazed at how calm Amanda could be, how coolly she could step back from her own feelings and speak clearly about them.

"I just wanted to say . . . I wish you hadn't gone to that game. I know I said it was okay, but after you left, I really wished I'd asked you to stay. Maybe it's silly, but I started kicking myself."

"I wish I'd stayed too," I said.

"Really? No fun?"

"No fun at all."

"Well, then, why don't you come home? Why don't you just grab your stuff and walk out?"

I hesitated. Nothing sounded better. Nothing sounded better in the world. Home. Amanda. Henry. Peace and quiet.

But I couldn't do it. Not yet.

"I wish I could," I said. "It's just that we only have six guys. And I'm about to go back in."

My heart shriveled in my chest. I pictured it as a dried-up black thing incapable of love. What kind of man lied to his wife? Twice in one night?

"Okay," she said. "I shouldn't have called. And I know you haven't been getting out for fun as much. Neither one of us has. And I have that weekend planned. You should plan something like that. Hell, do something with Blake."

"I'm just glad you called."

"I can't hear anyone," she said. "Are you playing the world's quietest basketball game?"

"I walked out. To the hallway by the court. But I have to go back. Look, I'll get out of here as soon as I can. I promise."

There was a pause. Then Amanda said, "Look, it's just . . ."

"It's just what?"

"There's so much going on lately, you know?"

Was she talking about life with Henry? Our lives as new parents? Or something else?

I remembered the way she said my name at home when I was going up the stairs . . . and the way the thought remained unexpressed and unfinished.

What was going on with her?

"I know," I said. "But we're getting the hang of it, aren't we?"

"Are we? I'm not sure. . . ."

"Of course we are—"

"Yeah, I guess you're right."

"I think I am."

"Look, I'm going to read my book, but I may be asleep when you get home."

She then hung up without saying good-bye.

CHAPTER EIGHTEEN

Blake rented one half of a redbrick duplex on the east side of town. He'd lived there for the past three years, ever since he moved from Lexington, where he'd been living near his parents, to Rossingville to take a job as a salesman for an auto parts manufacturer. I hadn't been thrilled when he moved to Rossingville, where I'd been living ever since college. I'd just gotten engaged to Amanda when Blake came to town. I had hoped to leave those events and memories from college behind, especially anything having to do with the accident.

For the most part, we avoided discussing that. Yes, we met for the occasional beer. And once we took a guys' trip down to Nashville for a bland, booze-soaked weekend of watching football, which I regretted pretty much as soon as I checked into the hotel. But mostly we interacted as adults. And Blake seemed to do well at his job, his ability to talk anybody into anything clearly a huge benefit for a salesman. When he and Samantha were in the "on" portion of their on-and-off relationship, Blake came as close to being a normal member of society as I'd ever seen him.

I'd never received a clear answer about why Blake left Lexington and took the job in Rossingville. Sometimes he said it was a great opportunity, too good to pass up. Once or twice he alluded to his father taking early retirement from his corporate job, but he was vague about why. Blake's dad was a classic workaholic, and I never imagined that he would leave his job when he was only in his late fifties. His dad's decision to step down seemed to have coincided with Blake's acceptance of the job in Rossingville.

The driveway in front of his half of the duplex was empty, and a lone light burned upstairs in the bedroom. The night had grown colder, the wind picking up. I still wore shorts, and I shivered as I walked up to the front of the house and rang the bell.

I left Jennifer's phone in the car for the time being. It was like an explosive device I didn't want to be caught holding when it blew. I'd seen enough to tell me I needed—really needed—to talk to Blake.

I waited with my hands in my pockets, my shoulders hunched to stay warm. The street was quiet, no neighbors in sight. I hit the bell again, pressing with as much force as I could muster, as though that might make the bell ring louder and summon Blake more quickly.

But I started to accept what I'd known all along—he wasn't home.

And I had no idea what he was doing.

I rang one more time and was about to walk away when I heard the lock being undone. I perked up, hopeful, and when the door swung inward, I saw Samantha standing there in a T-shirt, old sweatpants, and no shoes, her hair piled on top of her head in a messy bun.

She didn't look particularly surprised or dismayed by someone showing up on her doorstep late at night.

"Oh, Ryan, hey," she said. "I almost didn't answer. I thought it was kids playing a prank. No one comes to the door without calling."

"Is Blake home?"

I wanted to ask if they were living together. As she leaned against the doorjamb, her hand resting on her hip, I took a quick glance to see if an engagement ring decorated her finger, but I saw nothing.

"I don't know where he is, Ryan," she said. Sam usually spoke in a precise manner, her thoughts measured and orderly. But when I arrived at the house that night, she rambled a bit, her thoughts jumping from one to another without any noticeable connective tissue. "He was supposed to work late. And he needs to buy his mom a birthday present. Did you hear he stopped drinking?"

"I heard."

"Were you supposed to meet him or something?"

"Kind of."

Samantha remained in the doorway. She worked as a kindergarten teacher at a public school, and she always carried herself with the determined enthusiasm and peppiness that job no doubt required. It was too easy for me to joke—but I did anyway—that she was the perfect woman for Blake since she worked with five-year-olds all day.

But that night a measure of her usual easygoing cheer and ready smile was absent. She looked like I'd interrupted her in the middle of something. I knew she tended to work late, preparing lesson plans and classroom projects. Or maybe I'd rung the bell while she was starting to doze off. She rubbed at her eye absentmindedly, a gesture that made her look like a small child.

"Okay," I said. "Well, can you tell him I came by?"

She stepped back then. "I'm sorry. Why don't you come in? I was just—I was surprised when I heard the bell ring. I didn't know what was going on. I have to work tomorrow, of course, and I was organizing some things upstairs. But I guess you have to work too. By the way, how's Henry?"

"Am I interrupting your work?"

"No, it's okay. My mind is just . . . It's got a lot going on."

She talked as she walked back into the house, leaving the door open, so I followed her. She went into the living room and turned on two lamps, which cast soft light over the space, and then she took a seat on the couch. I followed her in, feeling a nervous energy urging me on.

"He's good," I said. "Getting bigger every day. And now his teeth are coming in."

"I love all the photos you post. You're so good at it. I feel like a failure at that kind of stuff. Maybe I can take a class or something. And Blake's no help. You know he refuses to do any of that."

It hit me I hadn't said anything about the wedding.

"Oh," I said, "Blake told me the good news. Congratulations."

For the first time, her full smile appeared, bright and warm, deep dimples standing out on her flushed cheeks. "Oh, yeah. Thanks! I know it's all kind of last-minute, but we've worked some things out. And neither of us wants to wait anymore. This spot at the Barn was open, and while I would have been happy to take our time and plan, plan, plan . . . You know how I am, right? Well, Blake just told me we should go for it. Get married, grab the brass ring. So we're doing it. Saturday."

"I get it. You guys know each other well now."

She suddenly turned more serious than I'd ever seen her. "And, Ryan, I'm so sorry you and Amanda weren't invited. I mean, I tried to talk to Blake about it. I did. But he's still kind of peeved about the thing with Amanda. You know, the thing with Henry and the lampshade."

"It's okay—"

"No, it totally isn't." She scooted to the edge of the couch, her face serious. "I wanted to call Amanda and tell her, but you're here now, so I can tell you. Please just come, the two of you, on Saturday. Just come. Blake wants you there. I know he does. And you know I love Amanda. She's so great, such a great friend. She reminds me so much of my friends from college. Smart. Hardworking. But fun too. She said a lot of harsh things about Blake. I know that. But hey, maybe I'd do the same thing if someone bonked my baby's head. That's what I like about Amanda. She's so tough. So fierce. I get it."

"Sam, I'm not worried about it. We just want you guys to be happy."

She placed her hands against her cheeks, and the flush deepened.

"But that's just it, Ryan. I'm not sure Blake *is* happy. He hasn't been acting like himself the last few days. He needs you, Ryan. That's why I'm a little flummoxed tonight. All over the place. I'm worried. Worried he might start to drink again. Or . . . Look, he really needs you in his life. More than ever."

CHAPTER NINETEEN

When Samantha lowered her hands from her face and placed them on the tops of her thighs, they were shaking. I'd never noticed that she chewed her nails, but they were gnawed to nubs. Her smile was long gone, her lips pressed tight together.

I sat in a leather recliner across from her.

"Do you want something?" she asked. "A beer or whatever? I was having some wine earlier. A couple glasses, actually . . . Blake wasn't home, and I've been laying off when he's around."

"I'm good. What's going on with him that has you so worried?"

She puffed her cheeks and let out a long sigh. "The last six weeks or so have been tough. He's been kind of distracted, short-tempered. 'Erratic' is maybe a better word."

"Erratic?"

"I mean, more than usual, you know?" She smiled with little cheer. "I thought it was the wedding. You know, we're throwing all of this together fast. It's stressful and busy. My mom and my sister are helping. Blake's family isn't coming down until tomorrow. But, you know, his unhappiness seems deeper than the wedding. And it started before we were engaged. He seems more on edge. Sometimes it's like he's electrified, and if you touch him, you get a shock. I guess I'm the one getting shocked. I feel awful about what I think sometimes."

"What's that?" I asked.

She took in a deep breath. "I wish he'd have a drink. Just one. A small one." She held her thumb and index finger an inch apart. "Something to soothe him. Or maybe some weed. I thought about buying some from a student teacher at work. Do those thoughts make me a horrible person? Am I an asshole for saying that?"

"Not at all. He's certainly more fun when he drinks."

"What were you and Blake supposed to meet about tonight?"

I scrambled to come up with a believable answer. "I think we were just going to get coffee or something like that. No beer, you know."

"And he stood you up?"

"Maybe I got my wires crossed."

"He's not home. I can tell you that. This late at night, and he's not home. It happens sometimes because he's working late, but so close to the wedding? I moved most of my stuff in here, but we want to buy a house. We're going to do that soon. My parents are going to give us a down payment as a wedding present. We want to buy something south of town, something that's new construction."

"Did you try calling him?" I asked.

"No. I don't want to be that kind of fiancée, the one who checks in all the time. Maybe that's the last thing he needs right now. But you know how this has gone in the past. How he gets scared. He freaks out about being committed forever. How do you deal with someone like that? In the past, I might have pushed, but then I feel like I'm driving him away. So I'm trying to be laid-back and chill, but maybe he doesn't need that. I feel stuck in the middle."

"I understand. It's like feeding a skittish animal."

"Although when we got back together this last time and decided to get married, he promised he'd communicate better. That was part of the reason he stopped drinking. To be more focused, to be more responsible and thoughtful. And he had been for a while, up until the last few weeks. I don't want to overreact to one night. Maybe he just needs some time to himself."

"Well, I'm sure—"

"When did you talk to him? If you knew about the wedding, that means you talked to him. When was that?"

"Earlier this evening," I said.

"And what did he seem like?"

I thought about my answer, and it was an honest one. "Same as ever. No, I don't mean that. Not exactly. I can tell he's healthier. Clearer."

When Samantha spoke again, her voice carried a sharp edge, something I didn't think I'd ever heard from her before. I worried I'd offended her. "See, that's just it, Ryan. He is different now. People don't want to give him credit for that, but he's different. He's grown-up. He works hard. He's good to me. You only see the guy you went to college with. We all do that with people we've known a long time."

"That's true, but—"

"You should see when he comes to my school and helps with the kids. They love him. They climb all over him. He has that gentle side. He's very loving. You've seen that, right?"

I had to admit I had. College. The time after my dad's death. Even later than that . . . When Amanda and I got married, he managed to track down a set of vintage dishes—Franciscan Starburst—that Amanda had mentioned wanting once in passing and he gave them to us as a wedding gift. How he remembered that detail and then acted upon it, I'll never know.

I didn't have any uncles I was close to . . . and no brothers. In the days leading up to the wedding, Blake had played the part of best friend and big brother and even a little of father, since mine was gone. It was Blake who made a sentimental toast at the rehearsal dinner, Blake who again helped me tie my tie, Blake who walked my mom down the aisle and danced with her at the reception. . . .

"Are you sure you don't know where he is?" I asked, hoping my question would jar her into thinking of something she'd overlooked. I didn't want to think the worst, and neither did Sam. "Do you have a guess?"

She looked away. I thought her chin started to quiver, but she quickly got it together and turned back to me.

"He'll be home soon. He will. He's probably working. And he's not drinking. I have to trust him. Oh, Ryan. Just a few days ago, I woke up, and he'd left me the most beautiful note on my pillow. He does that stuff all the time. Flowers, notes. He sent my grandma chocolates on her eighty-fifth birthday last week. I almost forgot her birthday, but not Blake. When we get married, my dad is going to hire Blake on at his company." She lowered her voice. "I don't know if you heard, but Blake's dad has been having money problems."

"He is? I thought he was loaded when he retired."

Sam looked like she didn't want to go on. She turned her head one way and then the other as though someone in the room might have been listening. Then she said, "Maybe not. Some kind of big problem at the company went down. I don't know all the details, but there are a lot of lawsuits flying around, and the stock is tanking and taking a big bite out of his net worth. It's been building slowly for a few years."

"I didn't know. I thought his family was set for another generation or two."

Sam nodded. "Blake thought so too. But in a way, it was good when his dad started having problems a few years ago. It forced Blake to be on his own more. He couldn't count on his parents for everything the way he had been. And when he moved here, we met."

"Sure."

"So my family's help is really going to matter. My dad has started warming up to Blake. They actually make jokes with each other now. They go fishing, Ryan."

"Fishing? Blake?"

"He loves it. And Dad's help will set us up for having a family. Like you guys have. A baby like Henry. A nice house." She smiled again, her eyes brightening. "That's what we both want. And it's right within reach now. More than ever."

I wasn't sure there was anything else I could say to her. And I sat in the one place I knew Blake wasn't. And I wondered if he had any plans to come home at all. If he'd hurt Jennifer, if he was on the run from something and not telling Sam . . .

He might never come back. He could have been driving away to a new life somewhere as Sam and I spoke.

I shook my head, although Sam wouldn't know what it meant. It couldn't be that. Blake was a lot of things . . . good and bad. But a killer? *No way.*

"Those are good things to have," I said. "They really are."

"I think so too."

I stood up, and Sam walked with me to the door.

"Thanks for asking us to come to the wedding," I said. "You know, just earlier Amanda was saying she needed to move on from the thing with Henry. She's been trying to work on forgiving and letting go. A lot of it stems from her sister's death, trying to move on from things and accept them. So I think that might be why she's trying to see Blake in a different light. It's healthier . . . to move on."

"I know," she said. "And I know her sister's death still hurts. Why wouldn't it? That probably makes her even more overprotective of Henry. Right? Besides being a new mom."

"Sure. New parents are pretty overprotective. I am too."

Sam leaned against the wall of the foyer and looked thoughtful, her arms crossed. "I remember when Amanda told me about her sister. It was tough for her to talk about, but I felt like we were closer after that.

She'd shared something deep and personal with me. It means something when people share in that way."

"She wouldn't talk about that with just anyone," I said. And it was true. Amanda distrusted sentimental feelings. She wouldn't share something deeply personal like her sister's death unless she really cared about the other person. "She values your friendship."

"Ugh." Sam shook her head. "Then Blake and the baby . . . that derailed everything. He loves kids, Ryan. He really does. He says he wants to have a houseful."

"He always said that. Even in college."

"I'll call Amanda," she said. "I will. She and I need to talk. I'm so glad to hear that she was open to Blake. That just . . . It makes my heart feel good. It really does. I hate negativity. That's why I hate my own thoughts being negative. I'm going to shake it off. All of it. At the very least, we can all get together after the wedding."

After the wedding . . .

To hear her making plans when she had no idea what Blake might have been involved in.

"Right," I said. "And if you see him—I mean *when* you see him—will you tell him to call me? I'd really like to talk to him."

Her smile returned in all its glory. "I will, Ryan."

She stood in the door, waving, silhouetted by the warm light from inside the house, until I started the car and drove off.

CHAPTER TWENTY

Blake knew I was looking for him—how could he not? Wherever he was, whatever he was doing, he didn't want to talk to me.

Or Samantha.

So I drove home. It was after eleven when I pulled into the alley that led to our driveway, and I expected to see a darkened house, Amanda long asleep with the baby monitor on the bedside table.

What I saw instead made me slam on my brakes.

Every room on the first floor of the house glowed, casting yellow light out onto the lawn and against the trunks of the trees in the yard. The same was true in every room upstairs, except for Henry's, which was dark, the blinds closed.

And a police car sat in the driveway, blocking my way.

I froze in place behind the wheel, my thoughts swirling like a swarm of insects.

Amanda. Henry. What had happened?

I parked at the curb and jumped out, starting for the house and slamming the driver's-side door behind me. I forgot everything that had happened, driven forward only by my desire to know that Amanda and Henry were okay.

I ran across the lawn, the dew cold and wet kicking up against my shins, and I yanked open the back door and went into the brightly lit kitchen, where Amanda was leaning against the counter, wearing a light jacket over her sweatshirt and yoga pants as though she was about to go somewhere. She'd exchanged the flip-flops for running shoes.

"What's happening?" I asked. "Are you okay? Is Henry?"

"It's about time you got here," she said. "The police were just leaving."

"The police?"

I'd been so intently focused on Amanda that I hadn't looked around the kitchen to see the two uniformed cops standing on the other side of the room. I turned to them, and they both looked back, their faces solemn, their silver badges glinting under the lights.

I faced the cops but asked Amanda, "Is Henry okay?"

"He's fine," she said, calm as anything. The eye of the storm. "We're both fine. You can relax."

"Then why . . . ?"

My mind raced to another place, somewhere it hadn't gone since I pulled up behind the house. Were the police there for me? Had they learned I was in Jennifer's house earlier? Had Blake told them something?

My heart, which had been a block of ice since I'd pulled up, started beating again. I didn't care. Better me than Amanda or Henry. As long as they were okay, I didn't care.

"I called them," Amanda said.

"To find me?"

"No." She moved to the window above the kitchen sink and turned that light off. She pressed her face against the glass. "What did you see out there?"

"Out where?"

"In the yard." She pointed out, her face still against the glass. "I heard someone out there. Just ten or fifteen minutes ago. That's why all the lights are on. That's why I'm up. And dressed. I thought I might have to grab Henry and run. That's when I called them and they came. It's crazy."

"What did you hear?"

"Sir?" one of the cops said. He was tall, with a goatee, and had razor burn along his neck. "Your wife called us because she thought she heard someone outside. A possible burglar."

Amanda backed away from the window and unzipped her jacket. But she left it on. She folded her arms across her chest. "Something bumped against the garbage cans. I heard them knock together. And it's not really that windy tonight. Not enough to rattle the cans like that."

"Maybe it was a cat. Or those raccoons we saw last week. Once they find a food source, they're going to come back."

"Of course I thought of that, Ryan. And if that was all that happened, I wouldn't be worried. But then I heard the back door rattle." She pointed to the door I had just come through, the one we used the most to enter and exit the house, the one that led right out to the driveway and the detached garage. "Ryan, someone was trying to get in here. I swear. They pulled on this door handle a few times."

Every nerve and fiber in my body was pulled as tight as an over-tuned guitar string. I'd expected to find peace and quiet at home. Not more craziness.

"Are you sure?" I asked.

Amanda gave me a withering look. Her head cocked to one side, and the corners of her mouth turned down. "You know I don't get riled up over stuff like this, Ryan. I'm not a scaredy-cat like some people we know."

She was right. Amanda had a friend named Jane who had called the police three different times when her boyfriend was out of town and she thought someone was breaking into her house. Once it was a branch rubbing against the roof. Once a cat. And once she called the police because a piece of siding had come loose and fallen into the backyard. She no longer stayed home alone when her boyfriend went out of town. She spent those nights sleeping in her childhood bedroom just down the hall from her parents.

"We looked around outside," the cop said, the one with the razor burn. "We saw some tracks out there, ones that went along the back of the house. Was there any reason for someone to be out there?"

"I don't know. Who knows when the tracks were made?"

"It's been raining a lot lately," the cop said. "They must be pretty new. Did you see anything just now, when you were coming in?"

"I ran in. I saw your car, and I thought the worst."

"Have you seen or heard anything unusual recently? Anything at all?"

Had I seen anything unusual? Yes, I wanted to say. A dead woman. On the floor of her bedroom. A dead woman who sent me a ghostly Facebook friend request.

Stone dead.

"Nothing," I said. "Nothing."

"No one suspicious hanging around? No property missing or signs of a break-in?"

I felt every breath I took. My heart rate slowed ever so slightly. Dawn Steiner. She was suspicious and odd. But she'd never been to the house. Not as far as I knew. But her deadline loomed . . . two days away. Had she grown impatient and come by to force the issue?

"Sir?"

"No. Nothing like that. It's safe here."

"You haven't had any problems like this any other night?" the cop asked.

"Nothing at all," I said.

Both cops considered me without speaking. They were big men—like linebackers with gleaming badges—and younger than I was. They looked eminently capable and smart, which set me on edge.

"Well," the only cop who had spoken said, "we can file a report, and we'll be sure to mention the fresh tracks. If anything else happens, feel free to call us. We'll be patrolling all night."

"Thank you," Amanda said. "I hope this wasn't a wild-goose chase for you all. I know you're busy."

"No problem, ma'am," the second cop said, finally speaking. He had a thick head of hair perfectly sculpted into place. "That's what we're here for."

"Your wife said you were at a basketball game tonight," the first cop said.

"What's that?"

"You were at a basketball game, right? At the Y?"

"Yes, that's right," I said.

"Must be the Thursday night league," he said. "My brother plays in that."

"That's right."

"Well?"

"Well, what?"

My eyes moved between them. They both kept the serious looks on their faces.

"What happened?" the second cop asked.

My throat went dry. I looked at Amanda, who was watching me.

I tried to swallow and couldn't. "What do you mean?" I asked.

Both the cops smiled.

"At the game," the first one said. "Your wife says you're not very good. How did it go?"

Then they were both laughing. And so was Amanda.

And I tried to laugh too, although it felt like coughing up rocks.

"She's right," I said. "I'm not very good."

The cops moved forward, and the second one clapped me on the shoulder.

"Like we said, if you need anything else, just call. We'll be around."

CHAPTER TWENTY-ONE

When the cops were gone and we were alone, Amanda looked at me, her face growing serious. "Tell me you know I wouldn't overreact to something like that."

"You're right," I said. "I know you're not like that."

"Will you go look around and make sure everything's okay?"

"Didn't the cops do that?"

"They did. But you know our yard better than they do. You can tell if things are out of place or missing. Just take a quick look."

But I really didn't want to. Given Amanda's usually calm demeanor and tendency not to exaggerate such things, it seemed there was a very good chance that someone *had* tried to come in the back door. And if that was the case, then who was it?

The same person who had killed Jennifer?

Did that person know where I lived? Had they come to the house to harm Amanda and Henry?

I couldn't believe it was just a random coincidence that on the night I stumbled into the middle of a murder scene, some burglar also decided to try to break into our house.

Should I have told the cops about all of that?

How exactly would I have explained that to them?

"You just had the cops here," I said. "They dealt with it. They weren't too worried. They wanted to talk about basketball. I don't need to go out there like I'm Han Solo or John Wick. You always say the police are there for a reason. We pay taxes. So we put them to work. You heard that cop—he said they'd be around."

"I know. They are. But just look yourself, okay? It would make me feel better if you did it. Check to make sure that entrance to the crawl space is secure. You know it comes loose sometimes. And make sure nothing's missing. Or I can do it and you can stay in here with Henry." Amanda watched me, her arms still crossed.

"Will this make you feel better?" I asked.

"Yes."

"Okay, then I'll do it. For you. And you're sure Henry's okay?"

"I went up and checked on him before you came home."

Before I went back out the door, I opened a closet in the hallway and brought out the battered aluminum bat I used in my summer softball league.

"Please don't lock the door behind me once I'm out there," I said.

Amanda didn't hesitate. "I won't."

"You'll help me if I scream. Right?"

"Of course. Unless you're being chased by the boogeyman. Then you're on your own."

I opened the door and went back out into the night.

CHAPTER TWENTY-TWO

The bat rested on my shoulder, and I kept two hands wrapped around the handle in case I suddenly had to swing.

Did I really think I'd be willing to swing a baseball bat at somebody's head? With the intent to harm or kill them?

And if I was right, the person who might have been sneaking around and trying the back door had already killed someone. They might be carrying a real weapon, a gun or a knife.

Maybe they'd seen me in Jen's house and came by to polish me off for being a witness. Maybe they wanted to peek in the windows and watch my response to getting mystery friend requests.

I felt like I was in way over my head. Like I'd stepped onto a frozen pond, and the ice around my feet had started to crack in all directions. And the freezing water was sloshing over my shoe tops as I stood there, watching it rise.

We lived in an older neighborhood near downtown where the houses, most built around World War One, were in the process of being renovated and sold to young couples and families. The houses were close together, and our yard backed up to a narrow pothole-pocked alley that saw a decent amount of pedestrian and vehicle traffic. Could someone have just been passing by? A kid playing a prank even that late at night?

I willed myself forward and walked around the perimeter of the garage. At each corner of the building, I expected a giant man dressed in black to come at me, menacing me with a knife or a club or a gun. But no one emerged from the shadows. Still, by the time I made it back to the house and the door I'd come out of, my heart had swelled like a balloon and was cutting off air in my throat.

I continued past the back door and headed for the other side of the house. We'd been drenched with rain a day earlier, a spring soaker, and when I stepped off the patio, my shoes squished in the soft grass. It was darker over there. Light from the kitchen windows provided some illumination, but that only went so far. Holding on to the bat with one hand, the taped grip rough against my skin, I took out my phone with the other and activated my flashlight. I directed it in front of me, a cone of brightness cutting through the dark, and adhered to the belief I'd held since childhood that the boogeyman and monsters disappeared when light hit them.

I really hoped that was true.

I squished along the back of the house, my phone casting light into the yard, and stopped only when I reached the far corner, where the property was bordered by a wooden fence. I saw no one. Heard nothing. A measure of relief passed through me at seeing and hearing nothing, and released some of the pressure from my heart. I told myself I'd done enough, and it was okay to return to the safety of the house. Amanda wasn't someone who overreacted, but since Henry's birth, she and I had both become bigger worriers, anxious about germs and car seats and chemicals in food.

I told myself we could only handle one crisis at a time, and the one with Jennifer and Blake was more than enough to keep me occupied.

As I came back to the door, the beam of the flashlight revealed the ground around the edge of the patio. The cops had been right. I saw footprints that weren't mine, deep and fresh. They went in two directions—away from the back door and toward it, as though someone had paced outside, perhaps looking in one of the kitchen windows before or after trying the back door.

My heart, which had been going back to its normal size, swelled again. It felt like it might burst out of the center of my chest. Someone had been there. Without a doubt.

I went back inside and quickly closed the door. Then I made sure to throw the bolt and use the chain, making the house feel like Fort Knox.

When I turned around, Amanda was walking back into the room. I figured she'd gone to look in on Henry and come down when she heard the door opening and closing.

"Well?" she asked.

"I didn't see anyone."

"So you think I'm crazy?"

"I didn't say that, did I?" I still held the bat, so I put it down in the corner of the kitchen by the back door. "The tracks were there, just like the cops said. Looks like someone in sneakers. It's pretty eerie. In fact, I'm going to go around and make sure all the doors and windows are locked. Just to be safe."

"And the crawl space entrance?"

"Secure. I looked."

"So I did the right thing calling the police?"

"Yes, of course," I said.

And I meant it.

"If we hear anything else, let's call them," I said. "Like I said, I'll check everything. Oh, and then I'll post on the neighborhood Facebook group. Did you check that yet?"

"No. I didn't think of it. That's your thing."

"Maybe somebody else saw or heard something. Or, at the very least, everyone else can be on high alert."

Amanda listened to me and then nodded. She seemed mollified.

"Are you going to bed now?" I asked. "Can you sleep? Or are you too amped-up?"

"I better. Sir Henry might be getting me up soon."

"I'll secure the place and then post in the group. I'll come to bed after that. You'll probably be asleep."

"Probably."

I went over and kissed her good night, letting my lips linger for a second. I wanted to do more. I wished the night were so simple I could lead her by the hand up to the bedroom and we could slide under the covers together like we used to do all the time before Henry was born.

I wished it were a night like that.

But it wasn't. I focused on my task of securing the house.

"I'm sorry I interrupted your game," she said.

"What's that?"

"I feel silly that I called you during the game. I should have just rolled with it."

I'd forgotten about her call. "No worries. I wish I hadn't gone too."

"Why? Did you lose?"

"No," I said, trying to be casual. "I just think everything would have been better if I'd been here with you."

She studied me for a moment, the light catching the green in her eyes. She seemed to be searching my face, wondering if something deeper lay beneath my words.

I'm not sure what she saw, but it must have been enough, because she nodded and said as I turned away, "I wish I hadn't gone to the store earlier."

I stopped and looked back. "Why? Did something happen?"

"No," she said, shaking her head. "I'm just being silly. I just wish . . . I should have been at home."

She turned then and went up the stairs without looking back.

CHAPTER TWENTY-THREE

Once I heard Amanda's footsteps recede up the stairs and move into our bedroom, I went into the small office I kept at the back of the first floor. I pulled out both phones—mine and Jennifer's—but before I looked at them, I did what I told Amanda I would do and opened my laptop to look at the neighborhood Facebook group.

A flood of notifications inundated me. It took me a moment to remember, but then I knew why. The photo I'd posted that morning of Amanda bathing Henry. I'd captured them together with the sun coming in through the window in the kitchen, and then posted the photo with a comment about how lucky I was.

Which felt even more true now.

And I also saw Jennifer's friend request. I hadn't accepted it. Obviously. But I hadn't denied it either. Something about saying no to her when she was dead felt strangely disrespectful.

But as I sat there in my house, my mind changed. With everything else going on, I desperately wanted to seize control of something.

This was a small thing. And easy.

So I rejected the request.

One push of a button and I felt some relief spread through me.

Ordinarily I'd go through and respond to every comment on my photo, most of which were agreeing with me or saying how beautiful Amanda and Henry were. But I put that off for another time, even though it felt unnatural to ignore those comments.

The neighborhood Facebook group—called the Heights Watch Group, after the name of our area—had existed before we moved there. In the group, anyone who lived in the Heights could post questions about repair people, comments about the weather, or announcements about events and activities like yard sales, parades, lemonade stands, et cetera. The group also proved to be an effective way for my neighbors to share information and complaints about scams, break-ins, and suspicious people on our streets.

Just the week before, someone had pulled up in a white van and let out a bunch of kids who fanned through the neighborhood to sell magazine subscriptions, supposedly to help the kids pay their way through college in another state. Why college students from another state would show up where we lived, selling magazine subscriptions during the semester to fund their studies, I wouldn't guess. But word quickly spread as neighbors posted about the kids, and someone even Googled the name of the company they said they worked for and shared information about how the entire thing was a scam.

Too often word spread in the group about anyone in the neighborhood who looked suspicious. All it took was for one young guy to walk down the street in a hoodie or with a baseball cap pulled low, and someone would jump on to warn us all that a "prowler" was in the area and we should all lock our doors.

I wondered if Jennifer's neighborhood had a similar group—one that was at that very moment sharing a description of me wandering around in the vicinity of her house late at night in my basketball clothes.

Nevertheless, the group provided useful, if occasionally hysterical and unreliable, information about the goings-on on the nearby streets.

So I logged on to see if anyone else had experienced someone in their yard earlier in the evening.

I hoped to see something. I hoped someone else's yard had been invaded by an unknown guy who'd squished around in the soft mud beneath their windows. Maybe someone had seen a woman who looked like Dawn Steiner. But no one had reported anything more than a dog that had been incessantly barking early in the morning for two weeks straight.

So I posted about someone being in our backyard. I told the group that Amanda thought she'd heard someone in the backyard and maybe trying the door around eleven o'clock. Had anyone else seen or heard anything weird?

It surprised me how many people were still up at that hour. Did nobody else have anything to do after eleven thirty at night? Sleep? Watch TV? Have sex? Or was everyone like me, attached to their devices, fearing that they might miss something?

I quickly received a few replies to my post. One mentioned the barking dog again. One mentioned a fire hydrant near the park that leaked water day and night.

And then there was a comment that actually seemed relevant.

I didn't know the guy who replied, but he gave the name of his street, which was three blocks away from us. He said they had seen a man in their backyard shortly before Amanda thought she heard the person at the door to our house. He described the man in a nondescript way. Medium height. Brown hair. Dark clothes. Nothing helpful.

But it allowed me a small measure of relief. Maybe this was the same person who had been in our backyard. And so maybe it wasn't connected to Jennifer's death at all, and Amanda and Henry had been safe. At least from the killer.

Or maybe the person who had killed Jennifer had come to our house . . . and just happened to pass through another yard a few blocks away.

I knew the more I thought about it, the crazier I would drive myself. So I closed the laptop lid and turned to Jennifer's phone, hoping for answers there.

Before I picked it up, my own phone buzzed.

Blake?

I was indulging in a juvenile wish. It wouldn't be him. I assumed it was another notification from social media, someone else with something to say about the photo I posted.

I thought of ignoring it, but like Pavlov's dog, I jumped when it buzzed.

When I saw the notification, I jumped again.

Almost out of my skin.

Jennifer Bates has sent you a friend request.

My breath quickened, like a summer storm rising. The hand that held the phone quivered like a seismograph.

"No. No, no, no . . . not possible."

That was when I heard the back door rattling.

Just like Amanda described it.

CHAPTER TWENTY-FOUR

"No, no, no."

I told myself I must have been hearing things.

My office sat too far from the back door for me to really know if someone was trying to get in.

Maybe it was the wind. Or a neighbor dragging his garbage cans down the driveway.

But who would have been doing that so close to midnight?

And it wasn't windy enough to make that much noise.

But the noise coupled with the new friend request brought me back to my mind-set inside Jennifer's bedroom.

Was someone hunting me?

I rolled away from the desk and used my fingers to pry open the blinds. But the angle prevented me from seeing the back door. I picked up my phone, ready to call the police.

They said they'd be around. *So where the hell are they?*

Instead I went out of the office and down the hall, stepping quietly over the creaking wood floors, hoping Amanda was well asleep and wouldn't hear me. Every light remained on on the first floor of the house. What kind of burglar would choose that moment to try to come in the back door? How did I know it was really a burglar?

Could it be Jennifer's murderer, intending to do me harm? First send the friend request again, and then show up and finish me off. Why? Because I'd seen her body.

Because I was a loose end . . .

When I entered the kitchen, I heard the rattling again. Someone *was* trying the knob on the back door. My heart thumped, and I walked across the room to where the bat still stood in the corner. I grabbed it, and lifted it with one hand while I swallowed hard.

My throat was dry as the desert. My knees felt weak, like tiny twigs that couldn't support me.

The knob stopped rattling, and then someone knocked lightly.

What kind of burglar knocked?

I shuffled to the door, the bat raised, and with my left hand, I undid the chain and the dead bolt. I pulled the door open, ready to swing.

And I saw Blake standing there on the patio, blinking like a dazed child in the porch light.

CHAPTER TWENTY-FIVE

I went right out the door, pulling it shut behind me with my free hand while holding the bat with my other.

Blake backed up as soon as he saw the look on my face.

I reached him before he could get out of my way and shoved him in the chest, sending him stumbling backward until he fell onto the soft grass with a dull thump. I dropped the bat and stood over him. He held his hands up defensively, his eyes wide, his mouth turned down in a grimace.

"What the hell is the matter with you?" I asked in a harsh whisper.

"I could ask you the same thing."

I wanted to pile on top of him and start swinging. I wanted to kick him in the gut while he was down. He and I had never had a fistfight, although many, many times I'd felt like punching him. But I'd never made the kind of contact with him I did that night. Shoving him down. Standing over him.

"Where have you been?" I asked. "I've been trying to call you. Sam is looking for you. What did you do to me? Did you set me up? Are you trying to get me arrested? And you're sending me these absurd Facebook requests."

My voice rose to a shout, so I cut my words off. I turned and looked up at the house, at our bedroom window. I hoped I hadn't made so much noise that I'd woken Amanda or Henry. My shoulders heaved as I breathed hard. The pent-up anger and frustration of the whole evening surged through me like a flammable liquid, putting me on the brink of losing control. I took a step back, tried to get a grip on my emotions.

Blake stayed on the ground, his hands up, still begging for mercy. "What's your problem, Ryan?"

My voice remained harsh in the darkness. "You set me up. You sent me in there, to a dead woman's house. I could have been caught. I still might get caught. And if I get caught for that, then everything comes out. What were you thinking? Everything you touch turns to shit, Blake."

Blake's hands lowered. His face fell, transitioning from fear to shock. "What are you talking about? Who's dead?"

If I'd had more time to think or if I'd been in a calmer state of mind, I would have hesitated or softened what I said. But given the long night I'd already been through and the amount of blame I placed on Blake's shoulders, I blurted the information out.

"Jennifer, of course. Jennifer's dead."

He stared at me, his face stricken. Then something seemed to drain out of his body, and he grew limp. He fell back into the grass and placed his hand over his eyes as though shielding them from a bright light.

"Jen? Dead?" he asked. "Don't say things like that. Don't talk about her like that."

"You didn't know? Are you kidding?"

It took him a moment to answer. "I went by there. A little while ago. I saw cops and an ambulance and everything. But it wasn't her. It's probably one of the neighbors. The couple next door is elderly. One of them probably fell or had a heart attack or something."

I tried to be sympathetic, to soften my tone. It wasn't easy.

"That's not it. She's dead, Blake. I saw her body on the bedroom floor when I went in to get the letters. I'm sure somebody killed her. She had blood on her head and in her hair . . . and the room was trashed. And the letters are gone, by the way."

Again, he remained quiet for a long time. If I'd just come across him without knowing why he was lying in my backyard, I would have thought he had fallen asleep. His chest rose and fell, and his hand still covered his eyes.

But he suddenly lowered his hand and sat up, lifting his torso off the ground. His eyes bored in on mine. "Do you really think I killed her? You really think I'm capable of that? Is your regard for me that low?"

"What else could I think? You lied about seeing her today. Did you do it? Why did you send me there?"

He continued to stare at me, in his eyes a mixture of anger and hurt. He started to shake his head.

"You think you know so much, don't you? In your house and your perfect life. With your wife and baby and the sunlight always coming through the window just right. Even though it's all built on a lie." He continued to shake his head. "Not everybody's life is like yours. Not everybody's life looks like a magazine spread all the time. Not everybody cultivates the perfect social media feed."

CHAPTER TWENTY-SIX

"What are you even talking about?" I asked. "Somebody's dead, Blake. Murdered. Your ex . . . whatever she was. Girlfriend? And we're talking about Instagram filters."

"It's a mess, Ryan. Everything is a mess. At least for the rest of us. This is what life is. It's chaotic and messy. Hell, it's like that for you too. People don't know about the accident. You can't neaten *that* up with the right filter. I'm in a big damn shit show right now."

"The letters were gone, you idiot," I said. "Do you understand? The letters, the whole reason I went in there, the things that are going to hang us both out to dry—they're gone. What are we going to do about that? Do you have a plan for that?"

"Are you sure?" he asked.

"Of course I'm sure."

"Did you panic and rush? Maybe you missed them."

"I looked in the drawer you told me to look in. Someone had been through everything. The place was trashed. Could she have moved them?"

"I don't know. She's very organized. She had a place for everything and everything in its place. I just don't know, Ryan."

I walked over to him, and he drew back slightly. He eyed me with suspicion, but I made no hostile gestures. I felt like an animal trainer trying to get a scared squirrel to take a treat.

I held out my hand. "Come on. The ground's soggy."

"I know. I can feel it."

He took my hand, and I hoisted him up so we stood face-to-face. "The cops have to be looking for you. They are going to go through everything in that house. They're going to connect you to her somehow. You had to leave a trail. Do her friends know the two of you were dating?"

"Some did."

"Then the cops will find out once they start talking to them."

"Obviously." He turned to the side and started pacing, running his hand through his hair. He came back to me. "Is she really dead?"

"Yes. Really. I'm sorry, but she is."

"Oh, God. Oh, God."

"How do you even know her?" I asked. "She works for that non-profit, the one that helps former prisoners find jobs. Did you know she was almost a client of ours? We were going to help them with a media campaign."

"How do you think I met her?" Blake asked.

"*I* didn't introduce you."

"Not directly." He stopped pacing and looked up at the sky for a moment. The clouds had slid away, revealing pinpricks of stars. "Remember about six months ago you had that fund-raiser at the Pig? What was it for? Pediatric cancer or something?"

"Yes, pediatric cancer. I remember."

"Do you remember you left early?" he asked.

I did. Henry had been born just a few weeks earlier, and Amanda's mom had come over while the two of us went to the fund-raiser. But not long after the event started, her mom called, saying she thought Henry had a fever. So we left and went home, and Henry ended up being perfectly fine. We called our pediatrician, who told us what to do, and Henry was asleep in fifteen minutes.

"I remember," I said.

"Well, Jen was there. Hell, you invited her."

"I didn't invite her," I said. "Maybe someone else at the office did. We have twelve employees at the firm. I don't know everyone who gets invited somewhere."

"Whatever it was, she was there. And you were gone. And I showed up, and she and I started talking. Once she found out I knew you, she perked up. I got the feeling . . ." He gave me a sideways look, one corner of his mouth curling up a little. "She asked me a lot of questions about you, to be honest. I was clearly her second choice."

"Just tell me what happened."

"Well, she knew how to have a good time. We drank together. We went home together. That's how it started. She and I shared a cynical sense of humor. It wouldn't be any good for me to be with someone like that forever, but for a short time while I was broken up with Sam . . . Yeah, it was a lot of fun. But I always hoped to get back with Sam. I love her. I need her."

"I'm not arguing with you."

"What are you saying about Facebook requests? You were raving about something when you were standing over me."

"When I was in her house, I got a friend request from Jennifer. How the hell did that happen? And then I just got another one while I was sitting inside. Right before you came to the door."

"How could I send a message from her account? I'm not even on Facebook."

"Do you have her laptop or another device? The cops will find out."

"You're nuts, Ryan. All of this is getting to you and making you unable to think."

I took a step toward him. "Okay, then let's clear this all up. Let's call the police right now. We can tell them everything we know, get it all out in the open, and put this behind us. You can marry Sam, and the cops can deal with this mess."

For a long time, he studied me. I thought I'd gotten through to him, that my calm, logical plea had busted through his thick skull and reached him. But then he smiled, his mouth crooked.

"Are you crazy, Ryan? Just call the police and tell them everything? And ruin what I have with Sam?"

"Ruin what you have with Sam?" I said. "You mean the job her dad is going to give you?"

Blake looked stung.

"I know. A job from her dad. And your dad out of money. Sam told me. Is that why there's such a rush to get married this weekend? To lock everything down?"

"That's really low, Ryan. That's insulting. We're friends. Why would you say those things?"

"Why else is all of this happening?"

"I don't know. And by the way, if you call the police, you know what's really going to come out? The truth about the accident. How you were driving and not Aaron. They'll want to know why you were in Jen's house. Are you going to lie to them about that? Are you going to mention the letters? It could all be out there for the world to see. You'd be facing the legal music, and my relationship with Sam and her family would be damaged. Do you want all that? Do you want to get arrested for vehicular homicide? They can still pop you for that, remember? There's no Instagram filter that can put a shine on that giant turd."

"What are you hiding, then?" I asked. "You lied to me. You said you hadn't seen her or talked to her for weeks, but you texted her this morning. Did you lie to me because you really do have something to cover up? Did you hurt her?"

"How do you know I texted her this morning?" he asked.

"Because I took her phone. I was looking for the letters. But her phone was on the floor underneath the bedside table. I just impulsively grabbed it because I thought it could tell me something about what was going on. I was just about to look through it more carefully when you showed up."

"You have her phone? Here?"

"It's inside."

"You idiot. You know they can track that shit. They might be on the way here now."

"The cops were already here once tonight. Somebody tried to break into the house. Was that you?"

"Why would I try to break into your house? Where is the damn phone?"

"Wait a minute. Why were you there this morning? At Jennifer's? What did you do there?"

"Get the phone, Ryan."

"Did something happen? Did you have a fight? Did she try to blackmail you with the letters?"

He lifted his hands to the stars as if he expected God Himself to deliver him from my obstinance and stupidity.

"It wasn't pretty, okay?" Blake said. "Does it make you happy to know that?"

"Was she alive when you left her?"

"Will you just go get the phone already? That's kind of more urgent than all of these questions. Okay?"

I stared at him. I tried to read his face. His words. Was he telling the truth?

"Go. Will you?" he said. "Just go."

CHAPTER TWENTY-SEVEN

Blake waited outside while I went in and downloaded everything from Jennifer's phone onto my laptop. While the information transferred, I silently cursed myself for taking the phone out of Jennifer's house at all, let alone bringing it back to my home. My only hope was that it was so early in the investigation, that Jennifer's body had been discovered such a short time ago, that the police hadn't yet started looking for the missing phone. They'd be processing the crime scene and examining the physical evidence there.

For all I knew, they were finding my fingerprints somewhere I forgot I'd touched in the house. But I couldn't worry about that either.

Blake had called me an idiot. Was he right?

When the information was transferred, I disconnected the phone from my laptop and started back outside. But before I reached the door, Amanda called to me from the top of the stairs.

"Ryan?"

I froze for a second. I slipped Jennifer's phone back into my pocket and walked over to the bottom of the stairs. Amanda stood at the top, her hair in slight disarray because she'd been asleep. She squinted into the light where I stood.

"What are you doing down there? Are you coming to bed soon?"

"Yeah, soon. I got caught up looking at the Heights Facebook group. Someone else saw someone in their backyard, so I was reading about that."

"I heard voices. Who were you talking to?"

I couldn't lie to her again. I couldn't just stand there in my own house and lie about every damn thing I was doing. I couldn't do it.

"It's Blake," I said. "He came by. Don't worry. He's standing outside."

"What is he here for?"

"He wanted to talk to me about the wedding."

"This late?"

I shrugged. "You know how he is. Don't worry. He's leaving now."

"Look, I don't care if he comes in."

"He's not coming in. He's going. Okay? And then I'm coming up to bed."

"Is he inviting us to the wedding?" she asked. "Find out about that."

"You'd go to his wedding?"

"You heard what I said earlier about moving on. And Sam . . . you know, I miss her friendship. We were starting to get pretty close. I'm just saying . . . let the past stay in the past, you know?"

"That sounds like a really good idea. Just go back to sleep. I'll be there soon."

I went out through the back door and into the yard, where Blake waited. He stood on the patio with his hands in his pockets, his shoulders hunched against the increasing coolness of the night. I handed him the phone.

"What are you going to do with it?"

"Throw it in the river. What else can I do?"

"You can't do that. That's tampering with evidence. It's obstruction."

"As opposed to taking it from the crime scene and bringing it here?"

"I acted impulsively. We're clearheaded now. We're thinking."

"I'm all over this phone, Ryan," Blake said. "Texts. Pictures. They'll see everything."

"Then you're on her computer too. The cloud."

He seemed to be listening. For a change. I let him think, even though a million questions remained unanswered.

"Okay," he said, hefting the phone in his hand. "I'll toss it in her neighborhood somewhere. The cops will think the killer just dropped it there."

"Fine, do that. I downloaded everything off it."

"You did?"

"I did."

He smiled. "Who died and made you James Bond?"

"Maybe the information can help us figure out what's happening."

"Okay. Fine. Good. But I'm going to toss this."

But before he left, I stopped him.

"Wait. Let me see that." I took the phone back. I went into the house again and used a kitchen towel to wipe the phone off. Every inch. The screen, the back, and the sides. I found a Ziploc bag and put the phone inside, sealing it shut. When I went back out, Blake was staring up at the stars, lost in thought.

"Here," I said. "Just open the bag and let the phone fall out. Don't touch it."

"You're turning into a pretty good criminal yourself. But I guess you've been hiding your role in the accident all these years, so maybe you're used to the double life."

"I think we should just call the police. We can tell them everything and be done with it."

Blake held up the bag and jiggled it. "You're done now, okay? This is the end of your involvement with this. Just keep your mouth shut and stay out of it from here on out. Okay? They're going to find out about the guy she just started dating. They'll lean on him harder than anybody. Hell, maybe he did it."

"I'm not done. The letters are out there. Whoever has them will know about the accident. So what are you going to do?" I asked. "After you get rid of the phone . . . what are you going to do? You said it yourself. The cops will come calling for you too. They'll know about you. They're going to have all kinds of questions."

"Don't worry about it." He waved his hand like it was nothing.

"And you still haven't told me what happened when you saw her this morning."

He backed slowly away, disappearing into the darkness of the yard like a ghost. "You heard me," he said. "Just stay out of it."

CHAPTER TWENTY-EIGHT

I tried very hard to do what Blake instructed me to do.

What I wanted to do—live a normal life.

I went all through the house and checked and rechecked every door and window. I wished we had an alarm. Or a giant dog. I wished we lived in a fortress.

I took the bat with me when I went upstairs, and I paused in the doorway to Henry's room. His night-light burned in the corner, casting his crib in a white glow. I went over and looked down at him, peaceful and calm. Did every parent feel like their heart would burst when they stared at their sleeping child?

Then I went on to our bedroom, placed the bat next to the bed, and slipped beneath the covers while Amanda slept. Once I was in and settled, she turned to face me.

"Well?"

"Well, what?"

"What did he say about the wedding?" she asked, her voice rough from sleep.

"Oh, that. I really don't think we should go. It's so sudden."

She said something I couldn't understand, her voice muffled by her pillow.

"What did you say?"

She said, "Whatever you want to do. I don't care. I just don't want Sam to be disappointed."

"I think she knows what she's getting into. Any commitment from Blake is tenuous."

"And I don't want you to lose a friendship. . . ."

Her voice trailed off, and soon she was breathing steadily as she slept. Her days with Henry were exhausting, and another one would start soon. The kid refused to let us sleep past six in the morning, which wasn't far off.

I tried to sleep. I closed my eyes, told myself to clear my mind. But every time I closed them, I saw Jennifer's face, her unseeing eyes. Her stiff body underneath the piles of clothes.

My hand touching her cool, lifeless skin.

I saw my phone lighting up with that friend request.

Twice.

I couldn't make any sense of it, but it made me feel cold. And jumpy. Like I lay on a bed of nails.

When I was a kid, trying to sleep alone in my bedroom, my imagination sometimes grabbed ahold of me. If I'd heard of a murder on the news or a plane crash or a disappearance, I'd become convinced that the dead or missing people were under my bed, and I'd lie there in fear of a clawlike hand reaching up to grab me as I slept. Sometimes the fear drove me to tears, or else I'd dash down the hall to my parents' room and wake them up. My dad might gently guide me back to my room and shine a flashlight under the bed, assuring me nothing was there that could hurt me.

If I proved particularly inconsolable, they'd let me climb into bed with them, and the three of us would sleep that way, allowing me to feel safe.

As an adult, I knew Jennifer's body wasn't under the bed. I knew no cold hand would be reaching up to grab me. But I felt the same surging, intense anxiety, the same freezing, gripping fear.

And there was no one to run to. No place I could crawl into and hide like my parents' bed. I was the adult. I was the one the full weight of everything rested on.

And those letters were out there. The ones that told the truth about the accident and my role in it. A truth only Blake and I knew. But if those letters went out into the world—and I had no idea who currently had them—then that truth would spill over like a clogged toilet, destroying everything. . . .

After an hour of staring in the darkness, certain that Amanda was deeply and fully asleep, I slipped back out of bed. When I stood up, I noticed something unusual. Amanda's phone sat on her bedside table next to the digital clock and the baby monitor. Amanda almost never kept her phone by the side of the bed. She hated the temptation to look at it during the night, to grab for it first thing in the morning.

I went down the stairs to the office, the floor cold against my bare feet, and opened my laptop, hoping to learn something—anything— from the information on Jennifer's phone.

I'd experienced some good luck. Not only was Jennifer's phone easy to access, but she used an iPhone and I had an Apple laptop, which had made it easy for me to back up the information from her phone to my iTunes account.

I'd never done such a thing with anyone else's phone before. Every device Amanda and I owned was backed up to the cloud, so accessing them was easy. I assumed reading through Jennifer's data would be the same way. But it wasn't. The files in the iTunes backup were gibberish, and I couldn't make any sense of them.

"Crap," I said out loud.

I thought I heard a floorboard squeak overhead. I froze, listening. Was Amanda up with Henry? Had she noticed I was gone?

But no other noises came. So I turned back to the computer, even though I didn't know what to do. I had a pretty good knowledge of computers and phones, but I wasn't an IT guy. We had people at work who did those things and solved those problems for us. Sure, I could have gotten in touch with one of them, but it was the middle of the night. And how would I explain to them why I was trying to search through information from a complete stranger's phone?

I did what anyone would have done. I Googled, searching for an answer. It didn't take long to learn that software existed—many different kinds of software—that made it much easier to read and search through the information downloaded from a phone. Some of it was used by law enforcement. I picked a program that looked reasonably easy to use and purchased it.

While I waited for it to download, I checked my own social media accounts. Everything people shared suddenly looked strange and alien. Pictures of dogs and kids, pictures of food and clothes. Everyone else had gone about their day, posting the most inconsequential moments of their lives for all the world to see, while I had gone into a house and found the woman who lived there dead on the floor.

But just that day, hours before I ran into Blake at the Pig, I'd done the same thing. I'd taken and posted the photo of Amanda and Henry, sharing it with the world as though I believed everyone wanted and needed to see what my wife and child looked like on an ordinary Thursday. And even after the events of that night, I felt a little rush, seeing so many likes and comments, so much appreciation for how beautiful my family was. Some part of me believed that every interaction increased my value as a human being.

I closed the window.

The software finished downloading, and I was ready to wade through the contents of Jennifer's phone, knowing I'd start with the messages between her and Blake.

CHAPTER TWENTY-NINE

I scrolled past the most recent messages Jennifer and Blake had exchanged, the ones in which he said he was coming over to see her just that morning.

It's a free country

Had he gone? And if he had, what happened when he showed up?

Jennifer must not have been too worried about him having access to her house since she never changed the code on her door lock. If she'd wanted Blake out of her life, which she apparently hadn't, that would have been the easiest way. That, and not responding to his messages. But she was also a person who used the same code on her alarm as on her phone. Was she just careless?

The two of them talked via text. A lot. They shared every detail of their lives. What they ate, what they saw, what they read. I felt sorry for archaeologists from the future who would have to wade through billions upon billions of abbreviated messages and photos of people's tacos. I knew I'd contributed more than my fair share to the avalanche of data with my photos of Henry and Amanda, my pronouncements about beer and music. Were we all just yelling into a void? Was anybody really listening?

Once I'd scrolled back farther, I found an exchange from a month earlier in which Jennifer appeared to be listening very carefully.

Jennifer: Look, I just want you to be honest with me about what's happening.

Blake: I'm trying to. It's complicated.

Jennifer: It doesn't have to be.

Blake: I wish that were so.

I lifted my hand to my forehead. I resisted the urge to bang my head against the top of the desk.

"Blake, you are a most magnificent idiot," I said to no one.

I went back a few more weeks and saw a very different exchange:

Jennifer: I don't ever want you to call me again.

Blake: I won't. Don't worry about that.

Jennifer: I won't be your backup plan.

The more I read, the more I felt like a person could get whiplash following their relationship. The rest of the messages between the loving couple were more of the same. Highs and lows. Mundane talk and intense professions of love punctuated by the occasional several-week break in which things were completely cool. Only to resume again when one of them reached out to the other, arranging a meeting at Jennifer's place.

I found it difficult to comprehend how Blake could almost blow the relationship with the person who was supposed to be most important to him.

And then I heard Blake's voice in my head, cutting through everything like a buzz saw: *Who are you to judge someone else for keeping secrets from the person closest to them?*

Involuntarily my eyes trailed across the room to the bookshelf against the far wall. It was crammed with novels, textbooks left over from college, some professional journals relevant to both of our careers. But on top sat a framed photograph of Amanda and her sister, Mallory. The two of them were teenagers, hugging each other close. A photo taken six months before Mallory was killed by a drunk driver.

Something acidic rose in the back of my throat, nearly choking me.

I'd done the same thing to another family. Taken their daughter away in an accident. That sick, bile-filled feeling was part of my DNA.

I couldn't argue with the disembodied voice asking who I was to judge for keeping secrets, so I tuned it out as I had so many other times, and tried to find something else, some other piece of relevant information in Jennifer's phone. Even though searching through another person's—a dead person's—most private messages made me feel like one of the lowest forms of life. I'd been in her bedroom after she died. I'd seen her dead body. Now I was combing through her private messages, things never meant to be seen by anyone but her.

I suddenly remembered Blake mentioning Jennifer having another guy in her life, someone she had started dating recently after she and Blake broke up, someone else who might be a suspect in her death. So I exited the message stream between Blake and Jennifer and tried to find someone else, someone who might have been more than a friend.

I saw a lot of names. A few of the names made a roiling nausea rise in the pit of my stomach.

Mom. Dad. Uncle Jake.

I'd managed not to think of this unpleasant truth until it stared me in the face, but Jennifer had a life. She had family, friends. Maybe siblings or nieces and nephews. Those people had perhaps just been informed of her death, a grim-faced detective delivering the news in a matter-of-fact voice. A mother crumpling to the floor. A father punching a wall in the rage of grief.

Was I just going to stand by, knowing what I knew, and not say anything?

I decided I had to come clean in the morning. I'd tell Amanda everything. And then I'd call the police.

What choice did I have?

My eyes were tired and bleary. My body felt worn out from the late hour and from the night of craziness. It seemed hard to believe I'd lain in our bed and not been able to sleep. If I went up there again and settled in next to Amanda, I imagined myself sleeping for two days straight.

I rubbed my eyes. My vision cleared, and I caught another name and recent messages. **Kyle.**

Kyle. A guy? The other guy?

I skimmed their messages and couldn't deny he sounded like a boyfriend. A jealous boyfriend.

Just two weeks earlier:

Kyle: I don't care. We can be together.

Jennifer: I'm working on it.

Kyle: So it's over with Blake?

Jennifer: It really is . . .

And then the rest of the messages came from Kyle. With no response from Jennifer.

Well?

Is it really over?

Why were you texting him?

Why aren't you answering me?

And finally, just one day earlier:

We need to settle this. I need to know where I stand. Now.

CHAPTER THIRTY

Light started to leak in from behind the curtains. I'd been through an insane number of texts, including many more between Jennifer and Kyle, and found little else of interest. If my eyes had been bleary and tired earlier in the night, by the time I heard Amanda's footsteps above me they felt like they'd been scrubbed with a Brillo Pad.

I stood up from the desk, my back creaking like a rusty gate. Any thought of work or the day's demands had rushed out of my mind like blowing sand. When I had been twenty and pulling an all-nighter before a college class, I could manage it. I knew when the class ended I could return to my dorm and crash into bed. Facing an eight-hour day at work with real responsibilities seemed impossible. Especially with so many unanswered questions swirling around me.

I grabbed my phone and jumped from one social media platform to another, looking for any information about Jennifer's death. Twitter and Facebook. The local newspaper and TV stations. Nothing. I almost threw the phone in frustration.

A second later I heard Amanda's steps in the kitchen, accompanied by Henry's gooing and gurgling.

"Ryan? Are you up?"

I went out and saw Amanda in her robe, her hair mussed by sleep, sliding Henry into his high chair. Once he was in, he started thrashing his arms around, his mouth a near perfect O of desire and hunger.

"Why are you up so early?" she asked. "And after you were up so late dealing with Blake."

"Couldn't sleep."

Henry held his arms out to me like he was Superman, then started banging his fists against the high chair. I went over and kissed him on top of the head, which calmed him a little.

"You never have trouble sleeping," she said. "Unlike your son."

"Maybe I had too much caffeine."

I felt jittery and caged up. Amanda started taking things out of the refrigerator, and I kept getting in her way. I couldn't concentrate on anything around me.

"Do you need something?" she asked, a polite way of asking me to move.

"I'll be right back."

I went to the office and sent e-mails to the appropriate people at work telling them I wouldn't be in that day. I claimed to be under the weather but didn't offer any details. I didn't need to, not really. One of the benefits of being a VP at a small company. And it was a good time to miss work. We'd recently completed a large project I'd been in charge of—a giant social media campaign for Rossingville's minor-league baseball team, the Roadrunners—so I'd stored up enough goodwill to miss a day. I could check my e-mail and be available by phone if anyone needed me.

When I came back out, Amanda was in a chair next to Henry, spooning yogurt into his mouth. He lapped it up happily and only half of it went across his cheeks.

Amanda gave me the side-eye. "Are you going to get yourself something to eat? Or maybe do something useful, like make coffee?"

"Sure. I'll make coffee."

I filled the coffeemaker to the rim and turned it on. I needed all of it. It was nice to have a simple task to perform. Then I didn't know what to do with myself.

"What's going on?" she asked. "You're pacing like I'm in labor all over again."

"Why was your phone next to the bed last night?" I asked.

"My phone?" She said the word like it was something foreign she'd never heard before.

"Yeah. It was on the bedside table. You never do that. You always plug it in across the room."

"That's why you seem agitated? My phone?"

"You didn't answer the question."

"I don't know. I just fell asleep that way, I guess. Do you know how tired I am at the end of the day? I'm lucky to get my clothes off before I pass out. What's really on your mind?"

"I don't think I'm going in to work today."

Amanda turned completely away from Henry and gave me her full attention. "*You're* not going in to work today? *You?* Missing a day of work? What's wrong?"

I barely heard her. I was scrolling through my phone again, checking for news. Finding nothing, I did something I almost never did anymore. I went out to the living room and clicked on the TV, thinking I might find breaking news there that they didn't have online yet. It was almost six, and I knew a local morning show came on right then.

I waited while the hosts—a young blond woman and a chipper young man—chattered through some opening inanities about the weather and the blooming flowers and the approach of Easter. I wanted to yell at the screen and tell them to hurry up, that we didn't need the happy talk. Just the news.

Then they transitioned, and the blond woman's face switched from shining happiness to grim seriousness. She started talking about a suspected homicide in town, her brow furrowed as she related the facts.

"The suspected victim was twenty-seven-year-old Jennifer Bates, a resident of the Kingston Manor subdivision. . . ."

Jennifer's face flashed on the screen, a vacation snapshot that showed her with a gigantic smile.

I heard the noise. The gasp. To be honest, I thought it came from me. I thought I'd made the noise when I saw her face and heard her name. Seeing it and hearing it on the news made it much more real even than touching her still body in her house. Seeing it on the news meant other people knew she was dead too. It meant I hadn't imagined the whole thing. I hadn't dreamed it.

"Ryan?" Amanda said behind me.

"Hold on."

I didn't turn around. I didn't know when she had come into the room. Was she the one who had gasped?

The story ended with the blond woman telling us that if we knew anything we should call the local police. As of now, she explained, they had no suspects and no motive in the crime.

Then she started talking about a classic-car show, something coming to town during the upcoming weekend.

Amanda crossed the room and muted the TV. She turned to face me.

"Where's Henry?" I asked.

"I can see him. He's going to town on his teething ring. Do you want to tell me what's going on?"

"I was watching the news," I said.

"You never watch the news. Not on TV anyway. Why are you watching it today?"

"We should check on Henry."

She leaned back. "I can see him. He's happy. You know that woman, Ryan. That's Jennifer Bates. You know her. Ryan . . ." She shook her head. "Ryan, do you want to tell me what's going on?"

CHAPTER THIRTY-ONE

Henry started whining in the kitchen.

"There, see. He's not fine," I said, hoping to change the subject away from me.

He couldn't stand it when we—and especially Amanda—were out of his sight for any length of time. And he liked to let us know it. He awkwardly banged his hands against the high chair, rattling his plastic bowl.

Amanda hesitated for a moment, her eyes locked on mine, and then she turned and went out to the kitchen to tend to Henry. But I knew the conversation wasn't over. I turned the TV off and followed Amanda.

She stood at the counter, pouring milk into a cup. She brought it over to Henry and gave him a drink. He calmed down then, stopping his banging. Amanda straightened up and looked at me.

"What's going on, Ryan?" she asked, emphasizing every word. "You're out last night playing the world's quietest basketball game. You're talking to Blake outside. Late. You're up all night. You say you're not going to work. And now you have the TV on because someone you know, someone who was almost a client, has been murdered."

Her words were accusatory and upsetting enough. But she placed a special emphasis on a few of them. She had said "almost a client" as though those words carried some kind of additional meaning, something both she and I knew. And that set me off-balance.

"Wouldn't you think it was disturbing if someone you knew got murdered?" I asked.

"Of course. But how well did you really know this woman?" she asked. "As I recall, she wanted your firm to bid on a project for her nonprofit. They wanted some kind of updated marketing approach, right? Print and social media? The usual? And you gave them the bid. And they went with somebody else because you guys were too expensive. So that's it. That's not a big deal. How well could you even know someone from that?"

"We had to meet a couple of times," I said. "With her and several of her coworkers."

But it seemed strange to me that Amanda remembered Jennifer at all. Sure, I talked about work at home. We talked about it a lot. But in the big scheme of things, my interactions with Jennifer Bates and her company would have been small. Insignificant. We bid on jobs from companies all over town, all over the county and even the state. Would Jennifer's company have even rated a mention with all the other stuff going on in our lives?

I started to understand that something else was at play.

"I think we need to sit down," Amanda said.

I didn't argue. Thank God Henry was only six months old. Amanda and I could discuss just about anything we wanted to in front of him, and he wouldn't have any idea what was going on. As long as we didn't yell or curse—since he was acquiring language skills right then—and as long as the milk and apple juice kept flowing to his mouth, he'd be content.

So I sat down across the table from Amanda, with Henry in his spot to my right.

"I know, Ryan," she said.

"Know about what?"

"I know about the messages that woman sent you on Facebook."

The overhead light bore down on me. Even Henry, pausing for a moment from his destruction of the teething ring, turned his wide eyes and rosy cheeks my way, as if curious to hear my response.

I certainly couldn't lie. I'd had my fill of that. I couldn't do it anymore.

"How did you know about that?" I asked.

"Why didn't you tell me?" Amanda spoke in a calm voice as usual. She didn't lose her cool or yell. She didn't sound panicky or frantic. "We tell each other everything. Or at least, I thought we did. Why didn't you tell me this woman was coming on to you?"

"Is that why you remember her name?" I asked. "I can't believe I would have ever mentioned her around here."

"Tell me what happened, Ryan," she said. "Why was she writing to you?"

"How did you find out? Did you check my messages? I didn't think you ever snooped around on my devices."

"I wasn't snooping." Her words came out more sharply, like nails from a nail gun. "Do you want to know how I saw them? It was about a week before Henry was born." When she mentioned his name, Henry turned her way. Maybe he thought his parents were having an important discussion about him. I hoped he thought that. "You remember how big I was then. I was like the side of a house. It was hell going up and down the stairs. I was miserable."

"I know. I remember."

"Well, I was down here one night. And you were out. I think you were playing basketball. Again. Anyway, I realized my phone was upstairs. Rather than waddle up there, I decided to use your computer to check my work e-mail. It was my last chance to feel like a normal working person for a while. I was wrapping stuff up before Henry was born." She tapped her fingers against the table. "You're right. I wouldn't snoop on your stuff. You have a lot of work things on there. I don't want to disrupt any system you have for organizing things. It's the same reason I don't want you logging on to my devices." She cleared her throat. "But I saw the messages. One of them came through and dinged while I was on the computer. I saw what she said to you about hoping your relationship went beyond the professional. Or something like that."

"That means you saw something else," I said. "You saw that I never wrote back. That she wrote to me a few times, but I didn't reply. That was it. I ignored her, and she went away."

"But you didn't tell me about it," Amanda said. "Why not?"

"You just explained why," I said. "You were about to have Henry. And you were stressed and uncomfortable. And you were ambivalent about quitting your job. I didn't want to add anything else to your shoulders. I didn't want to pile on."

Amanda said nothing. She appeared to be absorbing everything I'd told her. She stood up and used a napkin to wipe milk off Henry's face.

When she was seated again, I said, "You of all people should know about people flirting with you and coming on to you whether you want them to or not."

CHAPTER THIRTY-TWO

"You're really bringing that up?" Amanda asked.

"It seems relevant. Doesn't it?"

The year before, while Amanda had still been working her grant-writing job, one of the guys from the IT department started showing a great deal of interest in her. He manufactured excuses to come by her office and tinker with her computer or printer. He happened to bump into her during the lunch hour at nearby restaurants and coffee shops. He invited her out for happy hour.

"What was his name?" I asked. "Steve?"

"What's your point, Ryan? Some guy hit on me at work. So what? Do you know what it's like to be a woman in this society? When I was eight months pregnant and walking into the grocery store in sweatpants and a maternity top, two different guys whistled at me. That's what it's like for women to navigate a world of men. At least Steve never whistled at me. He was polite. And when I gave him the cold shoulder, he backed off. End of story."

"Just like Jennifer," I said. "I ignored her, and she went away."

"But I told you about Steve."

"And I wasn't eight and a half months pregnant when he asked you to coffee."

Amanda cocked her head. "That was the last time you heard from this Jennifer? When I was as big as a house?"

She had me there. And I couldn't deny it. Even though I didn't know how she knew.

"Somehow you know she wrote to me again?" I asked.

"Yeah. And you didn't tell me about that either. And now all of this." She waved her hand in the air, a gesture that seemed to be intended to encapsulate Jennifer's death, my all-nighter, my skipping work, and anything else odd that had transpired in the last twelve hours.

"She wrote to me once more. Just a couple of days ago. And I don't know what made her do that out of the blue. I hadn't seen her or talked to her. But I didn't respond to that message at all. In fact, when I got that message two days ago, I finally unfriended her on Facebook. I didn't realize we were still friends then. She friended me originally when we were doing the bid for her." My mind flashed back to the night before, standing over Jennifer's body and receiving the friend request. Then the other friend request right before Blake had showed up. I was no closer to understanding those requests than I was to understanding anything else. "How did you know about that if you're not snooping around on my computer or phone?"

Amanda sighed. She looked over at Henry, who bobbed his head between the two of us. "I looked last night. I hadn't looked since the first messages came. Since that night I was pregnant. I feel gross doing that. But last night . . . you were gone. It was weird. It was weird when I called the basketball game. It was weird the way you left. And I'm sitting here, feeling a little isolated, to be honest. You're basically working two jobs, and I'm working none. It feels like your life is going by like a speeding bullet. The job, the bar, the sports. And I'm here lactating and changing diapers. So I snooped. I couldn't help it."

"You know I would never . . . I wasn't."

"I know that. And I'm as disappointed in myself as anything else. That's not who I am. But then . . . what the hell is going on? You've been acting awfully strange, last night and this morning. And you're glued to the news about that woman being killed. And she was after you. What am I supposed to make of that?"

"It's not like that," I said, shaking my head.

And I was ready to come clean, to tell her everything. Wouldn't someone crack apart under the pressure of being two-faced all the time?

"Then what is it like?" she asked.

Somebody rang the doorbell. At the front of the house.

"Who the hell is that?" Amanda asked. "Who would come to the door this early in the morning?"

"I don't know. I'll get rid of them."

As I stood up, I noticed an unpleasant odor emanating from Henry's direction. Either the milk had given him gas, or he needed to be changed. Badly.

"Did you—"

"I smell it," Amanda said. "I'll take him."

"I'll get rid of whoever it is," I said. "And then we can finish talking."

Amanda pulled Henry out of his high chair and took a whiff of his bottom. Every feature on her face curled. "Ugh. Funny how you get to go to the door, and I get the pile of shit."

"We can switch if you want. Maybe it will be Blake. Would you like to talk to him?"

She shook her head. "He's worse than the smelly diaper."

"What happened to turning the page and moving on?"

"Oh, right. Okay . . . I'll be kind."

While she went upstairs, I went out to the front of the house. Before I opened the door, I peeked through the front window. I saw a woman in business attire—blue suit, white shirt—on the stoop. Middle-aged. Serious looking. As if she felt my eyes on her, she turned and looked at me, locking on to my eyes through the glass.

She waved. Not a friendly wave that said *Hello*. It was a wave that said *Hurry up and open this door.*

So I did.

"Ryan Francis?" she asked.

"That's me."

"I'm Marita Rountree, with the Rossingville Police Department. I'd like to ask you a few questions about an ongoing investigation."

CHAPTER THIRTY-THREE

Detective Rountree looked around the living room when she came in, sizing up the furniture, the letterpress prints on the walls. I offered her a seat, and she sank into the end of the couch while I opted for a chair. She had brown hair in long braids. She looked fit and wore a Garmin watch on her wrist, the kind you could use to track all of your exercise. I didn't see a wedding band on her long fingers.

"Do you know why I'm here, Mr. Francis?"

"Ryan. And, yes, I think I do."

She raised her eyebrows, encouraging me to explain.

"You're here because someone tried to break into our house last night," I said.

"Oh, I know about that, yes," she said. "But that's not why I'm here. Do you have another guess? I'll give you one more."

"I saw on the news that Jennifer Bates was murdered."

"And how did you know her?" Rountree asked.

I explained that we had once made a bid on a project for her non-profit. But they'd gone with someone else.

Rountree waited patiently. She looked like a woman with all the time in the world, even as her watch buzzed twice to indicate incoming texts. She didn't even look down at it. She clearly had more discipline than I did when it came to ignoring texts and notifications.

Finally, she asked, "Did you know her in any other capacity?"

I was thankful for one thing—the secret about the Facebook messages sent to me by Jennifer hadn't come out for the first time with the detective sitting there. Wherever Amanda was in the house—and I suspected she was still upstairs—I had no idea if she could hear us or not. If Henry was blathering and fussing while she changed him, she probably couldn't. Nevertheless, I was glad she'd heard it from me already.

"We didn't have a relationship outside of that one work experience," I said. Then added, "Although she tried to establish one with me."

Rountree's face remained impassive while I told her about the Facebook messages. The ones six months ago and the more recent one in the last couple of days.

"What did this message from a couple of days ago say?" she asked.

"Nothing really. Just that we should talk. Soon."

"Talk about what?"

"She didn't say."

"Just talk. Do you think it was work related?"

"I guess it could have been. Maybe. I just don't know. I unfriended her and didn't respond."

Rountree didn't show surprise, and I guessed, although I wasn't certain, she already knew what the messages said. Why else would she be at my house?

Unless something else had pointed her in my direction.

Fingerprints.

A witness, like the dog walker.

I said, "You know her job, that nonprofit—they worked with prisoners, men returning to the workforce when they get released. Could one of those guys have hurt her?"

"We're well aware of her job and the people she might have met. So, outside of this work transaction and these Facebook messages, you didn't know her. You didn't see her socially or spend time with her?"

"That's right."

"And just for my records, because I know my boss will ask about it, where were you yesterday?"

"What time?"

"Oh, any time. All day. Humor me. Account for all of your movements. Where were you?"

I summarized my day. Work from morning until evening. Stopping by the Pig after work. The coffee with Blake. Then home. And then . . .

"I played basketball at the Y last night. They have a league that goes late on Thursday."

She nodded. "But I want to go back to your friend Blake Norton."

I heard Amanda on the stairs, the wood squeaking as she came down. She swept into the living room, carrying Henry on her hip.

"What about Blake?" Amanda asked. "Did something happen to him?"

Rountree stood up and smiled when she saw Amanda and Henry. Her face showed more warmth than it had shown to me. I stood up as well and introduced them.

Rountree reached out and shook hands with Amanda. Then she turned her attention to Henry. "Who is this handsome little man?"

"This is Henry," Amanda said.

Rountree leaned in and rubbed her index finger against Henry's cheek, prompting him to smile toothlessly. She had no idea how lucky she was not to have shown up fifteen minutes earlier, when he smelled like a toxic-waste dump.

"Did you say something about Blake?" Amanda asked.

Rountree appeared reluctant to take her attention away from Henry, but she did, straightening up. And once she did, her face went back to being all business.

"Right, Mr. Norton. You all are friends with him, aren't you?"

"We are," I said.

"Mostly Ryan," Amanda said at the same time. "But, yes, we both are."

Rountree withheld comment. "Do you know where he is? We'd like to talk to him."

"Isn't he home?" I asked. "Or he'll be at work eventually."

"Wait. Why do you want to talk to him?" Amanda asked.

Rountree looked at both of us. "Because of his relationship with Jennifer Bates. Didn't you know he was romantically involved with her?"

Amanda gasped. For the second time that day. Her mouth formed an O that made her look like Henry. And then she raised her hand to cover her mouth.

"He was in a relationship with her," she said once she'd lowered her hand. "You mean . . . an ongoing one? Right now? What a . . ." She cut her words off, showing deference in the presence of the police officer.

"He broke it off when he got back together with Sam," I said.

"So you did know about that relationship, Ryan?" Rountree asked, turning to me.

I felt three sets of eyes on me, all of them, including Henry, staring at me with great expectation. "He mentioned it," I said. "He said it ended a few weeks ago."

"And he wasn't cheating on Sam?" Amanda asked, her voice skeptical.

"He says he wasn't. He told me last night."

"Last night? When he came to the house?"

I took a deep breath. "No. I saw him after work. We got coffee."

"You were talking to him and not Tony?" Amanda asked.

"No. I did talk to Tony about his boyfriend. I did. But when I was leaving, I ran into Blake. He said he wanted to talk, so we got coffee at the Ground Floor."

"And you didn't tell me?" Amanda asked.

Rountree lifted her eyebrows and looked at me.

"No, I didn't," I said. "He's been persona non grata around here. So I didn't tell you."

"So you saw Mr. Norton twice last night," Rountree said. "I think I need to know more about these chats with Mr. Norton."

CHAPTER THIRTY-FOUR

We all sat down, Rountree on one end of the couch with Amanda on the other, Henry balanced on her lap. I returned to my chair.

"What was Mr. Norton doing here last night? What time was this?"

I looked at Amanda and then back to the detective. "It was late. Amanda had gone to sleep already. Maybe midnight or so."

"And this was *after* someone tried to break into your house?" she asked.

"We don't really know if someone tried to break in," I said.

Amanda cleared her throat. "The back door rattled. And the two officers who came found tracks outside. So did Ryan. None of that is normal, is it?"

Rountree agreed by nodding. "And why did Blake come by?"

"He was following up about his marriage," I said. "He's getting married on Saturday."

"He told you about his marriage in the coffee shop?"

"He did."

I shifted my eyes to Amanda, and she was watching me. Brow furrowed, thoughts swirling. She knew I'd withheld the information about seeing Blake. Yes, I'd had a good reason, but that didn't mean she was going to like it. Her disapproval radiated off her body like summer heat from asphalt. Rountree had to have noticed. Any halfway intelligent detective would have picked up on it.

"Does he always come over late at night? Is that odd?"

"He's not a conventional guy," I said.

"Even though he knows you have a baby, he shows up late at night."

"I was awake," I said. "He came by and must have seen the light on in my office."

"Could he have . . . ?" Amanda said.

"What's that, Amanda?" Rountree asked.

She shifted Henry's weight from one side of her lap to the other. He found a strand of her hair and started tugging on it, making Amanda wince. She shifted him again, hoping to break his grip.

"Could he have been the one outside the house, trying to open the door?" Amanda asked.

"You think Blake was outside your house when you were home alone with the baby, but he didn't ring the bell or anything?" Rountree asked.

"He and I have had our differences," Amanda said. "Which I'm trying to get over. Although this news about this woman . . . Never mind. If he thought Ryan wasn't home, he wouldn't have knocked. He might not knock at all if he thought I was home."

"But the shoe prints," I said. "I'm not an expert, but the shoe prints looked smaller than Blake's would have. And Blake wasn't wearing sneakers when he came over. I don't know."

But I wondered, *Smaller feet. Sneakers. Dawn Steiner?*

Rountree arched one eyebrow as she thought about the tracks. "So we do know Blake came by around midnight, talked to you, and then left." She turned to me. "Where was he going?"

"I don't know. Home, I assumed."

"Have you talked to him today?" Rountree asked.

"It's pretty early."

"Do you know what he was doing yesterday?" Rountree asked, ignoring my comment. "Did he say? You saw him in the evening at the coffee shop, and then you saw him last night here. What about the rest of the day?"

"I don't know," I said. "He must have gone to work. I mean, I assume he did."

"Did he say if he went to see Ms. Bates?"

"I think . . . he might have mentioned that he went to her house early yesterday."

Rountree nodded, her face a portrait of sagelike patience. "Did he say why?"

"I'm not exactly sure," I said. "I assume to talk about their relationship. Probably to make it clear it was really over."

"And did he say how it went?"

"I don't know. I assume not well. None of it sounds good."

"No, it doesn't."

"Did something happen?"

"A neighbor saw him there yesterday," she said, drawing her words out. "Late morning, early afternoon. They're not exactly sure. And the neighbor thought he heard arguing. Shouts coming from the house. Faint, considering the distance and the closed windows and everything. But he heard voices raised. We don't know yet how that visit lines up with the time of Ms. Bates's death. But we'll know that soon."

I thought of the frozen watch hands: twelve fifteen. Likely the time of death, because wouldn't it make sense to think the watch broke when Jennifer was killed? And Blake had been there around that time. . . .

I felt hollow inside. Like a rotted tree trunk.

"You should talk to Blake about all of this," I said.

Rountree hadn't taken a note since she'd been in the room. I'd assumed all detectives took notes on little pads and then went back to the police station and typed their notes up on a computer. But Rountree must have had a good memory.

She ignored my question and instead waved at Henry, then stood up from the couch, adjusting her suit coat as she did. Smoothing it down, making sure it was in place. I thought she was ignoring my question, withholding the information from me. But then she answered.

"We haven't been able to get ahold of Blake," she said. "So if you hear from him or see him again, you need to let us know."

"He's not at home?"

"He hasn't been," she said. "And neither has Samantha. Samantha Edson. That's his fiancée, right? The woman he's marrying on Saturday? The wedding he came over here to tell you about, again, late last night?"

"That's her."

"If you hear from either one of them, let me know."

"Sam's not at work?" Amanda asked. "She goes in pretty early."

"We're about to check there," Rountree said. "Don't worry."

"She might have things to do for the wedding," Amanda said, sounding perfectly reasonable.

"True," Rountree said, her voice neutral.

Henry started to whine and fuss on Amanda's lap. She stood up with him, trying to keep him quiet. "I think he needs more to eat. Thank you, Detective."

"Thank you." She waved to Henry again as Amanda took him out of the room and back to the kitchen. Henry stared at Rountree, all wide-eyed fascination, until he disappeared out of sight.

I walked to the door with the detective. Her movements were smooth and unhurried. She walked like someone wandering through a garden on a spring day, not like someone investigating a murder. At the door, she held out her hand, and we shook.

"And you're sure, Mr. Francis, that there isn't anyone else who would want to harm you? Business deals gone wrong? Debts? Dissatisfied customers?"

Maybe because I'd thought of her just moments before, Dawn Steiner's face again popped into my mind.

"Nothing like that," I said.

Then Rountree spoke in a voice so low Amanda couldn't have heard over Henry's chattering.

"You're sure you didn't know Ms. Bates better than you said you did?"

Her words slipped out like a knife. They were meant to puncture me, force me to release something I didn't mean to admit.

"I didn't," I said. "That I can promise you."

She looked around the room one more time, taking it all in.

"Well, if you hear from either one of the lovebirds, you'll let me know, Ryan. It's very important that things not get held back in a case like this. You never know what detail could tip the scales the way we want them to go. We're talking to all the neighbors over by Ms. Bates's, anyone who might have seen something. We'll talk to your neighbors too about that possible prowler. More people are awake now. Who knows who saw something?"

She didn't wait for me to respond before she slipped out the door and back to her car.

CHAPTER THIRTY-FIVE

I went out to the kitchen after Rountree left. The news she'd brought—Blake was nowhere to be found, the cops knew he'd been at Jennifer's house and the two of them had argued while he was there—left me shaken almost as much as the events of the day before. Her words clouded my mind as though I'd taken a blow to the head, one that left me dizzy and slightly incoherent. It took effort to move my legs, I was so thrown by them.

Amanda had Henry back in his high chair, and she was spooning applesauce into his mouth. He greedily gummed it, his jaws moving like those of a wizened old man. She put the spoon aside, wiped her hands on a napkin, and started texting someone. The message whooshed away, and then she looked up at me.

"Who are you writing to?" I asked.

"Sam. I want to let her know what's going on. That the cops are looking for Blake and they want to talk to her too. She has a right to know all of this. If she knew, she'd do something about it."

"Have you heard from her at all today?" I asked.

"That's the first time I wrote. I haven't heard from her in a week or so." She picked up the spoon again and fed Henry more. "It's been a little awkward since the thing with Blake and Henry. But she's not a bridge burner. We keep up with each other. We keep trying to get together, but stuff comes up."

"Has she mentioned anything about Blake? Any trouble?"

"Not to me." She wiped her hands again. "What did you think of all that the cop told us?"

"I don't know. I can't conceive of Blake murdering someone. I just can't."

"You can't?"

"Amanda, we're talking about murder. Not being a jackass. Or bumping a baby's head against a lampshade."

"That's *your* baby he did that to."

"*Our* baby. And it was an accident. Not attempted infanticide."

"Isn't it obvious why Blake would kill this woman?" Amanda asked. "Isn't it clear the motive the cop was laying out?"

"I can see it. Maybe she made things awkward with Sam. Or she didn't want to break up when he ended it. Something like that."

"Pretty good motivation, isn't it?" Amanda said. "If he loses Sam once and for all, he loses everything. I always knew they'd get married. I knew he'd go through with it . . . for the money, if nothing else."

"I know. You always said that."

"And I'm right. Where does he want to work? He's always talked about it."

"Her dad's company. I know. And Sam's mentioned her dad might hire him. That's always been in play."

"He can't blow all that," Amanda said. "Hell, Sam's parents have plenty of money. And she only has one sister. Think of what they'll inherit."

"That's a little cynical, isn't it?" But as I said it, I remembered what Sam had told me about Blake's dad losing his job and maybe losing a lot of money and how that had led to Blake finding work in Rossingville. Blake had always been the rich kid. Had that been put in jeopardy?

"Does it sound like a fair assessment to you?" she asked. "You know Blake. Would that motivate him to get married?"

"I understand what you're saying, but I think there's more to it than that. Sam is a good balance for him. She brings out the best in him. You know that."

"Yeah. Maybe."

"Not maybe. You've said yourself it was true. They work well together . . . when they're actually together."

Henry was moving his head around as Amanda tried to feed him.

"Do you want me to do that?" I asked, pointing to Henry. "I'm just standing here. Not helping."

"It's fine. He and I have our routine. When I go back to work, we can share the duties more. We'll have to."

"I'm glad you're ready to go back," I said.

"I am too. I don't want to feel like I'm sitting on the sidelines while everyone else advances their careers. I'm sure Jennifer had a nice career. I'm sure Jennifer was making good money."

"She's dead, Amanda. Whoever killed her . . . she's dead."

She let out a deep breath. "I know. I shouldn't talk about her that way."

"If you're ready to go back to work, we can figure things out with Henry and everything. You know your parents would help too. They'd love to spend more time with Henry."

"You're right. I know."

Henry started grabbing for the spoon, as if he wanted to feed himself. He couldn't, not yet. But he would be there soon. And crawling and talking and walking all lay ahead. Everything with him would speed past like the scenery outside a fast-moving train.

"It's tough for me to be charitable to a woman who came after you," Amanda said, "and then was involved with Blake."

"We don't know what went on between Blake and Jennifer," I said. "But Blake said he ended it when he and Sam were going to get back together. I believe him."

Henry seemed content to play with the spoon. He tried to get it into his mouth. Then he banged it against the high chair tray. Amanda and I had both quickly grown deaf to the noise he made. The pounding, the rattling, the squealing. The spills and the mess. At some point we just let go, figuring all of these things were going to happen, so no need to get bent out of shape about them.

Amanda arched her back, stretching and groaning, and leaned against the counter.

"You saw Blake earlier in the evening yesterday," she said. "And you didn't tell me."

"Would you have wanted me to?"

"I told you, Ryan," she said. "I don't want to think we have secrets from each other. You kept this Jennifer stuff from me. You didn't tell me you had coffee with Blake last night. I said I can try to be more charitable toward him. To respect your friendship with him."

Bang, bang, bang went the spoon against the high chair.

"I heard all that," I said. "And I appreciate that. But it wasn't planned. I ran into him. But if you don't want me to hide my interactions with Blake, I won't. I'm not sure there are going to be too many more of them."

Amanda glanced at her phone. "Nothing from Sam." She set it down and looked up at me. "I don't want to turn into one of those couples who keep things from each other. The way my mom doesn't tell my dad when she buys something expensive. Or the way he doesn't tell her when he's going drinking with his friends. It's just . . . I don't know. Unpleasant, I guess."

Bang, bang, bang.

"But my parents were always honest with each other," I said.

"You always said that. And it's a shame your dad isn't here to see how you're doing. Or to meet Henry."

"I know." I went over and slipped the spoon out of Henry's hand. He barely noticed and kept waving his hand around like a conductor without an orchestra. "So . . . in the interest of honesty, I'm going to tell you what I want to do right now. No one can reach Blake, and I think he's in big trouble. And it's all trouble he brought on himself, I know. But . . ."

"You still want to go find him," she said, reading my thoughts.

"I think it's the best thing."

"And take him to the cops?"

"I just want to find out what's going on," I said. "Why he's acting this way."

Amanda nodded. "I figure I can't stop you. And for Sam's sake, I hope he does go and tell the cops whatever he knows. But can you do me a favor?"

"Sure. What?"

She looked up at me again. "Tell him if he was the one creeping outside the house last night to just knock the next time. I'll try not to bite him."

CHAPTER THIRTY-SIX

I dressed quickly upstairs. For all I knew, Blake had left town, fleeing like a thief in the night to avoid whatever trouble he might have found himself in. Given his refusal to answer calls from anyone—the police and me—was I willing or able to shift my opinion of him? Was it possible for me to accept that Blake might very well have killed Jennifer for the reasons Amanda gave?

Was I ready to accept it, Blake as a murderer, even as a remote possibility?

"No," I said out loud. And pushed the thought away.

But did I push with as much force as I would have once been able to summon?

Once dressed, I went downstairs and stopped in my office. I took the laptop, sliding it into my messenger bag.

I heard Amanda and Henry in the living room. I went in there to get my coat.

Henry was on the floor, squirming around on a blanket. Amanda sat in a chair nearby, trying to read for her book club. I knew she wouldn't be able to get much reading accomplished. It was tough to read a book with one eye on the kid.

"I guess it would be foolish of me to ask you not to go," she said. "To just let Blake deal with his own problems with the police and everything else."

"You know I have to do this."

"And you know I'm not going to beg," she said.

"I know that very well."

I put my coat on. But then I didn't know what to say or do next. I couldn't really tell Amanda all the reasons why I needed to go out to try to find Blake. I couldn't unroll the long scroll of secrets I had kept from her. My presence in Jennifer's house, my taking of the phone. My role in the accident all those years ago.

And I wasn't even sure what my involvement would do for Blake.

When the police found him—and I believed they inevitably would—he'd have to tell them the entire story. Which would expose everything I'd already tried to keep under wraps.

So was there any way for this to turn out well for me? Or Blake? Or Amanda? Or Henry?

A wave of hopelessness descended on me. Was there any way out that would leave my life intact?

"I just . . . Maybe you should do something else today," I said. "You could go see your parents or something."

"Why are you telling me to do that?"

"Look, I really don't know who was sneaking around last night when I wasn't here. Maybe Blake. He came to the house looking for me and saw you were home or something. But we can't be sure. We just can't."

"Are you saying you think Henry and I are unsafe?" Her voice remained calm. No hysteria. No loss of control for her.

"I doubt it. But . . . we don't really know what's going on. Do we?"

"Do you think Blake would come by and hurt us?"

"No," I said, and I meant it. "Not at all. Not Blake. I guess I don't know who all he might be mixed up with. If someone hurt Jennifer—"

"*Killed* her. Not hurt, Ryan. They killed her."

"Right. If someone killed her, and they know I know her, or they know I know Blake, is it possible they'd come looking for me?"

Amanda put her book on the end table, splayed open to hold her place. Color rushed to her face as she appeared to be processing what I'd told her. "Are you serious?"

"I don't know. I don't know anything."

Amanda stared at Henry on the floor, while I stood there with my coat on and my bag in my hand. I let her have the time to think and absorb the possibilities.

And I kept some of the possibilities to myself. Dawn Steiner. Amanda didn't know anything about her. And I didn't want her to. It was my problem to solve, something I hoped to keep her protected from.

"Okay," she said. "We'll find somewhere to go until you come home."

"I can drop you off if you want. Your parents . . ."

"No, I'll go. You're in a hurry. And I'm not sure I'm even doing the right thing. I feel like a little kid jumping at shadows."

"It might be best."

"Are you going to keep in touch while you're out?" she asked. "I want to know that you're okay. Even if you are doing something kind of stupid for a person who is definitely stupid."

"I'll keep in touch," I said. "I promise."

"You know what?" she said.

"What?"

"I have a feeling we're not going to get to watch that movie tonight either."

CHAPTER THIRTY-SEVEN

I should have been going to work.

As I drove through town, I saw school buses and cars, service trucks and delivery people, everyone going about their daily routines. I should have been part of that stream, with nothing more to look forward to than meetings over coffee and a boatload of e-mails to answer.

Instead I drove through Rossingville—a small city named for a Union general who quartered his troops here during the Civil War and then decided to stay and farm—trying to find an old friend who might have committed a murder. And was definitely a suspect in one.

A light flashed on my dashboard display, and a chime sounded. Low fuel.

"Great."

I'd planned on getting gas on the way home from the Pig the night before. Then Blake had distracted me and made me late. Then, when I went to Jennifer's house, I ignored it again.

And there I was with a low-fuel warning.

But I caught a break. Just outside of our neighborhood, I passed a gas station, and I pulled up to a pump and started fueling. The station had just opened, and a tired-looking clerk with a ponytail and an arm full of tattoos pushed a rack of motor oil out the door and into place. When he stopped moving, he stretched his back, pulled out his phone, and scrolled through with his thumb.

I reached for my own phone and started scrolling while the tank filled. I wanted to see the latest about Jennifer. Anything new. But as was so often the case, I saw only the same things repeated over and over.

A car door slammed, but I didn't look up. The sound barely registered.

A moment later I sensed someone standing near me.

"What are you looking at on there?"

My head snapped up, followed by the feeling of my chest deflating.

"Surprised to see me?" Dawn asked. She wore sunglasses and workout gear. Despite the early hour, her erect posture and crisp voice gave the impression of someone who'd been awake for hours. "We're overdue for a talk."

"Did you follow me? Were you at the house last night?"

"You're full of questions, aren't you?"

"Were you at my house? My wife called the police."

"You don't want me talking to the police, do you? Worlds could collide. Everyone would know things about you. Bad things."

The pump clicked off, and I let out a sigh. "Not today, Dawn. I've got other stuff going on."

"The clock is ticking on our agreement."

"*Your* agreement. *You* set the deadline and made the demand."

"And you have to pay. It's a simple transaction."

"I told you. We're having work done on our yard. I just had to put down a deposit on that. So you have to wait. A few weeks."

She started shaking her head before the words were even out of my mouth. And she continued to shake once I was finished. I looked at my watch. I wanted to get going. I didn't want to be dealing with her.

"I need the money."

"What do you even need it for? I'm sure you're not giving it to your family."

She lifted her sunglasses and squinted at me in the growing light. Her eyes were a cool green shade, and as I stared into them, I couldn't help but think of her two younger sisters. I saw the resemblance in the shape of the face, the thinness of her lips. It was like staring at a ghost from my past.

"I have things I need it for. More than just fixing up my backyard. It's my own concern."

"If you told me what it was, maybe I could help you in a different way. Or maybe I'd just be more likely to help. I don't like what happened to your family. If I could erase it all, I would. I promise."

Dawn took a step closer and spoke through gritted teeth. "Look, you have one job. Give me the money in twenty-four hours, and your name stays out of the headlines. Got it? You know, I did a little research. Whoever was driving that car that hit my sisters can still face legal jeopardy. Not to mention the civil suit that would follow."

"Someone already went to jail."

"But was it the right someone? If the right guy went to jail, why is the guy who sat in the backseat the one bringing my parents money? Anonymously?"

"Just drop it."

"You've never denied it. Not once. Why not just deny it if it wasn't you?"

I grabbed the pump handle and withdrew it from my car, taking care not to dribble gas on either of our shoes. The pungent fumes hit me in the nose and almost caused a cough. While Dawn hovered nearby I finished the transaction, making sure to ignore her and avoid any eye contact.

"Well?" she said. "What's the answer? If you want to drive to the bank, I'll follow you. You can make some of the withdrawal. Call it a down payment."

Her assertiveness struck the wrong note in me. I was starting to feel like a pinball, bouncing between people who wanted something, and they all seemed to feel a great deal of ease about telling me what to do. Blake. The cops.

I took a step closer to her, putting us toe-to-toe. Anger superseded my guilt.

And I noticed she wore sneakers. Clean and almost new.

"Look." I jabbed the air between us with my index finger. She flinched when I started speaking, acting as though I'd tried to strike her. "You'll get your money when I have it. I have other problems right now. Personal problems. So you need to back off."

"I can tell—"

"Tell who?" I asked. "Sure, tell the cops what you think you know about the accident. Expose me as a liar. But then what? The golden goose gets neutered. Where would you be getting your eggs from then? Hell, where else would your parents get that little bit of help I've been giving them?"

"You're too afraid to stop. You're too afraid—"

"*You* should be afraid—"

"Ma'am? Ma'am?"

The voice cut through our conversation.

Argument.

We both turned and looked. The gas station employee—the guy with the ponytail, the tattoos, and the phone—stood nearby, studying us. He was younger than he'd looked from afar, closer to twenty than to thirty. And his face showed concern. His eyes were dialed in on Dawn, and he expectantly waited for her to say something to him.

When she didn't, he said, "Are you okay, ma'am?"

"Okay?"

"Is this man harassing you?" the guy asked. "He made a threatening gesture to you. Like this." The guy imitated my finger jab, except he made it appear as though he was Norman Bates and my finger was a knife. "I've got my phone right here. And you can step inside if that makes you feel safer."

"Harassing her?" I said. "Me? You don't even know what's going on."

"Now, sir, don't direct your hostility toward me. That wouldn't be right either." He lifted his phone and tapped it. "I'm calling the police."

"No, wait." I held my hands out in a placating manner. "Just wait."

The man stopped tapping his phone. His finger hovered in midair. He turned his head toward Dawn, awaiting her approval. If she told him to keep dialing, he would. And I'd have the police called down on me.

But Dawn shook her head. And she looked imperious doing it.

"It's okay," she said. "You don't have to call. He just lost control of himself for a moment. He'll apologize. Won't he?"

Both sets of eyes turned toward me. A semitruck rumbled by the station, the noise and rush of wind it generated so great I wouldn't have been heard even if I had spoken. But the distraction gave me a moment to gather my thoughts. If I continued on the path I was on, if I gave the overly concerned gas station attendant reason to call the police, then I'd be getting nowhere.

Nowhere at all.

I'd have to explain why I was standing there, talking to Dawn.

And truth be told, she'd have to explain what she wanted from me.

I hadn't given her anything yet. How could I prove she'd been blackmailing me? And if I wanted to find Blake, I needed to get going.

"Okay," I said when the truck was past. "I'm sorry. I lost my cool. And I'm sorry. Okay? Is that okay with you?" I asked the attendant.

He took his time answering. He looked at Dawn and then he looked at me.

Finally he said, "Well, I guess so. If it's okay with her."

And then Dawn took her time answering as well. But she finally nodded. "It's okay," she said.

The attendant nodded his head a few times and started a slow walk back to the cashier area of the station. When he was out of earshot, I said, "I'm leaving. I have things to do."

"The money," she said. "Tomorrow."

"You'll get it. Or you won't. I may not be able to give it to you soon. But I have to go."

I opened the door and climbed into my car. Dawn had parked her car nose to nose with mine, so in order to get away, I'd have to back up. Before I could, she came to the window. I felt I had no choice but to power it down.

"What?" I asked.

"I showed you mercy today," she said. "Twenty-four hours. Have that money for me tomorrow morning."

"I can't—"

"See you tomorrow," she said.

CHAPTER THIRTY-EIGHT

I headed for Blake's house, still shaken by my encounter with Dawn, hoping I'd find either him or Sam at home. I hoped by the time I arrived the police would be there, talking to them. Straightening everything out. Moving everything along to a safe and logical conclusion in which Blake was not a murderer.

Even as I thought that, I knew it was foolish. Nothing involving Blake was resolved that easily. Our mistakes were lingering for years, like nuclear fallout, never completely forgotten and always willing to rise up and bite when least expected. Faces in dreams. Relatives seeking justice. A friend trying blackmail.

But I'd been right about something. When I turned down his street, I saw a police car sitting in front of his duplex. It partially blocked the entrance to the driveway, as though maybe it had just pulled up. Or maybe it was sitting on the house in case Blake or Samantha came by.

I didn't need to know anything else. I drove past, trying not to slow or stare. But my eyes trailed to the cop car ever so slightly as I rolled by. I saw a lone officer in the driver's seat speaking on a cell phone. He didn't seem to notice me, and I kept going, all the way up to the end of the block and the stop sign.

When I arrived and flipped my turn signal on, I took a look in my rearview mirror. The cruiser sprang to life like someone had plugged it in. The lights and siren came on. And then it launched out of its parking spot like a rocket. It came right for me.

I emitted a low noise, something between a gasp and a whine.

It had been years since I'd been pulled over, but I remembered well the feeling of seeing those lights behind me. My stomach felt like a rock, weighing me down in the depths of the driver's seat. My mouth went dry.

Should I just turn and keep going?

Even if I'd wanted to, I couldn't have moved. Maybe the police were looking for me. Maybe Rountree had sent my name and description around because they'd found fingerprints, a witness. One of the things I feared.

The cruiser came up, speeding so fast I thought it was going to slam into me. Then the driver swerved and went around, barely tapping his brakes before he made a left turn onto the cross street and accelerated away.

I remained frozen in place, my hands locked on the wheel. It took a full minute for my body to begin to relax, for my stomach to stop sinking and my heart to slow. I breathed again.

No other cars came up behind me. The street Blake lived on remained empty.

I resolved to get out of there. The cops were watching the place. Obviously. The one in the cruiser had been called away, maybe even for a break in Jennifer's case. But if not, he'd be back. Someone would be watching the place, waiting for Blake.

I turned right and then turned right again, retracing my route out of the neighborhood and making sure to go in the opposite direction of the cop who'd just scared the living daylights out of me.

After my second right, I was on the street parallel to Blake's, where the backyards of the houses ran up to the rear of his duplex. His sat in the middle of the block, and I could guess about where it was without being able to see it. When I reached that spot, I saw someone, a man, walking between the two houses that faced the street where I was driving. I slowed, curious. Was he a cable guy? A repairman?

He walked quickly with his head down, the collar of his jacket turned up high. He reminded me of myself slinking through Jennifer's neighborhood less than twelve hours earlier. The man's hair was dark. He had a beard.

Was it Blake? Had he been waiting for the cop to leave so he could go home? This man's hair was shorter than Blake's, but maybe Blake had changed his look?

I wouldn't have put it past him to call 911 to create a diversion to draw the cops away from his house.

So I turned right and then right again until I pulled up in front of Blake's house, stopping where the cop car had been parked. I looked and didn't see the man anymore, but if it was Blake, I couldn't let him go.

I turned the car off, climbed out, and started up the driveway toward the house.

CHAPTER THIRTY-NINE

I expected Blake—or whoever it was—to emerge from behind the duplex, but he didn't. I went to the front door and pushed the bell several times in a row. Then knocked and knocked, so hard my knuckles hurt.

But no one came. I tried the knob, and it was locked, refusing to budge.

The curtains were closed, eliminating any chance to see inside. I looked behind me, both up and down the street, expecting to see the cop coming back and catching me on the porch, but the street remained empty and quiet.

Had something happened in the back of the duplex? Or was Blake back there smoking a cigarette and staring at the sky?

I left the porch and went around the side of the house, heading for the back. It wasn't lost on me that I suddenly seemed to be a guy who spent his time slinking around other people's houses like a burglar.

My shoes skimmed over the bright green grass. The sun was bright, the sky clear. A beautiful day I couldn't enjoy. When I came into the backyard, I saw nothing. No sign of Blake or anyone else. Had I imagined the presence of that figure slipping between the houses?

But I knew Blake and Samantha had a back door, one that opened into their kitchen. Had Blake just gone in through there and decided to ignore me at the front door? Had he thought I was the cops?

As I approached the back door, I noticed that the window next to it—which also led into the kitchen—stood wide open. Had Blake gone in through the window instead of the door?

Unlikely.

My scalp started to tingle with anxiety, and the feeling spread down my back. I took two steps forward, moving closer to the open window. I stopped and listened but heard nothing.

"Blake?"

I kept my voice low, although that neighborhood, early in the morning, with everyone off to work or school, might as well have been the set of a postapocalyptic movie. The cop at the front of the house might have grown bored and sped off with his siren going just to try to break the monotony.

"Blake?"

I went closer to the window and bent down, trying to see inside. It was dark. I saw the outline of the kitchen table, a microwave, and a dirty dish on a counter next to a coffeemaker. I listened, thought I heard movement.

I was about to back away, to cut my losses and move on, when a face appeared in the opening. I jumped back so fast I almost fell over in the grass. And my heart skipped a couple of beats, like a scratched record.

The man, who looked to be my age, remained in place, staring out at me, his face set hard and his eyes burning.

"Who the hell are you?" he asked. "Why are you sneaking around here?"

His close-cropped hair was thinning on the top, and he wore a suit coat over a black polo shirt. His hands rested on the windowsill, the nail of his right index finger blackened by some injury. He stared out at me, his face framed by the window, and he looked like someone about to present the angriest children's puppet show ever performed.

"Who are you?" I asked.

The man studied me without answering. He looked me up and down, and some kind of recognition spread across his face. When his scrutiny had reached some point I didn't understand, the man nodded to himself and retracted his head. Then I heard the door's lock undone, and he pulled it open. He stood there, staring at me again, only this time he nodded, confirming whatever he'd been working through when his face was in the window.

"The Juniper Pig," he said, his anger cooling by a few degrees.

"What about it?"

"You own it. I've seen you doing those spots on Facebook."

"Right. That's me. And who are you? And why are you in this house? Why did you *break in* to this house?"

The man stood there, blinking. I thought the sun was in his eyes. Or else he had allergies.

But then I saw the tears forming just before he raised his hand and brushed them away.

He said something I didn't understand, the words muffled by his hand.

"You what?" I asked.

He shook his head and removed his hand from his mouth so I could hear him clearly.

"I loved her," he said. "I loved her and now she's gone."

CHAPTER FORTY

I followed the man inside and watched as he started opening and closing kitchen cabinets. The house was neat and quiet, most of the blinds drawn.

"What are you looking for?" I asked.

"I need something to drink."

"The one in the corner. On the left. That's where they used to keep it. Blake stopped drinking. . . ."

The guy opened the cabinet and started moving things around. Glasses and bottles clinked against one another, a tinny, irritating noise.

"Come on, come on," he said. He kept rummaging. "Who quits drinking?"

"Some people try."

"Ah." He took out a bottle of bourbon. He opened another cabinet and brought down two glasses, sticking his fingers inside to move them. "You're right. They never really quit. You want one?"

"No, I'm okay."

He unscrewed the cap and filled both glasses anyway, sloshing some of the amber liquid onto the counter.

"Who are you exactly?" I asked.

He lifted one of the glasses and swallowed all the contents, his Adam's apple bobbing. "Kyle Dornan. As if it matters to you. Or anyone else."

His mood had slipped from anger to sadness to teenage melancholy right before my eyes. The black polo shirt bore the insignia of a medical supply company in town, one that sold scooters and ramps for the elderly and the handicapped.

"Why are you here, Kyle?" I asked.

He picked up the other glass but didn't drink from it. He held it in his hand and stared at the liquid as if he expected something to materialize in it. "I loved her. That's who I am." Then he drank, swallowing everything in the second glass.

"You loved Jennifer," I said.

He put the glass down and leaned against the granite counter. It looked as though he would collapse to the floor without the support. "Yes," he said. "Jennifer. Jennifer Bates. My girl."

"Well, I'm sorry," I said. "I wish—"

"What do you know about her?" he asked, looking over at me. His eyes were tired, the skin around them dark from lack of sleep. "Did you know her at all?" Something crossed his mind, and whatever it was stiffened his spine. He straightened up, his chin jutting out as he considered me. "Did you . . . ? You weren't . . . ?"

I understood. He loved her. So he said. He wanted to know if I did too. I was more than happy to tell the truth.

"No," I said. "Nothing like that. We worked together, in a way. She was a potential client of my PR firm."

I opted to conceal the Facebook messages, the flirtation. And certainly all information about seeing her dead body on the floor. Lifeless and unseeing. No way he could handle that kind of detail. It wasn't my job to test him.

"And the cops informed you about her death because you worked together?" he asked.

"Yeah. Basically. They were working through anyone who had contact with her, I guess. I'm sure they're talking to everybody."

Relieved that I wasn't another suitor, Kyle turned his attention back to the bottle. He lifted it up, almost in a religious fashion, and then poured more into one of the glasses. "You sure?" he asked, nodding at the bottle.

"I'm good. It's kind of early."

He cut his eyes toward me.

"I mean, I understand why you want to," I said. "No judgment here."

"Sure. I'm supposed to be at work. Making sales calls." He pointed to the logo on his shirt. "You found out about her death in a better way than I did," he said, and drank again. "I went by her house last night. Late. Around eleven. I just wanted to see her. You know? We've been seeing each other. We had plans, you know? Late-night plans."

Then it came back to me—the messages on Jennifer's phone. She'd exchanged a series of texts with a guy named Kyle, ones in which he desperately tried to fan the embers of whatever their relationship was. And Jennifer simply offered no response.

So did they really have "late-night plans"? Had Jennifer responded with a phone call instead of a text?

Or had Kyle shown up uninvited and unwelcome?

Then I shuddered and was happy Kyle was focused on his drink and hadn't seen what must have passed across my face. He'd gone by Jennifer's house at eleven o'clock. Not long after I'd been there. What if he'd come earlier and walked in on me? Standing over her dead body?

"Do you know what I found when I went there?" he asked. "I pull up, and there are a bunch of cop cars. And an ambulance." The glass sat on the counter in front of him. "Then I saw it. I was broken when I saw it, I tell you."

Frozen in place, I waited for him to go on. I thought about what I was doing in Blake's house, speaking to a man I didn't know about a dead woman.

A dead woman he said he loved.

"I saw the coroner's van. It pulled up." He shook his head and slumped against the counter again. "When you see that—when you see that word, 'coroner,' as big as anything—and you know they're going right into the house where someone you love lives . . . and she lives alone . . . So it has to be her."

"I'm sorry."

I said it again, and the words still felt inadequate. Bland and unable to rise to the occasion.

"Thanks," Kyle said anyway.

I didn't want to press him any further, but I felt I had no choice. So I asked, "Why exactly are you here? In Blake's house?"

His head whipped toward me so fast I thought he'd hurt himself. "What are you? Friends with him? Obviously that's why you're here, nosing around."

"We're friends, yes."

Kyle looked disappointed, as though his assessment of me as a decent guy plummeted once I mentioned being friends with Blake. I didn't say it out loud, but that wouldn't have been the first time in my life someone's opinion of me dropped because of my association with Blake.

"Where is he?" Kyle asked.

"I don't know. That's why I'm here. Same as you, I'm guessing."

"No," he said. "Not the same as you at all. You're his friend, you say?"

My parents weren't very religious, but they did send me to Sunday school a few times. I remembered Peter in the garden with the chance to admit he was friends with Jesus or face the wrath of the Romans. While Blake was no Jesus, there was something inside me that refused to deny my friend. No matter how much he deserved it.

"We've been friends a long time," I said. "I'm worried about him."

"You should be worried," Kyle said. "He was such a jerk to Jennifer. He kept her around for his own reasons. He yanked her chain, breaking things off at a whim and leaving her high and dry. You have to wonder what kind of guy would do that to a woman. What else might he be capable of?"

CHAPTER FORTY-ONE

His certainty knocked me off my stride.

Here was a guy much closer to the situation than I was, a person who knew Jennifer and her relationship with Blake in ways I didn't. He sounded like someone who had seen behind the curtain of these events and had formed harder, more durable opinions.

Since the police seemed to be barking up the same tree, it made it all seem bad for Blake.

Very, very bad.

"I admit Blake might know more than he's let on," I said. "But he's never hurt anyone. Not like that."

"So he has hurt people?"

"We've all hurt people, Kyle, haven't we?"

I thought of the accident from college, the one I caused. Maggie and Emily Steiner.

If the memory of them ever slipped away, Dawn Steiner or Blake would be there to bring it back.

Once again Kyle leaned against the counter, his fingers splayed against the granite surface. "See, he came on all strong with her and then just dropped her when he went back to this other woman he'd already been involved with. He was careless with Jen's feelings."

I nodded, picturing Samantha in my mind. Did Sam even know Jennifer had ever existed?

"But he wouldn't stop," Kyle said.

"Stop what?"

"Calling her. Texting her. He kept her on the line, almost like he was afraid something wouldn't work out and he'd need a backup plan." He straightened up, lifting his hands from the counter.

I thought he was going to pour another drink, but he didn't. He ran both of his hands back and forth across his face, pulling against the skin until it stretched, his mouth forming a wide O. When he spoke again, he wasn't looking at me. He stared at the kitchen cabinets as though something important was being reflected back at him from their surface.

"Jennifer is strong. She worked with prisoners, ex-cons. She always said she was a sucker for a hard-luck case. She liked to help people who needed it. Give them second and third chances. Maybe that's why she liked me. But even strong people get hurt and feel vulnerable. You have to understand that." His voice became lower. "She's like anyone else. She wanted someone to care for her. We all do."

When I first showed up, I'd hoped to find Blake or, short of that, some idea about where he was. When I found Kyle instead, I hoped he'd have something useful to share with me. But here stood a man with a broken heart, a man who seemed less tethered to reality than even Blake. He said he'd just gone by Jennifer's house and driven away when he saw the police and the coroner. But did I really know what he might have had to do with her death?

Her murder, I reminded myself, trying to get used to the fact that word had become a part of my life.

Murder.

"I think I need to move on," I said. "I'm going to see if I can talk to some friends. Maybe someone else has heard from Blake."

"Do the cops suspect you?" Kyle asked, still not looking over at me. Still staring at the cabinets.

His question hit me with the force of a hurricane.

Did they? Was I a suspect?

Kyle went on. "You said they talked to you because you knew Jennifer. You had business dealings or whatever. Do they suspect you? Did you have to give an alibi and all that?"

"I did. I kind of assume cops think everyone is a suspect until they find out who the guilty party really is. They start with the people closest to the . . . victim and work their way out."

"Nobody had broken into her house," Kyle said. "The cops mentioned that to me."

I knew what I knew—Blake had the door code. It surprised me the cops would tell Kyle something like that if he was a suspect. But as if he had read my mind, he provided more information.

"See," he said, "they figure somebody knew her door code. That's what they kept talking about. That door code. They think that's how the killer got in without breaking and entering or whatever. And *I* knew that code. Jennifer just gave it to me recently. It's silly, but it felt like a step forward for us. You know?" He almost smiled at some private, happier memory. "We'd had some rocky times lately because of Blake. He kept trying to contact her, and I didn't like it. I don't know what he wanted, but he kept reaching out to her. But she told me she was really done with him. Absolutely. Sometimes she went to yoga late, and I'd meet her afterward. That's what we were doing last night. Or, I guess, trying to do before . . . Well, I went over there to surprise her."

"Surprise her? She didn't know you were coming?"

Kyle's eyes flashed. "Sure. Don't you ever surprise your wife? Chocolates? Flowers? A surprise. That's what it was."

I wasn't reassured, but I nodded. "Sure. Okay. Well, let's hope the police figure it all out soon." I took a step back, heading for the door.

"Where is he?" Kyle asked. "Blake. Where is he?"

The temperature in the room dropped. A cold sensation passed across my skin. Kyle's voice had taken on a different timbre. Something edgier. More desperate. More angry.

"I told you—I don't know. That's why I'm here. I'm looking as well."

Involuntarily, I took another step backward.

Kyle turned to face me. Finally. I saw his face. Pale. But something hot burned in his eyes.

"They're going to hang this on me, you know," he said. "We'd been dating. They always look at the boyfriend. And I knew the code. . . ."

"Maybe it was one of those convicts she worked with. That's something for the cops to look into."

"Maybe. Or maybe your friend."

"If I find him, I'm going to make him go to the police."

"I'm a suspect," Kyle said. "They told me not to leave town. They want to keep talking to me. They want me to give hair samples . . . DNA. . . . She really drove me crazy, you know. How much I wanted her . . ."

"I have to go," I said. "I have some other problems to solve in addition to whatever is going on with Blake."

But Kyle was shaking his head. And then he moved toward me before I could get away.

"I can't let you leave."

CHAPTER FORTY-TWO

I took yet another step back. And another.

I couldn't see behind me. I had no idea if I was about to stumble over a piece of furniture, an ottoman or a coffee table, that would send me flipping backward onto the floor, where I would be completely at the mercy of Kyle and his quickly darkening mood.

"I'm going," I said. "I have nothing to do with this. It's all very . . . different from what my life is usually like."

I lied. I very much had something to do with it. I'd found the body. I'd been in the house. I'd used the door code. I knew the man who was presumably the prime suspect.

And I was in his house with another man, who seemed to be either an avenger or a suspect himself.

Kyle remained in place in the kitchen. I thought—hoped—my words had frozen him. That I'd managed to slip enough steel and defiance into what I'd said about leaving that he'd decided to just let me go, to give up on any notion of fighting.

But then he surprised me.

He wrapped his hand around the bourbon bottle and smoothly,

confidently, as though he'd been practicing the move his entire life, flipped the bottle into the air, causing it to spin end over end. When the bottle came down, Kyle expertly grabbed it by its neck. Without hesitating at all, he swung the bottle, smashing it against the granite that had so recently supported his weight and leaving him with a jagged, spiked weapon that looked more threatening than a gun or a knife.

"Stop," he said, looking right at me as bourbon leaked from the bottle onto his shoes. He didn't look like the kind of guy who could have so smoothly executed such a move. But people were full of surprises.

So I stopped.

He moved closer, putting me within easy jabbing range of the end of the bottle. My eyes zoomed in on those points. The glass glinted in the sunlight coming over my shoulder. Kyle's fingers looked thick and rough as they gripped the neck.

I felt even colder. Almost enough to shiver.

I couldn't remember a time in my life when someone had threatened me to such an extent.

"I don't think you know how bad this can turn out for me," he said. "When they start asking someone for DNA, it isn't because they think he's a good citizen."

"You were in the house. You dated. Of course your DNA is in there. Just tell the cops that. They'll understand."

"I already told them that. Do you think they listen?" He stood still, the bottle in the space between us. "Damn. Do you think . . . Is it possible they think this was a sex crime? Someone raped her and then . . . ?"

"I really don't know what's going on," I said. "Not really."

Then my phone started to ring. The tone sounded insistent and urgent as it filled the space between and around us.

Was it Amanda calling me home? Was it the police?

Or . . .

I made a move to answer it, but Kyle jabbed the bottle toward me.

"This could be Blake," I said. "It probably is."

Kyle hesitated, and then he used the bottle to gesture toward my pocket, telling me to answer. But the caller ID screen told a different story.

Samantha.

I didn't tell Kyle who was calling. I just answered.

"Oh, Ryan, where are you?" she asked without any greeting.

Should I have said—*I'm standing in your house with a man waving a broken bottle at me*?

I kept it simple. "I came to your house, looking for Blake. Do you know where he is?"

"That's why I called you. I thought you might know."

I took a risk and turned my back on Kyle, moving a couple of steps away. I expected to feel the jagged points of the shattered bottle in my neck. . . .

I tried to lower my voice. "I don't, Sam. Did the police talk to you?"

"Yes." Her voice broke, and she sniffled. "Last night. Late. They came by to talk to Blake, but he wasn't home. I was honest with them. I didn't know where he was. And then this morning, before I left for work, they came by again."

"So you know why they want to talk to Blake?"

Samantha didn't answer right away. I chanced a look over my shoulder, expecting the bottle to gouge my eye out, but Kyle stood behind me, still holding the bottle but obviously intent on learning whatever he could from my conversation.

"I can guess," Samantha said, her voice low. "It's all over the news. This woman was killed, and Blake knew her somehow." Then her voice took on a harder edge, unusual for Samantha. "You knew her. Blake told me once that you introduced them."

"Kind of. Maybe. Did he tell you anything else about her?"

"So you don't know where he is?" she asked.

"I don't. I saw him last night. He came by the house. Late. But that was it."

"He came back to our house last night, after the police left. I was dozing off, but I heard him come in. I thought he would come up to bed, but he didn't. He left the house again without talking to me. And without saying where he was going."

I heard shuffling behind me. Kyle moving around. Again I turned to look, to see what he was doing, and I saw him disappearing to the front of the house, leaving me alone. Mercifully.

"Sam, I'm worried about Blake. I'm worried he's in over his head, and the police just showed up here and seem to suspect him of doing something. We have to find him."

"I know."

"Where are you?" I asked. "Are you out looking for him?"

"I'm at work."

"You are? Why?"

"I just got here. I wanted things to be normal. I can leave, I guess. But then I'd have to tell my principal why I'm leaving. How do I do that?"

Kyle was still out of the room. And the back door was just ten feet away from me. Broken bottle be damned. I wanted to get out of that house. I *needed* to get out.

"I'm going to come see you, okay? We have to talk. I can come to the school. But right now I have to go."

I ended the call and looked back one more time. Still no Kyle.

So I went for the door. And as I did, Kyle came running back into the room, as though the house had gone up in flames. I checked his hand. No bottle. But he charged right at me anyway, and I braced myself for a collision.

But he went past me, saying only one word.

"Cops!"

CHAPTER FORTY-THREE

The uniformed cop who came around the side of the house just as I emerged from the back door held his hand above his gun. When I saw that placement of his hand, I froze, one foot outside of the house, the other still inside.

I'd never been confronted by a cop that way before, but something instinctive, something that everyone in the human race who had ever seen a cop show understood, kicked in, and my hands went up above my head like I was signaling a touchdown.

The cop approached me, speaking into his lapel radio. His body was crouched like a wrestler's, although, thankfully, the gun remained holstered. I caught a glimpse of Kyle disappearing between the houses where I had first seen him.

"Officer," I said, trying to direct his attention that way.

"Quiet."

"Officer, that man—"

"I said, 'Quiet.'"

He approached me where I stood in the doorway, and then waggled his fingers, indicating that I should step all the way out. I did, with my hands still in the air, and when I came out, he took me by the left arm and spun me around. Before I knew what was happening, my face was pressed against the siding that covered the back of the house, and my arm was getting twisted around behind me.

"Sir, for your own safety and for mine, I'm going to pat you down to see if you have any weapons. Do you have anything in your pockets that's going to stick me?"

"My keys, maybe."

"No knives? No needles?"

"Of course not."

My outrage meant nothing to him. He patted me down—torso, outside of my legs, and then up the inseam and back down. All the way down to my shoes.

"You have identification in your wallet?" he asked.

"I do."

He removed my wallet from my back pocket. "Stay still," he said, his hand applying less pressure but still enough to keep me in place.

I had no intention of leaving without his permission.

"Why were you in this house?" the cop asked. "Do you have permission to be in there?"

"My friend lives here."

"Did your friend give you permission to be inside?"

"That man, the one who ran off between the houses over behind us— he opened the window and went inside first. I was trying to see what he was doing. I was worried. I think you need to talk to that man."

"What man?" the cop asked.

"Didn't you see him running off when you came into the backyard?"

"I didn't see anyone," the cop said, his voice dripping with skepticism.

"Are you kidding?"

"I don't kid, sir."

Out of the corner of my eye, I saw another cop emerge from around the corner of the house. She held her hand above her holster, and when she saw me pressed against the back of the house, she said, "Is that all you got?"

"I haven't been inside yet."

"There's no one else in there," I said.

"I'll check it out," the second cop said, and she went past us, heading for the back door of the house.

"Hey," my cop said. "Do you need a warrant?"

"Someone broke in. That's good enough for probable cause." And in she went.

"Sir," my cop said, "for your own safety and my safety, I'm going to place you in handcuffs right now."

"You are?"

He pulled my right hand back and brought it against my left. I heard the jangling of the cuffs, metal clanking against metal. The first one clamped onto my left wrist, tighter than I would have expected.

Before he was finished, I sensed someone coming around the side of the house. Someone in civilian clothes.

"That won't be necessary, Officer," she said. "He's okay."

"Are you sure, Detective?"

Rountree came all the way over to us and gave me a wry smile. She carried a walkie-talkie in one hand. "I'm sure. Why don't you go look inside?"

"Do you think we need a warrant, Detective?"

"We need to make sure everyone is safe. What if the homeowner is lying on the floor in there, bleeding? Shouldn't we help? Let him go and get in there, Officer."

I felt the handcuff being released from my wrist. I felt the officer step back, letting go of my arm and giving me space. It seemed safe to turn around, so I did. I was happy not to be pressed against the wall anymore, my nose and cheek rubbing against the aluminum siding.

Rountree studied me, the sun picking up the gold flecks in her brown eyes.

"Mr. Francis," she said, "you seem to be showing up everywhere I step. Sort of like dog shit. Do you care to explain this one? Or would it save time if I just had the officer put the cuffs back on you?"

"It's not what it looks like, Detective."

"Okay, I'll play along. Tell me what's going on. Because from where I stand, it looks like you broke into the home of a murder suspect. A man we've been trying to find for almost twelve hours."

CHAPTER FORTY-FOUR

"I didn't break in." The sun had fully risen over the houses behind Blake's, so I used my hand to shade my eyes. "That guy who was just here, Kyle Dornan. He's the one who broke in."

"Kyle Dornan is in the house?"

"He was." I pointed across the yard. "He ran off when he saw you coming. He went between those houses over there. I tried to tell the cop who put me in cuffs."

"Kyle Dornan," she said. "And he's on foot?"

"He was when he left here."

Rountree stepped away and raised the radio. She passed along the information about Kyle Dornan, giving his location and the direction he was heading. She listened as someone said something back to her, which I couldn't hear. Then she signed off and came back over to me. But she remained silent, which unnerved me. By design. Even though I recognized her strategy, it still worked.

I decided to break the silence.

"You think he did it?" I asked. "Kyle?"

"I don't know who did it, Mr. Francis. Why do you think Mr. Dornan is guilty?"

"He was involved with Jennifer. He came here and got into this house."

"Blake was involved with Jennifer at one time too. And you had a flirtation with her. Should I consider you a suspect, Mr. Francis?"

"You'd have to be the one to tell me."

"When I was at your house earlier, I got the feeling there were things about this matter that you didn't want your wife to know. I assume she knew about the flirtatious messages from Ms. Bates since you spoke so openly about them. Although my guess is it's still tough for a spouse to hear about such things. People get jealous. It's understandable. If someone was moving in on my partner . . ."

"That's a misunderstanding between my wife and me," I said. "It doesn't have anything to do with what's going on with Blake. Or this Kyle Dornan guy. It really doesn't have anything to do with Jennifer. I never wrote back to her."

Rountree crossed her arms and considered me like I was a painting on a museum wall. With the sun in my face and with the early hour and the stress of all the craziness, I probably looked like something surrealist or cubist, a distortion of a human figure. "What about Blake and Samantha? Does what happens between *them* remain private? How was their relationship? Any insights you have might help matters."

I thought back to Rountree's arrival at the house that morning. She said the police hadn't been able to find either Blake or Samantha.

"She called me," I said. "Samantha."

"She did. When?"

"When I was inside there with Kyle. About fifteen minutes ago. She called me, wondering if I knew where Blake was. And I told her I didn't. But weren't you looking for her earlier?"

"Where was she? Did she say?"

"She said she'd just got to work. You know she teaches at Cherry Lane Elementary, right? Kindergarten."

Rountree looked surprised. "She said she was at the school?"

"Yes. She said she went in because she wanted her life to be normal, to stick to her normal routine."

"That's odd," Rountree said. "We went by there looking for her an hour ago, and her principal told us she hadn't arrived, that she was running late. I guess I would think it odd for a woman to be at work at all the day before her wedding. Wouldn't you, Mr. Francis?"

"Yes, I guess it is. I've known people who worked right up until their weddings so they could save as much vacation time as possible for the honeymoon. Sam's a teacher. Maybe she can't miss too much."

"Did Samantha say anything else?" Rountree asked.

"She said she couldn't find Blake, and she was worried about him. I'm afraid I couldn't help much with that."

The two uniformed cops came out the back door and stood off to the side, waiting to make their reports to Rountree. She went over, and I heard them tell her they'd found nothing out of the ordinary inside. No signs of robbery. No sign of injury. Just a broken liquor bottle in the foyer and two empty glasses on the counter.

"That was Kyle," I said. "His method of persuasion."

Rountree looked over at me and then back at them. She appeared to be processing their reports, letting her eyes move away from the cops and over to the house.

She pointed at me. "Keep an eye on him for a minute," she said. "I'm going to take a look inside."

"Yes, Detective."

Before she went in, she looked at me. "You will behave, Mr. Francis?"

"Haven't I so far?"

"That's up for debate," she said, and went inside.

CHAPTER FORTY-FIVE

The cops ignored me while they waited for Rountree to come back outside. They stood close together, about ten feet away from me, and held a low conversation I mostly couldn't hear. Only scattered words reached me.

Can't believe it . . . does she think we missed something . . . overtime . . .

Their radios crackled. The cop on the right listened and then said something back. When she clicked off, she turned to her partner and spoke in a voice I could hear.

"They're trying to find that guy," she said. "The one he says was here."

"Kyle Dornan," I said.

They both turned to look at me but didn't respond. They went back to their conversation, speaking even lower so I couldn't make out anything.

So I waited. I leaned back against the house, letting the sun wash over my face. It was turning into a really nice spring day. I wished I was able to enjoy it. Go to the park with Amanda and Henry. Sit outside and drink a beer in the evening. Open the windows and air out the house.

Rountree came back out. She nodded at the two officers, and one of them told her about Kyle Dornan.

"They haven't found him yet," she said.

"I heard," Rountree said. "They'll keep looking." Then she turned to me and asked, "How did you say you knew Mr. Norton again?"

"We met in college. At Ferncroft."

"Freshman year?"

"That's right."

"Would you say he's a sentimental man?" Rountree asked.

It was such an odd question, delivered in such a casual tone. It took me a moment to understand she was serious.

"Blake? He fancies himself a romantic. I guess sentimental can go along with that."

"Is he sentimental about your college days?"

"No. No more than anyone else." We avoided a lot of talk about college because of the way it ended. The hazing. The accident. Like it was a healing scab, I tried not to put any pressure on it, although from time to time I bumped up against it accidentally, bringing on a new rush of pain. "Why do you ask?"

"What was Sigil and Shield?" she asked.

The sun suddenly felt warmer. The two uniformed cops had turned to watch Rountree's questioning of me like curious bystanders. A bead of sweat trickled down my back under my shirt.

Where was she coming up with all of this?

"Why are you asking about Sigil and Shield?"

"Can you just explain it to me?" she said, her voice weary. "You see, I had to go to a public university. Where I grew up in Nebraska. I paid my way through by working in a fast-food restaurant. Worked my way up to assistant manager in two years. We had sororities and fraternities, but nothing called 'Sigil and Shield.' Can you enlighten me on what that is? It sounds like a Dungeons and Dragons–type game, but I'm guessing it was more than that."

The two officers looked even more curious, watching from behind Rountree.

"It's a social club. At Ferncroft. We didn't have fraternities and sororities, but we had social clubs. A group you had to be invited to join. We did charity in the community. Social things."

"And you partied too?"

I swallowed. My back grew wetter from the sweat. My throat drier. "Of course. We were in college."

"And you and Mr. Norton were in this group together?" Rountree asked.

"That's right. With a lot of other people. We weren't officers or anything."

"But he wasn't sentimental about it? Not the kind of guy to go traipsing down memory lane? Not the type to reminisce about the good old days in Sigil and Shield?"

"We talk about the past. Sometimes. Why are you asking me this? I'm sorry I don't see what it has to do with—"

"You've been in this house before today, right?" she asked.

"Of course."

"So you've been all through it? Upstairs and down?"

"I have."

"You know Mr. Norton has an office upstairs? He has a desk, a computer, reference books for his job, all that kind of stuff. I'll give him credit. He keeps it pretty neat and tidy. Nothing out of place. Everything orderly. Is that him or his fiancée who insists on that kind of order?"

"Blake always kept his desk pretty clean. We roomed together for three years in college. He could go weeks without doing laundry or getting a haircut, but he kept his desk clean."

"Interesting."

"Are you going to let me in on the secret?" I asked.

Rountree looked back at the other officers, who stared at her like kindergartners waiting to see if their teacher was going to let them out for recess. She turned back to me and nodded.

"I went all through the house. They were right. There was nothing ransacked, nothing damaged outside of that bourbon bottle. Rowan's Creek. Good stuff too. A shame to waste it. But I did notice in the office that Mr. Norton had his college yearbooks out. What is it called? *The Bower*?"

"That's it."

"*The Bower*. Anyway, all four years of college yearbooks out on the desk. Nothing else out, nothing out of place. But there were those yearbooks. And one of them was opened to the page about the Sigil and Shield. From what must have been your senior year. It was the most recent yearbook. That's why I ask if he was sentimental. Why would he have those out and be looking through them now? It seems odd, given the complications with Jennifer Bates and his impending wedding. You'd think his mind would be on other things, right?"

"I don't know, Detective."

And I really didn't. There was nothing in the yearbook about the accident. Nothing about the Sigil and Shield being suspended for a year. They kept things like that out of a yearbook. No one wanted to look back on bad memories.

What Blake wanted from *The Bower*'s pages, I couldn't guess.

Rountree turned to the two officers. "Will one of you close that window and make sure everything is locked? Then sit on the place in case anyone comes back."

The two officers jumped to it. Rountree folded her arms again and studied my face. She even tilted her head a little, trying to get a better angle.

"I need a favor from you, Mr. Francis. I need you to answer a question. Something I learned a little earlier today just came back to me, and it's really sticking in my craw."

"What's that?"

"We had a witness come forward a little while ago. A gentleman who lives in Ms. Bates's neighborhood. It turns out he was walking his dog last night, not long before the body was discovered."

I stayed still, tried to keep my face neutral. I felt like an insect pinned to somebody's display board. Exposed. Helpless.

Desperately in trouble.

"He saw a man creeping around the area, and he gave us a description of the man. You weren't around there last night, were you?"

"I told you where I was."

"Not exactly an answer," Rountree said. She turned and started to walk off, but she abruptly stopped and came back to me. "You know what we can do, Mr. Francis? We can go down to the station. You can stand in a lineup and this gentleman can come in and, well, then he can tell us if it was you who he saw near the crime scene. How does that sound?"

"Not pleasant."

"It isn't." She toed the ground, her arms still crossed. "When those officers come out of the house again, I could get them to cuff you and bring you down to the station, whether you like it or not."

"I guess you could," I said. "And I could call a lawyer who probably wouldn't want me to stand in any lineups. I've already been cooperating with you."

"By trespassing in your friend's house."

"I need to go, Detective. I need to check on my family."

Rountree reached into her pocket and brought out an iPhone. She held it in the space between us.

For a second I thought it was Jennifer's. Recovered from where Blake had ditched it.

But it wasn't the right color. This was Rountree's phone.

"I could take your photo," she said. "Snap it right here and show it to our witness. I know you like Instagram. Which filter would you like? Crema? Juno? Hashtag no filter?"

I held her gaze. Steady. Unwavering. No blinks.

She lowered the phone.

"But we don't really need that. I can easily find a photo of you online to show our witness. I'm talking to him again today. I trust you're not leaving the area anytime soon, are you?"

"I'm not."

The two uniformed officers came out of Blake's house, and once they walked past, Rountree followed them.

"Good day, Mr. Francis. Do your best to make it a good day."

CHAPTER FORTY-SIX

I sat back in the driver's seat of my car.

Sweat—a river of it—still poured down my back, making my shirt stick to my skin like flypaper. I took short, sharp breaths, trying to get air into my lungs.

A witness. The dog walker. He had seen me. Rountree was going to show him my photo.

And I'd invoked a lawyer. I looked guilty as hell.

And I was.

My phone buzzed. Amanda.

Call me when you get the chance.

And then:

Call me.

And then:

Ryan, where are you?

I called, but she didn't answer. I let the phone ring for a while, hung up, and tried again. Still no response. I checked the time on the phone. Almost nine on a Friday morning. She gave Henry a bath around nine. I pictured her up to her elbows in sudsy water with a wet, squirming infant in her hands. She wouldn't answer.

And I'd told her to head out, to go to her parents with Henry. She might have been packing to do that. Or she might have been on her way, driving and not responding. Even with the Bluetooth in the car, Amanda refused to talk on the phone when she was driving Henry somewhere.

As Rountree had told them to, the two uniformed cops remained parked on the street, observing Blake's house. I felt certain they were observing me, wondering why I hadn't driven off like Rountree. I didn't need any more trouble with them, so I started the car and drove off, out of the neighborhood and away from the prying, curious eyes of the police.

A new strip mall sat a few minutes away, occupying a space where a small warehouse once stood. It held a check-cashing place, a Chinese restaurant, a dollar store, and a fitness center. I stopped on the outer edge of the parking lot, away from all the other cars, and decided to call Sam.

Rountree had sounded like she was ready to head right over to the school and look for her. It was possible Sam wouldn't answer, either because she was involved with her students or because she was being questioned. But she deserved a heads-up if the police hadn't arrived yet.

Samantha answered on the fourth ring. Her voice sounded buoyant and hopeful. "Did you find him?"

She'd placed a lot of faith in me, counted on me as his close friend to deliver the goods. But I hadn't been able to do that.

"No, not yet," I said.

"Oh."

The joy and hope went out of her like air from a balloon.

"Have you heard anything from him?" I asked.

"He called me this morning. Just a little while ago. He said I shouldn't worry, that he was taking care of some things for the wedding. Things that will make everything go more smoothly. I'm trying, Ryan. I'm trying to keep my sanity as all of this goes on. I'm not a fool. I'm trusting him. But . . . it's getting hard. Really hard."

"He must know the cops are looking for him by now."

"He does. He said he'll talk to them soon."

"He should go to them now," I said. Then I thought, *Probably. Maybe. Hopefully.* "I'm a little worried about you."

"Me? Why?"

"That Detective Rountree, she's looking for you. I'm pretty sure she's going to come to the school to talk to you. She may very well be pulling in the lot right now. I just wanted to give you fair warning."

"She's been calling me."

"I know. I saw her at your house. I went there looking for Blake."

"Well, I'm not at school anymore," Sam said. "I left about ten minutes ago. I came in a little late, trying to work a normal day, but my principal told me to leave. She knows I'm getting married tomorrow, and I guess I seemed kind of distracted."

"Then where are you? Are you going home?"

"Eventually. I have some errands to run for tomorrow. . . ." Her voice trailed off.

"Sam?"

"Ryan, do you think tomorrow's going to happen? The wedding? If I can't get ahold of Blake, and the police are looking for him . . . maybe we should just call it off. My God. It would all be so embarrassing if we had to stop it. But I'm trying to be reasonable. We threw this whole thing together in a rush. Maybe this is the world telling us to slow down. What do you think?"

"Where are you? Can we talk in person?"

"I'm on . . ."

I heard a rushing of wind, air through an open car window. Then the clicking of a turn signal.

"I just turned onto Bricker from Montero. You know where that is, right?"

"I'm right there. You know where that Chinese restaurant is? The one with the fortune cookie on the sign?"

"Oh, yeah."

"I'm in the lot there. Turn in, and you'll find me."

"Okay, okay. That's good. We can talk, Ryan. We can make a plan for finding Blake."

CHAPTER FORTY-SEVEN

While I waited for her to arrive, I called Amanda again. The call went right to voice mail. So I sent her a text.

Talking to Sam. Will call soon.

Soon enough, Sam pulled in and parked next to me. She climbed out of her car, her hair whipping a little in the wind and covering her face, and she slid into the passenger seat of mine. She let out a long, breathy sigh as she settled in and pushed her hair off her face, which looked tired and pale, as though she hadn't slept well. She wore a maroon sweater and formfitting jeans. I checked her hand and still didn't see an engagement ring.

"Are you okay?" I asked. "You seem a little frazzled."

"I am. There's too much going on, Ryan." She sighed again, adjusting herself in the seat. She flipped down the sun visor and checked her hair in the mirror on the reverse side. "I'm supposed to talk to the caterer and the florist today. About tomorrow, you know. But is it even worth it?" She snapped the visor back into its normal place. "I'm on the ledge here, Ryan. Can you talk me down from it?"

It sounded like an increasingly impossible task. She was planning on getting married in just over twenty-four hours, and her fiancé was nowhere to be found. And he was a suspect in the murder of a woman he'd recently been dating. After I talked her off the ledge, I could maybe part the Red Sea for good measure.

She lifted her hand to her mouth and chewed on a loose piece of skin. "Shit." She pulled the hand away. "I can't mess up my hands before the wedding. They're going to take a picture of the rings, which we don't even have yet. We were supposed to pick them up today. They take those pictures up close. And I need to get a manicure. I've already got these ragged-looking nails. I've been chewing them again. Ugh."

"The police do want to talk to you," I said. "I think you should talk to them. Tell them whatever they want to know."

"I talked to them already. Last night. They keep asking me the same questions over and over, and I don't know what else I can say."

The police were supposed to know how to be delicate. They'd tiptoed between the land mines of marital discord in any number of cases. I was entering the fray without training or experience, so I tried to tread lightly.

"What exactly have the police said to you about Blake? About why they want to talk to him about this woman's murder?"

Sam stared straight ahead and through the windshield like it was a giant screen. A few shoppers wandered around the lot in the distance. An older man pushing a cart. Two young women in workout clothes laughing and carrying cups of coffee.

Had Sam even heard me? She proved she had by saying, "I'm not an idiot, Ryan."

"I never said you were."

"Not in so many words, you didn't." She turned to face me. She looked younger than Blake and younger than me. She could still easily pass for a college student despite being the same age as I was. "I know what you all think about Blake and me. That he's difficult, and I'm naive. That I don't know what I'm getting into. That we'll get married, and he'll just walk all over me."

"It's none of my business what goes on—"

"Huh." She shook her head and looked back out the windshield. Foot traffic was picking up as the morning shoppers came out. "You're not denying it. You're just using that dodge. 'It's none of my business.' Well, why isn't it any of your business, if Blake is your closest friend? If Amanda and I are supposed to be friends?"

"I just mean that what you and Blake work out is between the two of you. No one can intrude on that. And you know, Blake and I haven't been quite as close—"

She turned to face me again. "And why is that? Why haven't you guys been as close?"

Rountree had nothing on Sam when it came to conducting an interrogation. She should have flashed a badge and read me my rights.

"We had a baby, Sam. Henry takes a lot of time and energy."

"And Amanda chewed Blake out. I know that."

"She's reconsidering all of that. She was just telling me she needs to look at Blake in a new light."

"I know. The lampshade-banging thing pissed her off. I get it. The drinking. I've always liked Amanda, regardless of how she feels about Blake. She's right about a lot of what she thinks of him. And I admire her for having a career and then being willing to put it on hold to raise Henry. I want to do that someday. I want to have all of those things. With Blake."

She presented me with an opening to steer the conversation back to the original matter, so I took it. "That's why we need to find him," I said.

But Sam wasn't ready to move on just yet. "You asked me what the police have told me about Blake and this woman. Jennifer, right?"

"Right."

"They've told me enough. And so has Blake. I know what it means that the police think he might be involved in this murder. I know they dated while we were apart." She chewed on the piece of skin around her nail again. She seemed to have forgotten about the close-up photo of her hand coming the next day. "He's not the only one who saw other people. I did too. I'm not a doormat, Ryan. But Blake told me the truth. It was over when we got back together and he proposed. It was over then. For good. Anyone who says anything else is lying. Blake and I understand each other. We do."

"I understand, Sam. I'm glad you feel that way."

She stopped chewing on her finger. "He told me other things, Ryan. He told me things about you too. He told me everything about the accident and who was driving that night."

CHAPTER FORTY-EIGHT

I'd kept the engine running, but the air in the cabin started to feel close and stifling.

I reached with my left hand and pressed a button, lowering the window next to me a few inches, letting in cooling fresh air. Traffic sounds came in, the whooshing of cars, the honking of horns.

"Why did he tell you about that?" I asked.

Sam leaned a little closer. Her hair fell forward across her face again, and she brushed it back. "When we got back together this last time, we wanted to know everything about each other, Ryan. We wanted to have all of that in the open. He told me Amanda doesn't know the truth about the accident. And I get it. Look at the lampshade thing. Amanda can be unforgiving. Maybe it's best if she doesn't know. I can't say. With what happened to her sister . . ."

I shifted my weight, letting my body fall back against the seat. I sank against the cloth material, felt the light breeze against my face. And it brought a small amount of relief.

"Do you think differently about me, knowing that?" I asked. "Knowing the role I played in the accident? Don't you look at me in a different way?"

She sounded believable when she said, "We all make mistakes, Ryan. None of us are perfect. You *and* Blake were there. You were driving, sure. But I love you both. Isn't it time to move on from that? To not have that grip you so tightly? We all do what we do in the moment, and then we have to live with it. Right?"

She sounded so wise. She made it so simple and clear. But I couldn't buy it all. Not yet.

"I don't know," I said. "It runs counter to who I believe I am."

"You can think about it," she said. "You were young and immature. Young men do stupid things all the time. I believe Amanda would understand. It happened in college. Before you even met her. Before you knew about her sister."

Sam could say all she wanted about how knowing wouldn't affect Amanda's view of me, and I worked to get my mind to believe and accept that. Amanda and I loved each other. We knew each other's strengths and flaws. Very well. We were committed. Wouldn't she understand anything I could tell her about myself? Especially something that happened when I was twenty-two?

Wouldn't I understand if I learned she'd done something horrible? Wouldn't I try?

Then my mind bounced back to something else. Something Rountree had told me back at Blake and Samantha's house.

"What prompted him to tell you all of this about college?" I asked. "When did he do that?"

"It was just a few weeks ago. Why?"

"He just unburdened himself of this out of the blue? You said you share everything, but you've known each other for a while. Why did this just come up recently? That seems random."

"Well, that article ran in the paper. The Good Samaritan one." Sam rubbed the back of her hand against her cheek while she thought. Her eyes narrowed. "Oh, I think I know. I think he ran into someone from college. Someone you guys were friends with back then."

"Who?"

"He didn't tell me the guy's name. I think it was a guy." She lowered her hand and tapped her fingers against her thigh. "Yeah . . . no . . . a guy? Anyway, it was someone he knew. 'A blast from the past,' he called it. Someone you were in that club with. The shield thing."

"Sigil and Shield."

"Right. Why didn't they just call them fraternities? That's what they called them at UK. Anyway, whoever it was triggered something in Blake, some kind of weird distraction. Since I didn't go to Ferncroft with you guys, it didn't matter what his name was."

"Why did he have his yearbooks out?"

"What yearbooks?"

"At your house today, just now, the detective went in and looked around. She said Blake had his college yearbooks out on his desk. All four of them out, and one open to a page about Sigil and Shield. Why was he doing that?"

Sam shook her head. "I have no idea. I don't go in his office usually. I knew he had those yearbooks from college, but I didn't know he ever looked at them. I've never seen him doing it."

"Maybe he was just feeling nostalgic."

"Could be— Wait. Why was a detective *inside* our house?" Sam asked. "What was going on?"

"Oh . . ."

I needed to explain that to her, but I didn't know how. *Kyle.* The strange man in her house drinking her liquor and looking for Blake.

Crying over Jennifer.

Before I could, my phone rang. Amanda.

Oh, good, I thought. "I have to take this. It's Amanda."

When I answered, she didn't greet me. She spoke in a rush, her voice clipped and panicked.

"You need to come home right now, Ryan. *Right now.*"

CHAPTER FORTY-NINE

Sam came with me.

I'm not sure how much of a choice she had. When I heard Amanda's voice and the panicked edge in it, I ended the call and started driving. Thoughts of letting Sam out of the car so she could go back to her life were secondary. Only after I'd made the first couple of turns did I think about it and turn to her.

"I'm sorry. Do you want me to take you back?"

"No, I'm going. I want to know she's okay."

We remained mostly silent the rest of the way. I concentrated on the road, my hands gripping the wheel until my knuckles hurt. The sound of rushing air through the window I'd kept open filled the space. Before I hung up and started driving, I'd asked Amanda twice if she was okay, and she just repeated her request.

Her order, really.

Come home. *Come home.*

Right now.

My mind swirled with possibilities. Henry hurt. Amanda sick. The police returning. Armed with an arrest warrant. Evidence of my presence in Jennifer's house.

I didn't care. They could take me away. They could end it all, as long as Amanda and Henry were okay. Unhurt. Safe.

I expected to see a dozen cop cars or crime scene vans when I turned down our street, but everything looked quiet and orderly. As placid and calm as any other day in the neighborhood. Shining houses, the windows reflecting the sunlight. The trash cans put away, the flowers starting to bloom. A place for everything and everything in its place.

I parked behind the house, stopping just outside the garage, and used my key to let myself in the locked back door.

"Amanda. Where are you?"

I heard Sam's footsteps behind me. She followed me into the kitchen, closing the door. I told her to lock it, to turn the dead bolt in case trouble was coming along in our path.

"Amanda?"

Footsteps on the stairs, squeaking against the wood. Amanda appeared. She was dressed—jeans, sneakers, a long-sleeved T-shirt advertising the Pig. She looked ready for action. Her cheeks flushed, her hair pulled back.

"Thank God, it's you," she said.

"Are you okay? Where's Henry?"

"He's upstairs. Asleep. Yes, I'm okay. I'm fine."

"Are you hurt? Either of you? Just tell me that. I need to know that."

"No, we're not hurt."

I placed my hands on her biceps, felt her firm, muscular arms beneath the soft material. I looked her over—face, head, everything—searching for signs of injury. For blood, rips in her clothes, or bruises on her skin, but I saw nothing out of order.

"Are you sure?" I asked.

"I'm sure."

I started for the stairs. "I want to see Henry. I need to see that my son is okay."

"He's fine, Ryan. He's asleep. He slept through everything."

"Everything? What everything? I want to see him, okay? I want to make sure my son is okay."

Amanda understood. Any parent would. She nodded, and I started up the stairs. As I went, I heard Amanda and Sam talking, hugging, and commiserating.

When I reached the top of the stairs, I turned right and went into Henry's room. My eyes ran over the dark blue walls, the jungle wallpaper. A pile of stuffed animals in one corner, the changing table in another. I caught the sweet scent of baby powder I so strongly associated with the space.

I crossed the room and leaned over the crib. He was there, splayed out beneath a blanket. He breathed perfectly. He looked perfect. Fresh and safe and clean and new.

I wanted to pick him up, to clutch him to my chest, but I couldn't wake him. Better to let him sleep, oblivious to whatever had happened in the house and to Amanda. Oblivious to everything the adults were wrapped up in.

I went back down the stairs, moving more slowly with less frantic energy. Amanda and Sam were still in the kitchen. I heard the sound of water filling the teakettle, their voices sharp and focused. When I came into the room, Sam was listening to Amanda with her hand clutched to her chest.

Amanda placed the kettle on the stove, turned the burner on with a soft whoosh of igniting gas, and turned to me.

"Okay," she said. "I started telling Sam, but I'll back up a little so you can hear everything. It started just about half an hour ago."

CHAPTER FIFTY

Amanda leaned back against the counter, the blue flame glowing next to her. Sam and I remained standing, waiting to listen.

"I'd just finished giving Henry his bath. I was about to get him ready to go. To get us both ready to go. I was going to head over to my parents' house since that's what you wanted me to do. I thought you were overreacting." She shivered. "I guess I was wrong."

"Why did you want her to go over to her parents'?" Sam asked.

"Someone was sneaking around outside the house last night," I said, not adding that it might have been Blake. "Amanda thought she heard them trying to get in the door."

"Oh." Sam's hand remained at her chest. "Wait. That guy broke into our house today. That's what you said."

"I know," I said, understanding what Sam was thinking. Amanda looked curious about it as well. "I can explain, but I'd rather know what happened here. Go on. Just tell us the story."

Amanda nodded. "I'd finished with the bath and dried him off. I got him dressed, and then I was going to pack some things to take with us.

Henry was in his seat, vegging out while I packed. And that's when I heard it. Again. Someone messing with the back door." She shook her head, her eyes widening with exasperation. "I thought I was nuts, hearing things. Maybe I'd allowed myself to get so worked up that I was imagining someone breaking in. Maybe I'd just been hearing things last night. I was seriously doubting myself. But I decided to check. I knew the door was locked. I'd made sure before I went upstairs. I always do, and especially after last night."

"Good," I said.

"So I left Henry upstairs and came down. I thought maybe it was you coming home." She looked me dead in the eyes, and I wondered if she might have been on the brink of crying. But she held it back and went on. "Or my mom might have come over to help. You know she does that sometimes. And she doesn't always bother to call, since she forgets to charge her phone."

The teakettle clicked as the water started to heat, the flame pulsing underneath.

"When I came down here and looked out the door, I saw a man standing there. I didn't know him. Never seen him before. But he was waving at me, telling me to come over to the door and talk to him. I was scared. Enough weird stuff has been going on around here to freak anybody out. But I thought maybe he was a cop. I don't know. The chain was on the door, and the lock was bolted. So I went over." She pointed at the door where the man had stood. "If he was just selling something, I could get rid of him."

"And you had your phone with you," Sam said.

Amanda looked sheepish. "Like a dumb ass I left it upstairs. If only six-month-olds could dial nine-one-one. Anyway, I went over and asked what he wanted through the glass. He wanted me to open the door, but I told him I wouldn't. I didn't know who he was. He looked pretty irritated, but he told me he was looking for you, Ryan. Or Blake.

Either one. When I asked him who he was, he wouldn't tell me his name, but he said he was a friend, that he knew both of you and needed to talk to you both about everything."

"Everything?" I asked.

"That's what he said."

"What did he look like?" I asked.

"Of course I'm kicking myself for leaving the phone upstairs." She did a face-palm. "If I'd had the phone, I could have taken his picture. I could have shown you and the cops. But I didn't have it. He wasn't much taller than you, Ryan. Maybe the same height. Not much hair. Kind of haunted-looking in the eyes, like he'd been kicked around by life pretty good. But clean. Not like a bum or a homeless guy. Just kind of pushy. He kept saying he needed to talk to one of you guys. And that he needed to tell me what was going on. If I'd just open the door, he said, he could explain everything, and it would all make sense."

"But you didn't open the door to him, did you?" I asked.

Steam started to come out of the spout of the teakettle, and within a few seconds, it whistled, a high, piercing shriek. Amanda turned the burner off with a flick of her wrist. Before she poured anything, she looked over at me.

"I undid the lock so I could talk to him through the little space the chain allowed," she said. "It was hard to hear through the glass. And it felt kind of rude."

"Rude?"

"The guy said he knew you. He said he was a friend of yours and Blake's. How could I know he wasn't? I still don't know that he wasn't."

CHAPTER FIFTY-ONE

"Damn it, Amanda." I clenched my fists, holding them down at my sides. "He could have kicked the door in once you did that." I knew my voice came out like a sizzling hiss through pressed lips. "Do you know how easy that would have been?"

Amanda calmly went about her business. She poured tea into two mugs—she didn't offer me any—and then passed one of the mugs to Sam, who took it with both hands and thanked her. Amanda then turned back to me.

"Do you think I don't know that, Ryan? Do you think I didn't learn that in my college self-defense class? Did it ever occur to you that I had my reasons?" Her voice rose a little in anger, although she kept it under control. "Maybe I want to know what's going on around here. Maybe I thought this random guy had some information that would clear things up. And if that meant I had to open the door a crack to a stranger, I was going to do it."

"But it's—"

"I know what it is. I also didn't know where you were. You ran out of here right after the police came. *You* could have been in danger. Or hurt. How was I supposed to know? So if this guy had information that might put my mind at ease, or that helped solve your problems, wouldn't it make sense for me to get it?"

She'd made her case coolly and clearly. And I couldn't argue. If I'd been in her shoes, wondering where she was, I'd have made the same choices. But I didn't have to be happy about it.

"Okay," I said. "I get it."

Amanda picked up her mug and blew across the surface of the liquid. I smelled the peppermint from across the room. She took a cautious sip, and so did Sam.

"Are you going to unclench your fists and hear the rest of the story?" she asked.

I hadn't realized I was still standing in such an aggressive manner, like I was ready to charge into a burning building. I opened my hands and loosened my posture as much as I could.

"Happy?" I asked. "Is that all this guy did or said? Did you get rid of him?"

Amanda put her mug down. Sam watched her and then me like a spectator at a tennis match. I felt certain she'd never seen any hint of marital discord on display between the two of us. Amanda and I managed to keep any issues that existed between us private. We didn't see any point in spilling our problems out for the rest of the world to view. If anything, we did the opposite. We only showed the happiest, most polished side of our lives on social media.

"Let me ask you something first," Amanda said. "When I described the guy, you acted like you might know him. Who is he?"

So I told her about Kyle Dornan. How he was over at Sam and Blake's house when I went there, how he was inside their house. And how he was very distraught over what had happened to Jennifer.

"They were dating or something like that, he and Jennifer," I said. "And so he's taking her death pretty hard. He's blaming Blake, but Kyle's acting pretty strange himself. When the cops showed up at Blake and

Sam's house, Kyle ran off. I mean, he ran out of the house like it was on fire. He must have come right over here after he did that. It's easy enough to look up an address. He knew me from the Pig. Maybe he thought he'd catch me here, or maybe he thought he could talk to you. But he's acting guilty. And the cops want him."

Amanda tapped her foot, her eyes squinting. "He didn't say Jennifer's name. I would have remembered that. But he did talk about her. He said it was terrible that the girl got killed, but that you and Blake knew all about it. He said you could tell me everything that happened to her. And so could Blake."

Samantha gasped. I looked over at her. She was shaking her head, her eyes wide. "Why did he say that about Jennifer getting killed? If he said it that way, it must mean he's the one who hurt her. Right? Why else would he be running around so obsessed about it?"

"If he did it, why wouldn't he just leave town?" I asked, not expecting an answer. "He's hanging around here a lot for a guy the cops are looking for. Blake is the one we can't find."

"Ryan, he's not—"

"I'm sorry, Sam. I am. None of this makes sense. And none of us have answers."

"You're right," Amanda said. "We don't know anything."

"Was this guy was alone? Did you see anyone else?" I asked.

"I didn't see anyone. But I was pretty focused on him. There could have been someone out in the yard. Or waiting in a car."

"You didn't see a woman with him?" I asked.

"A woman? Why would you ask me that? Women don't usually do this stupid bullying shit. That's what men do."

"I don't know. I'm scrambling."

But I really wasn't. I was thinking of Dawn Steiner. Had she come the night before? And then Kyle that day? Were they somehow working together to harass us?

"Was that it, then?" I asked. "Did the guy leave?"

Amanda let out a long sigh. She stopped tapping her foot and shifted her weight from one leg to the other. "He grew a little more aggressive. It was subtle. But he had his hand on the door, and I saw he was pressing against it, exerting more force. Maybe he was getting ready to kick it in. I don't know. I told him to leave. He said something about evening the score or getting even. I'm not sure which. But that scared me. More than anything else, *that* scared me. But then I caught a couple of breaks."

"What?" I asked.

"Henry started crying. And the guy heard it. 'Your baby,' he said. And he said it in a way like he knew we had a kid. Had you mentioned that to him?"

"I don't think so. But he heard Henry crying."

"It's the way he said it. Like he was confirming something, not like he was surprised. I began to worry he wanted to hurt Henry. But then the next break came. A car went down the alley. Slow, the way they have to back there. You could hear the tires over the gravel. The man—Kyle, or whatever his name is—turned to look, almost like he expected trouble."

"He probably thought it was the cops," I said.

"Maybe. When he turned and checked out the alley, I took my chance. I pushed on the door, slamming it shut. Then I threw the bolt and ran upstairs. He pounded on the door a few times. I heard him. But when I made it upstairs and picked up the phone, I looked through the window and saw him leaving. He went down the alley in the opposite direction of the car that had just passed. I called you right away."

When she was finished talking, I realized I may have loosened my clenched fists, but the muscles in my neck were as taut as piano wire. Fear and relief tumbled through me like charged electrons. All I could do was move forward to give Amanda a hug. I folded her in my arms and pulled her close.

"It's okay," I said. "I'm glad you did what you did. You were smart to slam the door and get up to Henry."

"And your baseball bat was right there in the corner still," she said, her mouth against my chest. "If he'd come in, I would have taken a few swings. He wasn't going to get near my baby."

"He doesn't know you started at third base in high school."

"Damn right."

I let her go, even though I really only wanted to hang on to her.

Sam had moved closer, the tea mug in her right hand. "We have to call the police," she said. "You heard that. This guy Kyle, he practically confessed. And he's out there looking for Blake for some reason. We have to call the police."

She was absolutely right. So I did.

CHAPTER FIFTY-TWO

While we waited for Rountree to arrive, Sam and Amanda talked about the wedding. Where it was being held, what kind of dress she was going to wear. If she was nervous with only one day to go . . .

The conversation felt strained and overly formal, mostly because it seemed so unlikely—at least to me—that any wedding could happen under the circumstances. But we soldiered on, trying our best to ignore the elephant in the room—who the hell had killed Jennifer, and did Blake know something about it? Or was he just a victim of circumstance? Was it Kyle Dornan who had killed Jennifer and put Blake in the crosshairs? Had Kyle hurt Blake as well?

Henry had woken up, and Amanda and then Samantha bounced him on their knees. He loved the attention, looking at Sam with wide eyes like she was the most fascinating person to ever set foot in the house.

"I hope we get to have one of these someday," she said.

Amanda reached over and squeezed her hand. "You will. Of course. You will."

"Just make sure you babyproof the lampshades," I said.

Nobody laughed. I wasn't as funny as I thought I was.

When Rountree finally arrived, entering through the back door, which Kyle Dornan had pushed against, she looked surprised to see Samantha there. She said, "You're a tough woman to get ahold of."

"It's been a crazy morning," Sam said, still holding Henry.

We all stood up from the table. Rountree eyed me, her face impassive.

"I'll say." Rountree raised her index finger in the air. Then she focused on Henry. "Well, hello there, mister."

Henry looked just as happy to see her as he had been to see Samantha. Maybe he was already growing bored with our faces. Rountree tickled his belly, then looked at Sam. "You hold that thought. About the crazy morning. I'll talk to you in a minute. But what about this man you called about? The one who tried to come in the back door?"

Amanda repeated her story, interrupted by a periodic question or request for clarification from Rountree. When Amanda told her that Kyle said it was terrible the girl got killed, Rountree's eyebrows rose, and she pursed her lips.

"He said it was terrible the girl had to get killed?"

"Yes."

"Did he say Jennifer's name?"

Amanda took her time answering. I could sense the wheels moving in her head as she scanned through her memory banks to be certain.

"No," she said. "It was a stressful situation, and I was worried he was going to get in and hurt Henry."

"I understand. That's your first instinct—to protect your baby. And it's the right one. Always. If someone was at the door like that and my babies were upstairs, look out."

"I'm just not sure what he said exactly. What I can tell you is that he was talking about Blake and Ryan, and then he said he was sorry the girl had to get killed."

"Had you ever met Kyle Dornan before?"

"No. Never."

Rountree looked at all of us. "None of you know him?"

We all shook our heads like obedient children.

"Well," she said, "we definitely want to talk to him. He's broken into one home and tried to get into another. He's making quite a name for himself. We have his description out all over. Even with the state police."

"Did you find Blake?" Samantha asked.

Rountree turned to face her. "No, we haven't found him either. But that's a nice segue for us to talk, isn't it?" She made a face at Henry, one that prompted him to giggle. "Ah, if only we could just talk to this little guy for a while. Right? It's been a long twelve hours or so, hasn't it?"

Sam nodded. She looked young and small in the kitchen lights, standing in front of the authority figure. Like Henry's older sister. Or a youthful-looking babysitter. "You can ask me whatever you want to ask me. It's okay."

"I hate to break up the party, but maybe you should give little Mr. Man back to his mama. That way you and I can drive down to our station and talk there. Do you have a car here?"

"No. Ryan drove me."

"Even better. I'll drive you back to your car when you're finished with us. Okay?"

Rountree sounded cheery and peppy. Her tone failed to match the mood of the circumstances.

Sam agreed to the plan, and she gently handed Henry back to Amanda. She kissed him lightly on the forehead before turning to Rountree.

"Okay, Detective, I'm ready."

"What about us, Detective?" Amanda asked. "That guy tried to get inside our house. He got into their house. Are we safe?"

"We can step up the patrols in the area, but it's a busy time. We're getting pulled in a lot of different directions today. Didn't you say something earlier about going to your parents'?"

Amanda nodded. "That's what I was getting ready to do when that man showed up."

"Then I say head over there," Rountree said. "I'm sure they'd be happy to see their grandbaby."

Rountree pointed to the back door, but Sam hesitated for a moment. She looked uncertain, like she couldn't decide what she wanted to do.

"Miss Edson?" Rountree said. "Are you ready?"

"Well," Sam said. "I just . . . the police station?"

"Yes," Rountree said. "The police station."

Sam stood there a moment longer, and then she nodded her head. "Right. Okay, sure. I'll call the florist on the way and let them know I'm going to be late."

Finally, the two of them walked out.

CHAPTER FIFTY-THREE

When Sam and Rountree were gone, Amanda went upstairs with Henry to finish getting everything together for their imminent departure. I felt a little at sea. I wandered around the house, once again making sure the doors and windows were locked. And they were. Still. From the night before.

I took out my phone and checked Twitter. I followed a number of local news outlets as well as the local police. I'd found they provided so much information I almost never read the local newspaper anymore.

Jennifer's murder still dominated everything. The police provided little information, just the most basic facts. While they said they wanted to question a number of people, no names were mentioned, meaning Blake and Kyle were kept out of the news. For the moment.

I made the mistake of checking some of the replies to the tweets from a local television station. Aside from giving a hint as to what people in the community were thinking, it was also a surefire way for me to lose faith in humanity. Sure enough, a number of increasingly bizarre and horrible theories were already bouncing around. Jennifer had been murdered because she owed someone money. Jennifer had been murdered because she was mixed up in drugs. Jennifer had been murdered by a member of a gang of illegal immigrants.

I closed the app.

But I still felt a little dirty. Twitter always made me feel that way. But not so much that I stopped looking.

Then again, I knew next to nothing about Jennifer. I knew nothing about what she might or might not have had going on in her life. I'd been fixated on blaming Blake—or Kyle—but how did I know it wasn't something else, something completely unrelated to any of the things I knew about?

I'd have almost preferred it was.

Without even thinking, I checked Facebook as well. More notifications about my photo, but they were slowing to a trickle.

And the second friend request from Jennifer. Lingering. Unanswered.

I was afraid to deny it because the last time I had done that, another one came right on its heels. I'd had enough of that. When I thought of those mystery requests, the ones that seemed to come from beyond the grave, my skin felt like a million ants were crawling over it. And it made me wonder again if someone was watching me, gauging my reactions like some kind of mad scientist or twisted psychologist who wanted to see how much pressure they could apply before I cracked like aging plaster.

Maybe it was Kyle in control of her account. Maybe he had watched me through the windows the night before when I was in Jennifer's house, since he said he was going by. Maybe he had watched me in my own house the night before, sending the request to see how I responded, and then come back again to harass Amanda.

Or maybe the ex-cons Jennifer worked with. Could one of them have gained control of her account? Could one of them have killed her and then decided to harass me?

I shivered.

To take my mind off that, and since I was standing there holding my phone, I decided to try Blake again, on the off chance he might pick up.

The trilling of the electronic ring went on and on, and then clicked over to Blake's voice. A cool, ironic monotone as he told the caller he wasn't available. And if you left a message, and he felt like it, he'd get back to you.

The sound of his voice struck a strange chord in me. I almost missed the jerk. It was like hearing the voice of or seeing a photograph of someone long dead. It reminded me of the years we'd spent together as friends. And now . . .

I tried again, and the line rang a few times before it sounded like someone had answered the call. But they didn't speak. The ringing stopped, and I heard the sound of dead air.

I waited, then said, "Hello? Blake? Hello?"

I thought I heard breathing. A few huffs and puffs of air. Someone was there, but they weren't speaking. Or they weren't able to. Was I hearing the sound of an injured or dying person?

"Blake?"

The call clicked off.

I immediately tried again, but the call went straight to voice mail.

I left a message, but it felt a lot like throwing a rock down a deep well and never hearing the splash. He hadn't called me back all day. Why did I expect him to now?

And why had he picked up and said nothing?

Had he seen my name on the caller ID screen and felt the same wave of nostalgia I felt when hearing his voice? Had he considered speaking to me, but then decided not to because of whatever trouble he was in?

I tried again, but it just rang and rang.

"Ryan?" Amanda called from the top of the stairs.

"What?"

"Were you talking to someone?"

"I tried . . . It's nothing. Just a wrong number."

"Can you come up here when you get the chance?" she asked.

I slid the phone into my pocket, trying not to think about the electromagnetic waves radiating next to my balls. I trudged up the stairs and found her in our bedroom. Henry sat on the floor in his carrier, a pacifier in his mouth. He looked content, like a little red-faced king on his throne. I let him take my finger in his little hand, loved the feel of him squeezing.

"I'm about ready," Amanda said.

"I can drive you over there. We can spend a little more time together."

"That's sweet. Sure. What did you think of all that? The police and everything?"

I could tell by the way she asked—her tone casual but only superficially so. She was trying too hard to be casual. Some thought or series of thoughts was coursing through her mind, and she wanted to see if I was on the same page without being prompted.

I extricated myself from Henry's grip and sat on the bed. Amanda stood in the closet door, sliding clothes around on the rod, the hangers making a scraping sound.

"This Kyle Dornan guy is bad news," I said. "He got into Blake's house. He came over here. He's jealous. Very jealous of Jennifer and Blake. Maybe he found out that Jennifer had sent those messages to me somehow. Maybe that's why he came over here. I don't know. It's scary."

"Sure, right. I agree with you about all of that," she said. She took a dress off the rod and stared at it. Why did she need to look at a dress when she was rushing off to her parents' house with a six-month-old in tow? I couldn't answer that. But I'd learned to never question her packing strategies. "I mean, I really agree. I stood here face-to-face with the guy. He didn't seem right."

I thought back to my own encounter with Kyle. And she was right. The broken bottle waved in my face. "Obsessed" seemed like far too mild a word.

"But I'm talking about Sam," she said.

"What about her?"

"What did you think about how she handled everything?"

Henry spit his pacifier out onto the floor as if he couldn't stand to hear his mother question Sam. I went over and picked it up, wiping it on my pants leg. Seven months ago, I would have run from baby spit. I no longer even noticed it. I stuck the plug back in his mouth.

"She's scared too. If Blake . . . if he did this, her life is over. Or, I guess, the life she thought she was about to have is over. Imagine if I had gotten arrested right before our wedding. Arrested for murder, Amanda. Blake could still be facing that. Even if he's innocent, he's a suspect. A lot of mud is going to stick to him."

"That's true." She put the dress back and nodded to herself about something. Then she turned and leaned against the jamb of the closet door, facing me. She rested one foot on top of the other and tilted her head. "You're probably right."

"What else are you talking about?" I asked. "You seem to have something in mind."

She took her time answering. "Sam just looked scared. That's all. And you gave a plausible reason why. She's getting taken away by the police because her fiancé might have been involved in a serious crime."

"Let's get you out of here," I said.

But Amanda remained in place. Her face wore a distant, thoughtful look. I knew she was working something out. She was always one step ahead of people, and it was one of the things I loved most about her. "She was afraid—that's for sure. But it was a different kind of fear. Something more . . . visceral."

"Really?"

"Yeah. When that guy was at the door, that Kyle guy, I felt that way. Like a caged animal fighting for its life. Everything just hung in the balance for a moment. I swear that's what Sam looked like when that cop led her out of our kitchen."

CHAPTER FIFTY-FOUR

Amanda finally finished packing, and I carried her bag downstairs while she made sure Henry was ready. Amanda checked Henry's diaper and saw that he'd chosen that moment to pee, forcing a delay. She called for me, and I went back up and grabbed him, and placed him on the changing table in his room to deal with the minor mess.

Amanda wandered off to the bathroom, and when she came back, I had Henry ready to go. But Amanda stood in the doorway, her forehead creased.

"What?" I asked. "Are you cooking up another theory about Sam?"

"Not that. Do you think it's okay to go to my parents' this way? What if this Kyle Dornan guy tracks me down there? Am I putting them in jeopardy?"

I shifted Henry to my left arm and balanced him against my hip. His dry diaper gave him renewed energy, and he squirmed, trying to escape. Then he started holding his arms out, reaching for Amanda, confirming my suspicion that he liked her better.

"This guy isn't looking for you," I said. "He's looking for me. Or, really, for Blake. He's not going to go track you down. Not over there. And he doesn't know your name, does he? Or their names?"

"No, I guess not."

"Look, you've got to be somewhere, and it shouldn't be here. Do you want to go to a hotel?"

"No. I'd feel more trapped."

"I think your parents' house is good. I know how protective your mother is. I think she'd be a pretty formidable opponent if Kyle tried to get in the door of her house to try to hurt her daughter or grandson."

She smiled. "That's true."

"The apple doesn't fall far from the tree. You fended him off on your own."

"Sometimes you just have to battle it out with people."

I expected her to laugh. Or smile. But her face looked serious. A little distant.

"What does that mean?" I asked.

She averted her eyes and looked at the floor as she spoke. Henry stopped moving, perhaps because Amanda wasn't rushing to take him. But he seemed to be listening too.

"I remembered something, something from my soccer days in high school. I haven't thought of it in a long time. Maybe I blocked it out to some extent. Senior year we went to state. We played a really good team from eastern Kentucky. These girls were good. And they were big and tough. They played to win. Really played to win. I went for the ball against one of them, and I tackled her pretty hard. A slide tackle. But I clipped her leg and knocked her down."

I wasn't sure where all of this was going. Or where it was coming from. I knew Amanda had played soccer and softball in high school and was pretty good at both. Good enough to get some scholarship offers from small colleges in both sports, although she passed and went to

Indiana University for her degree. I'd seen the photos of her in her various sports uniforms in the basement of her parents' house.

But I'd never heard this story before.

"Was she hurt?" I asked.

"Not really. More pissed than anything else. She popped right back up and glared at me. Then about fifteen minutes later, I had the ball, and she tackled me. And I mean hard. Harder than I took her down. And it was clearly intentional. It knocked the wind out of me. But she stood over me, taunting me. Calling me every name she could think of."

"Nice sportsmanlike behavior."

"It's competitive during playoff time."

"Sure."

"I said Sam looked trapped, and I felt the same when that guy was at the door trying to get in. It took me back to that soccer match. I jumped up when that girl taunted me. I got right in her face and shoved her. Hard. I'd have done more, except my teammates got in the middle. And her teammates held her back. But her tackling me was so unfair, so unwarranted, I just had to do something about it. You know?"

"You were defending yourself. I get it."

"I figured you would."

I shifted Henry to my other arm and hip. He kept growing every day, and sometimes he felt like a pile of bricks in my hands. "I don't blame you for standing up for yourself on the soccer field in high school."

"And I'm trying not to blame you for Jennifer messaging you that way."

I almost laughed. Out of confusion. "I didn't do anything. It just happened."

"I know. Things just happen sometimes. Things beyond our control to some extent. *That's* what I'm saying. I understand that very well."

"Okay. I get the feeling you're hinting at something deeper. Are you worried I'm hanging on to bad feelings from when that guy hit on you at work? Is that what you're wondering?"

"No, I wasn't really thinking about that. Not directly anyway."

My face must have looked like I felt, jumbled and confused. "So what is it? And answer quickly before our boy decides to pee again."

She shook her head. "I'm just thinking of everything that's going on right now. Blake. Sam. Even Jennifer. There are a lot of complicated and bruised feelings there. People trying to stand up for what they think is right. People trying hard to protect what's theirs. I'd protect Henry if he were in danger. My mom would. You would. Sam's fighting to keep Blake. Makes sense?"

"People fight to hang on to the things that matter to them. Their loved ones. Their pride. Their sense of honor on a soccer field. I get it."

"And sometimes that gets out of control," Amanda said.

"Are you talking about soccer? Or what?"

"We should go," she said. "It's not important."

"Amanda?"

"Seriously. Let's just go."

CHAPTER FIFTY-FIVE

It took fifteen minutes to drive to my in-laws' house.

We rode mostly in silence. Car trips lulled Henry into peaceful oblivion, so he remained quiet, strapped into his car seat. Amanda had tuned the radio to a local rock station, something that played classics from the seventies. I didn't mind the station, but it tended to rotate through the same songs over and over again, ad nauseam. I could only handle so many versions of "Free Bird" in one day.

Amanda liked it though. The station played "Fool for the City," and Amanda absently looked out the passenger-side window, her body swaying slightly to the music. But her mind seemed to be on other, more important things. No doubt she was reliving Kyle Dornan's appearance at our back door, his aggressive push to break inside. It might take a long time for her to feel safe in the house again. I had to accept she might never feel completely at ease.

Robert, one of the partners in the Juniper Pig, had had his house broken into once when he wasn't home. The thieves came in through a bedroom window and ransacked the place, taking little of substance. But they clearly enjoyed destroying Robert's possessions and disrupting all of his order. Robert told me he slept with the lights on in his house for two weeks. And it took another month before he slept through the night without freaking out over the usual noises and clicks that any house made.

I reached over and placed my hand on Amanda's knee. She jumped a little.

I smiled, and she smiled back in a somewhat forced manner. I kept my hand on her knee, squeezing through the soft denim. She placed her hand on mine but looked out the window again.

"All that stuff you were saying before we left the house," I said, "about fighting and standing up for things. Is there more to that?"

"Shhh."

I hadn't noticed that the music wasn't playing. Foghat's paean to city life over the country had stopped, and the DJ, who normally screamed into the microphone in a rich baritone voice, was quickly telling everyone listening that they were switching over to their sister station for a breaking news update.

The man's words registered with Amanda. She sat forward, her eyes wide and her lips pressed tight, and turned the volume up.

I leaned forward as well, waiting to hear what they had to report.

We heard the breathless voice of a reporter who told us she was standing at police headquarters downtown, where breaking news in the Jennifer Bates murder case was coming in. The reporter's voice went quiet for a moment. Muffled voices sounded in the background. A siren squealed. It all seemed so old-fashioned, like a blast from the past, waiting for a reporter to deliver news live on the radio instead of gathering it from Twitter.

Then the reporter came back on. She spoke quickly and urgently.

"I've been able to confirm with a source inside the police department that a suspect, actually a person of interest in the murder of Jennifer Bates—she's the local woman who was found dead in her home late last night, the victim of an apparent homicide—that police have located that person of interest, and that individual, who was wanted for questioning, has been killed by police as he resisted their attempts to speak to him."

The car drifted to the right into the next lane. A car over there honked.

"Ryan. Watch it."

I jerked back, trying to keep my hands steady on the wheel. I remembered Henry strapped into his car seat, Amanda next to me. *No more accidents,* I said in my head. *No more.*

But I felt hollow inside. Shaky and empty.

A man had been killed. A person of interest. I kept my eyes on the road, stayed in my lane. But I knew Amanda thought what I thought.

Blake?

"Police are not releasing the man's name at this time, but he has been a target of their investigation ever since Jennifer Bates's body was found in her home late last night. Details about how this shooting came about are sketchy right now, but apparently the man was located by the police not far from downtown. In fact, not far from the police station. And when they tried to apprehend him, he resisted. It's not clear if the man had a weapon and that led to police firing on him and using deadly force in this way. We're trying to get word from someone inside. . . . We're expecting a press conference any moment. . . ."

A horrible thought occurred to me. I said it out loud.

"Sam."

"What?"

"Sam's already down there. At the police station. That's where Rountree took her, to talk to her."

"We don't know that it's Blake," Amanda said. "We don't know who it is."

"But someone died. Someone else is dead because of this."

I arrived at the entrance of my in-laws' subdivision, an upper-middle-class enclave with redbrick homes and tidy lawns. My father-in-law,

Bill, had worked as a regional manager for a medical supply company. He and his wife were pretty tight-lipped about their financial situation, but judging from the cars they drove, the trips they took, and the size of the house, he'd done well for himself. Amanda had already had to tell them to ease up on the gifts they showered Henry with. He was six months old. New clothes meant little to him. A set of keys or the ribbon from a package occupied him as well as any toy.

I also knew, from Amanda, that her parents had received a nice insurance settlement from the accident that killed her sister, Mallory. Amanda never knew the exact amount, but a fair portion of it had been set aside for her and then for Henry's education when he was born. Mallory was something of a specter that hung over their house. She was seen—photos on the wall, the occasional old home video—but rarely spoken of. My in-laws tended to be overprotective and worrying, and I always tried to remind myself that parents could easily become that way when they'd lost one of their children.

I couldn't imagine the private pain both of them carried inside.

And I knew it must have been the same way in the Steiner house.

"I'd call Sam, but how can I reach her if she's with the police?" Amanda said.

"Text her. Maybe she can get it."

"But what if . . ."

"Look on Twitter. Is there any news there yet?"

"I'll check."

I wound through the subdivision, turning right and then left onto my in-laws' street.

"Anything?" I asked.

"Not really," Amanda said.

"Did you tell your parents why you were coming?" I asked.

"Not yet," she said. "I didn't need to be bombarded with all their questions. I just said I wanted to visit. I said you were about to get wrapped up in a work project, so I wanted to spend the night. I was hoping things would be resolved before we got there or shortly after. Then I wouldn't have to tell them the truth. They'll freak. Any threat, any problem, and they lose it."

"They're going to know something's wrong now," I said. "They'll read it on our faces."

"I know. And it will make them nervous. You know what it's like if they think something's wrong with me or Henry."

My in-laws lived halfway down on the right, a redbrick house with large windows and a three-car garage. I half expected my mother-in-law, Karen, to be standing on the lawn, arms wide, ready to snatch Henry out of the backseat and whisk him into the house. But she wasn't outside.

Yet.

I pulled into their driveway and stopped. But I kept the car running.

"Do you want to leave?" I asked.

"No. I'm sure they saw us. We'll just have to . . . I don't know. I don't want to tell them about Kyle coming to the house. Not right away. Or Blake. Or any of it. I'll try to keep it under wraps."

"Good luck. Their favorite pastimes are worrying and asking questions."

"Cut them some slack," Amanda said, repeating one of her favorite lines. "You know why they act this way."

As if on cue, the front door opened, and Karen came breezing out, on her face a smile as wide as the front yard. She wore a hooded sweatshirt, and leggings that emphasized the figure she kept slim through hours of tennis and yoga.

Amanda placed her hand on my knee. "Are you okay? You don't have to come in. You can just go. You can call Rountree and try to find out what's going on."

"She won't answer if she's in the middle of all that craziness."

"It might not be Blake," she said. "It might be someone we don't even know about."

"True. We don't know what all Jennifer was mixed up with. Or who."

I thought of the hateful comments on Twitter, the ones accusing her of everything from organized crime to drug trafficking. I scolded myself for thinking the same way, for letting that virus infect me.

I had no idea what was going on. None of us did.

But before I could regroup, the back door of the car was pulled open, and Karen was leaning in, unbuckling Henry from his car seat as he squealed for joy at the sight of her.

"There's our little guy," she said. "Look how big he's getting. I think he's bigger today than he was yesterday." She removed Henry from the car so fast you would have thought we were sinking in a lake and he needed to be rescued. "Come in, come in," she said. "I'm so happy to see all of you."

Amanda and I looked at each other. We felt we had no choice.

We unbuckled and followed grandmother and grandson into the house.

CHAPTER FIFTY-SIX

"Bill?" Karen still held Henry, and she called to her husband from the foyer. "Bill? They're here."

"Mom, where is he?" Amanda asked.

"He's glued to the TV. Where else? I'm sure he can't hear me."

"Then why are you yelling for him?" Amanda asked.

But Karen went on into the house, either ignoring or not hearing the question. Amanda rolled her eyes, a scene that must have been replicated ten thousand times during her childhood. We followed along in Karen's wake.

She led us back to the family room. Before we even arrived there, I heard the TV playing. And I could tell what Bill was watching.

". . . we go there now for more details on this police shooting . . ."

I looked at Amanda. She had heard it too. No choice. Bill's hearing had been declining for the last five years, and his TV volume went higher and higher each time we visited them. He always seemed to have the TV turned to either the news or a true-crime story. Murder and mayhem unleashed on the heartland seemed to appeal to him . . . but also made him more afraid of everything that moved. He once spoke openly of buying a gun, which prompted Amanda to say she wouldn't bring Henry to their house if he did. Given everything that had been going on, I kind of wondered if I felt differently about my father-in-law packing heat.

Bill waved to us but kept his eyes on the TV screen. I saw the police station, with a bunch of cars and news vans out front. A reporter stood stoically with a microphone in her hand.

"Honey, can you turn that down a little?" Karen asked.

"Are you following this?" he asked. I assumed he meant the question for Amanda and me. "The cops shot a guy downtown. They think he killed that girl they found dead last night. Did you hear about all that?"

"Yes, we heard, Dad," Amanda said. "Are they saying anything new?"

"That girl, the one who got murdered—they said she worked at a nonprofit that helped prisoners get jobs. How much do you want to bet—"

"Dad? Are they saying anything new?"

"Not really. They never do."

"Have they said who got killed?" I asked. I hoped I didn't sound overly curious. Or shaken.

"They're not saying," Bill said. He looked at us both for a moment as though he had just noticed we were standing there. "Well, why don't the two of you sit down?"

"Bill, why don't you get them a drink? We have some rolls left over from breakfast."

"We're fine, Mom."

And we both sat on the couch, staring at the TV. Karen placed Henry on a blanket she'd already laid out on the floor. She began handing him blocks and cars and toys, more than the boy could ever grab and suck on in a lifetime of trying.

"Can you believe this is happening here?" Bill asked the entire room, his hands wide, his eyeglasses slipping to the end of his nose. The top of his head was as bald as ice, and the fringe of hair that remained was completely gray. He answered his own question, not bothering to wait for a response. "A murder last night, and then this shooting today. Not that I think what the cops did is murder. I mean, if the guy drew on them or something to resist arrest, then what could they do? But how many murders do you think we had in Rossingville last year? Do you know?"

I shrugged. "Ten?"

"Four. Four." He held up his hand with four fingers extended for emphasis, his gold watch slipping down his arm. "This is the fourth one for this year. And it's only April. And this woman got killed in her own home. By some intruder. You all lock your doors every night, don't you?"

"Of course, Dad," Amanda said.

"Have you thought about an alarm system? Living downtown like that."

"We might actually," Amanda said.

"With a baby you need to be more careful. Someone might want to take him."

"Bill, why would you say that?" Karen asked.

"I'm just saying—kids . . . they're vulnerable. Really vulnerable."

His words brought an awkward silence over everyone. Only the TV kept the room from becoming as quiet as a church. I couldn't help it. My eyes trailed across the room to a portrait of Mallory, one taken when she was in the eighth grade and had only one year to live. She wore a white sweater and a smile with braces. She looked so much like Amanda that if I hadn't been told Amanda had had a sister, I would have thought it was a picture of her.

"Actually, I need to tell you something," Amanda said. And I could tell what she was going to do. She was about to tell them the truth. She and her parents had that kind of relationship, the kind where they really told one another things. The three of them were close, a relationship—so Amanda said—forged from the grief over their deceased daughter and sister. I'd lost my dad suddenly, but I still wasn't as open with my mom as Amanda was with Karen and Bill. She had said she wanted to keep everything quiet, but I knew she couldn't. Not with them. "Can you turn the TV down a little, Dad?"

"Well, they might say something important. Ryan acted like he wanted to hear."

"Dad? Please?"

Bill responded to the pleading in her voice and fumbled around for a moment before he found the remote, lifted his glasses to his forehead, and muted the TV. The silence felt as welcome as rain on a hot summer day. I could think.

"What is it, honey?" Karen asked. "Are you okay?"

"I'm fine, Mom. I just wanted to tell you about something that happened this morning."

Karen pointed to Henry, her face half-happy and half-surprised. "It's not . . . I mean . . . it's too soon, isn't it?"

"I'm not pregnant, Mom. Okay? Just listen."

"Okay," Karen said, but I could tell she was stung by Amanda's orders. "I just wanted to hear some happy news, and I'm afraid that's not what you're about to give me."

Bill turned his body to face us, reluctantly peeling his eyes away from the TV screen, which had shifted to a commercial for credit-card-debt relief.

"Do you remember Ryan's friend Blake? He was in our wedding."

Bill nodded. "The short guy who drank and talked a lot."

"That's him," I said. "He was my best man."

"Isn't he the one who hurt Henry?" Karen asked. "Didn't he drop him?"

"He didn't drop him, Karen," I said.

Amanda placed a calming hand on my knee. "He didn't drop Henry, Mom. No one has dropped Henry."

"Well, he did something. You have to be careful who holds the baby, Amanda. You heard your father. Children are vulnerable."

"I don't want to talk about that, Mom. Can we just talk about something else?" Amanda sounded like a kindergarten teacher trying to keep her unruly charges under control. "Look, as it turns out, Blake knew this woman who was murdered. Jennifer. They were"—her hand waved in the air as she decided which word to use—"friends of some kind. I'm not sure how close they were."

Her parents were both rapt. Lips parted, eyes wide. They had suddenly found themselves a couple of degrees away from a murder victim.

Amanda went on. "So the police want to question Blake, because they want to question everyone who knew Jennifer. That's logical, right? If there's a murder, they want to talk to everyone who knew the victim."

Bill nodded, and so did Karen. They'd watched enough *Law & Order* to get that.

"In fact," Amanda said, "they came to our house because they wanted to know if we had seen Blake."

For a moment, I wondered if she was going to mention my connection to Jennifer. How would that play with my conspiracy-minded in-laws? Me getting secret messages from a woman who ended up dead. I already knew not only would they not like or understand it, but they'd zero in on it for the rest of our lives. I'd always be the son-in-law who'd brought a trail of murder into their lives.

"They came to your house?" Bill asked. "Looking for this Blake guy?"

"Right. And we don't know where he is. But we're a little worried because we heard on the radio that a suspect in this murder was killed by the police. We don't know if it was Blake or not."

Bill sat up straighter. "You think the police might have shot Blake? That he's the killer?"

"We don't know," I said. "We really don't. But we're worried."

Karen and Bill exchanged a look, their faces pale.

"And we're worried about his fiancée, Sam," Amanda said. "You've met her, Mom. She came to the baby shower here."

Karen nodded as Henry squirmed on the floor next to her. "A sweet girl, yes. I remember her. The teacher."

"She's at the police station too. They wanted to talk to her about Blake. So it's kind of a stressful time."

"I hear you," Karen said. "But she's a smart girl. It's always up to the women to keep things together when the men do crazy stuff and go off the rails. Do you remember when your father wanted to buy a motorcycle and I had to talk him out of it?"

Bill ignored Karen as his face shifted from confusion to concern. "Do you want me to turn it off, honey? I can if it's upsetting either of you. A young girl dying like this. I guess it's upsetting to all of us. They showed her parents this morning . . . coming into the police station." He swallowed. Hard. "It's hell for them."

And my mind went to the Steiners. To Dawn. If Amanda's family found out about the accident, about my being the driver . . . everything would come up again. The old scabs and scars would break open like a fault in the earth.

"I know, Dad. But we want to watch it. We just . . . It could be difficult. For all of us."

"Keep the volume lower, Bill," Karen said.

The commercial ended, and first we saw the anchor in the studio, and then they threw the feed back to the reporter at the police station. She held a piece of paper in front of her and, just as Bill turned the volume back up, she told us that she had breaking news from a source inside the police department. They had learned the identity of the man killed by the police earlier that day.

My hand fumbled in the space between Amanda and me until it gripped hers. When it did, I squeezed tight, and she squeezed back. Her skin felt warm. Comforting.

I had no idea how much this announcement meant to me. I had no idea how much I feared hearing that Blake was dead. I felt a variety of emotions for him, many of them negative. And I had no idea what he might have done to Jennifer.

But to think of his life being extinguished, to think of him losing his cool so much that the police killed him, how could it even be possible? The fear I felt traveled through me like freezing water, chilling every outpost of my body. I pulled Amanda a little closer, hoping for warmth.

"Police say the man killed this morning and a suspect in the death of Jennifer Bates was twenty-eight-year-old Kyle Dornan, a resident of Rossingville—"

Amanda yelled so loud everyone looked at her. Even Henry.

She held her hand to her chest. Her eyes were wide, filled with emotion.

I tried to shuffle through my feelings. Relief, yes. I felt relief. Also shock. Horror. Fear.

Fear. That man Kyle Dornan. He'd come so close to our lives. He'd come to our house. And whatever he'd done with the police was enough for them to kill him.

"That's not your friend, is it?" Bill asked. "So that's good, isn't it?"

"It is good, Dad," Amanda said. "It isn't Blake."

"Are you relieved, honey?" Karen asked. "Why do you look that way?"

Amanda breathed deeply. Her chest rose and fell like she'd just run a fast mile. Her lips looked cracked and dry.

"He's not our friend," Amanda said. "Not at all. But we know him too. He came to our house this morning."

CHAPTER FIFTY-SEVEN

Bill and Karen bombarded us with questions right away, and it took Amanda long minutes of reassuring with calming words before they settled down to listen. Since it looked to be a longer conversation, Karen decided we all needed to eat something, so she went to the kitchen and started to take food out of the refrigerator and the cabinets. While she did that, the rest of us watched more of the news coverage, which offered little in terms of new information about the death of Kyle Dornan. Except when the reporter on the scene announced that sources inside the police department were telling her they believed Kyle Dornan was responsible for Jennifer Bates's death. Kyle had had a criminal record. He'd committed an assault while he was in college in another state. And he was currently wanted for another felony assault, something having to do with an altercation in a bar. I assumed it involved a jagged broken bottle and too much bourbon.

Police sources theorized he had resisted and taken a stand because of that outstanding charge. If he had gone into custody, he'd have faced the music. He had opted to go down swinging.

I checked my phone as much as I could, refreshing the Twitter feed in desperate hope of finding new information and growing agitated when none came. The fastest means of information spreading known to humanity, and it wasn't fast enough for me.

Amanda gestured to me, telling me to put the phone away, as we all moved to the dining room table, and while we ate—sandwiches and chips and some kind of insanely gorgeous and fresh fruit salad Karen seemed to have conjured out of thin air—Amanda finished telling her parents about Kyle's appearance at our house. She spared them no detail, and both of her parents gasped repeatedly and shook their heads, a combination of indignation at Kyle's craziness and fear for their daughter's and grandson's safety.

I added my own encounter with Kyle at Blake and Samantha's house. The way he had broken in, the bottle he had menaced me with, his rush to get out of the house and avoid the police. They showed less concern for me than they did for Amanda and Henry—only to be expected—but when I finished, Bill attempted to sum it all up nicely for the table.

"Well," he said, still chewing, a dab of mayonnaise on his chin, "good riddance to him. And you should get that alarm system. Listen to what I'm telling you. Innocent people, families—they're vulnerable. You know, I've been thinking of getting a handgun—"

"Dad, not the gun again. Okay? Not that."

My own feelings about those events we'd learned of on the news ran a more complicated gamut. I tried hard to reconcile my relief that Kyle would not be able to come back and menace Amanda or Henry or anybody else with the horror at the violent death of another human being. I certainly would have preferred that Kyle had surrendered, had a trial, and faced whatever music he needed to face without dying, but it was all beyond my control.

Could his death possibly signal a return to some semblance of normalcy? Did it mean Amanda and Henry could return home and have nothing to worry about?

While we ate, the news continued to play. A different reporter came on camera and told us that police were compiling a case against Kyle, one that included forensic evidence from the scene as well as the statements of friends and family who thought Kyle was growing too possessive and controlling of Jennifer in recent weeks.

"What a creep," Bill said. Mercifully, he'd swallowed his food first.

I exchanged a look with Amanda. I saw the relief in her eyes. She said to me what I was thinking.

"Maybe this takes the heat off Blake. Maybe he can come back from wherever he is."

"I hope so."

It was a measure of how crazy and upside down things had become that even Amanda summoned empathy for Blake, who had found himself a person of interest in Jennifer's death. While I harbored my own anger toward him for so many things, not the least of which was involving me in Jennifer's death by sending me into her house the night before, I shared that relief with Amanda. Some of the weight that had been pressing down on my shoulders had been lifted.

But I still had Dawn Steiner and her looming deadline to deal with.

One thing at a time . . .

"Just don't let him hold Henry anymore," Karen said. "You have to be careful with those things."

"Excuse me," I said, and stood up from the table.

As I left the room, I heard Amanda assuring both of her parents that Blake wouldn't be holding Henry anytime soon.

"He's getting married this weekend," Amanda said. "And Sam's a good influence. He might be ready to grow up. . . ."

As I walked to the front of the house, I started to recognize a shift in my perspective. Compared to Kyle Dornan, trying to break down the door of our house, Blake seemed like an okay guy. If the worst thing he ever did in Amanda's eyes was bonk our baby's head against a lampshade, then he seemed to be doing okay.

I went into the living room, which was small, overfurnished, and barely used. In fact, I didn't think I'd ever spent any real time in there. When Karen and Bill hosted parties—at Christmas, say, or for the Kentucky Derby—their guests usually just threw their coats on the couch in there.

I looked over my shoulder to make sure I was alone and then I called Blake. And I waited while the phone rang incessantly.

"Come on. Come on."

I heard the voice mail greeting again. I tried one more time, and on the third ring, he answered.

"Finally," I said.

"Hey. Sorry."

"Where have you been? What's going on?"

"It's a long story," he said.

"I can imagine. But I'd like to know what you've been doing. The cops have been looking for you. Sam is worried about you. And this guy, this Kyle Dornan guy—did you hear about him?"

"Yes, I did. I just heard it on the car radio." He let out a relieved sigh. "Yeah, it's pretty crazy, isn't it? I mean really, really crazy."

"Have you talked to Sam again?"

"I'm going to talk to her. Soon. You know, she's dealing with a lot too."

"She's at the police station," I said. "At least, she was the last I knew. The detective working the case wanted to bring her in and talk to her about everything that was going on. I guess mostly she wanted to ask her about you."

"Oh, yeah," he said. "Sure. I'll get ahold of her. The police really wanted to talk to her?"

"What do you expect? She's the person closest to you."

"Right."

"I'll let you go if you want to get on that," I said. "She's probably worried. And scared."

I chose not to tell him about Kyle trying to break into our houses. There wasn't enough time to explain it all, and I wanted to let him talk to Sam. She could explain it to him. And if he needed to know more, we could talk about it at another time, when things were less frantic and rushed.

"Okay, I'm going to let you go call her."

"Wait," he said.

"What?"

"There's something else I need you to do," he said, his voice level. "Something only you can do for me."

"Blake, what the hell else could you want? I went into that house. I risked everything."

"This is an easy request, okay? Just meet me at your house."

CHAPTER FIFTY-EIGHT

I drove back across town, back to our house to meet Blake.

I'd made my excuses to Amanda and her parents, telling them I had something to take care of. It took a little convincing to get Amanda to agree to stay behind. Having Henry in an unfamiliar place made it tougher to keep him on his schedule, although neither he nor his grandparents minded in the least. But I told Amanda it was better if she stayed, if she remained there a little while longer, until we were sure all the dust had cleared.

She walked with me to the door and told me how relieved she was that Kyle was out of the picture.

"I know I'm not supposed to feel that way," she said. "In fact, I feel awful just thinking those kinds of thoughts. But he scared me. He really did. And to think . . . he killed someone, Ryan, and he came and tried to get into our house. With Henry there."

"I know. I know."

We held each other longer than we usually did outside of our home. I breathed in her scent, a hint of vanilla from her shampoo. I didn't think she'd showered that morning, but it didn't matter. She smelled better than I did on any day. And I took in her scent like it was oxygen filling me with strength and resolve.

Amanda stepped back but not completely out of my grip. She looked up at me.

"I have a feeling I know who you're going to see," she said, her face showing concern.

"He finally answered his phone. We're just going to talk at the house. He's been through a lot the last day or so. It can't be easy to have the police looking for you like that."

Amanda remained quiet, still looking up at me. And my mind scrambled to come up with a counterargument as the TV played in the background, punctuated by the sounds of Henry's gurgling.

But Amanda continued to surprise me with her reaction to Blake.

"I know he's your friend," she said. "You've known him longer than you've known me."

"I like you better. You're much prettier."

"Seriously," she said. "I know he might be in our lives to some extent. I know that none of us are perfect. Maybe I'm trying to be more forgiving of everybody. I don't want to have such harsh reactions to people like I do sometimes. It doesn't make me feel very good."

"I just want to have you and Henry around. No one else matters."

We kissed before I went out the door. Before she shut it behind me, she said, "It will be nice to have all of this in the past."

I expected Blake to be waiting for me, but when I pulled up to the house, I found the driveway empty, everything placid. We'd left in such a hurry, we hadn't bothered to open the blinds or turn off the porch light.

As I approached the back door, keys jangling in my hand, I couldn't help but think about Kyle pounding the wooden surface just a few hours ago, as alive as I was. And so quickly he was wiped out of the world, extinguished like a fragile flame.

I went inside. The quiet in the house emphasized how much I'd grown used to the noises Henry and Amanda had made going about their day during the last six months. Henry's increased chatter and Amanda's steady, persistent conversation with him, the clacks and clangs of dishes and toys. Even when he slept, we listened to him breathe through the baby monitor. For a moment, I saw a flash of my life without them, and I breathed a little easier knowing Kyle was gone. Knowing Blake, one of my oldest friends, wasn't a killer.

In the office, I opened my laptop. Somehow, through a great application of willpower, I managed not to look at all the e-mails that had accumulated in one morning away from the office. I knew they waited for me, the number of messages increasing by the minute, but I'd promised Blake I'd take care of this for him.

He hadn't told me what he wanted to see. If Blake had dropped Jennifer's phone in her neighborhood, as he'd said he was going to, then the data on my computer might be quite valuable to the police, who were trying to put the finishing touches on her murder investigation. I tried to tell myself that since they had their man, they really didn't need anything I had. But I knew that was a foolish argument. Even being certain of Kyle's role in Jennifer's death, they still needed to be able to close the case, to prove what they believed and shut the book once and for all.

I had promised Blake I'd wait for him. But I had also told him I didn't know how long I felt comfortable keeping that information out of the hands of the police. He needed to show up and do whatever he wanted to do, and then we were going to hand it over.

Except he didn't show up.

I waited ten minutes. Then fifteen. I called him. Twice.

No answer.

So I texted. What gives? Where are you?

It took another five minutes before he wrote back.

Sorry, buddy. It will make sense soon enough. I promise.
Peace.

I stared at the phone. Something seemed odd about the text. Very odd.

Peace?

Blake had never, ever used the word "peace" once in his life. It didn't sound like him at all.

What was going on now?

CHAPTER FIFTY-NINE

But I wasn't sure what I could do about it. Or if it was anything worth thinking about.

Perhaps the events of the past night and day had worked together to turn me into a paranoid freak, someone who saw danger and conspiracy in the most mundane things.

I listened to the quiet house, heard the tick of a clock from another room. The information on the computer screen from Jennifer's phone waited for me.

I remembered the series of messages between Jennifer and Kyle, the ones I'd seen last night while Amanda and Henry slept above me. I looked at them again, and in light of the recent events, they struck me as particularly chilling. Especially the last thing Kyle said to Jennifer:

We need to settle this. I need to know. Now.

I looked around at other texts, focusing on messages Jennifer had exchanged with women. I wondered if she'd had friends she'd confided in, anyone who could have known Jennifer was in danger and could have stopped it. I found nothing to indicate that, and even if I had found such a thing, what difference would it have made? The image of Jennifer's body stretched on the floor, cold and alone, pulsed in my mind. Such a lonely way to die . . . and I wanted to believe something could have prevented it. Somehow I thought that would make it more sensible.

A fool's errand.

And what did it say about me? I felt like a ghoul, sifting through the electronic remains of a murder victim. We all spent so much of our time looking through and observing one another electronically, through social media photos and posts and texts. Scrolling through my social media feeds made me feel like a voyeur, but it was nothing compared to seeing someone's private messages this way.

But I kept looking, telling myself I would do it just a few minutes longer.

I finished looking at the text messages and decided to check something else. I started searching through the messages that had come through Jennifer's Facebook account. Those messages also showed up on the download, and the possibility struck me that Jennifer might have spoken to someone through that platform instead of a text. Maybe she had talked to someone there about her problems with Kyle? Maybe a friend or family member had offered her advice and comfort there?

I gave myself a five-minute time limit. When five minutes had elapsed, I promised myself I'd close the software and back away, leaving Jennifer's private conversations behind forever. Maybe by then Blake would have arrived. Then he could do what he wanted to do, and we could hand everything over to the police.

The list of messages unfurled. I scanned quickly, looking for familiar names. Kyle's was on there, but the messages he exchanged with her were mundane and rare. They made plans, sounded happy. I saw nothing from Blake, of course. He would have kept his communications with Jennifer limited to texts. When I clicked on some of the other names—friends, coworkers, acquaintances—not much was revealed. I saw exchanges about birthday parties, happy hours, a question about whether she was happy with the model of car she'd purchased the year before and what kind of gas mileage she was getting. And I saw the messages she had sent to me, the ones Amanda had encountered on my computer.

It all made me sad. A person's life reduced to these mundane discussions. What else had Jennifer left behind? I knew so little about her. She'd passed along the periphery of my life without leaving any real mark. If I'd known a man like Kyle had harassed her, maybe I could have helped. But how often did anyone confide in a stranger? And that was what we had been to each other when all was said and done.

I can't say why I clicked on the last conversation. The name of the person writing to Jennifer struck me as almost bland. Lily Rose. But no photo accompanied the name, which seemed odd if she and Jennifer were friends. Maybe that was why I clicked there, because the lack of a profile picture and the blandness of the name stood out to me amid all the other noise and messages.

What I saw froze me in place. I stared at the screen, my mouth dropping open.

This Lily Rose person had sent Jennifer a flurry of messages in the last twenty-four hours of Jennifer's life. They were read by Jennifer, but she'd chosen not to respond.

This isn't over.

You can't do this.

Who do you think you are?

It's going to get bad for you. Very, very bad.

I'm coming.

CHAPTER SIXTY

First, I took a screenshot of the conversation. Then I called Blake again, and this time when I received his voice mail greeting, I insisted he call me as soon as possible.

"I don't care where you are or what you're doing—you need to call me."

Kyle might have created a fake account, an alias, to be able to write to Jennifer and threaten her. I knew that people sometimes created fake accounts in order to reach out to people who might have blocked them. But if Kyle was heading over to Jennifer's house the night she died, had they completely fallen out?

And given the nature of the threats, wouldn't she have gone to the police?

Maybe she had. The cops felt compelled to tell me only things that involved me. Nothing else. When they referred on the radio to other suspects and evidence, that could have been it. They might already have known someone else had made threats against Jennifer.

Lily Rose's Facebook profile showed nothing. No photos, no personal information. A ghost. Spam accounts popped up all over social media, accounts meant to generate clicks and spread advertising, but I'd never heard of one being created just to threaten someone. Someone who later ended up being murdered on the floor of her own bedroom.

I considered sending a message to that account but decided against it. If I didn't hear from Blake, I'd go to the police on my own. I'd tell them what they needed to know and hope for no more involvement.

As if my mind had been read, the phone rang. It jarred me so much, the hard, insistent ringing, that I jumped in my seat, my heart racing like it had received a massive shot of caffeine.

"Thank God," I said. "Blake."

Except it wasn't. The caller ID screen told me Amanda was calling.

A dark shadow fell over my mind. Why was she calling? It made sense she would just be checking in, but something felt off—

"Hello?"

"I think you need to come over here," she said in the low voice she used when Henry napped.

"Did something happen? Is Henry okay?"

"He's okay. He's good. He's in the other room with my parents. I'm trying to keep them from hearing me."

"Why?"

"Look, can you just come back? Are you done with whatever Blake wanted?"

"He didn't show."

"Well, I'm sorry you went over there for nothing," she said. "Look, come back. Okay? We need to talk. I'd get my dad to drive me over there, but he'd just ask a bunch of questions. They both would. And I'm not up for that right now. I want us to talk first. Okay?"

"And you're not going to tell me about what?"

"So you're coming back over?" she asked, her voice brightening.

I heard Karen talking in the background. She must have come in, and was hovering over Amanda like she was a teenager plotting with her boyfriend.

"Okay. See you soon."

If Amanda's goal had been to light a fire under me, it worked. I rushed through the house, out to the back door. I dropped my keys and then kicked them, like I was in a one-man Three Stooges routine. When I straightened up from grabbing them, somebody called my name.

A familiar voice.

I looked over to the garage. Blake emerged from around the corner, looking like he hadn't slept in a month. His clothes were disheveled, his hair wild.

"What the hell happened to you?" I asked.

"I thought you were meeting me here."

"I was. Now Amanda needs me. And I'm sorry, but I take her wishes more seriously than yours. Especially when you're late."

"It was unavoidable."

"It must have been. You look like you couldn't avoid the tractor that rolled over you."

He sighed and leaned against the side of the garage. In the bright sunlight, I saw a bruise on his left cheek. His shirt hung out of his pants, and his shoes were covered with mud.

"I'm tired," he said.

"So am I. Tired of all of this. And I want it finished. I thought that's why we were meeting here today. We were going to do something together, and that would be the end of this. Kyle killed Jennifer. And he's dead. So what else is there?"

"I just wanted to look at that stuff from Jen's phone before we go to the police. I just want to see it."

"Why? Never mind. There's plenty to see."

My phone chimed. Amanda.

Are you on your way?

I should have been driving. She hated it when I glanced at my phone while I was driving. And my car was too old to have the most up-to-date Bluetooth technology that read your texts to you.

"I have to go," I said. "And after all the craziness of the last day, I don't want anyone in the house. Can we do this later?"

"It can't wait."

"Why?"

"Ryan, just let me in to see it. There are things going on with Sam. I just need to figure some things out. Okay?"

"Wait until I get back."

"Ryan. It needs to happen now. I told you—you could still be exposed. Do you want that to happen? Do you? Just let me see the data from the phone."

"No, get lost. Too many people have been hurt already."

"I agree, Ryan. Damn it." His voice rose higher than I'd ever heard it. His eyes were misted by emotion. "Just . . . Can you just do this for me? I know I've asked for a lot. Okay? I know I've stirred up a whole shit storm. I get it. And if you don't ever want to see me again when this is over, then so be it. Okay? Just do this for me. Okay?"

I'd never heard him plead that way. Never heard him being so achingly sincere.

"Are you in more trouble?" I asked. "Are you okay?"

"Just let me in. Then you can be done with me."

I wanted to say no, but I couldn't. I just couldn't.

"Okay. But get out of there before we come back."

I went over and unlocked the back door. When I turned, he still leaned against the garage.

"Come on," I said. "I'm in a hurry now."

He pushed off the garage and came over, his steps slow and deliberate. He looked like a kid on his way to the principal's office.

"What's wrong with you? Aren't you off the hook now?"

He nodded, some life and energy returning to his body. "Sure. I'm just tired. It's been a hell of a night. And day."

"Come on."

He followed me in, down the hallway, and to the office. While I opened the laptop and entered the password, he sank into a chair. I pointed at the screen.

"It's all there. Everything from her phone. Texts, contacts, social media messages. You should check out the ones from Facebook. Somebody was threatening her. Big-time. We have to tell the police about that. In fact, you should call them right away. Or I will when I get to my in-laws' house."

He nodded. Calm. He seemed unbothered by the threats.

"Call me when you're finished. I'm going over there to get Amanda."

I started to go, but by the time I reached the office door, he still hadn't said anything.

"Did you hear me?" I asked. "You'll call?"

"Yeah," he said. "I'm on it."

I left, but his voice stopped me again.

"Seriously, Ryan," he said. "Thanks for everything. You're a good friend."

"Are you feeling sentimental or something? What gives?"

"I'm just thanking you. Okay?"

My phone chimed again. I locked the door behind me and took off without saying anything else.

CHAPTER SIXTY-ONE

Since I couldn't drive and check my Twitter feed at the same time—something I silently lamented—I turned the car radio on as I headed back to my in-laws' house. News about Kyle and the investigation into Jennifer's death had slowed to a trickle. The radio mindlessly scanned through all the stations, beeping each time it landed on a new one, but only sports, information about a flower show, and a minister imploring us all to return to Jesus and give up our sinful ways came through.

The sky clouded over, and the wind picked up, shaking the trees and bushes as I entered the subdivision. The April weather was changeable, jumping from sun to clouds at random. I looked forward to the coming weeks when it would calm, when we could take Henry to the park and push him around the walking trail in his stroller, the flowers in bloom, the winter far behind.

I eased to a stop at the end of the driveway. Before I pushed the door open, Amanda came out and headed over to me. I watched her through the glass, struck by how much she looked like Karen. They both walked in the same brisk manner, as though they were always on a mission to accomplish something decidedly important. Amanda pulled her sweatshirt tighter across her body as she walked, protection against the rising of the chilly wind. Her hair blew across her face, and she brushed it away before opening the door and settling in the passenger seat.

"Are you sure you're okay?" I asked.

Her cheeks were flushed, her breathing faster than normal. "I'm fine. I guess. And Henry's perfectly fine. My parents are undoing any routine and structure we've established. But I guess that's what grandparents do."

"They do know something about raising kids, don't they?"

"Yes, they do."

"So, what is going on that I had to rush back here?"

I'd wondered the whole way if someone had tracked Amanda and Henry to her parents' house. Had it been someone like Dawn, jumping the gun on her own deadline?

But Amanda still didn't answer my question.

"Where's Blake?" she asked. "Did he show up?"

I couldn't lie. I just couldn't. The thought of not telling the truth made me feel tired. "He's at our house."

"Doing what?"

"He needed to use my computer."

"He's *in* our house?"

"You called me away, so I left him there. It's a long story. It was the easiest thing to do in the moment. At least Henry isn't there. If anyone hits their head on a lamp, it will be Blake."

"Why does he— Never mind. I don't need to know. I can tolerate you being friends with him, but there are limits."

"What is so urgent here?" I asked. "I thought everything would be quiet."

Amanda fumbled around and brought out her phone. She entered the pass code and clicked around. Then she extended the phone to me, almost pressing it against my face.

"Who is that?" she asked.

It took me a moment to take the phone from her hand and hold it in such a way that I could actually see the screen. Amanda seemed frantic, her energy odd and rushed. It felt like being in the car with a nervous cat.

I recognized the face on the screen. Immediately.

"That's Kyle Dornan. So?"

"Are you sure?"

"Of course. I saw him up close at Blake's house. I stood face-to-face with him while he waved a broken liquor bottle at me. You saw him too."

Amanda shook her head, her cheeks still flushed. Her eyes were wide and searching. Scared, I realized. She was scared. Rattled.

"What?"

"Ryan, that is *not* the guy who came to the house this morning. Whoever came to our door and said he was sorry the girl got killed, it was *not* Kyle Dornan."

CHAPTER SIXTY-TWO

The wind picked up even more outside the car. It gently rocked the vehicle from side to side. A storm brewed, the clouds darkening behind the jagged rooflines of the houses.

"You're wrong," I said. "You're just remembering it wrong."

"You're telling me how I remember something?"

I shifted my body to better face her. I handed the phone back. "You were under stress. You had this man, this maniac, pushing against the door. You thought you were fighting for your life. For Henry's life. You said that yourself. Your brain was flooded with adrenaline and cortisol. How can your memory be reliable?"

Her lips parted. A little disbelief. A little anger. "His face was six inches from mine. I felt spit hit my face when he was talking. I thought this man who came to the door, whoever he was, was going to come in and hurt Henry. You better believe I imprinted his face on my mind's eye. I wanted to be able to describe him to the police. I wanted to make sure of that."

"But when Rountree came to the house, when we talked about him, you agreed with the description. Short hair. My height. Clean-cut."

"Hell, Ryan, that's half the men on the planet. He was unremarkable looking. Unremarkable in general. Except he wanted to tear the door down and get at me for some reason. He was foaming at the mouth. Other than that, yeah, he looked like a regular guy. I thought we were talking about the same person. It seemed that way."

Rain splattered against the windshield. I stared out through the speckled drops.

"This doesn't make sense," I said. "You're saying someone else came to the house looking for me. Or Blake. Someone else said it was a shame the girl got killed. I don't get it. . . ."

"I don't either."

"You didn't see anybody with him, did you? You didn't mention anyone. But are you sure he was alone? Could there have been a woman with him?"

Amanda's face went cross with suspicion. "Why do you keep asking me about a woman? Ryan, you're acting like you know something I don't. What woman would be coming to the house?"

The front door opened, distracting both of us, and then Karen came out. She strode down the sidewalk and over to our car, holding an umbrella above her head.

"What the hell does she want?" I asked.

"Easy, Ryan," Amanda said. "I'll deal with her. She's my mother and she's worried. She's worried about you too."

Karen went around to the passenger side, and Amanda powered down the window. "What is it, Mom?"

"I didn't know you were coming out here. It's about to pour."

"We needed to talk about something," Amanda said.

Karen's eyes roamed over me and then back to her daughter. "Well." She wanted an explanation but didn't want to be seen as the kind of mother who asked for such things. She wanted one offered to her without having to ask. "Henry seems to be getting tired. Is it okay if he goes to sleep?"

"It's fine. Thank you."

But Karen stayed in place. Rain started to fall in through the open window, landing on the doorframe and Amanda's jeans.

Karen leaned over more. "Are you staying for dinner, Ryan?"

"I don't know, Karen."

"Okay. Well, you're welcome. You're both always welcome."

"Mom, really. Thank you, but can we just have a minute alone?"

Karen nodded, looking a little hurt, and walked away, finally allowing Amanda to roll the window back up. I watched her cross in front of the car and up the sidewalk to the door. She disappeared into the house.

"What are we going to do about this, Ryan?"

Amanda brought me back into the present moment, to our exchange in the car. Her voice always did that. Everything about her did that. She tethered me to the ground, which lately seemed to constantly be shifting. She was doing one of the things she did best—stepping back, focusing, trying to see things with the clearest eye.

"What did this guy look like?" I asked. "If he wasn't Kyle, then what did he look like? And we need to have more than 'average height.'"

Amanda folded her hands in her lap while she spoke in a calm voice. "He had brown eyes. Pretty eyes, really, which seemed incongruous while he was trying to attack me. He looked clean-cut, like I said, not like a homeless guy or anything." She pursed her lips while other details came back to her. "His teeth." She lifted her hand and pointed at her mouth. "They weren't as nice as the rest of him. Not white. Not like someone who regularly went to the dentist. In fact, I think he had one missing, along the side and near the back of his mouth. That seemed strange. Everything else about him looked well maintained, but not the teeth."

"Tattoos? Accent? Anything?"

"No. He sure seemed strong, pressing against that door. But maybe he wasn't as strong as he seemed. I held him off."

"You're pretty strong. Remember what you did to that woman at the soccer match."

"My crowning glory. Knocking down another woman."

Amanda appeared to be lost in thought, likely trying to summon other details of her encounter with . . . whoever he was. But my mind started down a darker tunnel, one with little light at the end. Amanda had been curious enough to look at my Facebook messages. Curious and insecure during her pregnancy. She spoke about feeling cornered, recognizing that sensation on Samantha's face.

And she'd gone out the day before when I was supposed to be coming home from work. And hadn't mentioned it to me until I asked.

Had all of it driven Amanda to pay a visit to Jennifer? And had it gone wrong?

Something hot and choking burned at the back of my throat. I swallowed, cracking the window a little to let some fresh air in.

"Are you hot?" she asked.

"I'm fine. It's stuffy."

Amanda studied me, her eyes narrowing with concern and curiosity. Had she read my mind and understood what I'd been thinking? If she had, she didn't let on. She went ahead, trying to solve the problem.

"I can't really remember anything else about him," she said. "You're right. It was stressful. And fast. But I know what I saw." She tapped her phone. "Kyle Dornan was not at our door. Not unless he went out and bought some kind of *Mission: Impossible* mask to hide his identity. We have to tell Rountree," she said. "We don't have a choice."

"You're right."

The rain started to fall with greater strength. The wipers were off, and soon the view was obscured by water.

"We didn't do anything wrong, Ryan," she said. "It was a misunderstanding. We all just assumed that man was Kyle Dornan. And the police believe he killed Jennifer. This doesn't mean he didn't do it. He was involved with her. It's always someone who was involved with the victim. We have to remember that. The suspicion always falls on those men who are involved with the murder victim."

"Usually it works that way."

"That's because usually it's some idiot man doing something to a woman. *Usually.*"

We still didn't even know exactly how Kyle had died. What he had done to bring down the wrath of the police. Where he'd been or why. But I felt acutely responsible for his death.

I felt the urge to take out my phone and check Twitter, but I knew Amanda would find that rude.

"If we hadn't said he was at our house, the police might not have been so hot to talk to him," I said. "Maybe he would have just left town. Or surrendered."

"He broke into Blake's house too. He threatened you. You just said he used that broken bottle. He had a record. And you *know* that was Kyle Dornan. They can still close the case against him."

Her words made complete sense. As much sense as anything else. But they brought little comfort.

"This means someone else came to our house," I said, working through the crazy news. "Someone else wanted to break in and do us harm. Someone else said it was a shame the girl was killed."

"It's terrifying." Amanda held the phone out to me. "Do you want to call Rountree? Or should I?"

I took out my phone and called the detective.

CHAPTER SIXTY-THREE

It took fifteen minutes to get ahold of Rountree. We sat in the car while we called her and left messages. Karen came out only one more time, an umbrella opened over her perfectly coiffed short hair, and received a firm but polite brush-off from Amanda. When Rountree finally answered, and Amanda told her about the man at the back door not being Kyle Dornan, the detective promised she would come over to Karen and Bill's house as soon as she could.

But as soon as she could might turn into an hour or more.

So we waited inside the house. While Henry slept, we sat around the dining room table, the remains of lunch long gone, and Amanda filled her parents in on the latest about Kyle Dornan, that he wasn't the man who had come to the house looking for Blake and me.

Karen and Bill listened to the new information with their hands raised to their chests. While it didn't take Amanda long to tell them, they both managed to gasp and exclaim three or four times as she spoke.

When she finished telling them, Karen asked, "Does that mean there's another maniac on the loose? Could he have followed you here?"

"He's not following us," I said. Although I really didn't know. I didn't know anything for sure. "If he was following us around, he would have been here already. And you have different last names than we do, so how could he associate you with us?"

"It's not hard to do," Bill said. "You look someone up on the Internet, and you see all the people they're connected to. He could do that."

Bill sounded so practical. Just like his daughter. I'd hoped for words that would bring greater peace of mind. But those words weren't coming.

"Okay," I said with less confidence, "but he hasn't yet. And the police are on their way."

"Maybe we should go to a hotel," Bill said. "We could take Amanda and Henry there, get them out of harm's way. If the cops want to talk to them, they'll have to call me, and I can tell them where we are."

"Ryan," Karen said, "why would this man want to come after you this way? Do you have any idea?"

Three sets of eyes turned to me. Had Henry been awake and bouncing in his seat, waiting for his next meal, his likely would have joined them.

"I really don't know. I can't think of who this man is."

"Could it be someone from work?" Bill asked. "Someone you fired or someone who feels they got cheated out of something?"

The same thing had started racing through my mind when Amanda gave me the news out in the car, and it continued to run beneath my conscious thoughts like an underground stream. Given a moment to sit and think about it, even with my wife and in-laws present before me, I brought those thoughts to the surface of my mind. I scanned through the catalog of recent events at work and at the Pig, hoping, really, that something would jump out. A disgruntled employee or client I could blame. A vendor who had walked away from work feeling cheated or misused.

Dawn Steiner with a male friend?

"I can't think of anything obvious. I work in PR, and I own a stake in a bar. The most anger I encounter or hear about there is someone thinking we charge too much for beer."

Bill leaned forward, scratching his cheek thoughtfully. "But this guy who came to your house, the one who banged on the door and tried to get in after Amanda and Henry—he mentioned you and your friend Blake. The one you were talking about earlier. Is there someone who could have a beef with both of you?"

"Big enough that he wanted to come to the house and act that way," Amanda said, her voice low. "Like a maniac."

"We don't work together. We don't have any connections like that. We haven't spent much time together lately."

"Someone like Blake has probably pissed a lot of people off in his life," Karen said. And all the eyes in the room swiveled to her. The word "pissed" coming out of her mouth struck us all as a bizarre breach of decorum for Karen, who usually peppered her speech with phrases like "Oh, heck" and "Cussy darn." She looked right back at all of us. "Well, he did drop my grandson."

"He didn't drop him, Mom."

"Well, whatever he did, I don't like him. He drank a lot at your wedding."

"What about the toast he made?" I asked. "Or the china he went out of his way to find after Amanda mentioned it?"

Karen hesitated for a moment. "Well, I don't like this. I don't like any harm coming to members of my family."

But my mind quickly shifted, trailing off in a different direction. Karen was right—Blake had no doubt made a fair number of enemies in his time. If he'd been involved with Jennifer while he was on and off with Samantha, there was no telling how many other women he might have dated. And any one of them might have had a jealous boyfriend or husband. Any one might come trailing their own version of Kyle Dornan.

But how did that connect to me? Why would a jealous or bitter boyfriend or husband decide to come after me? And why say something about the girl getting killed?

"Excuse me," I said, standing up. "I'm going to call him."

"Good," Karen said. "It sounds like he needs to be asked some tough questions."

I ignored her and walked out to the living room, the line ringing and ringing as I moved.

CHAPTER SIXTY-FOUR

I hung up and tried again, and I kept expecting him to answer.

He'd been there for me so many times. I'd counted on him for so much. Despite everything he had dragged me into with Jennifer, I still expected him to come through. To answer.

Maybe I was a fool. But how hard was it to let go of the belief we had in people we cared about the most?

How hard was it to believe he could be letting me down at the biggest moment of them all?

I never would have let him in the house, never would have gone along with any of it except for the looming threat of the exposure of my role in the accident.

I sensed someone behind me. I knew it was Amanda.

I tried again and received no answer.

"He's not there?" she asked.

"He's not answering."

"He's supposed to be at our house, Ryan. You left him there, using your computer. Shouldn't he still be there?"

"I don't know. He didn't tell me what all he was doing."

"You have to tell Rountree about that when she gets here. Tell her Blake was at our house. You said he looked ragged. Maybe she knows something else—"

I put the phone in my pocket, felt its bulk against my thigh. "I'm going over there."

"Why? You should wait here for Rountree. We need to tell her about the man at the door."

"You can tell her," I said, moving away from her. "You saw him, not me."

"But I need you here. I want you here. With me and the baby and our family. I don't need you running around and not knowing where you are."

I wanted to stay. More than anything else.

But I couldn't.

"I'll call you when I can," I said before I leaned in to kiss her.

"Ryan. Don't. Let Blake deal with whatever he has to deal with. This guy is out there. He could be back at our house, looking for you."

Amanda didn't understand, couldn't understand, that Blake and I were tied together by things I couldn't talk about. Things she didn't know.

"Rountree will be here soon," I said. "You'll be okay here. If anyone comes to the door or sets foot in the yard who you don't know, call nine-one-one. Immediately."

"Anyone like this woman you keep asking me about?"

I ignored the question. "Just do what I said. Okay?"

I stepped out the door into the light rain, which I barely noticed.

CHAPTER SIXTY-FIVE

When I reached our house, I stopped in the alley a few doors down from where we lived. I replayed the moment from an hour or so earlier when Blake had emerged from behind the garage, his face pale, his clothes dirty. I hadn't seen his car. He'd simply appeared from behind the garage.

I wanted to be cautious, to avoid announcing my presence in case someone else—the man who had already been to our house once that day, for instance—lurked inside, watching or listening for a car.

I saw no other vehicles in the alley, nothing in our driveway. Cold, light rain continued to splat against the trees and the houses, but otherwise the neighborhood was silent. I approached the house, my shoes skimming through the standing water. Rain ran down my neck and underneath my shirt, mingling with the sweat that had already been there.

The back door came into sight. It was closed, unmarred. Everything looked normal. I brushed a raindrop off my cheek.

If someone watched from inside the house, they'd see me coming. But what could I do about that? I calmed myself by deciding that I was overreacting, that no crazy man was chasing after us, that Blake wasn't answering simply because he was involved with whatever questions he was trying to answer. Once he had those figured out, he'd be his old self. Jovial, teasing, loyal.

I took my keys out as I approached the back door. But before I put the key in the lock, I tried the knob, which turned freely. The door opened.

I felt like an intruder in my own house, trying to sneak in quietly. But why? What if Blake sat at my desk, looking for whatever he wanted to find, my calls ignored for some innocuous reason?

When I stepped into the kitchen, I called his name. I heard nothing, just the sound of my own voice.

I closed the door behind me, and I couldn't help but think of the night before when I had stepped into another house. It too had been quiet.

My heartbeat quickened. As the rain on my forehead and the sweat on my back dried, it grew cool, and I felt a chill despite the humid air outside. I looked in the corner of the kitchen. The baseball bat sat there, and it was a no-brainer for me to reach over and pick it up. It brought a measure of comfort, and I was more than happy to take security wherever I could find it.

"Blake?"

Nothing.

"Blake?"

I took slow, cautious steps, trying to be quiet. But since I'd already called out, it didn't matter. If there was anyone in the house, they either couldn't respond or didn't want to.

Neither possibility was comforting. And I thought about turning around and leaving.

But I didn't.

I turned the corner and went down the hall to the office. For some reason, the office door was closed. I closed the door from time to time when I worked in there and needed to block out the noise from Henry or Amanda's book club. But if no one was in there . . . why was it closed?

"Blake?"

I took a deep breath and gripped the bat tighter with my right hand. With my left, I turned the knob and pushed the office door open. As it swung wide, I braced myself, jumping into a batting stance, ready to swing at someone who might be on the other side preparing to charge at me.

But the office was empty.

I scanned the room, taking in every corner as quickly as I could. Under the desk. Behind the small file cabinet.

Nothing.

There were no closets in the room, nowhere else to hide. I even looked at the ceiling in case someone waited to drop down on me. But I saw nothing except the long crack in the plaster I needed to patch.

My shoulders slumped, and I relaxed my pose a little while still gripping the bat. I tried to get my breathing to return to normal, hoped my heart would slide back down out of my throat and into my chest.

I nearly yelped when my phone started to ring. I silenced it.

Something on the desk caught my eye. Or the absence of something.

The computer was gone. Along with Blake, the computer was gone.

CHAPTER SIXTY-SIX

I put the bat down, leaning it against my desk.

The phone rang and rang in my pocket.

I impressed myself by feeling calmer than I should have. My computer was gone. All my work. All my photos and personal items. Passwords, financial records.

Maybe I was numb. Maybe I expected so little from Blake, this was just one more disappointment.

I didn't expect it to be Blake on the phone. And I was right. Amanda's name was spelled out on the ID screen.

"He's not here," I said. "He's gone. My laptop is gone. He took my laptop."

"Ryan—"

"He's always been a loyal friend, but I think he's involved with something I can't understand. I think this might be more than I can understand."

"Ryan. Listen. Rountree is here and—"

"There's something else happening, something that doesn't involve Jennifer—"

"Ryan, I've got to tell you something."

Amanda spoke with such a harsh, almost frantic edge to her voice it froze me in place, cutting off my worries about Blake. My mind jumped tracks to worry about her. Had something happened there? Had the man shown up again?

But she had mentioned Rountree. She had said the police were there at Karen and Bill's house.

"What is it?" I asked. "What's wrong?"

"The police are here," she said. "They're asking a lot of questions. Ryan, where were you last night? And I need you to tell the truth. The absolute truth. You said you were going to play basketball at the Y, and I called you there. It didn't sound like you were at a basketball game. Where were you?"

I stood in the center of my office, in the middle of my house. A house we'd lived in for several years. Perhaps the most like home any-place had ever felt, with Amanda and Henry and the entire life we'd made there.

But as I looked around at the walls and the furniture, it shifted and became unfamiliar to me, almost unrecognizable, as though I'd stumbled into a stranger's life and house by mistake. Or else woken up there with no knowledge of how I'd arrived.

Amanda's voice, that tether that held me to the ground, sounded different as well. Her question, so sharp, so pointed, could only mean bad things for me. If the police were there and she was asking that question . . .

"You clearly know I wasn't at the Y last night."

"I do. And so do the police. They checked the records. You didn't swipe your card. They can check that. And guess what. The guys you said you were playing with weren't there either. In fact the whole league was shut down last night because there was a plumbing leak in the locker room. So where were you?"

I went over and sat on the small couch I kept under the window. It served nobly as a place to nap or read, and I often sat there with Henry in the morning, trying to give Amanda extra time to sleep. The walls, which had already started to feel unfamiliar and strange, seemed to continue shifting, moving toward me, making me feel dizzy.

Words wouldn't come. My mouth was dry, my throat blocked. I couldn't say it to Amanda. I couldn't tell her. Everything we'd built would shift.

Everything.

"I'll make it easy for you," she said. "You weren't at the Y. They know that. And a man who was out walking his dog last night saw you in Jennifer's neighborhood, just wandering around. He knows who you are. First, he described you to the police. He said he'd met you at the Pig before. You bought him a beer once. And then the cops showed him your picture. Rountree did. And he said he saw you walking near Jennifer's house. They've taken fingerprints from everything at the crime scene. They're going to turn the place upside down, looking for every hair or fiber they can find. If somebody sneezed in there, they'll know. So where were you? Tell me. I've got Rountree and two other cops in the house in one room and Henry and my parents in the other. Tell me something. Okay?"

"I don't understand, though." I forced the words out with great effort. Each one felt like a boulder I was pushing up a large hill. "They got Kyle Dornan. He's the one who wanted to hurt Jennifer. He's the one who resisted arrest. He's the guy. What does it matter what I did?"

"Don't you know?" she asked, her tone blunt.

"Know what?"

"You're always on your phone. Weren't you checking? Did you miss all the breaking news?"

"What news?"

"Kyle Dornan had a rock-solid alibi. The police just announced it.

At the time of Jennifer's death, he was in an emergency sales meeting at work. With three witnesses. He was in the meeting for hours. He couldn't have killed her. There's simply no way."

"But he resisted. Like a guilty man. He was wanted for assault."

I replayed it all. The break-in at Blake's house. The broken bottle. The running away from the police.

"They think he was afraid because of the outstanding charges against him. He had a temper. He threatened you with a broken bottle. How do you think he responded to cops coming after him? Didn't he run away when they came to Blake's house and he was there? Maybe he decided not to run this time. Maybe he decided to fight."

If Kyle hadn't done it . . . who had?

"Okay, okay." Again my mind turned back to the night before, when I was standing over Jennifer's body. The watch with the cracked face and the frozen hands: twelve fifteen. "I have an alibi too. I was at work when she died. She died around noon. Right?"

"No, she didn't. The police can approximate the time of death to within a range of a couple of hours. They're saying late afternoon or evening."

"Are you sure?"

"It's the medical examiner who figures these things out. Not me. Ryan, do you understand what I'm saying?" Amanda asked. "You're a full-blown suspect in this murder now. They're looking for *you*."

CHAPTER SIXTY-SEVEN

Her words stung me deep in the center of my torso, like a shock applied directly to my internal organs.

I popped up off the couch, ready to dash out of the room and out of the house. Away somewhere else, looking for safety or escape.

But as quickly as I had risen to my feet, my fight-or-flight instinct engaged, I froze.

Where did I think I was going to go? Was I going to climb into my car and drive five hundred miles away? Head for a city or state on the far side of the country? Was I going to start my life over?

What would I be leaving behind?

Everything.

"Is Rountree still there? Did you say?"

I couldn't remember. My mind felt scrambled, like a radio with a busted antenna.

"She's here. She's right here with two other cops. I told you that. And she wants to talk to you. Ryan, they're asking me things about you . . . like they think you're guilty. I wouldn't be surprised if there wasn't a cop car on the way to our house already."

"You told them I was here?" I asked.

"Of course. That was the first thing they asked me. I told them you went there to meet Blake. Was I supposed to lie?"

"No," I said. "Of course not. Can you . . . ?" I took a series of deep breaths, tried to focus my mind. The images and thoughts swirling there came into clarity. As I thought of what to say and do, a calm came over me quickly. "Look, just tell Rountree I'm coming over there. Tell her I'm on my way to Karen and Bill's. I'll explain everything."

"What do you mean? Is there something to explain, Ryan?" Amanda asked. "What could it possibly be? Can you explain it to me first? Your wife."

"I'll tell you everything when I get there," I said. "It's Blake . . . but I can't blame him for all of it. It's me too. It's really about me."

The other end of the line grew silent. I waited, listening to the silence that meant Amanda was gathering her thoughts.

"Ryan, are you trying to tell me . . . Were you involved with Jennifer? Was there more to it than the Facebook messages I saw?"

"No, not like that," I said. "Nothing like that."

My phone buzzed. I held the screen out where I could see the identity of the new caller.

Blake.

I told Amanda he was calling.

"I think I should take it," I said. "I should see what he's doing. He needs to know about Kyle. And that the cops are looking for me. All of it."

"Then you're coming over here, right?"

"Right," I said. "I promise."

"Be careful. Okay? Just come over here, and we'll deal with all of it. I know you're not perfect. None of us are. I'm certainly not. And all of this is making me afraid. The police, the questions. The way they want to tear into everything about us."

I wanted to ask what she was talking about.

"Ryan, we can just go somewhere else. Maybe we should, somewhere all of this can't reach us."

"Why would you say that? What's going on?"

"I'm just trying to help. Forget I said that."

But Blake's call kept insisting on being answered.

"I'll be there soon," I said. "Tell the police."

I switched over to Blake's call, and at first, he said nothing.

"Blake? Where the hell are you? Where's my computer?"

The sound of breathing and then something shuffling.

"Ryan? I need you to listen to me."

"No, Blake, you need to listen to me. The cops have cleared Kyle. He had an alibi. It's us they're looking for. Me. They're looking for me. Some guy saw me by Jennifer's house. They think I know something. They might think I killed her."

"Ryan—"

"The cops are waiting for me, and I'm going to go over there and tell them what I know. They're probably testing hair fibers or fingerprints or something from Jennifer's house. You need to go along too. I can pick you up. But we have to come clean. Bring that computer so we can show them the stuff from Jennifer's phone—"

"Ryan, listen. *Listen.*"

He shouted the last word. The sound came through the phone like the slicing of a blade. It stung my ear, so I had to move the phone away and then back into place.

"Are *you* listening to me?" I asked.

"Ryan, I need you to do what I say. You need to listen very carefully because there isn't much time. And I have to get this out."

"What are you talking about, Blake?"

"Do you know that condo development out on Gap Springs Road? The one they started and never finished?"

"Hilldale Estates? Yes, why?"

"I need you to come out here. I'm already here. With your computer. You've got to get here too."

"Why? You're crazy. We have to get to the police. Now. Or they're going to lock us up and not let us out until Henry is a grandfather."

"No, we can't. You have to come here. Ryan . . ." It sounded like someone took the phone or placed their hand over it. Muffled sounds. Maybe another voice? And then Blake was back. "Come out here, or people will get hurt."

"Who?"

"Your family, Ryan. Amanda. Henry. Sam too. You've got to come out here."

"But—"

Amanda? Henry? I thought of the man who had come to the door, trying to get in. Looking for Blake and me. *It was terrible that the girl got killed.*

"I can't tell you more, Ryan. But when you get here, it will all make sense. But you can't tell the police where you're going. Or Amanda. If you tell anyone, it won't be good. If you tell anyone or call the police, Amanda and Henry could die. They really could. . . . I know you can't go to the bathroom without sharing it on Twitter, but don't tell anyone—"

Then the call cut off. No farewell. Nothing else. Just the end of the call.

"Blake? Blake?"

And once again, I really worried that Blake was in way over his head. And couldn't get out on his own.

And I was in danger of being pulled down with him.

Amanda and Henry were in danger of being hurt. If I didn't go . . .

I grabbed the bat and left the house.

CHAPTER SIXTY-EIGHT

Hilldale Estates sat on the far edge of Rossingville. A local developer—a man named Forsyth who had already made several fortunes creating subdivisions, strip malls, and office buildings—had decided that what the town really needed were luxury condominiums and townhomes on the outskirts of town, the kind of place that would be a neighborhood unto itself, complete with its own shops, restaurants, and even a bank.

To say Mr. Forsyth overreached would be an understatement. People in Rossingville didn't want to pay a lot of money for a luxury condo or townhome. They didn't want to pay exorbitant condo fees. To make matters worse, Mrs. Forsyth decided she no longer wanted to tolerate her husband's infidelities, and she filed for divorce, which left everything tied up in court. As a result, Hilldale Estates remained half-built and unoccupied, the buildings erected but unfinished inside.

As far as why Blake wanted me to go there, I couldn't guess except it was remote and quiet and unlikely to have anyone around to interrupt.

While I drove across town, the rain continuing to spit against the windshield, my phone rang twice. Keeping one eye on the road, I managed to glance at the ID screen. I really didn't need to. I knew who was calling.

Amanda. Both times.

She'd want to know where I was. She'd want to know if I was coming to talk to the police.

And I desperately wanted to answer. I desperately wanted to turn around and go to her. The desire burned in my chest so much, it hurt. Like a burning firework.

But I didn't answer. I didn't want to lie. I wanted to be done with Blake and have it all finished. He ran loose in the world, carrying my computer, and his knowledge of everything that had happened in the distant past as well as with Jennifer's death. Wasn't it time to escape from under the dark cloud all of these problems trailed with them, once and for all?

I drove past the edge of town by a half mile. The strip malls, gas stations, and warehouses faded from view, and then I saw the entrance to Hilldale Estates. The sign remained in place, optimistically and against all odds informing everyone that units were for sale or lease. Inquire inside! But I had recently read on Twitter that the management office had sat empty for six months, the door locked tight with a giant padlock.

I made a left turn, entering the complex, the bat I'd brought with me rolling on the seat and falling to the floor on the passenger side. The combination of rain and churned-up earth from construction meant the roads were muddy and littered with pebbles and sticks. There were no street signs, no guideposts of any kind, so I drove down the main thoroughfare past windows and doors that stared back like sightless eyes. Wherever Blake was, he must have seen me turn in, because my phone chimed with a text. I slowed, looking at the phone.

Take that road to end. Right and then left.

I did what he told me, my blood pressure rising. An absurd thought popped into my head—*I wish I had a drink*. To calm me. To anesthetize me. To give me courage.

I made the first turn, my tires rumbling over some debris I couldn't see. I wished to whatever controlled things that I wouldn't get a flat and be left out in the middle of nowhere with no means of escape. But the car seemed fine. I looked from side to side at the unfinished buildings, monuments to somebody's busted hopes and dreams. Would they ever be finished? Would anyone ever move in and nest there, making it their own?

I made the next left, and at the end of the road, which dead-ended against a stand of trees, I spotted a car I didn't recognize. As I approached, moving slowly, I saw it was about ten years old, with a dented bumper and a missing gas cap. I stopped behind it and looked around but saw no one. No sign of Blake. No sign of anyone else.

On either side of the road were unfinished town houses, the yards muddy, the sidewalks and driveways just gravel. A window on the upper level of the town house to my right, on the side of the street I'd parked on, was broken, the result of a thrown rock or another projectile. The jagged edges of the glass looked strangely menacing in the midafternoon light. It seemed like a good idea to remain inside the car. If I stepped out onto the dirty road, I'd be exposed to anyone who might be watching, including Blake, and since I didn't know what I was getting into, it felt more secure to wait as long as possible.

But, again, Blake read my mind. His next text came.

Come inside one closest to you. Door unlocked.

This was the last turning point.

I could easily turn and go. The car was still running. All I needed to do was drop it in gear and swing around over the messy road, heading back out toward town. I could travel straight to Bill and Karen's house, where I assumed Rountree still waited, and spill everything I knew. I'd face some nasty music, but I'd be safe. And so would my family.

I wouldn't be walking behind door number three, not knowing what waited for me.

The phone dinged again.

Coming? It's time.

It was. And I knew it.

I just didn't know exactly what it was time for. But I grabbed the bat, pushed open the car door, and started up the gravel sidewalk to the front door of the town house beneath the lowering gunmetal sky.

CHAPTER SIXTY-NINE

I placed my hand on the knob and turned. And the door swung open and wide. I stood in the doorway for a moment, the bat in my left hand, resting against my leg.

It wasn't lost on me that all of this had started because I agreed to go inside a house I didn't belong in the night before. I'd pushed open *that* door and gone down the wrong road. And there I was again.

The living room was open and bare. Exposed wires trailed from sockets. Dust and debris littered the floor, and the sweet scent of freshly sawed lumber hung over everything. The cool air brushed over my body, bringing a shiver. My eyes scanned the room, seeing nothing, the bat resting against my shoulder. An open doorway at the back of the room led to the kitchen. I started that way, my shoes scraping over the dirty floor. The kitchen looked as unfinished as the living room. More so. The spaces for appliances were empty, the cabinets not installed. A balled-up paper bag sat in one corner of the room next to an empty Coke bottle, two cigarette butts, and a dead cricket with its legs pointed at the ceiling.

I risked making noise.

"Blake?"

I listened, straining my ears. It was so quiet. No traffic sounds. No people. Only the random chirps of a bird or two. Had Blake led me there for . . . what? Nothing? A wild-goose chase? An elaborate, strange joke?

"Blake?" I said, louder. My voice echoed through the empty space.

I took a step toward the back door, planning on stepping out and seeing if he waited there. But then I heard my name. Faint and muffled.

I listened again, turning my head toward a closed door that led off the kitchen.

I barely heard what came next. "Down here."

I made out what he said. I went to the door and turned that knob, finding myself at the top of a staircase that led down to the basement. The steps were wood, unfinished. And the light from below was faint and weak. I'd assumed there was no electricity in the house, but something provided a measure of illumination in the basement. And I couldn't hear a generator or another power source.

I took a deep breath, gripped the bat tighter, and started down the stairs. They creaked beneath my weight.

I took them slowly, cautiously placing one foot in front of the other. About halfway down, I paused.

"Blake? Do you mind telling me what's going on? Why are you out here?"

"Just come on," he said, his voice strained. "It's the only way."

"For what?"

Someone coughed. Or grunted? And I wasn't sure if it was Blake or not. I didn't bother asking if he was alone. I knew it was too late for those questions.

So I went on, taking the remaining steps at an even slower pace. When I reached the bottom, I turned to the left, taking in the rest of the basement. I was ready to swing the bat if need be.

About fifteen feet away, two droplights hung from the ceiling, providing a circle of illumination. Blake kneeled on the floor, looking even more disheveled than he had at our house. His hands were raised and clenched behind his neck, so he looked like a prisoner facing a firing squad. Behind him, a shadowy figure loomed, one I couldn't make out in any detail at all.

"Blake? What is this?" I asked.

"It's history," he said.

"What are you talking about?"

"It's the past refusing to die."

I waited for the other person to step forward, to resolve into someone I could recognize. But they remained still and silent.

"I'm calling the police," I said, reaching for my phone with one hand while hanging on to the bat with the other.

The figure behind Blake shifted and came forward. It reached up and angled one of the droplights so it shone on his face. A gaunt face, pale. With brown eyes that caught the light and seemed to glow with some combination of anger and manic energy.

"Put the phone away, Ryan," the man said. "And the bat."

My head cocked at the sound of my name. Had I heard him correctly?

I kept quiet, watching him, studying him.

But I shifted my weight, lifting the bat.

"I don't . . ."

"You don't know me, do you?" he asked.

"I'm sorry. I . . ."

He angled the light so more hit his face. And he smiled. I saw the missing tooth, the brown eyes. The short hair.

This man had come to our back door and harassed Amanda.

But it wasn't just that. Something about his face scratched at my memory. I knew him. I'd seen him before. It had been years, but I knew him.

"Come on, Ryan," Blake said from his spot on the floor.

"Yeah, come on, Ryan," the man said. "The last time you saw me, I was driving toward my own doom. Surely you remember that night, don't you?"

It all came back, like a torrent of rushing water. Ferncroft. Sigil and Shield. The night Maggie and Emily Steiner collided with a drunk driver.

The man grinned wider, the missing tooth a cavelike gaping hole.

"Hello, Aaron," I said. "Long time no see."

CHAPTER SEVENTY

Aaron shifted his weight from one foot to the other. When he did, the gun in his free hand, black and sleek, caught the glow from the light above. Aaron pressed it against the side of Blake's head, forcing him to slump ever so slightly as the force increased. Blake winced.

"Easy, Aaron," I said. "I don't want anyone to get hurt. Nobody does."

"Oh, you don't? All of a sudden you care about other people in a way you never did before."

"Aaron, look . . ."

"Look?"

He took a step back, moving into the darkness again and sweeping the gun back and forth from Blake kneeling on the floor to me. Aaron let go of the droplight, and the bulb swung free on its cord, casting all of us alternately in light and shadow, like some kind of carnival-fun-house effect.

Aaron's breathing increased. I could hear it bouncing off the walls in the empty concrete space.

"Look," he said again, but this time the word was a command instead of an expression of incredulity. "Look at me. People have been hurt. Badly. Very badly. And killed, even. And we're going to settle all of that right now. I've finally got the two of you assholes in the same place, so we're going to settle some things."

"Just listen to him, Ryan," Blake said.

"Shut up." Aaron jerked the gun toward Blake and pressed it against the side of his head again. Blake cringed like a whipped dog. "Just shut up. And you. Drop the bat."

I did what he commanded. The bat clanged against the concrete floor, sending a ringing echo through the space.

"Okay, I'm listening," I said. "Say what you want to say. And to be honest, you can do whatever you want to do to me. Just leave my wife and son out of it."

Aaron's face lit up when I said that, like an obscene jack-o'-lantern. He looked happy, almost gleeful, and I immediately regretted mentioning Amanda and Henry.

"Your wife and son," he said. "Right. I met her. Nice girl. But she slammed the back door on me and wouldn't let me in. Isn't that typical? I couldn't even set one foot into your house. It sounds familiar, doesn't it? Like another group I wasn't able to set foot in back in the day."

While he spoke, I studied his face and tried to reconcile the gaunt, slightly crazed man I saw before me with the memory of the younger man—almost a boy—I had known in college. The two images failed to line up, even though I clearly saw the shadow of that college student in the face of the person before me. It was him, without a doubt. But gone was any lightness, any of the almost joyful naivete that other Aaron had displayed when he first came around Sigil and Shield, hoping to gain admission. We kidded him then, compared him to Opie Taylor from *The Andy Griffith Show*, which we all used to gather around and watch on Nick at Nite. But none of that remained. His face was all hard lines and paleness, his eyes lit by a fire of rage and not a sense of wonder.

"If you want to talk about all of that, we can," I said. I held my hands out, placating, hoping for calm. "But if you just put the—"

"Your wife is pretty," Aaron said. "I didn't see your son, but I know his name. Henry, right? I've seen about three million pictures of the kid on Facebook and Instagram. Most people try to keep their kids off of there, but not you. No, sir. That's the most photographed and shared kid in the world. He could be a Kardashian."

"Aaron—"

"I made a mistake, didn't I?"

He seemed to want me to answer, but I had no idea what he was talking about. "A mistake?"

"At your house."

"You mean, you tried to break in?" I asked. It seemed like a much smaller transgression when compared to waving a gun around at us. But I was in no real position to argue with him.

"I didn't try to break in," he said. "I'm not a thief." He seemed genuinely offended by the implication. "I've never stolen anything. No, the mistake I made was leaving your house at all this morning. Because she saw me. And she can identify me. She can tell the cops I was there, and so they'll know what I've been up to and anything I might have said."

His words came back to me, the ones Amanda reported he'd said to her: *It was terrible that the girl got killed.*

He went on. "But that's a loose end I'll have to tie up. That's something I'll have to go back and take care of when all is said and done. When I'm finished with the two of you here."

My bladder felt full to bursting. And every one of my joints ached as a chill passed through me. I considered running, just turning and dashing up the stairs, but unless Aaron was the worst marksman in the history of mankind or he really wasn't ready to pull the trigger of that gun, I stood no chance of getting away.

And given the way he looked, the flaring hatred in his eyes, I harbored no doubts about his readiness to cut me down if I ran.

I consoled myself with the knowledge that Amanda and Henry remained at my in-laws' house, with the police there. But I knew the cops couldn't stay forever. And Aaron seemed to read my mind.

"Even if she isn't home," he said, "if she goes to a hotel or a relative's house, I'll find her eventually. Hell, there are enough photos of your stupid baby with his grandparents on social media as well. I can find them. You're such a foolish idiot, you've drawn me a map."

If he wanted to scare me, he did. More than anything in my life ever had. To the point that my body felt dissolved by the combination of cold, adrenaline, and a racing heart. I wasn't sure I could have moved even if I'd wanted to.

"But first things first," Aaron said. "It's time to deal with the two of you."

CHAPTER SEVENTY-ONE

"Let him go," I said.

The words were unplanned. They spilled out of my mouth without any thought on my part. But once they were out, they felt right. And I knew I'd had to say them.

"Let him go," I said again. "And then leave my family and everyone else alone. *I'm* the person you want. *I'm* the one you need to deal with. Okay? Just let . . . just let everybody else be."

Aaron looked surprised by my declaration. For a moment, he stared at me as though I were an exhibit on display in a zoo, a strange creature who performed some bizarre, unexpected act. I kept my eyes locked on his, so I had no idea what Blake was doing.

"A hero, then," Aaron said. "Saving the day for everybody."

"Not that. Not that at all. It's just the right thing, okay? Your quarrel is with me. I'm the most to blame for what happened that night."

For some reason, Aaron continued to hold the gun against Blake's head. Maybe he deemed Blake the greater threat. Or maybe he felt he could keep me from running off by maintaining the pressure on Blake. If I made a sudden move, either to leave the basement or to charge

Aaron, he could easily pull the trigger and kill Blake with a head shot. Maybe he figured pointing the gun at me wouldn't have been as much of a deterrent for Blake.

"Are you?" Aaron asked.

"Don't you know what really happened? After all these years, don't you?"

"I know now," he said. "I was pretty well concussed that night. And drunk. So I went along with what I was told by the cops. What they thought happened. But somebody finally filled me in. But you tell me what you think happened. Let's see if it matches what I know."

"Who told you?" I asked. "Was it Dawn?"

Aaron's face scrunched. "Dawn? The sister? Forget her. Just tell me the story."

His desire to have me speak first so he could compare stories put me further on edge. I wanted to ask more questions, to know where he'd been hearing things from. But the look on his face, the primal urgency displayed there, told me I needed to speak.

But I remembered the letters . . . what Blake said had been written in them.

Had Aaron read the letters? Had he been in Jennifer's house?

Had *he* killed her?

"Go on," he said, waving the gun.

"Okay, okay. We were all drinking. You know that. And we pushed you to go out of town and take that sign from Gnaw Bone. Look, we knew how much you wanted to get into Sigil and Shield. We played on that. We all did. It's no different than that gun you have there. That gun can get us to do a lot of things, if you're willing to use it. We used your desire for acceptance in the same way. I pushed you to do those things."

"The accident," Aaron said.

"I was drunk too. And it was fuzzy for me. But we were in my car. And when I woke up in the hospital that night, I could remember that we'd all walked to the car together. I remembered getting in. And I was behind the wheel. And I remembered driving away from campus."

"You did. You were driving."

"So it's me. I'm the one you have the problem with. I should have been arrested. Let Blake go."

"Let Blake go? What about this . . . ? How did the cops come to think I was driving if you were really the one behind the wheel?"

His words froze me, and I looked at Blake, who was staring at the floor.

"Well?" Aaron said.

"Blake moved us," I said. "Before the cops came, he moved me to the back and you to the front. He staged the scene. And when the cops arrived, they found you behind the wheel. You were so out of it you had no idea. Blake told me when I came to in the hospital. And we went with that. . . ."

"You went with that," Aaron said. "You make it sound so fun. So casual. *Oh, we just went with that.*"

"Aaron, it was wrong. I wanted to tell the truth. My father had died. I was barely paying for school. I covered my own butt because I was afraid I'd lose everything. Everything my mom was working for to help me finish school. She went back to school, worked nights and weekends.

"It was stupid and selfish and wrong of me. And many times I wanted to call the police and tell the truth, but I always found a reason not to. I'm not proud of it. Not at all." I felt sick just saying the words. But I was also glad for someone else to hear them. For Aaron to know the truth. "Call the police. Bring them here, and I'll tell *them* the truth. There isn't a statute of limitations in Kentucky. I'll go to jail. I'll lose everything. Just make the call and end this. . . ."

Something flashed in Aaron's eyes, something I hadn't seen in the short time we'd been face-to-face in the basement of the half-completed town house. It looked more like joy than the anger that had been simmering there, and for a moment, I couldn't understand the reason for the look. And I never would have understood it if he hadn't started talking and explaining it.

"That's what happened that night?" he asked.

"It is. Ask Blake."

Aaron's eyes trailed down to Blake, who still cowered under the pressure of the gun. He looked small and insignificant on the floor, like a child.

I waited for him to say something, to speak up and interject as he always did, but he remained silent, as if the pressure of the gun against his head cut off his ability to speak.

"I did ask him," Aaron said.

"And he told you the same thing, right?" I asked. "He had to."

It took a moment for Aaron to answer, but then he did. "We ran into each other. . . . What was that, Blake? A couple weeks ago?"

When Blake stayed quiet, Aaron pushed against his head with the gun. "Yes, weeks."

"An accident, really," Aaron said, not relaxing the pressure against Blake's head. "I was over in Cave Springs, working my job in a shitty Chinese restaurant. A job as a dishwasher, which is about all you can get when you've served time in prison. *And* never finished college. So I'm outside, taking a smoke break, when I see this one"—he pushed against Blake's head again—"walking through the parking lot with a beautiful woman. I recognized him right away. He hasn't changed much since college. A little fatter. A little shorter if that's possible. But the same guy. Same shit-eating grin on his face, like he didn't have a care in the world. A rich kid's look. That sums it up, right?"

"Yeah, sure," Blake said.

"You nearly jumped out of your skin when I called your name," Aaron said. "Like you'd been electrocuted. And I kind of wondered why you jumped so high. You and that woman you were with suddenly looked like you were in big trouble."

Why would Blake have jumped and looked guilty when someone called his name unless he had been with Jennifer and not Sam?

"At first he didn't want to talk to me," Aaron said. "But then he sent his ladylove over to his car so he could speak to me alone. And when we were there talking, and I asked him about that night and what really happened, he suddenly seemed very eager to tell his tale. I just really wanted to know what the truth was. Because I'd started to have my own doubts while I was in prison. I'd replayed it over and over, and I started to remember that you, Ryan, were behind the wheel when we left Sigil and Shield."

Everything grew silent. The absence of noise felt oppressive, like an unseen force filling the wide-open basement. I waited for Aaron to go on, but he didn't. I couldn't stand the waiting and the silence.

"What did he tell you?" I asked. "The truth, right? What I just told you."

Aaron cut his eyes toward me, and then he nodded slowly, like a man who knew a secret.

"That is what he told me," Aaron said. "He told me the same version you just gave. The truth."

But Aaron laughed a little after he said it.

"The truth," he said again, looking down at Blake. "Is that still the story you want to stick with?" When Blake said nothing, Aaron asked, "Well, is it, Blake?"

CHAPTER SEVENTY-TWO

I waited for his answer. Anticipating.

Aaron wore such an eager, excited look on his face, it unnerved me. He seemed like a man who knew something the rest of us didn't. But for the life of me, I couldn't guess what it was. So I waited along with Aaron in the cool, dark basement. And I watched Blake like he was an oracle about to intone.

After what felt like half an eternity, Blake nodded his head, an almost imperceptible movement. It failed to satisfy Aaron, who pushed harder with the gun.

"What was that?" he asked.

"Yes," Blake said. "That's the story. That's what happened that night. We kept feeding you drinks. We told you to get the sign. And Ryan was driving when we had the accident. And I made it look like you were driving, Aaron, and you took the fall for it because you couldn't really remember. And Ryan couldn't either. I set the whole thing up."

The words, spoken out loud the way they were, sent a hot wave of shame-induced nausea cascading through my body. The rush came on so strong I almost staggered backward, and I wished for something to lean against to support my body. But nothing was there, nothing nearby. I had no choice but to stand on my own while those awful words and memories swirled around us like angry bees.

"It was Ryan driving," Aaron said.

Again, Blake was slow to answer. Finally, he said, "Yes, it was. I was in the passenger seat, and you were in the back. Until I moved you."

"And that's what really happened that night?" Aaron asked.

"It is." Blake didn't hesitate this time.

A look of relief passed across Aaron's face, as if those were the words he desperately needed to hear. Like that of a doctor giving you the all clear when the test results come back, or a lover responding with *I love you*.

Aaron looked over at me, some of the fire and glee out of his eyes. "Did you hear that, Ryan?"

"Are you working with Dawn Steiner, Aaron?" I asked.

"Dawn Steiner? What a joke."

"Are you?" I asked.

"Did you hear what Blake said?" Aaron asked.

"I heard it," I said. "I heard it today, and I knew it already. That's why you can let him go. Just be done with him. Yes, he staged the accident . . . but I went along with it. I should have spoken up back then. Or anytime since. It's on me, okay? Not my family. Not really Blake. He's about to get married. Let him be. And let my family be."

Aaron leaned down and spoke close to Blake's ear. "Is that what you want, Blake? You want to get out of here and get married?"

"I don't want anyone to get hurt," he said.

"But you want to get married, right?" Aaron didn't wait for an answer before he continued talking. "You want to get married, even though you were spending time with another woman. The one who is now deader than a doornail. You see, I've watched all of this unfold. Blake running around with other women. Ryan, I've seen your happy life all over social media. The vacations and the nice dinners. The fancy drinks and the concerts. The wife and baby and house and business. I see it all. The whole house of cards is there for everyone to see. One little puff might blow it down."

"Ryan's right," Blake said. "Leave everyone else out of it."

"Leave Samantha out of it?" Aaron asked. "Is that what you mean? Samantha? Isn't that her name?" He leaned even closer, so close I saw spittle fly out of his mouth and land on Blake's face. "She might be interested to learn about this Jennifer. She might be interested to learn a lot of things. See, that night when you left the Chinese restaurant, I followed you. It was easy. I'm sure you were more interested in your date than who might have been driving behind you."

Blake cut his eyes at Aaron but didn't say anything.

"And I saw where she lived," Aaron said. "Jennifer Bates."

His statement struck me like a jolt of electricity. And our encounter started to move in a direction I'd already suspected—*It was terrible that the girl got killed*—but wished and hoped it wouldn't. Because if it moved that way, if Aaron was the one responsible for Jennifer's death, then the line from that death to Aaron's accident led directly back to me.

"Aaron," I said.

"Shhh. I went there, and I saw where she lived. And I found out her name. It's not hard to do. Isn't the Internet a remarkable thing? You can see how wonderfully other people's lives have advanced while you're stuck in neutral. You can learn the name of a woman you want to talk to. So I went back another night, and I talked to the lovely Jennifer."

"Did you know her already?" I asked. "Had you met her through her job, Aaron?"

A look of recognition spread across Aaron's face. "Oh, I get it. I see. You think I knew her because she worked with prisoners as they transitioned to the outside. It's that simple, right? Blame the ex-con."

"You know what her job is," I said. "Is that how you knew her?"

"I know what her job was because she told me when we talked,"

Aaron said. "And yeah, we talked about my record a little. But mostly we talked about the two of you. I told her I was good friends with Blake from college. And with you, Ryan. She was suddenly very interested. And willing to talk. We talked. . . . We even had a drink. She said a few times, 'This is totally nuts, me talking to you like this.' But she didn't send me away. I'll give her credit. She was a ballsy chick. Not a shrinking violet at all. And eventually I explained the whole thing to her. How I knew you two in college, and what happened the last time we saw each other. The drinking, the hazing, the accident. How Ryan was the one behind the wheel, and how I took the fall because I couldn't remember. Did you know we talked about that, Blake?"

Whatever color remained in Blake's face drained away. He shook his head. "I didn't know that," he said. "But she and I . . . We weren't . . . close anymore. We'd broken up. That night you saw us at the restaurant, we'd already broken up. I was letting her know that things were really over, once and for all. That's why we were there together. The relationship was over, and I was engaged. She didn't know me as well as she thought she did. She—she didn't understand everything about me anymore."

"I guess she didn't," Aaron said. "She didn't seem to."

Blake looked uncertain. His eyes narrowed, but he remained quiet, waiting for the next shoe to drop.

"Because," Aaron said, "she told me a very different story about what happened that night, the night that ruined my life."

CHAPTER SEVENTY-THREE

Blake's posture stiffened. He moved his head up, pushing against the gun Aaron still held in place. Blake suddenly seemed injected with more energy than he'd displayed at any time since I'd been in the basement with them.

"You killed her," Blake said.

"Don't change the subject," Aaron said.

"No," Blake said. "You killed her. You just said you knew where she lived. You wanted to hurt me, so you hurt her. And then you went over to Ryan's house and threatened his family. That's why you won't let that go. That's why you say you're going to hurt Amanda and Henry if you leave here."

"Don't be simple," Aaron said.

"Hold it," I said.

They both looked at me as my voice bounced off the walls, silencing their bickering. They'd been acting like I wasn't there, like they were deeply engaged in their own private spat.

"What do you mean, Jennifer told you a different story about that night than Blake told you?" I asked. "Jennifer wasn't there. We didn't even know her in college. She didn't know what happened that night."

Aaron looked at me like *I* was simple. He shook his head. "Somebody in this room told Jennifer all about that night."

My eyes went to Blake, and our gazes locked on each other for a moment. I wasn't sure what I saw there—shame? fear? anger?—but he quickly looked away. And he remained quiet, as though ceding the floor to Aaron.

So I looked over at him. "I still don't know what you're talking about, Aaron," I said. "You've been saying a lot of things, but none of them make any sense."

"Then let me enlighten you." Perhaps sensing whatever was building in Blake and putting the steel in his posture, Aaron took a step back from him while still holding the gun in his direction. But it no longer touched Blake's head. "It seems that our friend here liked to talk to his girlfriend more than anyone else. Apparently he had the habit of occasionally throwing back too many drinks and then having true-confession time with Jennifer. Even though he was supposed to be quitting." Aaron looked over at Blake. "He told her lots of stuff during the times they were together. His sexual exploits. And shames. The times he cheated on tests, the papers he plagiarized. The time in junior high he helped bully some kid who then tried to commit suicide. I guess he told her all the things he couldn't tell Samantha. Maybe those things didn't fit the image he wanted to project to her. Maybe those things would ruin their future prospects. Maybe he thought her family wouldn't tolerate the embarrassing aspects of his past."

I looked at Blake, who stared at the floor. I knew him well. He'd told me many things over the years, and, yes, he tended to get loose-tongued when drunk. And when I knew him well, he was frequently drunk. But he hadn't told me the things Aaron had mentioned.

Was Aaron right? Had Blake spilled his guts to Jennifer because she was so far removed from his world?

From the corner of my eye, I caught a glimpse of the bat. It was out of my reach unless I dove for it.

But it was there.

Aaron's voice drew my eyes back over to him.

"Are you listening, Ryan?"

"He quit drinking. He opens up more when he drinks, but he quit."

"Oh, right. Well, Jennifer says he always tried to quit. But he fell off the wagon. Hard. After he saw me at the Chinese restaurant. She said it was like he'd seen a ghost. Like he was Ebenezer Scrooge or something. He showed up at her place the next night with a bottle of Jim Beam and a loose tongue. He *really* unburdened himself when he told her about the night of the accident. The night that changed everything for me and nothing for the two of you. Although maybe not in the way we once thought."

"What do you mean?" I asked, not sure if I wanted to hear but desperate to know.

"He's lying, Ryan," Blake said.

"Why would I lie?" Aaron asked. "Why would you lie when you were drunk? Why would Jennifer? She said she knew you had already gone back to your old girlfriend. Sam. The one with the money and the rich daddy and the job. She knew that, but she was willing to listen to you one more time because you seemed so pathetic and needed someone to talk to."

"What did Jennifer say about the accident?" I asked.

"What do you remember about that night, Ryan?" Aaron asked. "What exactly do you recall happening when we drove off and wrecked everything? Eighteen months in jail. No degree. No way to get a job. What happened during that ride?"

My mind scanned back through the years, pinpointing that night I'd thought about so many times before. I remembered the drinking, the smell of stale beer, the wooziness and sloppiness the alcohol brought on. The music pounded as we poured shots and pushed them toward the fresh-faced kids who wanted to join Sigil and Shield. I remembered someone handing me a joint, which I might or might not have smoked. I remembered dancing with someone I might or might not have known.

And I remembered Aaron. Young. Eager. His clothes not quite right. His attempts at jokes not quite landing. And the desperation to belong oozed off of him like sweat. It covered every inch of his body. He followed Blake around like a puppy. He drank what Blake handed him. He fetched Blake beers when he needed them. At some point, a song came on, something stupid and cloying, and Blake told Aaron to dance. So Aaron danced, making a fool of himself in front of everyone. We laughed with him. But mostly at him.

And then . . .

"We went out to get the sign," I said. "That was my idea. It used to be a tradition with Sigil and Shield. They'd done it for years, but the club got in trouble for stealing it before we started at Ferncroft, so we had to stop. But we always wanted to get it one more time before we graduated. I'd always talked about doing it with Blake, but that night, I told you to do it. And we went in my car. And you know what happened. We all do."

"Do we?" Aaron asked. "How did you find out about the accident?"

I remembered that. Vividly.

I woke up in the emergency room. My head was pounding. My body hurt. I knew we'd been in an accident, and when Blake came into the room, I asked him if anyone had been hurt. He said Aaron had been banged up pretty good.

And he told me he just didn't know about the other car. But he thought it was bad.

Very bad.

Deep shit, he said. *We're going to be in deep shit.*

"He told me I needed to be careful about what I said and did," I said to Aaron. "That the cops were going to ask questions, but if I played it smart, it would work out. He said he'd arranged things at the scene so it looked like you were driving and not me. And I said I didn't like that, that I wanted to tell the truth and face whatever music I needed to face, even though the thought of it made me sick. But Blake reminded me of my mom and the money she'd borrowed for me to finish college. And he told me my life would be over, ruined, if I took the blame for the crash. And he said everyone was going to think you were driving. He told me to keep my mouth shut about my role."

"*He* told you," Aaron said. "Blake."

"Yes, he did. I was so foggy. I was drunk, and I hit my head in the accident. . . ."

"Then you didn't remember anything," Aaron said. "Blake told you what you did. Blake supplied all the details and all the information. Blake planted the whole story in your head."

It was my turn to take a step back. A shakiness started in my hands and felt like it passed through my entire body.

"That's not possible," I said. "I was there. It was my car. I did—"

Then Blake spoke up. His voice rose above mine.

"You didn't, Ryan," he said. "You didn't do any of it. I know because I did it."

"That's not—"

"It is," Blake said. "I was driving that night. I was the one behind the wheel when the accident happened."

CHAPTER SEVENTY-FOUR

After Blake spoke, he exhaled what had been a deeply held breath. His posture, which had become rigid and stiff, relaxed some, and he even lowered his hands from behind his head, where they'd been clenched as long as I'd been in the basement.

"You don't have to say that, Blake," I said. "It's not necessary."

"It is," he said. "I told Jen the truth that night when I fell off the wagon. He's right." He jerked his head to his left, indicating Aaron. "He knows the truth and so did Jen. And now you do too. You weren't driving the car that night. I was. That's what I put in the letters to her. The letters exposed me, not you. That's why I needed you to get them out of the house. I asked her to give them back, and she refused." He looked up at Aaron. "You can let Ryan go now. Let him go back to his family and his life. I'm the one you want, okay? Is that what you wanted me to admit? That *I* did it? Well, okay, I admit it. I drove that night and then I staged the accident to make it look like it was you."

I took a step toward Blake. "Don't say that. Don't say those kinds of things if they're not true."

"They are true. You started driving, but you clearly weren't able. So we pulled over and switched. You got in the backseat, and Aaron was the passenger."

"Why?" I asked Blake, taking another step closer. "Why would you do that to me? To your closest friend? Why?"

Blake used his tongue to moisten his lips. "Just go, Ryan. Get out of here and go."

"No. Why?"

Blake's eyes flashed. "Because." The one word cut through the space, freezing all of us in place. When he went on, he spoke in a lower, more controlled voice. "Because I got tired of always being the fuckup. I got tired of being the joke. Everywhere we went, I stood in your shadow. You were the winner. I was the clown. And let's face it. I deserved that reputation. I'm not saying I didn't. But damn, it gets old, having everybody see me that way."

"I didn't see you that way," I said. "We were friends. You were my best friend. You're the reason I finished school, the reason I survived my dad dying."

"Everybody else saw it that way. And when that accident happened, and you didn't know if you were driving or not, I saw an opportunity to level the playing field a little. To bring me closer in line to you."

"That's nuts," I said. "Blake, that's truly nuts."

"But look what happened. . . . You graduated and went on your merry. And when you moved here and married Amanda, nobody knew about the accident. Nobody knew what really happened. It was just a blip that occurred in the past at a small college. Everybody knew about Aaron. He did the time, while the rest of us moved on."

"I didn't. I've been living with that guilt over what I did."

"Oh, I know. You beat yourself up. But you never talked about it, not with anybody else. No one saw it. No one knew the truth. Everyone only saw what you wanted them to see. You never told anyone you'd fucked up that bad."

"Apparently I hadn't."

"And I thought many, many times about telling you. I really did. But the longer it went on, the longer the years stretched, it was harder and harder to do. And then this thing with Jen and the letters . . ."

"So you used it against me one more time."

"I didn't want it to end that way. I didn't want any of *this* to happen. You have to know that."

I took two more steps, until I stood over Blake. Years of guilt, years of hot wires of recrimination searing my insides.

Years of stuffing it away from Amanda . . . when I didn't need to.

My fist came back and forward with as much force as I could muster and cracked him across the jaw. The feel of my knuckles against his flesh satisfied me more than I could have imagined, and the jolt of pain that shot up my arm seemed like a small price to pay for knocking Blake off his knees and onto the floor. I stepped in for more, hoping to hit him again, but Aaron took hold of my arm and pulled me back, spinning me across the room so that I stumbled and landed on the floor.

"Enough," he said. He waved the gun back and forth between the two of us. "Am I the only sane one here? You two are a couple of prizes, aren't you? Liars and home wreckers and frauds. I don't care who did what now. All I wanted was for the two of you to see how worthless you both are. It's time to tie up all the loose ends. Hell, they'll find you in this basement in about twenty years when someone finally shows up to finish these town houses."

"Aaron, just leave my family out of this—"

"No chance. It's a going-out-of-business sale. Everything must go. Everything and everyone." He pointed the gun at me. I stared down the menacing hole at the end of its barrel. "You first, so I can better enjoy killing him."

"Aaron, don't. . . . If you and Dawn want something . . ."

My full bladder nearly burst. Images of Amanda and Henry flashed before me. Smiling. Laughing.

I'll never grow old, I thought. *I'll never have another child. Never have a grandchild. I'll never see Henry do anything. . . .*

From out of the darkness across the room, Blake lunged toward Aaron, grabbing him around the legs and taking him to the floor as a shot fired in the quiet space.

CHAPTER SEVENTY-FIVE

I spent a moment in a state of disbelief.

A shot had been fired somewhere. At me? Near me?

I looked down at my body in the dim light. I saw no injuries. No blood, no torn clothing. And I felt no pain.

But next to me, a struggle raged. Blake had landed on top of Aaron, and the two men grappled for control of the gun. Aaron's arm was extended toward the ceiling, his hand gripping the weapon. And Blake reached for it, trying to stop his movement and keep another shot from being fired.

But Aaron proved to be stronger. He managed to work the gun around so that it pointed toward Blake. Blake's efforts momentarily kept him from firing, but it was only a matter of time.

I scrambled across the floor and reached for the bat. I wrapped my hand around the handle and drew it to my body. If I thought I'd had more time, I would have stood up, measured the distance, and swung the bat in an efficient, focused manner.

But I didn't have time.

With one hand I swung, aiming—I hoped—at Aaron's hand. The one that held the gun.

I missed my target but managed to bring the bat down against Aaron's forearm. He held on to the gun, despite my efforts, and worked his finger free. He squeezed the trigger, causing another loud boom in the hollow space. The bullet ricocheted off the concrete wall across from us.

I swung again. This time the bat connected with the back of Aaron's hand, but on my follow-through, the bat hit the concrete floor and came out of my hand and rolled away.

Blake repositioned his body. He raised his fist and swung it at Aaron's face. Once. Twice. He did it again, scoring direct hits that landed with sickening thuds. Aaron grunted the first two times. Then the third time, he made a low groaning noise.

His hand loosened its grip. I pried his fingers off the gun one at a time until I could take it away. I held the strangely heavy, unfamiliar object. It was like I'd picked up a bizarre, unrecognizable sea creature off the beach. I wasn't sure what to do with it.

Blake delivered one more blow to Aaron's face, and that time Aaron made no noise at all.

"Stop it, Blake," I said.

He reared back again.

"Just stop it." I grabbed his fist with my free hand and looked down at Aaron, who wasn't moving. "He's had it. Just stop."

"He tried to kill me."

"He tried to kill both of us. And he did kill Jennifer. But let someone else sort that out." I took the gun across the room and placed it on top of the water heater. Then I took out my phone and called 911. "I'm calling the police now. They can cuff him and take him where he needs to go."

I told them where we were and what the situation was. I mentioned Jennifer's name, and they promised to send help immediately. When I was off the phone, I went back over to where Blake stood over Aaron.

"Is he okay?" I asked.

Blake looked at me. "Why do you care?"

"Because he's a human being." I looked down. Aaron's chest rose and fell steadily. His eyes were half open and glassy. I hoped for the best. He'd been battered, but I thought he would make it without any real damage. "Haven't we done enough to him? Or should I say, haven't *you* done enough to him? Six years ago and today."

"Whatever." Blake made a dismissive wave with his hand. "He tried to kill us. He tried to hurt your wife. That should be enough. *You* should want to pound him. Instead you hit me."

"You're lucky that's all I did to you. After you gaslit me for six years."

Blake again waved, this time with both hands. "We don't have time for that," he said. "We need to get our stories straight before the cops get here. I know they're on their way."

He seemed to be speaking a foreign language. "Get our stories straight? What is there to get straight? I'm telling them the truth. I'm telling them exactly what happened here."

"Right." He nodded with enthusiasm, as though we'd finally agreed to resolve a long-simmering dispute. "We had a beef from college, and he tried to kill us. And he killed Jen to get back at both of us. Right?"

"Right. Sure."

He nodded his head, a look of satisfaction on his face. But I sensed we weren't completely on the same page.

"I'm telling them everything, Blake. Everything. About Jennifer's house and the phone and all of it. I'm coming clean."

He cocked his head, and his mouth fell open. Then he threw his hands up in the air in disgust. "What are you talking about? You can't tell them that."

"I can, and I will. This is over, Blake. And the only way for it to truly be over is to tell the cops everything. They need that information from Jennifer's phone. They need to know all of it." I looked around the basement. "Where's my computer?"

He took a long time to answer a simple question. "I have it."

"Where?"

"It's safe."

"What did you need off of there?" I asked.

"It's nothing," he said. He took a step forward until we were uncomfortably close. Before he spoke, we both heard it. Sirens. The police were in the neighborhood and coming down the street, heading for this unit. They knew we were in the basement. "You need to think about this. Fast."

"What?"

"That computer. The story. I threw the phone away, but there's stuff on the computer." He placed his hand on my chest, letting it rest there. He patted me and then squeezed the material of my shirt. "People can get hurt by those things on there. People who don't need to get hurt."

"You mean Sam? Doesn't she know about Jennifer?"

He scrambled to find the right words. "It's . . . People can get hurt. That's all I'm saying. Think about whether you want all of that to happen."

The door opened above us. Footsteps moved across the floor above us.

"Rossingville Police."

"I want the truth to come out," I said. "All of it."

I saw the veins in his forehead, the pores on his cheeks. "You don't know what you're doing, Ryan. Just be careful about what you say. A lot of people can still be hurt here."

"What are you worried about? Losing a job with Sam's dad? Is that all you care about?"

"Be careful."

"You're going to face legal jeopardy for the accident. Remember? No statute of limitations. I'm telling them everything. And Sam's family will know. Everyone will know."

The cops started down the stairs. I saw their black shoes, their guns drawn.

And I said one more thing to Blake. And I hoped to stick to it forever.

"And then you and I really and truly won't ever see each other again."

CHAPTER SEVENTY-SIX

When we first arrived at the police station in Rossingville and before the questioning began, Detective Rountree allowed me to call Amanda on one of their landlines. They'd removed my personal effects, including my phone, so I sat at an empty desk and resorted to using a beat-up and out-of-date phone book, the cover so battered it fell to the floor, to find my in-laws' number. I didn't know it by heart. I hadn't dialed it that way in . . . ever.

When Amanda came on the line, I told her what I could tell her in the few minutes I was allotted, straining to hear her voice over the din of the police station. Ringing phones and chattering conversations, a siren wailing outside. More than anything I made sure she and Henry were safe, and I told her Aaron was in custody, unable to come near or harm anyone else.

Our conversation paused for a moment. In the background on her end of the line, I heard Henry making a series of noises, including his habitual banging of the spoon against the high chair tray. And I heard Karen's voice talking back to him, telling him how grown-up he was. Those sounds pierced my heart. How I wished I could have been there.

How I wished to sit by Henry and feed him mashed-up food. I'd even have settled for changing one of his stink bomb diapers because it would make life seem normal again.

"I have so many questions," Amanda said. "So many."

"And I'll answer them all. I promise. But the cops have a bigger claim on me right now."

"Just let me come down there. I can explain some things. There's so much more to this."

"No, you don't have to come down here. Stay with Henry."

I heard her breath on the other end of the line. "Do you need a lawyer?" she asked, again showing her practical side. "Is it that serious? I don't want you talking to the police without being protected."

I considered the possibility. "I'm not sure. Maybe."

"I'm going to ask Dad. He knows every lawyer in Rossingville."

I wasn't sure what to think. It hadn't all sunk in yet. The deep shame I'd carried with me for years, the belief that I'd killed someone in that accident . . . none of it was true. But I couldn't bring myself to feel relieved.

Maggie Steiner was still dead. Emily was still hurt.

And Jennifer Bates was gone too. Along with Kyle Dornan.

Such a waste. So much waste.

Rountree emerged from a back room and pointed at her watch. I looked around. I had no idea where they'd taken Blake or Aaron. I assumed they were being held in their own rooms, and they'd keep us all separate as we told our tales. At least that was the way it happened on TV.

"I have to go," I said. "I don't know how long this will take. I really don't. I'll try to call again if I can, but . . ."

"I get it. I'll be here with Mom and Dad."

"Okay. I love you."

"I love you too."

I started to put the phone down, but Amanda's voice came through the line, stopping me.

"What's that?" I asked.

She paused for a moment. Henry's banging increased in frequency and volume.

"I just said . . . I understand that there may be some things you tell them that are delicate. I get it. I do. I know sometimes these things come out whether we want them to or not. It can all get very tangled."

I wanted to ask her for clarification because it sounded as though she was speaking about something else, something besides the events that had spun out from Jennifer's death.

But Rountree came over to the desk and tapped her watch again, this time more dramatically. And there was no way to say or ask anything with any presumption of privacy, if that presumption had even existed in the first place. So I told Amanda good-bye and hung up, and then followed Rountree back to the room where I was to be questioned.

And the police devoted hours to questioning me. To say it was unpleasant would be the understatement of the century. In order to explain to them how I ended up in that basement with Aaron and Blake, I naturally had to go back to college and start the story there. And then it continued all the way up until the events of the previous twenty-four hours, including how I had ended up in Jennifer's house the night she was killed, the removal of her phone, the withholding of those details from Rountree the first time she came to the house.

All of it.

Rountree came and went. Sometimes I sat for long stretches by myself, and during those times, I replayed the events of the past day, especially everything that happened in that basement in Hilldale Estates. I'd spent the past six years of my life burying and secretly making amends for something I hadn't played as large a role in as I'd always thought. Blake had been driving that night. And he'd not only lied to me about it, but he'd used it to coerce me into going into Jennifer's house.

But knowing those things brought me no great relief.

Blake, someone I once considered a close friend, had lied to me for years.

And setting aside how much I feared exposure at his hands, I had made the choice to give in and go along with entering Jennifer's house the previous night. I shouldered the blame for that. I might face criminal charges for it. In fact, I couldn't see how I wouldn't.

What I'd thought while talking to Amanda was true—it was much better to have it all out in the open.

But my life would never be the same afterward. I'd never be looked at the same, and I wouldn't be the same. The uncertainty surrounding that scared me more than any criminal charge that might have been coming.

Everything felt new and out of control. No social media post or Instagram filter could put the right shine on my past decisions.

Shortly before midnight, Rountree returned for the final time. She told me we were just about finished, and I'd be able to return home under certain conditions.

"You can't leave town," she said. "And if we call you because we have more questions, we need you to jump. And I mean really jump."

"I'm not going anywhere," I said. "I just want to spend time with my family again."

She held a small notebook and flipped through the pages. I'd stayed focused on her questions the rest of the day, but with our time nearing its end, I worked up the nerve to ask a question I'd been thinking about for hours.

"What is happening with Aaron?" I asked. "And Blake?"

Rountree kept looking at her notes, but she answered. "Our friend Aaron Knicely is in quite a bit of trouble. He has a lawyer on the way, so things with him might take a while to sort through. That's all I can really say about that."

She added nothing else and kept turning pages.

"And Blake?" I asked.

She looked up, closed the notebook, and tucked it into a pocket inside her jacket. "He's in his own sinking boat. We're going to be looking into this car accident from the past. He faces legal jeopardy over that. I can't tell you more. And we'll be deciding about possible criminal charges related to everything you did. Going into that house, taking the phone."

A few hours earlier, Rountree had brought me some crackers and a bag of pretzels from a vending machine. Except for those, I hadn't eaten in hours. Despite that long stretch, my stomach felt nauseated, not empty. And when I said Blake's name, the nausea increased along with a sour taste in my mouth. I wanted to feel relieved to be done with him, but the imagined freedom and lightness refused to come.

"He's asked for a lawyer about the accident, so it could take a while to get sorted out," Rountree said. "But Aaron is telling the same story you are about the accident and the events in that basement. If that makes you feel any better."

I thought about it for a moment, looking at the scarred top of the beat-up table where I sat.

"I'm not sure it does," I said. "I understand it, but it doesn't make me feel any better. Someone was killed. And someone still got hurt. Bad. And I was there for part of it, acting like an idiot. Nothing can absolve me from that."

Rountree nodded in a sagelike manner. "Not even envelopes of cash stuffed in a mailbox."

I looked up.

"Yes," she said, "everyone's going to know you've been giving the Steiners the money. There's no way people will think Blake did it."

Her words started to sink in.

"Do you think the Steiners knew what Aaron was coming to do to us?" I asked. "I told you about Dawn Steiner. Could this relate to them in some way? Could they all be in on this with Aaron? Getting revenge together? You don't know who killed Jennifer yet, do you? Was it Aaron? He said he was with her."

"We'll look into everything. We always do. But you were the goose laying golden eggs. They didn't seem to want that money to stop coming."

"Yeah," I said, accepting it all. "But I guess you can't buy your way out of guilt."

Rountree stood up. "Maybe understanding that is the first step toward moving on."

CHAPTER SEVENTY-SEVEN

Amanda managed to sleep fitfully, while I once again stared at the ceiling and paced the house.

When I had left the police station, around one thirty, I went by my in-laws' house to pick her up. Mercifully, Bill and Karen were asleep, and so was Henry, and Amanda had already arranged with them to leave the baby there overnight so the two of us could have distraction-free conversation in the morning. I desperately wanted to lay eyes on the little guy, but I knew he was safe with his grandparents. And I agreed with Amanda's assessment that it would be nice to talk without interruption.

Since I was up long before Amanda, my mind swirling with the events of the previous evening, she at least came downstairs to the aroma of brewing coffee filling the house and the sight of me at the counter buttering toast.

She smiled when she came into the room, and we shared a kiss. But there was a strain in her smile, something that showed across her face. She wore a hoodie and baggy shorts, and I wished it were simple to pick up and return to our regular lives.

But I knew it wouldn't be.

And I knew Dawn Steiner's deadline loomed over the morning.

But would she really show up? Wouldn't she be scared off by the news that everything was out in the open? She held no more leverage over me. She had nothing to push me with. For all I knew, the police had her in custody as well.

Before we sat down at the table with our steaming mugs, Amanda went out onto the stoop and grabbed the morning paper. She reluctantly slid it across the table toward me, and I saw Jennifer's death and Aaron's arrest taking up most of the front page. And when I saw the large type and Aaron's mug shot, my heart jumped to a pace suitable for NASCAR.

"I thought about hiding it from you," she said. "But what's the point? Isn't everything supposed to be out in the open now?"

"It is." But I sounded less sure than ever.

I spread the paper out and scanned the first story. It revealed less than I knew and relied on a lot of "sources say" and "police aren't sure." I felt some relief that I hadn't been mentioned, but that lasted about one minute. In the second story, which detailed the circumstances of Aaron's arrest in greater detail, I saw my name. "Ryan Francis, local PR executive and small-business owner." While it withheld many of the details—it didn't mention my presence in Jennifer's house the night she had died—it did say that the potential crimes being investigated stemmed partially from an "alcohol-involved accident during college." And it made sure to tell the readers that additional charges could be filed against all of the men, including Blake and me.

I'd turned my phone off when I came home from getting Amanda, hoping to shut the world out so we could sleep. But something compelled me to reach for it. I went down the hall to my office, noticed the space on the desk where my laptop should have been resting, and picked up the phone. Amanda appeared in the doorway right behind me.

"Ryan, maybe don't . . ."

But I'd already seen. Text after text after text. And calls and voice mails. I scanned the first few.

Hey, man . . .

Is this you?

Do you need anything?

Are they serious?

I looked away, my face burning.

Amanda took a deep breath in the doorway. She pushed her glasses up to the bridge of her nose. "The same thing happened on my phone. And Facebook and Snapchat too. I thought you might want to avoid that for a while."

"I thought people didn't read the newspaper anymore. Do we know the only people who subscribe?"

"Well, you know the newspaper reporters Tweet all their stories. And the paper shares its stories on Facebook. At least people care," she said. "We have a lot of friends offering support."

"It's ghoulish," I said. "They just want prurient details. They want a glimpse of the disaster."

Amanda remained quiet, but she wore a knowing look.

"What?" I asked.

"Look, Ryan, live by social media, die by it. We put a lot of our lives on there, so naturally people think they can ask whatever they want. It happens."

"Just what I need to hear. Logic."

She came across the room and took me by the hand, the hand that didn't hold the phone. "Come on out to the kitchen. We can talk. You know, face-to-face like human beings used to. You can respond to those later. Or ignore them all. You don't have to jump every time that thing chimes. None of us do."

"Sure."

But I made the mistake of taking one more glance at the screen. Another text popped up.

I know you're pissed and I get it. But lets talk sometime.

"Crap," I said.

"What?"

"Blake. Of all the nerve . . ."

"All the more reason to ignore that stuff." She tugged on my wrist. "Come on."

"Wait," I said, slipping free of her grip. "I'm going to do one more thing."

"Ryan."

"Hold on."

I went through and blocked Blake. I blocked his texts and his calls. I made sure he couldn't contact me, no matter how hard he tried. I looked at my desk, where our barely used landline sat, the one we'd had installed when Henry was born. Amanda wanted a backup in case cell service went down and there was an emergency.

"Can you block someone on that?" I asked.

"Just don't answer," she said.

I went over and pulled the plug.

"Okay," I said. "That actually felt good. Now you have my undivided attention. You should always have it."

CHAPTER SEVENTY-EIGHT

I told Amanda everything that morning. Over coffee and toast and so much more coffee that my body started to jangle like a singing electric wire, I told her what I now knew about the accident. That I'd always believed I'd been driving that night and had allowed Aaron to take the blame for what I thought I'd done. That while I'd let Blake guide me to that decision, I had no one to blame but myself for going along with it. I was trying to cover my own butt, trying to save my own skin and finish college without getting into trouble.

Amanda's face flushed as I spoke, and her eyes narrowed. "All those years you thought you'd been driving that night? As long as you've known me, you thought that?"

"I did."

"And you knew how I felt about that issue because of Mallory? But you didn't say anything to me."

It was my turn to flush. Just because things were now out in the open didn't mean it would be easy. Getting it all out felt like passing a kidney stone. A big one.

"That's right," I said. "And I'm sorry. I always wanted to tell you, but I couldn't. Because of Mallory. Because of the pain her death caused your family. I was protecting myself that night, and it's the biggest mistake I've ever made, because I wasn't honest with you."

I explained about the money I'd been giving to the Steiners over the years, the amounts I'd taken out of our savings account. All because I'd thought I was behind the wheel.

"I saw the money being taken out," she said. "I mean, I'm not a dummy. But you pay most of the bills. At some point it wasn't really enough for me to worry about. I knew you had to put some money back into the Pig at one point. And then the work on the yard . . ."

I went on and told her about Dawn Steiner, how she'd asked for that big chunk of money that I didn't have. And the deadline she'd given me.

"I think the police are after her now," I said. "Since the story is out, she doesn't have any real leverage. And for all I know, she might have been working with Aaron to harass us. That's why—"

"That's why you asked if Aaron had a woman with him when he came to the door."

"Right."

"And all because Blake wasn't honest with you." She shook her head. "What a bastard."

I swallowed hard and told her about Blake coming to me outside the Pig, using the guilt over what I thought I'd done to the Steiner family to get me to go into Jennifer's house and retrieve the incriminating letters.

Her face changed, and changed significantly, when I reached the next part of my story. I told her what she had already figured out—that I'd lied about the basketball game the night I really went to Jennifer's house. And added insult to injury by lying again when she called me, asking me to come home. I sat across the table from her in our strangely quiet house, the absence of Henry's banging and chattering more noticeable than ever, and her eyes filled with tears. She fought them off and put on the best face she could, but I stopped, reached across the table, and squeezed her hand, which felt cold.

"I'm sorry," I said. "I feel like an asshole."

"That's the correct way to feel," she said.

"Do you want to stop talking?" I asked.

She shook her head. "No. I want to hear the whole thing. I want to know about yesterday and how you got away from this crazy man."

"You're sure?"

"I'm sure, Ryan. I'm a big girl, remember? I've been through an MBA program and also sixteen hours of labor. I can handle this."

So I finished the tale. All the way up to and through the stuff in the town house basement out at Hilldale Estates. The firing of the gun, the struggle on the floor. Holding Blake off so he didn't pound Aaron into oblivion.

"I even punched Blake once," I said. "When I found out he'd been gaslighting me over the accident. I couldn't stop myself. I punched him in the face."

"Good. Was it a hard punch?"

"As hard as I could make it," I said. "I'm not really an expert on such things."

"Good. I'd like to do the same thing to him."

"I get it, but we're not going to do anything with him anymore. We're done. I'm done. He leaves a trail of destruction wherever he goes."

"You're right." Her voice sounded distant and low.

I leaned farther across the table, moving my hand from hers to her forearm. "I'm sorry. About all of it. I lied, and I can't do anything about that except to say I'm sorry."

Amanda didn't pull away, but she didn't reciprocate my affection or contact either. She remained stiff in her chair, her eyes distant and distracted.

"What is it?" I asked.

She took her time, choosing her words carefully. She looked past me, not meeting my eye. "The lying," she said. "It hurts. It really fucking hurts. How could you just look me in the eye and tell me something that wasn't true? Even if it was just about a stupid basketball game. But it wasn't just about a stupid basketball game, was it? It led to all of this. It put us in danger. Both of us. And Henry."

I felt stung. I deserved it, but her words still stung. "I know."

"Are you sure there wasn't anything going on with you and Jennifer?" she asked. "You ended up going to her house, even after you were supposed to be done with her and her little flirtatious advances. And then she just happens to be dating Blake. It all seems so . . . I don't know. Convenient."

My face stung, but that time because it felt like it had been slapped. And hard. "Haven't we settled all of that? You saw everything between the two of us. Hell, you saw whatever you wanted on my phone and computer."

She kept looking away, but her cheeks flushed. We were a pair of red-faced lovers separated by a table-wide gulf of misunderstanding and suspicion. I pulled my hand back.

"I don't mind talking about all of this," I said. "But at some point, I want to move on and forget it."

"But doesn't all of this show that when you don't fully deal with the past, it comes back to bite you in the ass?" She looked at me now. Straight on. "Isn't that what we've been through the last couple of days?"

I couldn't argue. No way. But the excavation felt like digging up a lost and buried city. How long would it take?

"What do you want me to do?" I asked. "Amanda, I'm facing potential legal jeopardy here. I tampered with evidence. My name is all over the news. I'm going to pay the price. And I know you and Henry will too. Of course I'm sorry for that. More than anything else."

Amanda looked up at the clock above the sink. "I don't know what else to say. But I should go get Henry. Mom and Dad have somewhere to be later. I said I'd pick him up. And driving will clear my head a little."

"Let me go get him."

"Do you really want to go over there and face the Spanish Inquisition as performed by Bill and Karen? Besides, I could stand to get out of the house. I've felt like a prisoner lately. Hell, I was afraid to go anywhere for fear I'd get murdered. It will be nice to go and not worry about that."

"Okay," I said. And I knew she was right. The last thing I wanted to do was endure the inevitable barrage of questions about Aaron and Blake and Jennifer that my in-laws would fire my way like a series of missiles. "I understand."

When she went upstairs to get dressed, I felt lonely and pointless, cut off from everything. Normally I reached for my phone when I felt that way, but the phone and social media landscape offered no escape. I knew everywhere I scrolled or clicked I'd see news and questions about Jennifer and Blake and Aaron.

It seemed to take Amanda longer than normal to get ready, but eventually she came back down, dressed and ready to go. She stood across the room, her keys in her hand, the look on her face tense and guarded. "We can talk about this more," she said. "I know there's more to say. I guess I have more to say. And I'm trying not to be unfair and lay everything at your feet."

"It's okay. I get it."

She started to go and then seemed to remember something. She came over and pecked me on the cheek, a gesture that seemed strangely chaste and forced. "I'll be back as soon as I can."

"Okay. It's not such a long drive. You're making it sound like you're going to be gone for hours."

But she didn't respond to that. She went out the door, and once she left, I started looking for something to distract me in the real world instead of the virtual one.

CHAPTER SEVENTY-NINE

The police had seized my computer from Blake at Hilldale Estates, so I couldn't work. It hadn't been made clear to me yet exactly why Blake needed the computer. I knew he wanted to access the messages from Jennifer's phone because he'd tossed the phone away, but I didn't know why. Without the laptop in the house, and with the inhospitable landscape of social media at that moment, I felt like my right arm had been severed from my body.

In the fifteen minutes after Amanda left the house, I couldn't count how many times I glanced at my phone, lifting it toward my face, prepared to click on an app, only to realize I needed to heed Amanda's advice and not look. But then I asked myself a deeper and more profound question, one I'd refused to contemplate before that day: *How many times in an hour do I look at my phone? Fifty? One hundred?*

How did I get anything accomplished in my life? How did I talk to Amanda or interact with Henry with my face buried in my screens?

I held the phone with a tight grip and resisted the urge to throw it in the trash can in our kitchen. Instead I plugged it in, allowing it to suck up its vital electricity, and wandered out to the living room, where

I plopped onto the couch and picked up a novel I'd been attempting to read for the past month.

The house remained quiet. The smell of the coffee and the toast still filled the air. It felt strange to sit down and read with the phone so far away. It took me a few pages to remember what was going on in the story, because it had been days since I'd looked at it. But slowly things came back to me. A teenage boy during the Crusades had been apprenticed to a powerful knight. They prepared to set sail for the Holy Land. The author described the ringing of steel blade against steel blade, the smells of horses and cooking meat. I fell into the story. My mind cleared as I concentrated on one thing at a time and one thing only. I forgot about Blake and Jennifer and everything else that had happened, so much so that when the doorbell rang, I jumped about a foot off the couch.

Amanda?

But no. She'd come in the back door. And she never forgot her keys. And it was too soon for her to be finished with picking up Henry and talking to her parents. They'd never let her—or their only grandchild—get away so quickly.

I reluctantly set the book aside, using the subscription insert from a magazine as my bookmark, and went to the door. I thought about going to the kitchen and grabbing the baseball bat but decided against it. The boogeyman was gone, secure in the jail downtown, surrounded by cops and lawyers and bars. Aaron made a sad picture in my mind, locked up as he was, his life derailed by that night in college. And now Blake would be up to his neck in it for that night. I looked longingly at the book and the escape it promised to the Middle Ages.

I peeked out the window that afforded me a view of the porch. When I saw who was outside, I wished even more that I could go back to reading. I went over and undid the locks, opening the door to Detective Rountree. My hands shook as I stepped back, an involuntary reflex in the presence of cops, and one intensified by everything Rountree knew about me.

What could she possibly have shown up for?

She nodded to me as she came into the room. She looked around, although I wasn't sure what she was seeking.

"Is everything okay?" I asked.

Rountree stood with her back to me. If she intended to make me more nervous, and I think she did, it worked.

When a sufficient amount of time had passed, she turned and faced me. "Is your wife home, Mr. Francis?"

"No, she isn't. She went to her parents' house to pick up our son. Is something wrong?"

I caught a slight whiff of cigarette smoke in the air between us. I'd never noticed it on Rountree before, but maybe the stress of the past day had driven her to steal a few puffs in her car.

"Is she coming back soon?"

I replayed Amanda's somewhat odd response about how long she'd be gone. But I told myself it was nothing.

"Probably. Can you tell me what this is about? Why are you asking about Amanda?"

Rountree thought about it for a moment, and then nodded to herself as if she'd reached a conclusion inside her head. "I'm trying to tie up some loose ends and questions from our investigation. I thought Amanda might be able to shed some light on a few things."

"Amanda? Can't you just ask me?"

"Can you call her and see when she's heading back?" Rountree asked, her voice casual, making the request seem as simple as asking for a glass of water.

"I can. So you're not going to tell me what this is about?"

"If you give me her number, I can call her."

I let out an exasperated sigh. I went out to the kitchen and unplugged my phone from the wall. I saw more texts, more Facebook messages. None of them from Amanda.

I dialed her number, and as it rang, I walked back to the living room. "I'm tired of this cloak-and-dagger stuff. Can't you just tell us what's happening?"

Rountree ignored me. She stood in the center of the room with her hands clasped behind her back, tapping her right foot in time to a rhythm only she heard.

The call went to voice mail. I heard Amanda's peppy greeting asking me to leave a message. Which I did, asking her to call me as soon as she could.

"She's probably dealing with Henry. Or she's driving. She never answers when she's driving. She wouldn't answer while driving even before we had Henry."

"Won't she put it on speaker?"

"She won't. Not if he's in the car. She doesn't want any distractions. You know her sister—"

"I know. Can you try again? Just to be sure."

Her tone left little choice. And I didn't think I could refuse a cop. So I tried once more, receiving the same result. Voice mail. I skipped leaving a message.

"She'll probably be here in five minutes."

"Do you have your in-laws' number?"

"Yes, it's programmed in my phone."

"Can you try it?" she asked. "Like you said, maybe she's tied up with the baby. At least if they answer, they can tell you where she is. There. Or on her way back here."

I felt no desire to argue. The shaky feeling in my hands that started when I opened the door to Rountree grew in intensity, only its source became worry and concern over Amanda. And Henry. What did Rountree know? Why was she so adamant about tracking Amanda down?

"Can you just tell me why you need to know all this?" I asked.

"Like I said—loose ends."

"How did Amanda become a loose end? She doesn't know about any of this."

"Make that call, please."

So I did. The phone rang for a while, so I turned to Rountree and asked, "Did you look into Dawn Steiner? She could be involved in this too."

"She's part of this investigation."

Before she said more, Karen picked up, her cheerful hello likely loud enough for Rountree to hear.

"Hi, Karen. Look, is Amanda there? Or has she left yet?"

"Amanda?" She repeated the name like she'd never heard it before.

"Yes, is she there? Or is she heading back here?"

"Well, I must have my wires crossed. Or something. Amanda called me about fifteen minutes ago. She said she had something to do, and it might take all afternoon. Ryan, she told me you were going to come over and get Henry and that I shouldn't call her because she'd be busy."

CHAPTER EIGHTY

When I hung up with Karen, I made a special point of not looking at Rountree. I knew she knew I'd learned Amanda wasn't there, and I sensed she was ready to pounce with more questions. So I acted like she wasn't in the room and dialed Amanda's number again.

And again, it rang and rang.

I tried two more times with the same result.

"What about Dawn Steiner?" I asked. "Is she here in town?"

"We're working on accounting for her whereabouts. We have a lot of irons in the fire. But that's not your concern right now. Let me do my job."

"I get that. But we know the answer to the big question. It was Aaron who killed Jennifer. He was with her. He has a record."

I stared at the phone. A useless instrument.

"Mr. Francis?" Rountree said.

"Hold on."

I texted Amanda, asking her to call me. Then I sent another text, telling her she really needed to call me because the police were in the living room looking for her.

"Mr. Francis? I assume you don't know where your wife is right now."

I let my arms drop limply at my sides. The wind disappeared from my sails. "No, I don't. She's supposed to be . . ."

"So I gathered. But she told her parents she had somewhere else to go, and you don't know where that is. Right?"

"I don't know where she is."

"Do you track each other on your phones? Do you use a friend finder app or anything like that?"

"No, we've never used those." The next words I said came out with more difficulty. I still wasn't looking at Rountree. "We trusted each other. We said we wouldn't even do that to Henry when he was older."

Rountree took a few steps across the room until she'd moved into my line of sight. She made it impossible for me to pretend she wasn't there. "Do you want to sit down? Maybe she'll get your messages and call back. Let's give her a few minutes."

It was nice of her to say, and she spoke in soothing tones. But I could hear the undercurrent of doubt in her voice. She didn't really think Amanda was going to call me back. Not anytime soon.

Rountree took the lead and sat on the couch. What else could I do? I followed along and sat on the opposite end. My palms were sweaty, and I wiped the one that wasn't holding a phone against my pants leg.

"I should offer you something," I said. "Coffee or water?"

"I'm fine. Do you know why I'm here looking for your wife?"

My mouth felt dry. I wanted water. But I stayed rooted in place on the couch. "No, I don't. But I assume it has something to do with all of this craziness that's been going on. Like I told you when you first came in, Amanda didn't know anything about it. She didn't know Jennifer or Aaron. She didn't know I went over to Jennifer's house. Of anybody remotely tied up in this, she knew the least and did the least. Aaron came over here and threatened her. She could have been hurt."

Rountree nodded, her face full of sympathy. "I know Amanda isn't working now, not since she had the baby, right?"

"That's right."

"But before that she worked at Global Educational Enterprises. Right?"

"Yes. She wrote grants for them and brought in a lot of money. Once Henry gets a little older, she's going to go back and consult or freelance. Why does any of this matter?"

"You and Amanda both spend a fair amount of time on social media? You're both pretty active there?"

The direction of her questions irritated me. "What is this? Some kind of anti–social media screed? I can't get ahold of my wife, and you have a murder to investigate. In fact, don't you have Jennifer's murderer down in the jail? Or maybe it's one of those other ex-cons who killed her. The ones she helps at work?"

"We have a suspect in jail. But it's my job to explore all avenues that come up. I can't have tunnel vision and zero in on one person too early in the investigation."

"He tried to kill us," I said. "He wanted to. He fired a gun at us. And Blake . . . he killed somebody with a car."

"Your friend Blake has asked for a lawyer. And we're looking into that accident. It's been a number of years, which makes it tough."

"He admitted it. In that basement, he admitted it."

"He's being less cooperative now. But the guilty will pay a price for their behavior no matter what."

"What are you saying, then?" I asked.

"What I'm saying is that Amanda works in educational research and grant writing. But she also spends a lot of time online. Is she pretty adept with technology? Or are you?"

"I know how to hook up a printer. I know how to use apps. But I'm not an IT guy or anything. Neither is Amanda."

Rountree sat back against the cushions. She scratched her neck and seemed to be considering what to say next. She pointed at the phone in my hand. "Anything there?"

I looked at the screen. Nothing. But I could tell by the "read" receipts that Amanda had read my texts. She had seen them. Or someone had. Someone who had access to her phone. I told Rountree, and she nodded.

"Detective, is Amanda in some kind of danger? You come over here asking about her, and asking strange questions about social media, but you're not telling me what's really going on. If my wife is in danger, then I want you and me out there looking for her, not just sitting here on the couch talking in circles about stuff only one of us appears to understand. So can you tell me what's happening? Or else I'm going to get up and go find her."

Rountree scratched her neck again, and then she appeared to have reached the conclusion she'd been searching for. She leaned forward, placing her hands together in her lap.

"Do you know anything about hacking someone's Facebook account?" she asked.

CHAPTER EIGHTY-ONE

Her question threw me off. If she'd asked me how to build a rocket and fly to the moon, I wouldn't have been more surprised.

"I think I know what you mean," I said. "Are you talking about someone getting your password and then doing something to the account?"

She nodded. "Basically. Someone sends you a message that looks like it's really coming from Facebook, and it asks you to log in. When you do, the sender captures your ID and password. And then they're free to do what they want with your account."

"Okay, I get it. And I've had those messages sent to me before. But just because I use social media a lot doesn't mean I'd bother doing that."

Rountree looked skeptical. Maybe all cops looked skeptical all the time. "Are you sure about that?"

"I'm not lying, Detective. I've never done anything like that. Hell, I'm not sure I know anybody who would. Aren't those usually Russian hackers or scam artists? Why are you asking me about that?"

"Why do you think? We discovered that someone hacked into Jennifer Bates's Facebook account. We're not sure why they did it, but it means they could have been reading her messages."

"I had no interest in that. I wanted to stay away from her."

Rountree paused for the slightest moment before she asked, "Would Amanda know how to do that?"

The gears locked into place in my mind. She'd shown up looking for Amanda, and then she'd started asking about Amanda's ability to hack into someone's social media account.

"Amanda? Detective, you're going to have to speak some kind of English for me to follow all of this. What does this hacking stuff have to do with us? If Amanda wants to look at my social media accounts, she does. Lord knows she has."

Rountree rubbed her hands together as though she was cold. But I doubted that explained the gesture. She looked like she was working up to something, taking a slow approach to broaching a difficult subject.

"Do you remember how you received a friend request from Jennifer Bates while you were standing in her house the other night?"

"You mean, when I was standing over her dead body? Yes, Detective. I haven't managed to forget that moment. And I told you another one came through while I was sitting here in the house."

"Odd, no doubt. And disturbing. And of course, it doesn't make sense. How could she send you that request while she's dead on the floor? Right?"

"Good question," I said.

"Unless someone else had control of her phone or computer or other device. But all the devices were accounted for. Her computer. Her iPad. And you took her phone, as we know. Nothing else was missing from the house. That helped us rule out robbery. Someone had been in the house to kill her, but they hadn't taken anything valuable."

"Okay . . ."

"But someone sent the request. Well, now that we've been looking through her belongings and her online profiles, we believe we know how that might have occurred. Someone had apparently hacked into her account. They must have used a phishing scam and acquired her password and logged in that way. Anybody who has a Facebook account can look to see if someone else has logged in to their account from another device. And it gives an approximate location of the person who logged in. Most people don't know the feature exists, and most of us don't use it. I never have. But I will now. So we think someone did that with Jennifer's account. They could see everything she was doing. All her messages and everything else. They could take over the account and use it just like Jennifer could. And if they wanted, they could send a friend request that would appear to come from Jennifer Bates. And they did that the night you were in the house. Jennifer wouldn't have to have anything to do with it. In fact, even if she were alive, she wouldn't necessarily know anyone was viewing her private information or using her account. The average person wouldn't know or maybe even think to know. And most hackers don't want you to know they're there, so they wouldn't send a friend request that way. It stands out as odd behavior for a hacker."

Someone in the neighborhood turned on a saw, and the sound of it chewing through wood reached us in the quiet house. My phone sat quiet and still in my left hand. I wanted it to buzz or ring. I wanted to hear from Amanda.

"You said you can see where this person logged in from."

"We can. But it's very general. For example, it just says someone using a Mac computer logged on to Jennifer's account in Rossingville. Not very helpful. But do you all use Macs? You seem like the type."

"We do."

"What web browser do you prefer? I like Safari."

"I use Safari."

"And Amanda?"

I thought about it for a moment. "Yes, Safari. It's the best one for a Mac, isn't it?"

"Above my pay grade. Well, it turns out whoever was using Jennifer's account was using Safari."

"But that could be anybody."

"It could. I'm playing a hunch here a little bit. You see, I knew about those Facebook messages that Jennifer Bates sent you a while ago. The ones Amanda knew about too. And then you told me Jennifer sent you a friend request after you'd found her body. We've been pressing both Aaron Knicely and Blake Norton about this hacking, and neither man claims to know about it. Mr. Knicely hasn't really stayed up on technology. He doesn't have a lot of money to spend on it. And Mr. Norton, as I'm sure you know, is a self-proclaimed Luddite, someone who avoids that stuff as much as possible. Now, that doesn't mean they couldn't do it, but I tend to believe their denials."

"You do?"

"I do. And we know your wife saw those messages, so she might have a reason to look more closely at them. A jealous wife. Home with a baby. And you told me last night . . . you don't know where she was at the time Jennifer Bates was murdered. We know Jennifer was alive in the morning because Mr. Norton was over there. But in the afternoon, Amanda said she went to the store. Did she?"

"I don't know."

"But you called her. And?"

"She didn't answer."

"You thought Jennifer died at twelve fifteen because of the broken watch. Logical. That was our initial thought. But it turns out, she broke the watch last week while jogging. Her grandmother gave it to her, and she was wearing it until it got fixed. Her mother told us she felt horrible about damaging her grandmother's watch. That's why she kept wearing it. The medical examiner believes she died much later than twelve fifteen. You said her body felt cool when you touched it but not cold. Right?"

"Right."

"If she'd died around noon, she would have been cold. Late afternoon or evening, cool. It's not scientific, but it backs up what the medical examiner concluded based on her body temperature. About the time you called Amanda and got no answer. About the time she said she went to the store."

"You're throwing a lot of stuff at me, Detective," I said. "Amanda wouldn't know how to do something like this hacking." My words were true. It wasn't some weak defense, offered out of blind loyalty. I meant it. "She couldn't have. I would have known if she could do that. She used tech, but she wasn't a gearhead about it."

"Did she know anyone who could do that?" Rountree asked. "If not you, was there someone else?"

The protest rose within me, adamant and forceful. But as quickly as it rose, it withered and died inside my chest.

The answer was right there. And I knew it.

Of course.

Steve. The IT guy she used to work with. The one who was in love with her.

CHAPTER EIGHTY-TWO

I asked Rountree to give me a moment, and she agreed. Although she also said, "Time is urgent now. So just a moment. A very short moment."

I went down the hall to the half bathroom we'd renovated shortly after moving in. I turned on the water in the pedestal sink and splashed the coldness against my face over and over. The bracing coolness felt good.

As I toweled my face off, I looked in the mirror. None of it seemed real. Like I was staring at a picture of a TV character or someone on the news and wondering how their life had ended up so far down the wrong path. But the face belonged to me. And so did the life.

When I finished wiping the loose drops off my face and neck, I went back out to the living room, where Rountree was sitting, her thumbs working over her phone as she sent a text.

She looked up and waited patiently while I returned to my seat. She listened without showing any surprise while I told her about Steve the IT guy and how he could have been the person to help Amanda hack into Jennifer's Facebook account.

"Do you know his last name?" Rountree asked.

"Detective, maybe I should talk to Amanda first."

"Why?"

"Because you're saying all kinds of things that are bigger and more dangerous than anything I could have imagined. What you're saying is crazy."

"Maybe it is. But the sooner I talk to Amanda, the sooner she can be cleared. That's how it works. So, do you know this IT guy's last name?"

"I never knew it. I didn't want to know it. I was so disgusted by him coming on to Amanda in that way."

"Did he harass her? Was it something she needed to report?"

"No. Not like that, I guess. He just asked her out. She didn't feel like it crossed any lines of legality or ethics."

"So it was the same as Jennifer writing to you, right? Basically."

"I guess. Look, talk to that guy. You can find him at her company. It's out on Old Lexington Road. I'm sure he still works there. You can get his name and contact information from them."

"We'll look," Rountree said. "We'll talk to him."

"Hell, maybe Amanda's with—" But I cut off my own thought. I couldn't bear it. And it couldn't really be possible, could it? I'd been the distant and absent one lately. I'd been the one working too much. Had I driven her away?

But why that morning? Where would she have had to go without telling me or her parents what she was doing?

The thought of calling her again crossed my mind, but did I really want to know the answers to all of these questions? What if what I learned was worse than anything I could have imagined?

Had I told her everything about my past only to have her keep something huge from me?

"I've taken up enough of your time, Ryan," Rountree said. "And we certainly have some information to use going forward. I suggest you stay here, close to home, in case Amanda comes back. And if she does, you need to notify us right away. We do need to talk to her."

"Sure. Of course."

Rountree stood up, but she made no move for the front door. She held her phone in one hand, and she leaned down, studying my face. "Are you okay, Ryan? Would you like me to call someone for you? A friend? Another family member? Maybe your in-laws?"

"No." My voice was distant and small. My mind raced through the events of the past couple of days, trying very hard to piece things together. And one piece of the puzzle stood out and refused to fit. "Detective? I told you that when I saw the data on Jennifer's phone, there were Facebook messages that sounded threatening. I pointed those out to you when I turned everything over."

"I remember. Are you going to ask me who we think those messages came from?"

"Do I want to know any of this?"

Rountree straightened up and glanced at her phone. Whatever she saw there failed to interest her. "We don't know who they came from. Those have been hard to trace."

"Can't you find the IP address or whatever?" I asked.

She shook her head. "It's not that easy when someone uses a personal computer. A computer in your home may not even have a fixed IP address. What we do know is that someone threatened Jennifer Bates via Facebook message on the day she died. We know that person said they were going over to her house to see her. And Amanda's movements at the time of Jennifer's death are unaccounted for."

"She was . . . ," I said. I almost said, *She was home.* Then I remembered.

"You told me she was out," Rountree said. "You told me last night she called your mother-in-law to come and babysit Henry while she ran an errand. One we can't trace."

"She went to the store."

"Did she? Will the bank records show she purchased something? What did she need to buy so urgently that she suddenly was calling her mother to come over and watch Henry?"

"I don't know."

"And we don't know where she went."

"This is completely absurd. What you're saying is completely absurd."

"Let me ask you another thing. Does your wife own a pair of gloves? Black winter gloves? Last night you told me there was a glove on the floor of Ms. Bates's house. And you were right. We did find that glove there. A lady's glove. We thought it might belong to Ms. Bates, but then why would it be out in the middle of the floor when it's not that cold outside? So maybe we're rethinking things. Maybe the glove was dropped by the killer. We're checking it for DNA, of course."

"Lots of people own black gloves."

"But likely only one DNA profile will be on there. Maybe two if it touched the victim."

"I don't believe any of this."

"Why don't I just have a look at her devices? Laptop, iPad? It won't take long."

"Do you have a warrant?" I asked.

"Not yet."

"You're wrong. You're wrong to even think these thoughts. Just let it be."

"Prove I'm wrong, then," she said. "Find your wife and let her explain it all. Then everybody can move on." She started walking to the door and didn't look back, even as she said, "I'll be back with a warrant, then. It won't take long."

CHAPTER EIGHTY-THREE

I refused to sit around.

I refused to wait.

I stood in the middle of our living room surrounded by the photos of our life. A wedding portrait. The "For Sale" sign in the yard the day we moved in. Henry on Amanda's stomach moments after he was born. We'd built all of this. A life together.

Did it mean nothing?

But it was me. From the first day I'd met Amanda, I'd been lying. I never told her what I thought was the truth about the accident. I lied to her about going to Jennifer's house.

How could I expect honesty back from her? I'd started the lying. Had she built on top of it?

I took the risk of calling Karen and Bill. I hoped against all evidence to the contrary that Amanda had come to her senses, completed whatever task she was involved in, and returned to her parents' house to get Henry. As the phone rang at their house, I moved to the kitchen, remembering that just over an hour ago Amanda and I had sat down to coffee, hoping to begin the process of turning the page on everything that had happened. I walked past the spot where we sat together and looked out the back window, seeing the dogwood tree in my neighbor's yard sprouting white blooms. I hoped to see Amanda's car pulling in, Henry strapped in the back, life on the cusp of returning to normal.

But no one was there.

When Karen answered, I asked her if Amanda had shown up to get Henry.

"She sure hasn't." A TV played in the background, and I expected Karen to place her hand over the phone and ask Bill to turn the volume down like always. But she didn't. "Bill is out right now running an errand. Ryan, can you tell me what's going on over there exactly? I've started seeing these things on the news, and then you call here like you don't know where Amanda is."

"That's because I don't know where she is."

"Ryan, they're saying that someone tried to kill you. That you were mixed up in an accident that caused a girl to get killed when you were in college."

My throat constricted. Mallory. I couldn't imagine the pain the news summoned up in her and Bill.

"I was there, yes. A girl was killed in an accident. Another girl was hurt."

"Were you driving?"

"No, I wasn't."

There was a long pause. I thought she might hang up on me.

"Ryan, you know Bill is a very good listener. If you'd like to, come over sometime and talk to him. Or maybe the two of you could go out for a beer or something when he gets back, even though it's early. I could take Henry to the park and leave the house to you. It's important to talk. Maybe you could get some perspective. We know Amanda very well, and she can be difficult if she feels she's been betrayed. She seems very rational and calm most of the time, and she is. But betrayal and dishonesty can really get her. She just needs time to come to her senses—"

"Karen. Karen, it's fine. Just take care of Henry for us. Okay? It gives us peace of mind knowing he's with you."

I hoped the flattery would work, that it would redirect her away from the questions about the events of the last couple of days. It did.

"Well, you know we just love to have him here. He's a doll."

"Yes, we know. Now, are you sure Amanda didn't say anything about where she was going today? Anything at all?"

"She was pretty evasive. . . ."

The volume of the TV increased. It felt like Karen had moved closer to the set, almost like she'd placed the phone up against the speaker. I angled my phone away from my ear to get some relief.

"Karen?"

"Ryan, is Amanda okay? I'm concerned about all of this. She's our daughter . . . our only . . . and if you can't find her and she didn't tell us where she was going, then we're going to start worrying. All these things you men do. The drinking and the driving. The stuffing away of feelings. It ends up hurting people. Please tell me something that will set my mind at ease."

"There's a lot of stuff going on right now. I think Amanda just needed time to clear her head. She learned a lot of things pretty quickly, even some things about me she didn't really know."

"Are you the one who's been giving money to that family? The girl who was hurt in the accident? They're saying that on the news."

"That's part of it, okay? Yes, I have been doing that. And Amanda didn't know about it."

"Oh, my. I bet she's angry. She can get her back up with the best of them when she's pushed. But where is she now?"

"Karen, can you do me a favor? If Amanda calls or texts or comes by, will you have her call me right away? The police need to talk to her."

"The police?" Her voice rose an octave. Louder and higher than the TV. "Ryan, Amanda didn't do anything. She didn't do anything at all, did she?"

"Are you sure she didn't say where she was going today? Think hard. Even just the smallest hint about what she might have been doing."

"She didn't tell us anything, Ryan," Karen said. "Maybe you're right. Maybe she's just clearing her head. I'd like to think that. Wouldn't you?"

"Yes, I would. I'm trying to."

But in the back of my mind, I thought of the threatening messages sent to Jennifer by someone. Amanda leaving the house without telling any of us where she was going.

"A couple of days ago, Karen, Amanda asked you to come over to the house to watch Henry while she went out. Do you remember that?"

"Sure. Of course."

"Did she say where she was going that afternoon?"

"Let's see. . . . She said she had an errand to run. She was gone about an hour. Maybe a little more. I thought maybe she went to the store, but she didn't have any bags when she came back."

"How did she seem?"

"Oh, frazzled. Like most young moms are. I think Henry was being difficult. You know, I wouldn't have cared if she just wanted to go out and have a glass of wine with a friend. That would be okay with me. Maybe she did, although she didn't seem any more relaxed when she came back than when she left. But she didn't tell me anything."

"I see. . . ."

From time to time, I lost sight of how smart my mother-in-law really was. While she could seem distracted and fuzzy as she grew older, she also managed to surprise me with pointed insights when I least expected them. That day looking for Amanda was no different. The most important things failed to get past her.

"That's the day that girl was murdered, wasn't it?" Karen said. "The day she asked me to come over to watch Henry."

"Yes, it was."

"And on the news they're saying that was about the time she died. Late afternoon."

"Karen, if she calls or comes by, please tell her to call me. Immediately."

"Ryan, all of this makes me wonder what was going on. With you. And her."

I chose not to clarify who she meant by "her." Was it Amanda? Or Jennifer?

I didn't have time. And it didn't matter.

"Just take good care of Henry," I said, and ended the call.

CHAPTER EIGHTY-FOUR

I'd spent the morning ignoring texts, voice mails, and social media messages from concerned friends who had seen my name splattered all over the news. Hours had passed with me swimming in a self-imposed news-blackout bubble.

So when I started calling Amanda's friends, a number of whom had already reached out to me, they assumed I wanted to talk about Jennifer or Aaron or Kyle or something related to that mess. When I cut their questions off, trying as much as possible to be courteous, and asked them if they'd heard anything from Amanda, their confusion and then their suspicions only grew.

"Amanda?" they asked. "Don't *you* know where Amanda is? Isn't she with you?"

I stammered over my responses, even though I knew the questions would be coming.

"I'm not sure where she went," I'd tell them. "And I just really need to talk to her."

I left out any mention of the police. Or the hacking of Jennifer's Facebook account. Or the mystery of Amanda's whereabouts on the day Jennifer died. I sacrificed a chunk of the truth in exchange for protecting Amanda from the suspicion of her friends. If they wanted to cast blame, they could cast it on me, the doltish husband who kept secrets and embarrassed his wife. I hoped no one would ever find out what Rountree had told me. I hoped Amanda would be found, and there would be a simple explanation for everything.

After a series of fruitless calls, I headed upstairs. Amanda kept an office in the room next to Henry's. When company came, we put them on the couch in my office because it folded out into a bed. And then our guests were far away from us at night.

I almost never went into her office when she wasn't in there. It was her private space, a room where she could retreat and get her work done. Or she could hand Henry off to me in the evenings or on the weekends while she shut the door and polished her résumé or stayed up to date in her field. I understood the need for that designated work space.

Unlike me, Amanda managed to keep her desk clean and orderly. A place for everything and everything in its place. Files and cabinet drawers were labeled. Pencils, pens, and Sharpies were neatly arranged in a cup. Every office supply—stapler, Post-its, paper clips—was within easy reach and functional. More often than not, I couldn't find my stapler. And when I pushed down on it, I'd find out it was empty.

Amanda's laptop sat in the middle of the desk, a silver island amid all the clean space. I'd never gone on there without her permission. And even when I had permission, it felt strange. Sort of like—

Sort of like being in a stranger's house when they weren't home.

Or scrolling through a stranger's texts and social media messages after they were dead.

I opened the lid of the laptop.

Her screen saver greeted me. A photo of Henry in his crib smiling like he knew the secret to a happy life. And a request for the password.

I knew it. Amanda had told me over a year ago, when she'd bought the computer, what the password was in case I ever needed it. I hoped she hadn't changed it since then. If she'd changed it and hadn't told me . . .

I entered the password. The name of her favorite book when she was a child along with the number she wore on the softball team in high school. WindWillow43.

It worked. Everything on her neatly organized desktop appeared to me. I sat down and used my finger on the pad to move the cursor around until I opened her text message app. I imagined archaeologists way in the future trying to decode our language of emojis and abbreviations. Our one-sentence and fragmentary communications. Would they find anything worth digging up?

I saw my name. Sam's. Karen's. Bill's. Several friends', and the name of Amanda's cousin in Los Angeles.

But right at the top, clear as day: Steve.

I felt a little jab in my guts, a sharp twist of jealousy. The back of my neck where my skin met my shirt collar grew warmer. Sweat formed there.

I knew how Amanda had felt seeing those messages from Jennifer.

She and Steve had been talking just twenty minutes earlier. In other words, right before Amanda left the house, supposedly to get Henry. But really not.

So what was she doing?

I scanned the messages, and a few phrases jumped out.

Someone threatened this Jennifer.

Police can't trace it.

Someone named Lily Rose. Do you know who that is?

Oh, God. I have to go.

Lily Rose? Threatened Jennifer?

Why did Amanda have to go once she read that name?

I remembered the other threatening messages from that account.

I entered Steve's number into my phone and hit CALL as I started down the stairs.

CHAPTER EIGHTY-FIVE

Steve answered by the time I reached the kitchen. I took my keys and wallet off the counter, left the bat resting in the corner of the room, even though a part of me wanted to grab it.

"This is Amanda Francis's husband," I said. "Ryan."

"Oh," he said. "I see."

"Yes, you see. Where is she?"

I started for the back door. If my collar had been hot when I was upstairs, it reached the boiling point when I heard his voice. My actions were frantic. I dropped my keys twice as I walked to the door, the phone cradled against my shoulder. My heart thumped, and I wanted to shout. Really shout.

I wanted to reach through the phone and throttle him.

"I don't know."

"Who is Lily Rose? What's going on here? You know, the cops are looking for you. They're going to track you down. They know about the hacking. Do you think you can skate on this?"

I stopped by the door, my hands shaking. I wanted to make sure I really heard what he had to say.

"Look," Steve said. "I can tell you what I know."

"Where's Amanda?"

"That I don't know."

"Don't lie to me." I saw Henry's high chair, his plastic cup sitting on the dish rack. A copy of his birth announcement still on the refrigerator. "You're in the middle of this."

"Maybe I shouldn't be talking to you."

His voice was so calm, so reasonable, that I wanted to shout. Then I saw my hurried movements and shaking hands from the outside for a moment. I was stomping around like an angry kid. And what was it accomplishing? Nothing. None of my theatrics would tell me where Amanda was. Or who Lily Rose was.

I took two deep breaths, felt the sweat on the back of my neck cool a little.

"Don't say that," I said. "What do you know?"

"I don't know where Amanda is," he said.

I hated hearing him say her name. Hated it.

He went on. "I texted her this morning. I looked over the messages on that Facebook account we hacked when I heard all the details of the murder. This Jennifer's murder. I saw that someone had been threatening her. Someone named Lily Rose. So I wanted to tell Amanda about it. I knew she was dealing with the police. I thought she could put the detectives in touch with me. But Amanda . . . she acted very upset and scared when she saw that name. Lily Rose. It's like she knew who that was."

"And who was it? Is it someone you work with?"

"She didn't say. She said she had to go. I tried calling her, but she didn't answer."

"That's it?" I asked. "That's all you know?"

"That's it. Okay? If I knew more, I'd tell you."

"Well, you can tell the cops," I said. "They're going to be coming to talk to you."

"They're on their way over now. I can show them everything I have. Which isn't much."

Again, he sounded so calm. So rational. I wanted to say something. Insult him. Call him a name.

But nothing came to mind.

So I said, "If you hear from her, tell her to call me."

"I will."

I poked the red END CALL button with as much force as I could muster. It in no way felt satisfying.

CHAPTER EIGHTY-SIX

Lily Rose.

Who the hell?

I gripped my keys tighter and pulled the back door open. The cool morning air brushed over me. Someone was mowing their lawn, and the sweet smell of freshly cut grass hit me, mocking me with its invocation of more innocent times.

I pulled the door shut and started to lock it.

"Hold it."

I froze. That husky voice. The time of morning.

I spun. "I can't deal with you, Dawn."

She stood ten feet away, her hip cocked, her hands stuffed into the pockets of a hoodie. Her features were set as hard as marble. Her hair was loose from her ponytail, and dark circles showed under her eyes.

It must have been a long, sleepless night for her as well.

"You have to," she said. "This is the time."

"It's over, Dawn. With you and me and all of this. The secrets are out. And I have to go."

I started to move past her and she moved along with me, blocking my way. Her running shoes scraped against the pavement of the driveway like a basketball player's.

"Get out of the way," I said.

I reached out, intending to brush her aside, but she held her ground.

And pushed her hand forward in the pocket of her hoodie. Something long and firm pointed at me. Something that wasn't a human finger.

"Dawn? This is crazy."

"You didn't lock the door yet. I was watching. Get back inside."

"No."

I tried to move past her with greater speed, and again she moved along with me. She came close enough to press the object in her pocket against my ribs. She applied so much pressure it hurt.

It was sharp. Metal.

A gun barrel. For real.

"Get back inside," she said.

For the second time in less than twenty-four hours, a nutjob threatened me with a gun. While more sweat poured down my back, my insides turned to ice.

"Go," she said.

Did I have a choice?

I backed up slowly, making no sudden moves, and pushed the door open. Dawn followed me inside. Her eyes were narrow, the pupils like polished river stones. She left the door open behind her, the view of the green grass and the car beyond taunting me with the possibility of escape. But it was so far away from me with her in between.

I thought of yelling or screaming, but if she was desperate enough, she might just cut me down as soon as I shouted. I had no idea how far she'd go. But at that point, she seemed determined to go as far as she could.

"I don't have the money for you," I said. "Even if I wanted to give it to you, it's not here. And the bank is closed on Saturday. I could get a few hundred bucks out of an ATM, but that's all. Come back Monday."

I'd positioned myself when I came in the door so that the table was between us. I harbored some faint hope that if a bullet flew, I could drop down and find some shelter or protection. But as I spoke, Dawn moved around the end of the table, coming closer, that threatening object in her pocket always zeroed in right on my torso.

"Monday's too late," she said.

"Too late for what?"

A change passed over her face. Her chin quivered ever so slightly. And the hardness went out of her eyes and was replaced by welling tears. Her cheeks flushed.

For a moment, the gun wavered inside her hoodie as though she'd grown momentarily weaker.

"You'd never understand the loss my parents suffered," she said.

"I know. I can't."

"Everything they'd dreamed of stripped away. Two children's lives cut off."

The cold inside me turned to nausea. "I'm sorry. I am."

"And me . . . what have I done for them? They couldn't count on me either."

"I'm sure that's not true."

I caught movement out of the corner of my eye. I'd been so intently focused on Dawn—on the object in Dawn's pocket—that I hadn't been watching the door.

But someone slipped in. They moved stealthily, like a cat.

A familiar figure . . .

And then they were behind Dawn. Pressing something into the small of her back.

"Drop it," Bill said. "Just take it easy and drop it."

CHAPTER EIGHTY-SEVEN

Bill reached around Dawn's waist and took the object out of her hoodie pocket.

It was a gun. Black and sleek, the light from the window above the sink reflecting off the barrel. Bill adroitly racked the slide and ejected the clip.

"Nothing," he said. "It's not loaded."

I breathed a sigh of relief. I wanted to slump down on the floor and let every tense and corded muscle in my body unclench.

Dawn appeared to feel the same way. She took a hesitant step forward and pulled out one of the kitchen chairs. She dropped into it, letting her body weight crash into the seat. Her shoulders slumped, and for the first time since I'd met her, her body looked limp and powerless. She put her head in her hands, as though Bill and I weren't in the room.

"Bill, what are you doing here?" I asked.

"I was out, running an errand. Karen called me and said something was going on with Amanda. You couldn't find her, and you might need help, so I came over. I saw the open door. I thought someone might have broken in again."

"Did you buy a gun?" I spoke in a whisper, knowing Amanda's opposition to his talk of arming himself. I'd agreed with Amanda's position in the past, but in the moment, I was glad my father-in-law had arrived ready for action.

"No," he said. "Are you kidding? I don't want Amanda mad at me." He reached into his pocket and brought out a screwdriver with a worn yellow handle. "I used this. I stuck it in her back. She fell for it. Fortunately."

"And if she hadn't?"

Bill shrugged. He hadn't had a plan B.

Dawn made a low noise from her position at the table. I looked her way, listening, and couldn't tell if she was laughing or crying.

"I'm calling the police," Bill said.

"Go ahead," she said, her words muffled.

"What brought this on, Dawn? It's all over. It was over yesterday."

She said something else, but the words were too low and again too muffled for me to understand. I asked her to repeat herself, and she lifted her head and said, "My parents."

"What about them?" I asked.

"I did it for them," she said.

"I was already giving them money. Why didn't you just ask me to give them more?"

She leaned back, tilting her head until she stared at the ceiling. Her eyes were full of tears, but they didn't spill. Her compressed lips and taut jaw told me she was fighting to keep them back. She lowered her head and said, "It's not to give to them. It's to give them something." She tapped her fingers against the table. *Rat-a-tat-tat*. "To give them a grandchild, another chance after they lost Maggie. And since Emily isn't going to get married. And I'm not close either."

"What is she saying, Ryan?" Bill asked. "Buy a grandchild?"

"Not buy," Dawn said. "They *have* a grandchild. I gave a baby up for adoption when I was in high school. I got knocked up like an idiot, and they made me give the baby up. They were right, but it also means they didn't get to see the kid grow up. I got a picture every once in a while, but that's hardly the same. The kid's only twelve now, and I can't really have contact with her until she's eighteen. But I know the parents. They were willing to let my daughter—*their* daughter—see my parents if I gave them enough money. That's why I was putting the squeeze on you. I needed the money for that. And to just try to get the kid away from those awful people. I can't scrape it all together. I'm a freelance illustrator. I don't have that kind of money just lying around, so I went to you."

"That's blackmail," Bill said. "I'm calling now." And he did, punching in the three numbers that summoned the police.

"My father has prostate cancer," Dawn said. "He can hear the clock ticking. They didn't mention it in the article, but when he talked about medical bills and insurance, his illness was a big part of it. I wanted him to meet his grandchild now. Probably the only one he'll ever have."

Bill hesitated for a moment, the phone in his hand. Then he nodded as though confirming something to himself. "I'm still calling."

"I'm sorry, Dawn," I said. "I am. But I have to go. Bill? Have you got this?"

"I do. Where are you going?"

"I'm finding Amanda."

"I'll go with you."

"Stay here. Wait for the cops. I'll let you know when I find her."

"Do you know where to look?" Bill asked. "I thought you didn't know where she was."

"I don't know, Bill." And the enormity of the task froze me. No, I didn't know where to look. I could only guess. Friends' houses. A park. The library. All of them long shots, all of it slow and uncertain. "I'm just guessing. I'm trying anything."

"Aren't you going to your friend's wedding?" Dawn asked.

"What are you talking about?"

"Your asshole friend, the one the news is saying *really* killed my sister. He's getting married today. I saw it on his fiancée's Facebook page. Her stuff is public. I guess she wants everyone to know she's getting married. I thought about just going out there and killing him. I really did. It would have been pretty satisfying. But it wouldn't help my parents as much as meeting their granddaughter would."

"Are you sure?" I asked. "Blake was being questioned by the police last night. I guess he could be out already. But getting married?"

"Deer Valley Barn. I saw a picture of the stupid bridesmaids drinking champagne this morning."

"But Amanda wouldn't go there. . . ."

I was thinking out loud, and my voice trailed off. She wouldn't. But she and I would know a lot of people there. It was the greatest concentration of our friends I would be likely to find.

And maybe Sam had heard from her. . . .

"I'll be in touch, Bill."

And I went out the door.

CHAPTER EIGHTY-EIGHT

Deer Valley Barn sat five miles east of Rossingville, nestled in a series of rolling hills and surrounded by farms and grazing cattle and wide-open spaces as far as the eye could see. I headed out there, navigating my way along the narrow two-lane road, dipping and rising past freshly disked fields, the rich, dark earth already planted and ready to yield the summer's crop of corn and soybeans.

I thought of Dawn. So desperate to do something for her parents, something to ease their pain. How far we would go for those we love. To protect them. To care for them.

How far had Amanda gone to try to keep the person she loved?

The Barn had come into existence about five years earlier when a local farmer died and no one in his family wanted to hang on to the land, so they sold it to an event planner who realized money was to be made by renting out a renovated barn to young couples who wanted to get married in a rustic setting. The perfect Instagram filter at the right time of day, with cows and gently swaying grasses and trees in the background, made for beautiful wedding photos. Amanda and I might have said our vows in a similar place except that Bill had refused to pay for the wedding—and we'd had no money at the time to do it ourselves—unless we got married in his and Karen's church.

I crested the last rise, and the Barn came into sight. As it did, my phone rang. Rountree's name popped up on the car's display. I pushed the button to hear her.

"Have you found Amanda yet, Mr. Francis?" she asked without offering any greeting.

"Not yet."

"Where are you?"

"I'm out. Looking. Is that all you called for?"

"Where do you and your wife grocery shop?" she asked, her voice cool and detached. "I know there's only one Kroger store close to downtown where you live. And it's the nicest one. Is that where you shop?"

A small sign marked the entry to the long driveway, and as I turned in, the lush grass on either side greener than emeralds from the recent rain, I wondered about what I'd find there. I certainly didn't want to see Blake. If I did, I wasn't sure what my reaction would be—overwhelming sadness at the loss of our friendship or all-consuming rage at everything he'd put me and everyone else through. I counted on the amount of activity required of a bride and groom before a wedding—the picture taking, the fussing with clothes, the greeting of relatives—to ensure that we didn't cross paths. All I needed to do was see one friend of ours, one person with insight into Amanda's whereabouts, and then I'd be gone, zipping back down the driveway and out of the countryside like an alien observer.

"Yes, that's right," I said. "That Kroger store. Why?"

"One of my colleagues checked the CCTV footage. It was all right there, and Kroger was more than happy to cooperate with us."

"So?"

"So Amanda wasn't on there. She didn't go to the store at that time on Thursday. No sign of her. Do you have another guess as to where she was?"

It took three tries, but I finally managed to hit the END CALL button with my index finger. And then I saw I was driving too fast and hit the brakes, slowing the car.

The small parking lot was half full. Blake had told me it would be a small wedding, and from previous experience, I knew the Barn sat only about one hundred people. It advertised itself as an intimate setting, one where your closest friends and family could celebrate with you on your special day. I circled the lot, watching mostly young people step out of cars, the men in suits with no ties, the women in floral dresses and sandals. I looked for a familiar face and saw none. I stopped on the far side of the lot, waiting while two more cars came in and gave up their occupants. A young couple and a middle-aged couple, no one I knew.

Was I even in the right place? I found it hard to believe I wouldn't have recognized someone by now, but maybe Blake led a life I didn't know about. That seemed to be the theme that had taken over my life— did I really know anything about anybody close to me?

If Amanda hadn't gone to the store on Thursday, then where had she been?

At the time Jennifer was killed . . .

I took one more turn around the lot. When I reached the other side, I craned my neck, peering down the side of the Barn itself to the back, where a catering van stood with its rear doors open, and three guys with long hair and neatly cropped beards carried guitar cases and a snare drum. Behind them, and at a slight distance from the Barn, I saw a familiar figure.

Amanda.

She was talking in an animated fashion to a woman in a light blue dress who wore her hair piled on top of her head. Something about the woman's body and the way she tilted her neck looked familiar, and I would have sworn it was Sam, except Sam would have been wearing a wedding gown and not the simple dress this woman wore.

I stopped the car, jamming it into park.

My heart thumped fast enough that the guys in the band would have struggled to keep up if they tried to play along. Why was she here when we had turned down the invitation?

Amanda and the woman who I then recognized as Sam's younger sister, Wendy, spoke with more intensity, and the sister threw her arms up in the air as if she'd reached the brink of exasperation. I started walking toward them, moving slowly, even though Amanda was so focused on whatever she was saying that she never would have seen me coming.

Until the other woman threw up her hands again and made a quick pivot on her heels and disappeared through a door that led into the back of the Barn. When she was gone, Amanda turned away and faced off into the distance, where a handful of dark cows lazed near a small pond, looking like the living embodiment of ease and leisure.

When I came close enough for Amanda to hear me, I said her name.

She spun as quickly as Wendy had, her lips parted. She looked slightly surprised to see me but not unhappy. She let out a little breath, an acknowledgment that my sleuthing skills had impressed her.

I looked behind me at the Barn, expecting Wendy to come back out at any moment, but the door remained closed. The band and the caterers had disappeared inside as well, leaving us the only two people in the vicinity of the back of the building. I checked my watch. Ten minutes until noon. Almost time to start.

"What are you doing here?" I asked.

"I could ask you the same thing."

"I'm looking for you. And here you are at a wedding we said we wouldn't go to."

"I'm not here for the wedding," she said. "You should know that."

"Then what are you here for? Because it sure as hell looks like they're going ahead and having a wedding today."

"I listened to your messages," Amanda said. "I know the police are looking for me."

"So you came here . . . why? Because you thought the cops wouldn't show up at a wedding? I don't understand. You should have called me back. You should have come home. Your parents are worried. I'm worried. I'm scared too."

"Why are you scared?" she asked.

"Because of what the police found," I said. "In Jennifer's Facebook account."

The corners of her mouth turned down. Her shoulders slumped. She looked away, off into the distance, and I saw her in profile. Young looking. Beautiful.

Scared.

"What happened, Amanda?" I asked. "Is what the cops are saying true? You didn't go to the store on Thursday. Where were you?"

Her eyes looked deadly serious as she nodded her head.

"It's true," she said. "But I want you to understand why I did what I did."

CHAPTER EIGHTY-NINE

Amanda turned to face me when she started explaining.

The ground felt unsteady beneath my feet. My knees shook, reminding me of the kind of fear I had felt as a child when I was expected to go off the high diving board or deliver a speech in class.

Except the stakes here were much, much higher. As I stared at Amanda's face, I saw Henry there. Our son. Sitting with his grandparents, unable to comprehend what we were doing.

Would he ever comprehend it? Would he ever know his mother?

"You know some of it," she said. "When I saw those messages from Jennifer on your computer, I felt like crap. Jealous, of course. You know the kind of condition I was in then. I was going to stop working. I was getting bigger and bigger." She pointed to her now-flat stomach. "I felt tired, hormonal. You worked all the time, and I felt like the world had left me behind. I was wondering if I'd ever get back to work again. Would I ever be anything but a mom, sitting at home, changing diapers and cleaning up snot?"

"You know that would never be true."

"But I felt it. The feelings were as real as anything to me. And I thought you might not find me as appealing anymore. So I wanted to know what was going on with this woman. I wanted to know if you were talking to her all the time. And what kinds of things you might be saying to her. Or doing with her."

"Why didn't you just ask me?"

"You didn't tell me about it," she said. She swallowed, controlling herself. "Why didn't *you* tell me? You must have been hiding it. And if you were hiding it, then there must have been a reason." She shrugged, a slight movement of her shoulders. "So I got in touch with Steve. From work. I knew he liked me as more than a friend, so it felt good to talk to him online. And in the course of our conversations, I told him about my problems . . . our problems . . . and he came up with the solution of phishing so I could spy on Jennifer's account. Then I would know if you and she were doing something."

"Why didn't you just track *my* account?"

"I thought of that. Of course. That was the first thing that came to mind. But you have a lot of devices and accounts. You have things at work I don't even know about. And if you were doing something behind my back, wouldn't you be on the lookout for stuff like that? I figure you're too smart to fall for a phishing scam. But *she* wouldn't be so careful. *She* had nothing to lose by disrupting our lives. So it would make more sense to watch her. And Steve knew how to do it. He knew how to create a message that would get her password, and once you have that done, you can see everything she does. He made it all look very easy. Frighteningly easy, to be honest."

"That's quite an invasion of privacy."

"Like going into her house to steal her love letters? How is that any different, except one is in the virtual world and one is in the real? Or can we even tell the difference anymore?"

I offered no argument, because she was right. We'd both done the same thing, for stupid and vain reasons. We'd both failed. And where did we go from there?

"The police know, Amanda. That's why I was calling you and looking for you. They suspect about the phishing. Did you send those friend requests from her account after she was dead? Why the hell would you do that?"

"I didn't know she was dead when I sent the first one. I sent it because you'd lied to me that night. You lied about where you were going. And I suspected. She'd written to you again, and then you lied and said you were going to a basketball game. Supposedly. I guess I just sent the request to prove my point, to shake you up if you were there. With *her*. And I was right. You were with her. I wanted to scare you back to your senses."

"But I wasn't with her for that reason. You know that now. I was there because of Blake. And why did you send the other one? Once you knew she was dead?"

"Because you weren't talking to me. I knew you were keeping something from me but I wasn't sure what. I wanted to see if the bizarreness of the request would get you to tell me something. Anything."

"Those requests scared the daylights out of me. I thought someone was watching me, tracking me."

"I wanted to shake you up, not terrify you."

"Why are you here?" I asked. "Of all places. When the police are looking for you . . . and you left the house saying you were going to your parents' to get Henry."

I struggled to say the next words, to force them out of my mouth.

"The police, Amanda. They want to know where you were the day Jennifer was killed. During the time of her death . . . you called your mom and had her come over. And you went somewhere. You said you sent that friend request because you thought I went to see her. But when I did that for Blake and went to her house, I didn't know she was dead. I truly didn't."

She stared at me. She cocked her head to one side. Her lips parted in an almost expectant fashion.

"And?" she asked.

"I didn't know she was dead but . . ."

"You can't even bring yourself to ask the question, can you? You came over here ready to talk to me, but you can't ask what you really want to know."

"Because I'm afraid of the answer."

She brought her lips together and then spoke. "You're afraid to ask me if I called my mother that day so that I could go over to Jennifer's house. You're afraid to ask if I'm the one who killed Jennifer."

CHAPTER NINETY

Amanda took a step back. She placed her hands on her hips and looked at the ground, apparently taking the time to choose her words carefully.

"I don't know what I think of that question," she said. "And I don't know how to respond to it. Not really."

"Just tell me the truth. I can handle it. . . . I just want to know what's going on. I don't want to believe it. I don't believe it. But I don't know what else to think. . . . We've both acted crazy."

She looked up at me. "I'm surprised, really surprised, that you would even ask me that question. As long as we've known each other . . ."

"I've lied. We've made mistakes. If you went over there and something went wrong . . . Look, I'm the one who drove you to do it. I wasn't attentive, or whatever I needed to be. I wasn't aware of what you were going through." My thoughts ran together, like cars colliding on a freeway. I tried to make it as simple as possible. As simple and as frightening. "Just tell me everything. I know you didn't go to the store. And the cops know that too."

She remained in place with her hands on her hips. But she nodded her head, ready to share it all. "I did go over there to have it out with Jennifer that day. That's why I called Mom. That's why I needed a baby-sitter. I'd seen that she'd reached out to you again just a couple days before, and at that time, I guess the two of you were still Facebook friends."

"I told you I unfriended her after that last message. That's why you were able to send those creepy requests."

"Yes, and I felt like I was being attacked. Like my family was being attacked by her. Not just me. But you. And Henry. All of us. And I felt vulnerable. And I wanted it to end. I just wanted it to end."

I swallowed hard. "What happened?"

"I found her address. I drove to her house. I looked at it, wondering what was going on inside. Who the woman was who lived there. What had she been through? What did she think about? Were we that different when you got right down to it? I saw on Facebook she worked at a nonprofit, that she was doing important work. I guess it would have been easier to hate her if she was some vapid bimbo." She shook her head. "How was I to know what her life was like? Or what motivated the things she did?"

"So . . . ?"

"I stared at her house for almost thirty minutes. Frozen. And then I left. I went and got a giant coffee at Starbucks, sat in the park, in-dulging myself for a while, and then I went home and back to my normal life. Except you lied to me that night and went out . . . and I sent that first friend request. And when Jennifer ended up dead . . . I didn't know what to think. She might have been dead while I was sitting outside her house. But I didn't see or hear anything."

Days' worth of tension and anxiety had built within me. Like a wall of water held back by a dam, the pressure had grown and grown. When Amanda said those words, when she told me the truth about her where-abouts on the day Jennifer died, something slipped inside me. The pressure and tension loosened, and so too did nearly every muscle in my body. I thought I might fall over. My head swirled, and I expected to see the ground rushing up to meet me.

But I held on, remaining upright.

I willed myself forward, moving toward Amanda. And she opened her arms to me, looking as weak and spent as I felt.

We fell against each other, holding each other up.

I kissed the top of her head and pulled her as close as I could.

I told her I was sorry over and over again. I told her I loved her. The words all felt insufficient to the moment. Words always did.

I wanted nothing more than to get Henry and go home with him and Amanda. That was all I cared about. I wanted my world to encompass nothing more than those two people.

I didn't know how much time had passed. My grip loosened on her body. She moved back so I could see her face.

"Let's go," I said. "Let's go get Henry and get out of here."

But Amanda surprised me by shaking her head. "We can't."

"Why? Do you want to go to the wedding? After all this?"

Again, Amanda shook her head. "Aren't you wondering why I'm out here? Why of all places I came here?"

I had been wondering when I first pulled up and saw her talking to Wendy. But then those thoughts went away as I started talking to her.

But now . . .

"Okay," I said, "why are you here?"

"Because I needed to talk to somebody about everything that's been going on. Somebody who knows what really happened . . ."

Before I could ask who she meant, a voice behind us called Amanda's name.

A female voice.

I turned and looked.

Sam.

CHAPTER NINETY-ONE

Sam had stepped outside the Barn, and she stood ten feet away from us in her wedding dress. Her hair was piled on top of her head, like her sister's, but also woven with flowers. Her makeup looked Hollywood perfect and, set against the white of the gown, gave her a beautiful, healthy glow. She looked like a vision of marital vitality.

"What do you two want?" she asked, sounding less than pleased to see us. "I'm about to go down the aisle. Blake and I are ready for this. You said you weren't coming, so why are you here now?"

"Sam." Amanda took a step away from me and closer to the bride. "I never dreamed I'd be here on the day of your wedding. I wouldn't be here if I didn't think it was important."

Sam's eyes moved back and forth between Amanda and me. "You shouldn't be here." Her eyes landed on me. "You have both said you never want to have anything more to do with Blake. You've both said awful things about him. He invited you here in good faith, and you said no. And all that trouble from college. He's facing charges from the accident now. They're going to come after him for vehicular homicide. So why are you here? You say you don't want to interrupt—then don't.

Leave. Just let us finally get married, okay? We've worked it all out, so leave us be."

Amanda moved even closer. She reached into her pocket and brought out her phone. "I know, Sam. You sent those threatening messages to Jennifer Bates. You sent them on the day she died, and you said you were coming over to her house."

Sam's eyes moved slowly from me to Amanda as she spoke. And outrage spread across her face as she understood what Amanda was saying.

I had no idea what Amanda was implying. Or why.

"You're both crazy," Sam said. "You'd both do anything to ruin the wedding. Please leave. Okay? Just leave."

Sam lifted the hem of her dress, elevating it above the gravel and dirt, and turned back to the Barn. But before she went back in, Amanda said, "Lily Rose. That's the name you used for the fake account when you wrote to Jennifer. You threatened her from that account."

Sam closed her eyes. She looked like we were a great burden, trying the last ounce of patience she possessed. "Please. Not today."

"Amanda," I said.

Amanda shook her head at me. "Lily Rose. The cops don't know, at least not yet. But remember, you told me once." Amanda laughed a little at the absurdity of it all. "We all played that stupid drinking game when we went out for your friend's bachelorette party. Seven months ago, a month before Henry was born and we stopped speaking to Blake."

"*You* stopped speaking to him," Sam said.

"What would your stripper name be?" Amanda said. "It's always the name of your first pet and the street you grew up on. Everybody knows that. They do those stupid things on social media all the time, and people share it. But you were laughing that night. You said, 'Wouldn't it be funny if your stripper name was the names of your two grandmothers?' And you said yours would have been Lily Rose and how that sounded like an old-fashioned stripper from the Wild West." Amanda looked over at me. "It was the stupidest thing to laugh at. But everyone was drinking, everyone but me because I was pregnant, and so I remembered. It was a pretty name. That's what I thought. Lily Rose." She looked back at Sam. "Mine was Margaret Lynn. We decided it was the worst stripper name ever."

"This is all very charming, but I have to go get married. . . ."

"You threatened Jennifer using that name. I saw it on her social media accounts. You went over there. You knew something had gone on between her and Blake, so you went over there that day . . . and I don't know what you intended to do, but it must have gone horribly wrong, because that's the day she ended up dead. And Blake must not have known yet, because he sent Ryan in that night to get the letters back. Right? You killed her, Sam. You must have killed her because you didn't like the way she and Blake were carrying on. Then the two of you could get married. You must have just been driven by jealousy."

Sam remained frozen in place, her hand still clutching the material of the wedding dress. She stared hard at us, her eyes narrowed, the irises shining like dark marbles. She breathed a little heavier, a little quicker.

"You think I was jealous of her?" Sam asked. "You think jealousy would drive me to do anything so rash?" She looked at both of us again, her face sneering in contempt. "The two of you don't understand anything about us, do you? You never have. You're both just kind of simple and so perfect. *Simply* perfect. You'd think something as basic as jealousy would be a reason to do anything. It's not. Not for us."

"Then why did you do it, Sam?" Amanda asked.

I still wasn't sure Amanda was right. I wasn't sure about anything. If the Barn had exploded and the landscape around us had gone up in flames, I wouldn't have been surprised.

Before Sam said anything else, the door to the Barn opened again. Blake stepped through and saw the two of us talking to his bride.

CHAPTER NINETY-TWO

Blake took the whole scene in. He wore a black suit and a black tie with a crisp white shirt. His hair looked slightly wet and plastered into the kind of order I'd never before seen on him. He kept his eyes on Amanda and me but spoke to Samantha.

"What is this all about? It's time, honey. It's time to do this thing once and for all."

"Blake, I think you're going to want to hear this," I said.

He smiled, but there was little warmth in it. He looked at me like I was a stranger, someone he needed to tolerate for just another moment. "I don't need to hear anything from either of you. You were invited, but you said no. So . . . that's probably for the best. I told the truth about what happened in college, and I'm going to get in some trouble for all of that. And none of that is sitting well with Sam's parents. They're not even here."

"And that's fine," Sam said. "We can do it all on our own."

"Sam was just about to tell us something important," Amanda said.

For the first time since he'd stepped outside, Blake turned and looked at his bride-to-be. And then he spoke to us while he stared at her. "She doesn't have to tell me anything else. I know what happened. And I know why Sam went to Jennifer's house that day. Why do you think I wanted your laptop? I started to suspect Sam had done it, and I wanted to check the information you downloaded. When I saw the messages from Lily Rose, I knew. I've played the stupid drinking game with her. But none of that's important. Our wedding is."

He reached out and took Sam by the hand, gently tugging her in the direction of the Barn and their wedding guests.

But Sam stayed rooted in place, resisting the pressure. She fixed her eyes on me.

"It's not jealousy," she said. "Do you know why I went over there to see Jennifer that day?"

"Baby . . . ," Blake said.

"It's okay," she said. "They'll understand. Ryan will understand. He will." She sounded calm, logical, perfectly in control of her story. "Blake told Jennifer all about Aaron Knicely and the Steiner girls. He told Jennifer who was really driving that night. Not you, Ryan. Him. Blake. He told Jennifer that he was driving. He did it because he slipped up and drank again. And you know as well as I do that makes him loose-tongued. I'm not thrilled he told someone else before he told me, but it was the drinking that did it. That's why he had to stop when we got back together." She spoke about Blake as if he wasn't there, like he was her child and she was sharing her struggles with him at a support group. "When he ended the relationship with her to get back together with me, she threatened to tell. Maybe she was bluffing and just wanted to make him squirm, but how could we take that chance? You know what that's like, Ryan. When you don't want your dirty laundry aired for all to see. She . . . Jennifer . . . was going to tell the police that Blake was driving that night and put him in legal jeopardy. Hell, she tried to tell you, Ryan. Why do you think she reached out to you just a few days ago on Facebook?"

"I thought she wanted something else. Something . . . romantic. I didn't imagine . . ."

"She told me that day when I went over there. She was trying to tell *you* the truth about the accident. That Blake was driving, and you were off the hook. She was going to show you the letters. But you ignored her. If you'd responded and talked to her, you would have known then. Instead, I went to get the letters back. To keep Blake from legal jeopardy. To keep everyone from knowing. And then Blake and I would get married, and it would all be settled."

"What happened at her house?" I asked.

"I thought she'd listen to reason. You know, one woman to another. I just slipped over there in the evening. I didn't think it would take long. And if I hadn't gone there, everything we'd planned would have been out the window. All of this." She gestured to the Barn, the surrounding landscape, everything that was to come in the future. "We couldn't have that, could we? Not when we were so close to having it all worked out."

Her words were calm and reasonable. She didn't allow for the possibility that there could be any objection to anything she said.

"What went wrong when you got there?" I asked.

Sam reached up and brushed at a corner of her eye. Either a tear or a makeup smudge. I couldn't say which.

"She wouldn't listen to reason," Sam said. "Blake didn't know I was going there. He really didn't. That's why he sent you that night, Ryan. I didn't tell him I was trying to solve the problem on my own. I got the feeling she didn't really want to get Blake in trouble. She wasn't hanging on like a woman scorned. But she clearly wanted us both to squirm. She liked having that power over us. And she used it. So I offered her money, money I've received from my parents over the years. Not a small amount. And that set her off. She was offended, and she shut down. So things escalated from there. I wasn't leaving without those letters. We couldn't have the loose end dangling."

"Escalated until you killed her?" I asked. "Smashed her over the head or whatever you did?"

"I got angry because she was so unreasonable." Her voice caught. For the first time she showed something besides defensiveness and anger. Sam looked up to the sky. She again lifted a finger to her right eye, which was perfectly framed by eyeliner. She seemed to be trying to keep a single tear from falling. "I just wanted the letters. That's it. So I tried to just take them. You know, just grab them and go. If she wanted to call the police or make a stink later, she could. But I didn't think she would. Not really. Not if I took them and left."

Blake watched her with an intense protectiveness. And a look that resembled admiration.

"I went into the bedroom and started looking in the closet and ruffling through the clothes. I was scrambling. I had to get out of there as fast as possible, and I thought I'd be going empty-handed. For a minute or two, Jennifer watched me from the bedroom doorway. She was almost laughing at me. Then I started opening drawers, and when I pulled open the one in the top of the dresser, she came into the room behind me."

"That's the drawer you told me to look in," I said to Blake.

"That's where the letters were," he said.

"And before I could grab them, she grabbed me. By the hair. She pulled me back and told me to get out. She pulled so hard my eyes filled with tears." Sam shivered at the memory. "I don't like it when people think they can push me around. They think I'll take anything and not give it right back. You thought that, Ryan. You thought I was just the little woman sitting idly by while Blake did whatever he wanted. Well, I'm not. And I pushed back against Jennifer. Hard."

"How hard?" I asked.

"She had a trophy or something on the dresser. I just reached out, and it felt like a heavy stone in my hand. And I swung. Just once." Her eyes were wide, her hand cupped as though she was holding that heavy object again. "I knew it was bad. The sound it made. The way she fell. I knew." She swallowed hard. "I took the letters and the trophy with me. That trophy . . . It was some kind of employee-of-the-month thing. . . ."

"Where is it?" I asked.

"In the river. And the letters are burned."

"And the glove?" I asked.

"That could be a problem," Sam said. "I didn't even know the gloves were in my pocket. I hadn't worn that coat recently, and they were in there. And one of them fell out, I guess. I didn't want it to go that way, but it did. You would have done the same thing, wouldn't you? Wouldn't you, Amanda?"

Blake placed his hand on Sam's arm, and she went along as he guided her toward the back door of the Barn. But before they went inside, I spoke and Blake stopped and looked back.

"Did you know the truth about this, Blake? Did you know Sam did this?"

"I had my suspicions. Sam wasn't answering her phone during the time when all of that supposedly happened. When we talked about all of these things, about Jennifer's death, she was evasive. And cold, really. And . . . her hand. Her nails on her right hand . . . They looked like . . . They looked like she'd been changing a tire. They were all broken and chipped. And she'd been chewing them again. Her hands never look like that. But I found out for sure that day I came over to get your computer. I wanted to see what was on there. I wanted to know how bad it was."

"You're willing to cover for Sam, knowing she did this."

"I am," Blake said. "That's what you do for people you love."

"But you'll go to jail. The accident. The murder."

"Maybe we won't come back," Blake said. "We're getting married. We're going on a trip. Sam has money from her parents. They're going to cut us off, but we can make it on our own somewhere. That's why we're still getting married today. I think it's clear there's no need to tell the police about this. We all understand why Sam did what she did. Let's just move on and have a wedding. The cops won't know who Lily Rose is unless you tell them."

I reached into my pocket and brought out my phone.

"You can't do that," Blake said, leaning forward. "We're friends. We've been friends longer than you've been friends with anybody. Longer than you've known Amanda."

I dialed 911.

"I'm going to do the right thing at the right time, Blake."

"Are you serious?" he asked.

When the dispatcher came on the line, and I told her where I was and to notify Detective Rountree, Blake didn't hesitate. He let go of Sam's hand and went inside the Barn, saying as he went, "My keys are inside."

CHAPTER NINETY-THREE

Once Blake went inside to get his keys, Sam turned and stared at us.

"You're ruining our wedding," she said. "Why can't you just leave us alone? We want the chance to have what you have. We want to have a perfect life too."

"A perfect life?" Amanda said.

"The baby, the house. Everything you do and share on social media, it's so perfect. We were going to lose that if Jennifer shared the truth about the accident. Even just my parents finding out has ruined so much. But it's not the end for us. After all, Aaron already went to jail for the crime. And those letters . . . they're long gone. Burned. Gone. Who will they believe now?"

"I told the cops everything I know," I said.

Sam waved me away, a dismissal.

"Our life isn't perfect, Sam," I said. "Far from it. That seems pretty obvious."

"Well, it sure as hell looks that way."

Blake came back and took Samantha by the hand, and the two of them moved off behind the Barn, where a few cars were parked, including a black SUV that belonged to Sam. They dashed away, leaving Amanda and me standing in their wake.

"Are we just going to stand here and watch them go?" Amanda asked.

"No," I said.

I took a step forward, but then I heard the sirens.

I looked back and saw the police coming up the long driveway. . . .

Blake drove the SUV around the far side of the Barn and then re-emerged, heading down the driveway. In the direction of the police.

Amanda and I watched from a distance.

She reached out and grabbed my hand, her nails digging into my flesh.

I wanted to shout, to tell Blake to stop. But he seemed to be speeding up as they approached the cops.

The police cars skidded to a stop, angling across the driveway and blocking the way.

Then Blake slammed on the brakes, making the tires squeal.

He backed the SUV up fifty feet, and then paused.

"My God, Ryan, do you see that?" Amanda asked.

"I do. He's going to ram them."

"No, Ryan. He can't. . . ."

But it looked like he was going to do it. Like he was going to slam his foot down on the accelerator and fire forward, either plowing through the cops or hoping they would move out of the way.

Or maybe causing a fiery crash.

Was that how this would end? Another car accident?

And I felt powerless to do or say anything. Blake wasn't my friend. He wasn't anything to me anymore.

But did I want to watch him die? And take others down with him?

For a suspended moment, the vehicles faced each other, cops on one side and Blake and Sam on the other. No one made a move.

Through the windshield I saw Sam waving her arms around, urging Blake to do something. She seemed to be pleading.

Then the driver's-side window of the SUV came down, and Blake's arm came out. Sam was shaking her head. The sleeve of his suit and the crisp white cuff. Something metallic dangled from his fingers. He dropped the keys onto the driveway. And his hands came out the window in surrender.

Two cops emerged from their vehicles, hands near their weapons. They moved slowly toward Sam's car, like soldiers on patrol, and then ordered the two of them to step outside.

One cop went to each side of the SUV, and when Blake and Sam came out, the cops took them and moved them up against the car. It took me back to my own experience outside their duplex when the cops pushed me up against the siding and searched me.

Except it hadn't happened to me in my wedding suit.

The cops patted them down and placed cuffs on them. For attempting to flee the scene . . . and then everything that they would now be able to prove.

Despite my desire to be done with Blake forever, I felt bad for them. Embarrassed.

Although I shouldn't have. They'd both done horrible things and had finally been caught.

That was when Amanda let go of my hand and nudged me.

"Are you seeing this, Ryan?"

I thought she meant the arrest. How could I not? But then I followed her gaze and saw what she meant.

The wedding guests, who had been sitting inside patiently waiting for the ceremony to start, had come out of the Barn, and they stood fanned out across the lawn. They all gawked at the spectacle happening before them.

And most of them, almost all of them, held their phones up before their faces, filming and taking photos of Blake and Sam being led over to and then placed into the back of a police cruiser in their wedding clothes. A cop placing his hand on Sam's perfectly styled hair to make sure she didn't hit her head as he maneuvered her in.

No one stepped forward to offer help. No one said anything.

They filmed and photographed. And looked happy to be doing it.

CHAPTER NINETY-FOUR

It took hours to untangle things with the police.

Both Amanda and I had to go in and meet with Rountree and a team of assorted detectives and attorneys we'd never met before. We told our stories separately, over and over again.

I'd just been through the whole routine the day before in the wake of Aaron Knicely's arrest, and being back in the police station so soon and having to again talk for so long made me tired.

Very tired.

In the back of my mind, I worried about Amanda. Not that I didn't think she could handle herself and stand up to anything anyone threw her way. I knew she could. I knew she could probably better than I could.

I hated to think of the strain brought on her by my friends, by people I'd brought into our lives. And I knew she didn't want to be away from Henry that long. Neither one of us did.

In the early evening, Rountree came to me and said I could go. When I asked about Amanda, she told me to sit in the lobby and wait. She also told me that Dawn Steiner had been questioned thoroughly that morning. She was going to face charges of an undetermined severity.

"But her father is sick," Rountree said. "Her whole story checks out. The baby, the adoptive parents. We'll see."

It took another thirty minutes for Amanda to emerge, looking tired but none the worse for wear. I stood up and hugged her as hard as I could. We were free to go home.

We were still going to have legal problems to resolve.

The police were discussing whether to charge me with tampering with a crime scene for taking the phone. They might charge Amanda for hacking into Jennifer's Facebook account.

We'd deal with it as best we could.

And we'd deal with it as we began to repair the fractures the past days had brought to our marriage. That was the most essential piece of all.

Amanda went to pick Henry up—and give her parents a Cliffs-Notes version of the day's events. I swung by our favorite Thai restaurant and got us carryout. I beat them home, but when I saw Amanda pull into our driveway, I nearly cried with relief. And I ran outside to get Henry out of the car and bring him inside.

We ate in stunned but happy silence. I think we both stared at Henry as much as we looked at our food. I couldn't believe we were home and safe. The three of us.

When we were finished eating, I took Henry upstairs, changed him, and slipped his squirming body into his pajamas. I held him for a while, rocking in the rocker in the nursery, but spending the day with his hovering, smothering grandparents must have worn him out. He nodded off with ease and didn't budge when I placed him in his crib.

I'd be lying if I said I didn't stare at him a little longer than usual that night. If I said that seeing his face, safe and sound in our house, didn't feel sweeter that night than it ever had.

I must have been so lost in my thoughts that I didn't hear Amanda's voice the first time she called my name. I don't know how many times she called before she shook me from my stupor.

But it sounded like something was wrong.

There was an urgency in her voice, almost a panic, that made me run.

Down the stairs and into the living room, where she sat on the couch, her phone in her hand.

"What is it?" I asked. "What?"

Amanda looked . . . scared?

No. She looked stunned.

She held her phone out to me, so I walked over and took it from her.

Her Twitter account was on the screen, and it took me a moment to figure out what I was looking at.

Then I understood.

Photos. And videos. Of Blake and Samantha being arrested in their wedding clothes. The scene that had played out before us just hours earlier.

I looked to the side, and sure enough, I saw the hashtags.

Trending. Nationally.

#weddingarrest

#brideandgroomjail

I couldn't even look at it.

It had to have been started by people who knew them. And then it spread.

I couldn't look.

"That's sick," I said.

"It is."

"Do you know what I want to do?" I asked.

"I think I do. And I'm willing to do it if you are."

I went and sat by her on the couch. I handed her phone back and slid mine out of my pocket. I took a deep breath.

"Are you ready?" I asked.

"I am." She paused. "Are you?"

"I am. Really."

We sat side by side and used our thumbs. Our opposable thumbs, which could be used for so much more.

It took only minutes, but we deleted all of our social media accounts.

THE
REQUEST

DAVID BELL

Questions for Discussion

1. Ryan and Blake were close friends in college, but their friendship has cooled now that Ryan is married and has a child. Is it typical for friendships to change in this way as people move from college and into their mid- to late twenties?

2. Despite the cooling of their friendship, Ryan feels loyalty to Blake because of the things they went through together in college. Do you understand why Ryan still feels this loyalty to Blake?

3. Ryan has a seemingly perfect life. And yet he feels it is defined by his part in the accident. Do you understand why Ryan wants to keep his role hidden from everyone in his life? Would people understand that he made a youthful mistake?

4. Even though she had a career and even made more money than Ryan did, Amanda feels insecure about her place in the world and in her marriage after Henry is born and she stops working for a time. Is it to be expected that she would feel this way?

5. Ryan spends a great deal of time on social media and seems unable to stop measuring his life by what he shares there. Do you understand how someone can be consumed by their social media feeds? Do you think this is a problem in our society? If so, how?

6. Everything that happens in the book grows out of the lies Blake told in college. Has it been your experience that one lie only leads to more and more lying?

7. Blake admits that he has always harbored resentment for Ryan because Ryan was always seen as the golden boy and Blake as the screwup. Do you understand why this would lead Blake to attempt to tarnish Ryan's sterling reputation?

8. Amanda admits to being hurt by the lies that Ryan told her. Do you think the two of them will be able to repair their relationship and move on?

9. Do you understand why Samantha and Blake are together? What does each get out of the relationship?

ACKNOWLEDGMENTS

Thanks to the IT department at Western Kentucky University for fielding my calls and answering my questions about hacking and phishing. Hey, I swear I'm not the one sending all the weird e-mails to everyone.

Special thanks to Ann-Marie Nieves and all the wonderful folks at Get Red PR.

Massive thanks once again to all the great people at Berkley/Penguin. Thanks to Eileen Carey for the great cover design. Special thanks to Jin Yu and Bridget O'Toole for their marketing wisdom. Special thanks to Loren Jaggers for his publicity wizardry. Superspecial thanks to my editor, Danielle Perez, for her continued brilliance.

And superspecial thanks to my wonderful agent, Laney Katz Becker, for her continued guidance and knowledge.

Major thanks to all my family and friends.

And more thanks than I can express to Molly McCaffrey for everything.

Photo by Glen Rose Photography

David Bell is a *USA Today* bestselling, award-winning author whose work has been translated into multiple foreign languages. He's currently a professor of English at Western Kentucky University in Bowling Green, Kentucky, where he directs the MFA program. He received an MA in creative writing from Miami University in Oxford, Ohio, and a PhD in American literature and creative writing from the University of Cincinnati. His previous novels include *Layover, Somebody's Daughter, Bring Her Home, Since She Went Away, Somebody I Used to Know, The Forgotten Girl*, and *Cemetery Girl*.

CONNECT ONLINE

DavidBellNovels.com

🅵 DavidBellNovels

🐦 DavidBellNovels

📷 DavidBellNovels